From **TANSTAAFL Press**

Demon novels by Bruce Graw

Demon Holiday
Torval, Demon Third Class, Layer Four Hundred Twelve of the Eighth Circle of Hell, has been in the business of chastising sinners longer than he can remember. Delivering punishment is the only job he's ever known—the only job he's ever wanted. After Torval witnesses something unexpected, his demonic Overseer demands that he take time off to resolve this personal crisis. And so Torval, the demon, finds himself sent on vacation ... to Earth, the proving ground of souls!

CorpGov Chronicle novels by Tom Gondolfi
An Eighty Percent Solution – CorpGov Chronicles: Book One
In a world where corporations suborn governments as a part of good business practice and unregistered humans can be killed without penalty, Tony Sammis, a midlevel corporate functionary, finds himself unwittingly a pawn in a guerilla war between a powerful cabal of business leaders and an elusive but deadly underground movement. His final solution to the biological terror unleashed mirrors Tony's own twisted sense of justice.

Also by Tom Gondolfi
Toy Wars
Flung to a remote world, a semi-sentient group of robotic mining factories arrive with their programming hashed. They can only create animated toys instead of normal mining and fighting machines. One of these factories, pushed to the edge of extinction by the fratricidal conflict, attempts a desperate gamble. Infusing one of its toys with the power of sentience begins the quest of a 2-meter tall, purple teddy bear and his pink, polka-dotted elephant companion. They must cross an alien world to find and enlist the aid of mortal enemies to end the genocide before Toy Wars claims their family—all while asking the immortal question, "Why am I?"

Demon Ascendant

Bruce Graw

If you purchased this book without a cover, you should be aware that it was an unauthorized sale. All books without a cover have been reported as "unsold and destroyed." As a result neither the author nor the publisher received payment for the sale of this "stripped book."

TANSTAAFL Press
1201 E. Yelm Ave,
Suite 400-199
Yelm, WA 98697

Visit us at www.TANSTAAFLPress.com

All characters, businesses, and situations within this work are fictional and the product of the author's creativity. Any resemblances to persons living or dead are entirely coincidental. TANSTAAFL Press assumes no responsibility for any content on author or fan websites or other publications.

Demon Ascendant

First printing TANSTAAFL Press
Copyright © 2014 by Bruce Graw
Cover illustration by Tony Foti

Printed in the United States

ISBN 978-1-938124-15-0

Chapter 1

An angel ...

Christine is an angel.

An *angel*!

Some part of Torval thought that he must've known, or at least suspected this, all along. She was so kind and helpful, so genuinely *good* ... how could he ever expect to find a human with such overwhelming qualities?

And yet, he hadn't known. The possibility never even occurred to him, at least not consciously. In an instant, everything he'd experienced during the last few days flashed before him, as though mocking his many failures.

He remembered witnessing his first Transcendence, when one of the tortured souls on his route finally escaped from Hell. In response, Torval made the mistake of asking what that meant and why things worked the way they did. That ill-timed conversation earned him this accursed holiday on Earth, where, in some kind of cruel cosmic joke, he arrived in the body of a freezing street bum during a bitter snowstorm. Somehow, he managed to claw his way out of that predicament, but only thanks to the kindness of others, or sheer blind luck. One misadventure followed another as he stumbled about the city, trying to find his way and improve his lot as best he could. Only when he'd finally secured employment, however pathetic it might seem, did he finally begin to understand what it meant to be human.

Throughout all that, Christine was there, helping him, offering advice or assistance, or just being in his thoughts, one way or another. For reasons he'd never fully understood, she'd intrigued him since the moment he first saw her in the soup kitchen. At first, he simply assumed his frail human shell was attracted to her in some inexplicable way, but he later came to realize it was more than that. Their attraction was more than simply physical. He liked her for who she was, not what she looked like, and he desperately wanted to get to know her better. Best of all, she seemed to feel the same way. Once he worked up the courage to ask her out, he'd dared to believe he might have a chance, however slim, of finding love.

Now, in a single, frozen instant, as he saw her true shape for the first time, all those hopes were dashed. Christine wasn't human at all, but an angel in disguise. He'd never expected to meet an angel, but now that he had, their relationship would have to end. After all, angels were the Other Side, the Opposition. Demons and angels aren't permitted to interact, at least not until Judgment Day, when the armies of Heaven and Hell would be loosed upon each other in the final Apocalypse that would cleanse the world and change Creation forever.

At least, that's how Torval understood things, in his limited recollection of how that was all supposed to work. In fact, he was probably violating the Compact right now, just touching Christine like this.

With that final thought, he suddenly jerked his hands back. The faintly glowing, golden form before him reverted instantly to the human Christine Anderson, her lovely face now twisted into an expression of abject horror. She backed away, trembling, almost gasping for breath, staring at him with such intensity that it almost felt painful.

"You—you're a *demon*!" she blurted, almost spitting the word. "Get away from me! Away!"

"Christine, I—" Torval began, but his voice caught in his throat. What could he possibly say? That he hadn't known her true nature? That he didn't know what to do now? That he was sorry? Nothing seemed to be enough, and so many words rushed to his lips that he couldn't say any of them.

"Shut up!" she yelled, pointing a quivering finger at him. "You—you *fiend*! Creature from Hell! Whatever you were trying to do—whatever your mission is—just stay away!"

She moved sideways now, away from him and up the staircase, making for the door to her building without taking her eyes off Torval. She now wore an expression of mixed horror and fear.

"Please," he managed to sputter. "I never intended to deceive you. I have no mission—I am only on vac—"

"I don't care what you are, or why you're here!" she spat, fumbling with the keys until the door finally opened. "Just keep away from me! I don't ever want to see you again!"

"But, Christine, please—I just want to—" Torval sputtered, taking a few steps toward her.

It was too late. She retreated hastily inside, slamming the door in his face. He could hear her there, breath coming in ragged gasps, until finally her footsteps scuffled away. He also thought he might've heard, amidst those retreating sounds, a muffled sob.

But it could've been his imagination.

* * *

Torval didn't know how long he stood there. He lost all track of time, mentally going over what just happened, repeating it over and over in his head.

The date went well—he was sure of that, from the end result. The kiss they shared was sheer perfection. For a single, enduring moment, he held a human woman in his arms, pressed his lips to hers, and understood so many things. For an instant, he thought he felt the first faint stirrings of love.

Then everything was gone, ripped away just like that. The woman he thought of as Christine wasn't really a human at all, but an angel, an agent of Heaven, here on some mission for the Other Side. The heavenly equivalent of Prelz, perhaps, not a Tempter but—what? What missions did angels perform, anyway?

He knew nothing about angels. Nothing at all, except their appearance, and that from only this brief encounter. Doubtless they looked different depending on their tasks, just as demons did. And what did she see when she looked at him? Something foul, judging by her reaction—a horrible and disgusting creature, unbearable to even look upon. Well, that much he understood, at least. Of course his demonic form would be repulsive to something as lovely as herself.

Torval sighed heavily. He wished she wasn't an angel. He wanted Christine to be human again, a woman that he could pursue, and fall in love with, and be a part of his life for the duration of his stay on Earth. Now that, like everything else, had been yanked away. She no longer wanted anything to do with him. All he'd sought to accomplish, with the date and everything else, was lost—nothing but a wasted effort, gone forever.

If only he'd known before this! If only they'd touched—but they hadn't, he realized now, thinking back on their previous encounters. In the cab, at her apartment, even during the date tonight, they'd never actually made physical contact. On the few occasions that they came close, he recalled feeling a faint spark, the barest hint of something like electricity, but he dismissed that as some sort of natural physical attraction designed by nature to help human beings locate potential mates. Now he knew better. He wouldn't be fooled like that again.

He could only press on, he finally decided. His efforts with Christine had failed. She had ordered him away, and even if he wanted to, they could never see each other again. The Compact prohibited it. Angels and demons weren't permitted to interact. That was the way things were, and for good reason. He didn't want to be the one to precipitate Armageddon, after all.

So he turned away at last, heading slowly down the windswept street in the direction of his waiting job. He still had that, at least. He had a place to go where he could be warm and comfortable, and perhaps put these miserable thoughts out of his mind. He would have to forget her somehow.

That wouldn't be easy. He didn't want to forget her. He had to, though. He had to at least try.

He felt cold now, bitterly cold in the early night wind, so he pushed his hands into his pockets and shuffled along, shivering. As he did, he glanced back over his shoulder once more, trying not to think about Christine, or the fact that several tears were even now turning into frozen droplets on his face.

High above, in one of the distant windows, a pair of curtains fluttered shut, but Torval didn't notice as he shuffled his way slowly down the darkened street.

* * *

"There you are!" came a familiar voice out of the shadows, even as Torval finally reached the Roxton warehouse. "I was wondering how late you'd be!"

"I am not late," protested Torval, looking longingly at the inviting door behind Prelz, its promise of warmth almost beckoning to him. Glancing again at his brand-new watch, Torval added, "I am five minutes early."

"Then you're late for sure, 'cause I'm gonna bug you at least that long," chuckled the other demon. "Come on, fork over some details! I've been waiting here all evening for your sorry ass to show up—the least you can do is feed me a few juicy tidbits."

"I do not wish to discuss it," complained Torval. "I am cold and distraught and I wish only to work so I can forget all about Christine Anderson."

"Oh, shit, no," replied Prelz, shaking his head sadly. The look on his weathered face betrayed his disappointment. "You screwed it up, didn't you? I'm so sorry, man, sorry to hear it. I should've told you more about what to do, or maybe what not to do, hmm?"

"It was not you," Torval sighed, realizing he wasn't going to get out of this conversation easily. He shifted position so that Prelz blocked the wind. "The date itself was not the problem. In fact, everything went extremely well. When it was over, we walked back to her apartment, and I could tell she had a good time."

"Did you get lucky?" inquired Prelz curiously. "You seem to have a knack for that, y'know."

"No, not this time," replied Torval, too depressed to get irritated at the insinuation. "We did, however, exchange a kiss."

"You did? Sweet!" Prelz looked pleased, even happy, as he clapped Torval on the back. "Well done! You got to first base!"

"First ... base?" Torval raised his eyebrows.

"Never mind, never mind. What I mean is, she must've liked you, if she let you kiss her after the first date. Nice work. You're on the right track, it sounds like."

"Yes, I thought so too," sighed Torval.

"Well, what happened? Did you slip her too much tongue, or what?"

"No, it was perfect." Torval hung his head in disappointment. "It was exactly as I hoped it would be. For a moment I felt what it was to be truly human, Prelz! To truly understand it all. Attraction, intimacy, mortality ... perhaps even love. All of that flashed before me when our lips touched, and I held her close to me ... " His voice trailed off in a sad, forlorn sigh.

Prelz raised his bushy eyebrows. "My friend," he said after a moment, "I do believe you have the heart of a true romantic! All of that sounds great and all, but you still haven't told me what went wrong. What was the problem?"

"The problem was Christine," explained Torval wearily. "After the kiss, the truth was revealed to me. She is an angel."

"Oh, yeah, don't I know it!" agreed Prelz at once, slapping one rag-covered knee in affirmation. "She's so damn nice all the time, no matter what's happening, and so gorgeous, too." He paused for a moment, looking at Torval with head cocked sideways, before suddenly realizing what was going on.

"Wait a minute ... ! You don't mean—you mean she's *really* an angel?" He pointed a half-covered finger up at the sky. "An angel from Heaven?"

Torval nodded slowly. "Yes. That is exactly what I mean."

Prelz looked stunned, and in fact settled to the ground, dropping roughly onto the hard concrete steps leading up to the side entrance to the warehouse. He rubbed his frayed and mismatched gloves together as much in contemplation as for warmth.

"An angel," he muttered slowly. "You don't say. A real, honest-to-God angel."

"Yes, that's what I said," repeated Torval, sitting down beside his fellow demon and huddling next to him, keeping out of the wind as best he could. "We touched, and I saw her true form, and she saw mine. I thought that such revelations occur only between demons, but apparently it works for anyone who is not truly human."

"I guess so," Prelz agreed with a shrug. Quickly overcoming the initial surprise, he began to chuckle. "Hey, do you know what this means? You kissed an angel! A demon, kissing an angel! That's great! Oh, how I would've liked to have seen her reaction! Too bad I wasn't there. Damn, I missed a good one!"

"It was not," Torval replied gruffly, "particularly pleasant."

"I'm sorry, I don't mean to make fun of you," Prelz added after recovering from his sudden mirth. "So what happened then? I guess she didn't invite you inside, huh?"

"No, she was upset. Very much so, in fact."

"I bet she was. Well, she'll get over it. When do you think you two will get together again? So I can hide in the bushes and watch, of course."

"Never." Torval shook his head sadly. "When she found out what I was, she ordered me away. We cannot see each other again. She is an angel, and I a demon. We are not permitted to interact. Our relationship is over."

"Ah, what a load of horse hockey!" snapped Prelz. "Is that what's got you down? Nothing's over, my friend. She's a woman and you're a man, and that's that. You're both in human bodies here on Earth. You liked each other before you found out what you really were—so you have a connection. So keep at it! Love is blind, y'know, or at least that's what they always say."

"But the Compact—"

"—doesn't mean jack shit!" interjected Prelz swiftly. "Do you know what that thing says, exactly? Have you ever actually *read* it?"

"No, I am afraid not," replied Torval with a sad shake of his head. "Perhaps I should have, but it never seemed relevant to me."

"You couldn't have understood it anyway, not at your rank," Prelz pointed out, "and besides, you're absolutely right, it wasn't relevant. Not to you, until you came here. I'm just surprised you weren't forced to read it before Transitioning."

"The subject never came up," said Torval with a shrug.

"Whatever. Well, *I've* read it." Prelz put out his right hand, wrapped in a black glove with two missing fingertips. He held up a trio of slightly shivering fingers. "There are only three things that are really important in all that steaming pile of dung they call a Compact. Do you want to know what those are?"

His friend nodded eagerly. "Yes. Definitely."

"One," said Prelz, holding up a single finger, "no angel or demon shall enter the Middle World in their true forms, nor shall they purposely reveal their true natures to a human."

"But what about Father Michaels?" interrupted Torval. "He has seen both of our true forms. Is he not human?"

"He is, or at least I *think* he is." Prelz shrugged. "He's not a demon or angel, though, I'm sure of that. So if he's human, I suppose technically we violated the Compact, didn't we?" He grinned, gave a chuckle, and then coughed a few times. "I'm not sure what that means, exactly, but then, I didn't exactly purposely reveal myself to him, did I? He saw me himself, not because of anything I did. Same with you. Assuming he *is* human, and I'm pretty sure he is, he must just have a gift that lets him see us as we are. Second sight, they call it. Still, I avoid talking about demons with him, or the nature of Hell, just to be sure I have plausible deniability."

Torval nodded, not sure what to make of that, but then it probably didn't matter. If the Compact had been broken, surely something would've happened by now, wouldn't it?

"Anyway," went on Prelz, holding up another finger, which looked slightly blue from the cold, "the second thing is that no magic or miracles shall be employed by angels or demons. Here in this world, everything works the way it's supposed to, as can be explained through science and reason, using the natural laws that run the Universe—the laws the Creator set up when He made everything the way it is."

Torval shrugged. "I cannot do magic," he commented, "so that one does not matter. However, I do recall that when Father Michaels told us the stories of the Bible, there were miracles aplenty."

"Hmm, well, I'm not sure if those were real, or just some strange events those primitive people couldn't explain and just attributed to magic," suggested Prelz. "Anyway, if all of that was to be believed, it was God who took the form of Jesus, not an angel or demon. Of course the Creator can do whatever He wants, as He isn't bound by the Compact."

"Of course," agreed Torval, for the explanation sounded reasonable enough. "What is the third rule?"

"This is the one you want to listen to," explained Prelz, with his third finger up now. "Angels and demons shall not come into conflict until the Day of Judgment, at which point open warfare will result and, at least as we demons see it, the world will be destroyed."

"That is what I'm talking about, then," Torval pointed out. "That is the rule that binds me. Angels and demons cannot interact."

"Cannot *conflict,*" corrected Prelz. "That's the key word, my friend. We can't come into conflict with angels, but that doesn't mean we can't interact with them at all. Not that we usually have any desire to, of course, but at least now one of us has a reason."

For the first time, Torval felt a faint stirring of hope. "Are you certain?" he asked firmly. "You are sure you aren't misremembering the wording?"

"No, I'm not," insisted the older demon. "I'm quite clear on this. They even gave us instructions on the subject, in case we ever ran into an angel down here. Presumably it happens on occasion. There aren't many of us on either side, of course, but eventually some of us would have to meet, if only by pure chance. Hmm ... what are the odds of that, I wonder?"

"What instructions did they give you?" demanded Torval, not at all interested in any other speculations.

"Well, if you must know, we're supposed to avoid them at all costs," said Prelz with a sigh, "but that's because our goals on Earth would probably be polar opposites. You don't have to worry about that, my friend, since you don't have an assignment here. You can do whatever you want—you have the advantage of free will, right?"

"That is true," agreed Torval, remembering what Geezon said just before the Transition. "I can do whatever I like, as long as I am not interfering with another demon's work."

"And Christine isn't a demon, is she?" said Prelz with a sly wink.

"No," Torval replied, allowing himself the very briefest of smiles. "No, she most definitely is not."

* * *

When he finally managed to disengage from Prelz, Torval headed quickly inside, into the gloriously heated warehouse and its accompanying office. He stood there alone for a moment, enjoying the warmth and considering the ex-Tempter's words carefully.

He and Christine could definitely continue to see each other, at least according to the Compact. That news at least brightened Torval's mood somewhat. However, there was still the matter of the harsh manner in which she ordered him away, insisting that she never wanted to see him again. Was that because she, too, believed the Compact prevented their interaction? Or simply because he repulsed her physically? Or was there something more to it?

Did she think he had betrayed her trust by lying about his true nature? Torval considered that as he massaged his nearly frozen fingers, wishing he'd purchased better clothing for protection against the cold outside. If she did indeed hold him at fault for a deception, well, she'd done the same, had she not? She didn't reveal her own true nature any more than he had, so they were both equally at fault. Not that they could've done otherwise—the Compact was clear on that. They were both required to keep their true natures secret, at least as long as they believed the other to be human.

So the problem had to be Torval's status as a demon, and nothing more. He wanted to believe, as Prelz suggested, that their true natures wouldn't be a barrier, but of course they would. Torval knew he didn't want to forget Christine or end their relationship, simply because they weren't human. He liked Christine, and they definitely had shared something in that brief instant when they kissed—or at least he thought they did. He wanted to experience that moment again, if at all possible. The only way he could do that was to convince her, somehow, that it would be all right to try.

Exactly how that would be accomplished, he had no idea. If the way she reacted to his demon form was any indication, he had a difficult challenge ahead of him.

He heard footsteps tromping up the stairs from the basement, and after a moment the tall and lanky form of Pete Roxton stepped into the room. "Ah, you're here," said Pete with an affable grin. "Sorry if I kept you waiting, but I was making sure you had the Internet running down there. Everything should be good, I think."

Torval nodded, not really understanding what the other was talking about. "I only just arrived," he replied.

"Oh, okay, well, come down here and I'll let you play around with the computer before I head out. Gonna hit a few bars tonight and see if I can get lucky, y'know? Heh-heh."

The demon shrugged and followed. Somehow Pete didn't seem quite as charming, now that Torval knew how his boss had treated Christine during their brief date. Pete was still the same person, obviously, but there was now an air of tawdriness about him. He clearly intended to go out this evening, find some desperate woman, and have cheap and meaningless sex with her. If the female desired the same, thought the demon, then perhaps this wasn't in and of itself a sin; but that couldn't change the fact that it seemed at its core rather desperate and pathetic.

Torval thought about commenting as he followed Pete down the rickety stairs, but he didn't really know enough about this subject. He'd only been human for a few days, after all, so he stayed silent.

"Okay, have a seat," said his boss upon arriving in the now-open "secret" room in the basement. The computer waited, this time with its screen active, showing a scene of a barren hillside, azure sky above flecked with wispy white clouds. Several small images lined the left side of the view, while a tiny arrow floated in the middle of the scene.

Torval sat down, studying the display. The picture seemed quite serene, but he wondered what it had to do with anything. Was this something like television or the movies, where projected images were used to tell some sort of story?

"Okay, here's your manual," said Pete, slapping a hand on the book sitting to Torval's right. "Computers for Dummies" read the title, which seemed vaguely insulting. "Everything you need is right here. Read and practice and play around all you want. I've got virus checkers installed, so if any windows pop up with warnings, make sure you deny everything."

"Very well," replied Torval with no small amount of confusion. "I will deny everything."

"Anyway, I'm outta here," Pete went on hurriedly. "Meeting some friends downtown. Have a good time!"

Torval stared at the computer for a moment, not really comprehending the strange machine and its odd attachments. "Wait," he called out finally, "what exactly am I supposed to accomplish?"

There was no reply. Pete was already gone. The sound of the door slamming, followed by the turning of a lock, was all Torval heard.

He stood there, at a loss. Always, before, he'd had clear instructions on his goals for the night. Now all he had was a manual and the mysterious machine before him, with no specific task, other than to read and practice.

He did recall, when he last visited this place, that the Roxtons intended for him to somehow record their business transactions on this device. However, he had no idea how that might done. *Perhaps the manual will explain*, thought the demon. *Might as well get started.*

He began to read. The computer, it seemed, consisted of several component parts. The large, rectangular gray box contained all the inner workings, which the book actually avoided discussing. Apparently he had no need to know what the things inside did, at least not at this point. An advanced chapter dealt with taking off the case and fiddling around within, but Torval figured that was beyond the scope of his initial training.

Several other items were attached to the computer's main body. The "monitor" and its "screen" produced the background image, and contained things called "icons" that somehow represented objects he could work with in some way. Then there was a "keyboard," where he could type in requests or enter information, and a "mouse" which served as a kind of pointer and could activate mysterious items called "applications." According to the book, there might also be other peripherals, such as printers, scanners, and speakers, but glancing around the otherwise empty room, Torval saw no such items. The

Roxtons' computer lacked anything other than the bare minimum of add-ons, apparently.

The mouse, it seemed, controlled the computer. He discovered very quickly that simply moving the pointer caused the arrow on the screen to slide about. The oval-shaped device also had several buttons, and when he pointed the arrow at an icon, he could press a switch (i.e., "click") to activate its power. Following the instructions in the book, he could locate and use several tools, such as a calculator and notepad.

He played with these for a while, following Pete's instructions to practice, until he felt fairly confident in his abilities. Then he moved on, activating an application called "Internet Explorer." Immediately the hillside image on the screen vanished, replaced by a large white window containing a very large word that Torval didn't recognize. The word was "Google."

He consulted the book. Apparently the Internet Explorer application allowed one to "surf the Internet," or move from site to site looking for information. Torval nodded, now beginning to understand. He could recall now from his initial trip to the library how the woman Karen had mentioned the Internet somewhat disdainfully. Apparently its presence caused people to avoid libraries. Did that mean the same things available there could also be found using the Internet?

Apparently so, as he found out quite readily. Using the text box in the middle of the screen, he could type in any word or phrase, and after a brief moment all sorts of relevant articles would appear. Each of these represented something called a "website," where further information could be found. The act of moving from site to site was, apparently, referred to as "surfing."

As an experiment, Torval tried a word, carefully locating the appropriate letters on the keyboard one at a time. He typed in "demon" and hit the Enter key, as the manual instructed. Instantly a page full of sites appeared, all with that particular word in their title. He clicked on one of the pages and began to read.

After a few minutes, he tried another word, and read another page, and another. There was so much information here, and so many images! No wonder people didn't go to the library, if they had access to the Internet! They could find whatever they wanted, just by using a computer.

Torval closed the book and set it aside. For the moment, he had everything he needed. Perhaps he would return to the manual later, when he was done surfing the Internet, but for now he just wanted to explore and learn whatever he could. After all, he now had the entirety of all human knowledge at his fingertips.

And, at least for the rest of the night, he managed to forget about Christine.

Chapter 2

Nelson Rockefeller served as governor of New York from 1959 to 1973 ...

On traffic signals, red means stop, green means go and amber means prepare to stop ...

The tallest skyscraper in the world is the Burj Dubai in the United Arab Emirates ...

The Great Depression began with the stock market crash on October 29, 1929, a day known as Black Tuesday ...

Carbuerator electrical conduction truck driving Empire State Building computer subway Yankee Stadium foreplay asphalt New Testament public library 2007 five boroughs deficit spending G-spot movies United States of America ...

Torval awoke.

He was on the floor, as usual, but he didn't remember how he got there. He vaguely remembered surfing the Internet—drinking up information like a thirsty man in the desert suddenly confronted with a functioning water fountain. He remembered being tired, and having difficulty holding his eyes open, but every page he clicked on simply led to more and more questions, and more and more clicks on website links.

He wanted to know how computers worked, but that led him to sites explaining electricity, which themselves forced him to learn about atoms and electrons and protons, and the electromagnetic force, and on and on and on. He tried to find out how cars functioned, only to discover there were so many parts he could never fully comprehend them all. There was so much to learn, so much information that his human brain simply wasn't capable of holding everything.

He sat up and rubbed his eyes. His neck and back hurt from sleeping on the hard floor, and he felt weary and tired, even more so than usual after waking. Mind still awash in jumbled facts and half-remembered details, he stumbled to the shower. Minutes later he stood under the massaging flow of hot water, which helped him fully awaken and regain his focus.

The computer knew everything, it seemed. Torval could ask literally any question he had, and answers would be provided. Sometimes he had to try several of the possible choices in order to find what he was looking for, but the answer was always there. And each answer just led to more and more questions ...

He had lost himself in the Internet, hadn't he? He'd intended only to practice with the computer, to try to understand how it worked so he could better do his job, but his curiosity overcame him. There was so much to know. So many things he wanted to find out.

He knew now that he'd Transitioned into a place called New York City, located on an island known as Manhattan, on the east coast of a country named the United States of America, on the continent of North America, one of the world's seven continents. The year was 2009, and it was February 22, a Sunday. This was exactly the sort of information he needed to know, and would be expected to know as a human being residing in this place and time. The computer provided the perfect means to discover such things without giving away his true nature.

Yet he hadn't stopped there. He kept asking for more and more information, first about things he deemed important, then about anything that interested him. He stopped caring if what he was reading mattered—he only wanted to learn more and more, soaking up data like a sponge. He lost control of himself.

As the hot water soothed his body, invigorating him and washing the last vestiges of sleep away, Torval tried to remember how long he'd sat in front of that screen. He had no idea. There was a point, somewhere along the way, where he yielded to his body's demands and hastened to the toilet, but all he did while there was think about the next question he might ask. After that he never left the computer again. His lower back started to hurt from being in the same position for so long, and his eyes became droopy and his vision fuzzy, but he kept at it, clicking and typing and absorbing more and more until finally he must've overloaded and collapsed.

Even now he wanted to visit the computer again. He had still more questions to ask. He wasn't about to do that, though. He might never leave that room.

He washed himself off, keeping his thoughts on the present.

What had he learned that helped his current situation? Other than his present location in the world, very little. He hadn't discovered anything that would help him resolve the Roxton issue, or that would enable him to better deal with Christine. In fact, information on angels and demons was rather sketchy, most of it just speculation and quite a bit of it wrong. He doubted any of what he read about angels would be of any help.

Furthermore, when he attempted to discover helpful information about romance, he was led to websites featuring prominent images of women in very little clothing. Many of these locations seemed to be more interested in enticing the viewer to pay money for even more nude pictures. Although many of the ladies portrayed there were quite beautiful, they did nothing for Torval and didn't help him with his current troubles. Eventually he gave up trying to acquire further help in that area—apparently, much like the library, the Internet could provide hard facts for general issues, but nothing to aid him with his personal, unique problems.

The water began to cool, so Torval finished his shower and dried off, then shaved and brushed his teeth, completing the daily hygiene ritual that had started to become routine. Briefly he recalled that he'd left his latest purchase, the deodorant, with Prelz prior to last night's date, but what became of it thereafter, he had no idea. The other demon hadn't returned the item to him, so there was no telling where it might be now.

Torval dressed himself, using another pair of clean underwear, but otherwise putting on the same shirt and jeans he'd worn the day before. The clothing was noticeably dirty, but he had nothing else to wear, and worse, he'd run out of funds. Until the Roxtons saw fit to give him another bonus task, he was broke.

Torval stepped out of the bathroom and looked around. The door at the top of the stairs stood open, so obviously Pete or someone else had returned to let him out. Yet the building remained silent, and the light in the hallway stayed off.

He climbed the stairs and looked around. "Pete?" he called out, but received no answer. Curious, he went to the building's main entrance, but again, found nobody present and the lights were off. Had Pete simply come in, unlocked his door and departed? Was Torval supposed to simply leave?

While glancing around, he noticed the wall clock, and his

eyebrows went up. It was almost noon! How late did he stay up reading those websites, anyway? Far too late, it seemed.

He headed back further into the building. Surely he wasn't expected to leave the warehouse unattended, especially since he didn't possess the keys to lock the door behind him. Someone was still here—they had to be.

Sure enough, as soon as he stepped into the actual warehouse area, he could hear distant voices. He pressed on, moving along the rows of pallet racks and stacked crates of auto parts, until he got close enough to hear the words. Approaching from behind an idle forklift, he stopped cold when he heard his human body's name.

"Yeah, we could always use Joe," someone said. The voice of Pete Roxton, Torval realized at once. "He's been pretty reliable so far, and when we tell him to do something, he damn well does it right."

"I don't care how you do it, just get it done!" came the gruff-sounding reply. Torval also recognized that voice, too, but it wasn't as familiar. Still, it held an obvious tone of authority, as if whoever spoke was Pete's superior in some way. Yet it clearly wasn't Lincoln Roxton—Torval was sure of that.

After a moment's pause, the still unidentified voice went on. "As long as you don't do anything that can be traced back here, it doesn't matter to me," the unseen speaker said dismissively.

"What about the money?" asked Pete, sounding somewhat worried. "Jacques is breathing down my neck again, and if I don't—"

"You'll get paid when I'm satisfied, and not before!" snapped the other. There was a pause, and then a low chuckle. "Don't worry, Pete, you'll get what's coming to you. Now get to work! I should have another delivery for you later this week."

"Yeah, whatever," said Pete, a tone of frustration obvious in his reply. Footsteps followed, and Torval found himself crouching down behind the forklift, trying to stay out of sight for reasons he didn't even fully understand. There was something about that other person's voice that was familiar, and even disturbing.

The footsteps drew closer and then passed. He risked standing, to get a better look at the scene, but stayed slumped and kept his head low. Pete had his back to him, apparently going through something in an unmarked box on the floor, while the other man, tall and well dressed, headed away, toward an exit. For a second, the imposing figure glanced back, an imperious smile on his face, and Torval felt his blood chill, for he knew who it was at a glance. He'd seen him in the police station the day before.

He was Lieutenant McCord!

* * *

Torval remained frozen in place behind the inert forklift, trying to control his suddenly difficult breathing. His heavy rasps sounded loud enough to alert Pete to his presence, but his boss was obviously too busy to notice.

What was going on? Why would the police lieutenant be here, talking directly to Pete? Why was Pete expecting money? What were they up to?

The questions fluttered around in Torval's head like so many butterflies, but he had no answers, and the more he thought about the situation, the more confused he became. The only thing he knew for sure was that *something* strange was going on here, and like it or not, he was involved.

The first and most obvious thing to do was stand up, approach Pete, and simply ask what was happening. Not so long ago, Torval might've have done just that. This time, though, something in the back of his mind told him not to—at least, not right away. First he had to think this through.

While he didn't know exactly what was happening here, he did know Pete was involved in something mysterious and secret. Since the police were involved, perhaps that meant Pete might be helping with some kind of official investigation, which could explain the pay he expected to earn. If that were true, then it might also make sense to employ some third party, such as the formerly homeless Joe Sampson, for certain tasks.

Torval found that theory plausible, but something about it didn't ring true. The interaction between Lieutenant McCord and Pete Roxton didn't sound like what would be expected between a police officer and a cooperative informant. Instead it sounded downright hostile, as if Pete had been coerced somehow.

The other possible option, at least as far as Torval could put together as he huddled down behind the forklift, was that the two men were involved in something illegal. That a policeman might be involved didn't surprise Torval in the least. There were plenty of law enforcement officers in Hell for one reason or another, usually stemming from some form of abuse of power. In one of his cells, for example, there dwelled one Sheriff Eugene Carlton, who once ruled a small Southwestern town named Stone Falls with an iron fist, gunning down anyone he even suspected of being a criminal or outlaw. As his punishment, he got to spend eternity playing cards in the same dusty saloon, endlessly losing games to those he murdered in life. Since he couldn't cover the bets, the victors took their payments directly from his flesh.

But if McCord was indeed a crooked cop, what was the extent of Pete's involvement? Was he forced into doing the officer's bidding, or did he participate willingly? Did he truly need the money for some debt, as his comments suggested, or was there something else going on? Again, Torval felt the impulse to simply stand up and ask, but if he did that, and revealed himself, what would happen then?

If Pete was working with the police, either for good or ill, his actions remained a secret. Torval obviously wasn't supposed to know that secret, or he already would've been informed. So they probably had a good reason for not wanting someone like Joe Sampson to know anything else. If he revealed that he'd learned something, what if the Roxtons decided they couldn't afford to have him around? They could fire him ... or worse, if the secret was particularly crucial, they could ...

They could get rid of him.

Torval shuddered. He didn't want to die—not now, not with so much of his vacation still incomplete. He wasn't finished here yet.

How strange that he should feel that way! A few days ago, upon arriving on Earth, he would've been perfectly happy to perish and start over somewhere more comfortable. Yet now he felt exactly the opposite. He didn't want to go—he still had ten more days of life here to experience. Ten more days to sample new foods, see new places, learn more about humans ...

Ten more days to find out more about Christine.

When it all came down to it, that's what Torval wanted most. He wanted to talk to Christine again, more than anything. He couldn't leave now without doing that, and couldn't afford to take any risk that might result in his premature death, before he could see her once more.

So he waited, cowering in the shadow of the machine, forcing himself to calm down as he listened to Pete fiddling with whatever was in the box and muttering what sounded like curses under his breath. Eventually, a kind of slam sounded, and Torval heard footsteps tromping away, heading deeper into the warehouse.

Seeing his chance, Torval got to his feet and hurried back the way he'd come, hoping Pete wouldn't notice the sound of his departure.

* * *

On his way back to the basement, where he intended to retreat, Torval noticed a faint aroma coming from a nearby hallway. His stomach growled immediately, and he felt himself salivating, for he recognized the unmistakable scent of a fresh jelly-filled donut. He felt his feet turning in the direction of the large central office where he'd tried donuts once before, upon the conclusion of his first work shift. Sure enough, he found an open box on the table there, containing donuts of several types.

He was halfway through the second one when Pete arrived, poking his head into the room curiously. "Ah, you finally got up!" he remarked jovially, showing no hint whatsoever of the frustration he'd shown in the warehouse. "I thought you were gonna sleep all day. How was the computer?"

"Intriguing," remarked Torval, once he'd managed to swallow the incredibly tasty bite he'd been working on. "I must apologize, however. I spent very little time reading the book you gave me. Instead, I occupied myself surfing the Internet."

Pete chuckled. "Figured you might. As long as you didn't get too many viruses from the porn sites, I've got no problem with that."

"I stayed away from the pornographic material," explained Torval, "although I do admit I did reach some of those pages by accident. Instead, I occupied myself studying such captivating subjects as electricity, architecture, film, history, and finance."

Pete raised his eyebrows and gave a knowing chuckle. "You skipped on the porn to read up on *finance*? Whatever for?"

"I was curious," explained Torval. "For example, I have heard several references to something called the 'Great Depression,' and the Internet was able to explain it. Apparently in 1929 there was a stock market crash and—"

"Yes, believe me, I know all about the Depression!" interjected Pete, rolling his eyes in a protracted manner. "You should hear Grandpa yammer on about that shit all day long! How hard things were and all the bread lines and on and on. Believe me, I don't want to hear any more about that crap!"

"I apologize. I will not bring it up again."

"Oh, that's okay, Joe, my bad," said Pete with a conciliatory tone, clapping Torval loudly on the shoulder. "Didn't mean to jump all over you. I'm not having a real great day, I guess, and I shouldn't take it out on you. You could say I got some bad news, I suppose, but it's nothing you need to worry about. Anyhow, as long as you got comfortable on the computer, that's all I was wanting you to get done, seeing as it was Saturday night and all. Don't want to work you too hard on the weekend, y'know."

"Nonetheless, I feel as though I did not accomplish my task," said Torval, "but if you are satisfied, I suppose I should be as well. Is there anything else I can do?" He allowed a hopeful tone to creep into his voice without realizing it.

"Not today," came the reply, and Torval's shoulders slumped. "Tell you what, though," Pete added hastily, "if you're up for it, I do need you to do something for me tomorrow morning. Another delivery, I suppose you might say, but this one may take a bit longer."

"The time does not concern me," Torval answered eagerly. "I will do what I must, for I am out of funds and require more."

"You're out of money already?" Pete looked at him with head cocked slightly sideways. "What the hell did you spend it on? It's only been a couple of days!"

"I required clothing," replied Torval, indicating the jeans he was wearing, "as well as numerous hygiene products. Plus I bought myself several meals when I was not here."

"That's still not—well, okay, I get it, yeah, I can see how you spent most of it, I guess. All that stuff adds up, huh?"

"I am afraid so." Torval decided it best not to mention his date with Christine. Since he now knew that Pete's date with her didn't go well, he felt it prudent to simply not discuss the matter.

"Hmm," Pete said thoughtfully, rubbing his stubble-covered chin as if in thought. He obviously hadn't shaved this morning before coming to the warehouse. He reached into his pocket and took out his wallet, fiddling around inside until he found what he was looking for.

"I guess if you're out of cash, you can't very well get lunch, can you? Here, take this. We'll call it an advance on your payment tomorrow, okay?"

Torval reached out and took the twenty-dollar bill. "Thank you," he replied sincerely, tucking it into his own wallet. "That will help immensely."

"No problemo. You've done everything we asked of you so far, so it's the least I can do. Now if you don't mind, I'm gonna close up shop for now and go home—it's the last week of regular season basketball, y'know, and March Madness is right around the corner. Take one more donut if you want, and I'll catch you later."

Torval didn't have a chance to ask what this madness march was all about before Pete hustled him outside. He stood there for a moment, expecting his boss to follow him, but instead Pete locked the door on the inside and disappeared without a wave back into the building.

* * *

Torval waited, finishing the last of his donut, but Pete didn't return. The day was overcast, and as the demon watched, an occasional snow flurry fluttered down out of the dark clouds, drifting slowly along the windswept street to join with other swirls of snowflakes, forming strange little waves on the black asphalt. When cars drove by, they whipped the white dust into miniature whirlwinds that spun and danced before smoothing out again.

Torval shuddered. Even though it was midday, he still felt quite cold, and his light jacket didn't provide much protection against the weather. The last thing he wanted now was to get sick again, so he needed to get inside, where warmth and comfort awaited.

He began to walk in the general direction of the shelter, not really sure what else to do. The mysterious situation with his employers left him confused and distraught, so he forced it out of his mind. He couldn't possibly learn more without asking questions, and if he asked, he might get himself in over his head. Perhaps it would be best to just pretend he didn't know anything and see if he could figure out what was happening on his own.

Prelz, too, might be able to help. The ex-Tempter had already clued Torval in to the possibility that the Roxtons might be operating a "chop shop" at their facility. In fact, with the help of the Internet, Torval now knew exactly what a chop shop was and how it operated. However, such places were usually larger, with wide open areas capable of holding several vehicles, many people, and all the automobile parts they collected. Furthermore, all the waste products from the vehicle would have to be disposed of, and would no doubt leave stains and other remnants behind.

The Roxton warehouse was packed with row upon row of pallet racks, each filled with crates, with no room for cars to be broken down. There were no telltale stains or remnants of broken vehicles, or even the tools used to tear cars apart. Unless he'd missed some secret corner of the building, or the Roxtons were capable of moving all those racks out of the way when needed, the warehouse just didn't seem like it could possibly support a chop shop.

Nonetheless, Prelz's contacts had reported that the Roxtons were up to something in that building. Perhaps the older demon simply leapt to the conclusion that a chop shop was involved. Maybe that same source, whatever it was, might be able to gather more information that could help determine what was really happening there.

Prelz was likely at the shelter, so Torval angled toward it, wondering if perhaps Christine would be there as well. On a workday she would be at her office, but this was Sunday. Torval half wanted to see her and half didn't. How would she react to his presence now that she knew his true nature?

He wanted to talk to her very badly. He had so many questions! Yet he feared she'd reject him again, and order him away. Bless it all, why did she have to be an angel, anyway? If only she could be human—but there was no sense worrying about such things. He couldn't change her true nature, any more than he could change his own.

In due course Torval arrived at the rundown building that housed the familiar soup kitchen. A short line blocked the entrance, but it didn't quite extend outside the door, so he slipped inside without worrying about trying to get any food. The donuts would tide him over for now. He moved in amongst the tables, looking for Prelz, but there was no sign of the older demon.

He was still searching about when his eyes fell upon a very angry-looking plump black woman holding a still-dripping ladle in one accusing hand. "What the devil do you think you're doin' here?" she all but screeched. "Get the hell out before I throw you out! And don't think I won't!"

Devil? Torval cringed at the word. Did she know the truth now, too? Had Christine told her what he was? But no, she wouldn't have done that—it must be just another of those strange human euphemisms.

"Why?" inquired Torval worriedly. "What have I done? I do not require soup today—I am merely looking for—"

"You know perfectly well what you did!" Lakisha hissed, waving the ladle about like a weapon. Torval thought she might strike him if he got too close, so he took a cautious step backward. "You upset Christine, you damned fool! The kindest, nicest person in the whole world and you had the gall to—why I oughta just clean yer clock right now!"

"That's enough, 'Kisha," Christine called out. Torval immediately turned to the back room, where she stood just around the corner, head poking out so he could see only half her face. "Just tell him to go away. No need for violence."

"Oh, come on, maybe just a little?" Lakisha replied, looking noticeably disappointed.

"Thanks anyway, but no." Christine managed a kind of wan half-smile, then turned her gaze back to Torval. Her voice became firmer and more controlled. "Go away, Joe. I don't want to talk to you."

"But I—" the demon started, but she vanished instantly behind the corner. He took a step forward and found his way blocked by Lakisha's meaty arm, still clutching the soup-stained ladle.

"You heard her, boy," growled the woman. "An' just 'cause she said no violence don't mean I ain't gonna slap you if you try gettin' past me!"

"Then I will speak from here," replied Torval with a sigh.

"Christine!" he called out, choosing his words carefully, "I apologize for what happened last night. You must believe that I did not plan on any of this. Can we not simply talk? That is all I wish to do. I will not harm you."

"No!" she yelled back. "I don't care what you want. I just can't trust you anymore. I can't believe anything you say, and I don't want to see you again, ever! Have a nice life, Joe Sampson."

"But Christine, I—"

"Just can it!" snapped Lakisha, pushing him roughly. "You had your say, and she had hers. Now knock it off!"

Torval sighed. Trying to talk with Lakisha here was hopeless—he couldn't say the things he really needed to say, like how he was here on vacation, and not on some assignment, or that the Compact didn't forbid their interaction, only direct conflict between them. If he wanted to speak with her about such things, they would have to be alone.

The Compact wasn't the reason she didn't want to talk to him, though. She said something about trust. That meant she felt his demonic nature made him inherently deceitful, which seemed like nothing more than prejudice. Torval knew all about deception, but since coming to Earth he'd tried to avoid such things and and practice goodness whenever possible. That meant steering clear of lies, which were inherently evil in nature. He'd only lied to Christine when discussing his false identity. Had he known she was an angel, he wouldn't have bothered.

Still, he *had* lied—there was no getting around that. Regardless of the reasons, he'd been untruthful, and while she had done the same, that didn't absolve him of his own guilt. He had to regain her trust somehow, at least enough to get her to talk to him. He had to find a way to show her that he wasn't evil—he remained the same person she'd helped find a job. The exact same person she'd spent time with, and shared a movie, and dinner, and a walk home, arm-in-arm.

And, most importantly of all, with whom she'd shared a kiss.

How could he possibly earn her trust? What could he possibly do to change her mind? There must be some way—something she wanted, that he could provide. A gift, perhaps, but what?

He thought about the twenty dollars in his wallet. That would buy very little. She wouldn't want a physical gift, anyway. Not something material. There was something else, though. Something tickling at the edge of his memory, something she'd said she wanted ... what was it? Something he could do for her. She'd said it ... when? During the date, he remembered. During dinner.

Now Torval remembered. In a flash of inspiration, he knew exactly what he had to do.

He stepped away from Lakisha, who continued to watch him warily. Then he turned his back on her, hoping she wouldn't take the opportunity to brain him with that menacing metal implement of hers. Raising his voice, he called out, "Everyone, please, if I may have your attention. I would like to say something."

The shelter was a quiet place by nature, although there were a few muffled conversations here and there, as well as a constant clanking of silverware and pots and pans. All of this came to a halt in a few seconds, as everyone turned their eyes to Torval. Lakisha, apparently uncomfortable being so close to the center of attention, scuttled off behind her pot of soup, while Torval began to speak once more.

"Perhaps you know me and perhaps not," said Torval loudly. "My name is Joe Sampson and I was once one of you. A few days ago I was sick and hungry and cold in an alley outside, during the snowstorm. Like you I had given up hope, but then I thought of this place, of how warm and comfortable it is, and how there is food to be found here. And I thought, if only I could have such things for myself all the time, how much better that would be! Perhaps you have had such thoughts as well, but felt like things would never change.

"I can tell you, it is possible to change. The people who work here, like Lakisha and Christine, are willing to help you as they helped me. It is possible to find work, and acquire better clothing, and a place to live. It is possible to not be cold and hungry and homeless any more. I am proof of this. All you must do is ask them, and they will help you, because that is what they do.

"You may return to your meal now. That is all."

There were a few muffled comments, punctuated by a few hoarse laughs, and the clanking of silverware began anew. Torval put down his arms, which had mysteriously gone up in the air during his speech, and sighed. Although no one seemed to take his advice immediately, he still nonetheless felt a stirring inside himself, a feeling of satisfaction and well-being. He did good, he knew, even if it didn't produce any obvious results.

Lakisha stared at him with a mixture of surprise and confusion. "Why did you do that?" she asked after a moment.

Torval shrugged, looking past her toward the back of the kitchen, hoping to see Christine. She wasn't there, but for a second he thought he saw a shadow slip back into the darkness.

"Because," he replied as he turned to leave, "she asked me to."

Chapter 3

Torval waited a few minutes outside, hoping Christine would seek him out, but she didn't. He still felt good about what he'd done, but at the same time disappointed. Still, he'd at least accomplished something, making at least some progress in repaying some of the debt he owed her.

He could do nothing more at this point, since she refused to speak with him, and Lakisha wouldn't let him pass. He thought about waiting for Christine to finish at the shelter, perhaps intercepting her as she went home, but he had no idea how long she intended to stay. He didn't want to spend the entire day waiting outside, in the cold.

In fact, the chill air was already getting to be a problem. The wind wasn't nearly as severe as the day before, but the cold felt like knives stabbing into his exposed skin. With that in mind he began to walk, keeping his hands in his pockets and face toward the pavement, shivering.

In due course he came to the drugstore he'd already visited several times before. Stepping inside, he rubbed his half-frozen face and looked around for some solution to his current problem. After surveying the aisles, he discovered a rack with what he was looking for—gloves, scarves, and the like. Even better, they were on sale, as winter neared its end. Apparently the store had them clearanced in order to get rid of them quickly, which was fortunate for Torval.

After some searching he located a pair of gloves that fit, as well as a heavy cloth hood that covered his ears and most of his face. Together they cost almost twelve dollars, but that still left him enough money to purchase food later in the day, so he spent the cash and left the store, now able to endure the cold a bit more comfortably.

He passed by the shelter again, hoping to find Prelz, but didn't see the other demon anywhere. Now what? With no one left to talk to,

Torval found himself at a loss.

He kept on walking, thinking back to what he'd learned about New York City from the Internet. There were several places of interest fairly close by, as he recalled. Rockefeller Center, for example, although he'd already been there. There were tours available, but of course those cost money, which was in short supply. He needed something free.

He did recall, from the map and several descriptions online, that a natural area called Central Park dominated the center of the city. There were often free events, shows, and musical performances held there, so he headed in that direction.

After a few blocks he came to the park, which proved impossible to miss. In fact, the place stretched as far as he could see in either direction, filled with trees, open fields, pedestrian walkways, fountains, and the like. This was Torval's first experience with anything other than asphalt and buildings, and the sheer openness of it all took him by surprise.

All his life he'd lived in confined spaces, dwelling in a small cube-like room and spending his days walking through narrow halls from one cramped cell to another. To be able to suddenly see so far, to a distant horizon capped by a row of tall skyscrapers, was quite captivating. He stood for several minutes just mesmerized by the view, until finally a cluster of passing pedestrians jostled him into action. He crossed the street with them and wandered, still somewhat awestruck, into the open park.

There were people all around, some walking on the paths while others lounged on the open lawns, picnicking despite the cold. They seemed not to mind the occasional drifting snowflake or gust of wind. Here and there couples walked hand in hand, heavily dressed bicyclists flashed by, and joggers dressed in sweatsuits tromped along, breaths heavy with frost. A few birds stirred in the leafless trees, whistling and chirping, as if eager for spring to finally come.

Torval made his way to one of the paths and strode along, quickly forgetting he was even in a city at all. The park was immense and there were people everywhere, some exercising, others talking, and a few even locked in romantic embraces on the park benches. Here and there he came to groups involved in some activity, such as a team of runners jogging together, or a cluster of musicians playing drums and several different types of stringed instruments. Torval listened for a while, until he saw that viewers were expected to pay them by dropping money into a hat. Unwilling to spend any of his remaining cash, the demon moved on.

After a short walk, he topped a small rise and came to a round fountain, which was currently deactivated considering the cold weather. The water within had frozen, and a thin dusting of drifting snow coated the ice. Nearby, Torval saw several rows of tables, where a number of men and women sat facing each other, studying some sort of puzzle on a board in front of them.

No, not a puzzle, Torval realized after a moment. These were chess boards—he recognized them from the movie he'd seen with Christine. In fact, the tableau before him resembled the scene portrayed early on in the film. The main character, John Ramos, played chess at tables exactly like these.

Intrigued, Torval moved up and started to watch one of the contests. The two men, both fairly old by the look of them, were completely engrossed in their game. Next to them sat a wooden device consisting of two clocks, each with their own trigger in the form of a bronze peg jutting up out of the wooden frame. At present, the man on the right, who wore thick glasses and a wide-brimmed hat, had his clock trigger up, indicating it was his turn. Torval remembered from the movie that when someone made a move, they would press down on their button, so his opponent could move next.

Torval studied the pieces. During the movie, the games were played quickly, so he had no real idea of the rules. It seemed to him that the audience was supposed to understand the game already, so the individual moves didn't matter, only the result. He waited, expecting the man in glasses to move a piece, but he didn't right away. In fact, several minutes passed before he finally lifted up a horse-like token and set it down in another spot. Then he pushed his clock button, adjusted his glasses, and settled back to wait.

Torval continued to watch but very quickly became bored. The game seemed to take extremely long, totally unlike the movie suggested, and since the demon had no idea how to play, he felt lost. Unlike the film, in which the main character and his opponents frequently exchanged dialogue, these two men didn't speak or even look at each other. In fact, none of the other players seemed to be doing very much talking, either.

Torval moved along, examining some of the other boards. Some were filled with pieces, and others had very few, but none looked the same. One table seemed to be moving fairly quickly, so he watched that for a bit, trying to understand what was going on, but he couldn't make any sense of it. The pieces could jump around or move and even take other pieces off the board, but how this worked eluded him.

"Care for a game?" someone said. Torval turned to see a middle-aged man dressed in a heavy overcoat, wearing a thick checkered scarf. His head was wrapped in a dark brown skullcap, allowing only a single lock of black hair to escape, where it fluttered over his forehead. He wore a well-trimmed salt-and-pepper beard and glasses that rode low on his cherry-red nose.

"I would like that," agreed Torval, "but I must confess I do not know the rules. I have been watching, trying to understand, but cannot make sense of it."

"Oh, never played before?" inquired the man. "That's okay, I'll show you the rules if you want. Nobody to play anyways—too cold for most of the gang to show up. Have a seat."

He sat down and began to move the pieces, placing them in what appeared to be a very organized fashion. When he was finished, two rows of black tokens sat on his side of the checkerboard, while Torval's side contained the white pieces.

"Name's Fred, Fred O'Connell," said the man, putting out a hand in Torval's direction. "Yours?"

"Joe Sampson," said Torval, returning the handshake. "I saw this game in a movie recently."

"'Queen Takes Pawn,' I betcha," said Fred with a nod. "Haven't seen it myself, but it's good to see chess out there in the media, especially that kind of movie. Us chess nuts are usually portrayed as nerds or geeks, y'know?"

"I suppose," replied Torval, not at all understanding what those terms meant, but figuring by context that they referred to particularly undesirable subsections of humanity. "So, how does it work?"

"Well, you know anything about it chess all?" inquired Fred. "Anything about the pieces?"

"I know the smallest one is called a pawn," replied Torval helpfully.

Fred nodded, immediately grasping that Torval had no clue whatsoever. "Okay, well, I'm not promisin' anything but I'll at least get you started. Yep, these are pawns, and they move forward one space, like this." He demonstrated the move. "When they move for the first time, they can go two, if they ain't blocked, but that's up to you. Once they move they can't do that anymore, but move one space at a time only. Got it? Oh, and another thing, they can only capture at angles like this. If something's right in front of them, they can't do anything but sit there."

"I see," replied Torval. He wanted to ask why this was so, but Fred didn't wait, pressing on with his explanation of the next piece, something called a "rook." In fact, Fred moved on very quickly, almost overwhelming the demon with his explanations.

The entire briefing took several minutes, but when it was finally done, Torval felt he understood the basics of it. Each piece could move in a certain way, and capture other pieces simply by moving on top of them. Most pieces, except the pawn, captured in the same way they moved. Some, like the rook and bishop, moved down lines or rows of squares, while others could only move one space, like the king. Capturing a piece ended your move, and the presence of other pieces blocked the movement of every piece except the knight, which could jump over others and moved three spaces at a time—"two out and one over, no more and no less," as Fred described it.

The objective of the game was to capture the opponent's king. Placing a piece in such a way as to threaten the king was "check," and putting him in a position where he couldn't avoid capture was "checkmate." That explained some of the terms Torval heard in the movie, and he could see how those words might work their way into normal speech.

Often, as it turned out, the game would end long before checkmate actually occurred, usually because one player became so disadvantaged they had no way to possibly secure victory. Also, sometimes a game could simply result in a draw, either because a player lacked enough pieces to force checkmate, or for certain other reasons. The sheer number of complications confused Torval, but he felt sure he'd figure them out eventually.

Once the explanation ended, Fred concluded with, "Okay, that about explains it. Got any questions?"

"Yes," said Torval. "How do we begin?"

Fred grinned. "I was hoping you'd say that. Splainin' this game takes so damn long! Okay, since you're white, you go first. White always starts."

Torval looked at the board. The row of pawns blocked most of his pieces, except the knights, limiting his options, but he still had no idea what to do.

"Let me make a suggestion," said Fred after a moment. "Most of the game is focused around controlling the center, from which you can launch attacks anywhere on the board. So you want to try to establish control there first, meaning you might want to move one of your middle pawns out. Don't forget they can go two spaces on their first move."

Torval nodded and selected the pawn in front of his queen, which seemed logical since that was the most powerful of the pieces. Moving that one out into play, where it could be useful, seemed a good idea. He pushed the pawn two spaces forward and looked at Fred curiously.

"Good, that's a good opener," the chess player told him. He reached out and repeated the move, placing his own queen's pawn in front of Torval's. Both pieces now blocked each other from further movement. "Now you might think about moving a knight out, to help secure the center, or maybe that bishop."

Torval considered his options, finally shrugged, and moved his king's knight up two and to the left one. It seemed like as good a move as any. His opponent countered by sliding a bishop out four spaces on a diagonal. Torval didn't see the purpose of that move, but suspected it had some use considering how quickly Fred placed it there.

The game progressed slowly, with Fred frequently suggesting moves and Torval taking advantage of the advice. About halfway through, though, the man fell silent, and Torval realized he was now on his own. He made a few more moves, haphazardly attacking some piece or other, while Fred first defended and then, when he had a break, began a series of attacks of his own. After exchanging a knight for a bishop, he suddenly moved first a rook and then his queen all the way across the board, to an area Torval formerly considered safe. With a start, Torval realized he was in check, and could only move his king to one spot, and as soon as he did, the next move put him in checkmate.

"Not bad," said Fred once the defeat was obvious. "Really, for your first game, you did fine. Think you've got the basics down now?"

"I believe so," replied Torval. "I understand how the pieces move. The rest of the game is more difficult. It seemed to me as if you acted with some sort of plan, but how you did so eludes me."

"I looked ahead," explained Fred helpfully. "When I saw you move your knight out there," he went on, pointing at the board, "I realized I could make a couple of moves that would look like attacks on that piece, while setting me up for the strike on your king's position. That sort of distracted you, I know. Once you get better, you'll see through stuff like that."

"I see. So what you are saying is I must anticipate moves? And plan ahead for what I intend to do?"

"Exactly, that's what the game is all about," Fred agreed. "Want to play again? I'll tell you what, I'll play defensively and let you make some attacks, so you can try looking ahead a bit without worrying about what I'm up to."

"Very well," agreed Torval. "I appreciate the instruction."

"No problem, that's why I'm here." He started to set the pieces up again, back to the exact same original starting positions, except for one slight difference. "Now, this time, you get to play black."

* * *

Torval played for several more hours. First, Fred simply shuffled his pieces around, letting his opponent plan and execute a few attacks. Then they played another game in which the human held nothing back, annihilating his demonic foe within the space of about fifteen minutes. Much to Torval's surprise, afterward Fred pronounced him a skilled beginner and moved him to another table, where he took on another beginning player, a young man named Mark.

Mark was a teenager, dressed in a heavy leather jacket and also wearing glasses. His face was covered in a kind of wrapping so that very little of his face was visible, and other than a cursory hello, he said nothing at all. He and Torval played three times, and after two defeats, the demon surprised himself by winning the final game. He used something called a "Knight fork" to secure Mark's queen by simultaneously putting the king in check. Mark had no choice but to move his vulnerable king, and thereby lost his most valuable asset. Torval then proceeded to exchange pieces, a technique Fred had demonstrated to great effect in their last contest, until he easily overwhelmed Mark's remaining defense. The youth spared himself the inevitable by symbolically knocking his king over, signifying surrender.

After that, the young man stood, muttered a barely audible

"Thanks for the game, see you later," and shuffled off, hands in his pockets. Torval wasn't sure if he really meant that, or was simply frustrated at losing. Perhaps he blamed himself for making a mistake, but then, he was a beginner, after all. Torval had made his share of errors, but liked to think he'd learned from them.

Chess was certainly an intriguing game. There were so many pieces and so many possible moves that every game would always be different. The strategies were intricate and he found himself constantly wrestling with the possibilities—if he moved *that* piece *there*, and his opponent responded with *this* move, then what would he do next? He had to mentally visualize what the board would look like two, three, or even more moves ahead.

In fact, he'd been concentrating on such things for so long that his head actually hurt. He checked his watch and saw to his surprise that it was now close to four o'clock. Somehow he'd managed to spend several hours here without even realizing it!

I need food, he realized immediately, for his stomach rumbled in complaint, the morning's donuts long since gone. Furthermore, he needed to relieve himself as well, not to mention warm up his chilly fingers and face. *Time to go,* he told himself, standing up and rubbing absently at his sore behind. Hopefully, before work he could find Prelz and inform him of the latest developments, as well as ask for some advice.

Torval turned to leave, but as he did, Fred spotted him and got to his feet. "Had fun, did you?" he asked with an affable smile.

"Yes," agreed Torval. "The game is quite challenging. Thank you for taking the time to teach me."

"Well, if you want to play again, the Midtown Chess Club meets at this same spot every weekend," replied Fred. He pointed at a large glass jar on the end of a nearby table. "We don't have dues or anything, but we do accept contributions, if you like. The money goes to buying chess boards, repairing the timer clocks, and so on."

"Oh, I see," Torval responded, understanding automatically. Fred wanted something similar to a tip, which seemed perfectly reasonable considering he'd kept the demon entertained for the better part of the afternoon. Torval reached into his pocket, found his wallet, and pulled out a couple of dollar bills, which he dropped into the glass jar, where they joined a smattering of change and a single other lonely note. In doing so he left himself with what he hoped was just enough to afford lunch.

"Thanks, Joe," Fred said amiably. "That's more than most people bother with. Feel free to come back anytime."

Torval was about to depart, seeing as how he'd just been dismissed, but another thought occurred to him. Perhaps he could learn something from this game, something that could help him with one of his current dilemmas. Drawing from what he'd learned of chess, he decided to think ahead.

"Fred," he said hastily, catching the other's attention before he moved too far away, "is there any way I could have one of these chess pieces?"

"Just one?" inquired the man curiously. "Whatever for? Do you have a set somewhere that's missing a piece?"

"Not exactly," replied the demon. "However, I need to use one for another purpose not related to chess. Is it possible to borrow one, and return it to you next weekend?"

"Oh, that won't be necessary," said Fred with a shrug. "I've got a box over here that has a few random bits in it. Every so often we lose a piece or two setting up, or one falls out of a box, so we keep one partial set around to scavenge from. Grab whatever you need, and you can keep it if you like. I don't care."

"Thank you," replied Torval, employing a smile, which seemed like an appropriate gesture. He sifted through the proffered box until he located what he needed, slipped the token into his pocket, and started the long walk back toward the shelter, where he hoped he might find Prelz.

* * *

Unfortunately, Prelz remained frustratingly absent. Torval checked inside, admittedly only briefly for fear of catching Lakisha's attention, and then walked around the block, but saw no sign of the ex-Tempter anywhere.

Torval found himself feeling a certain amount of anxiety, which was somewhat disturbing. He hadn't realized how important Prelz had become to him. His fellow demon had been around ever since this ill-conceived trip to Earth began, and he always leaned on Prelz for help and advice. Now Torval didn't have that option, and he felt ... what? Not really anxiety, but something else. What was the human word for it?

He wasn't sure. Loneliness, perhaps? Yes, that was it. Torval felt lonely. He had no one to talk to, and the distress he felt was palpable.

The irony of this wasn't lost on him as he enjoyed a quick bite to eat at the nearby KFC. Not so very long ago, walking his route in Hell, he'd been perfectly happy being alone. Talking with imprisoned souls was an automatic, conditioned response, while having a chat with fellow demons was virtually unheard of. Even when someone like Geezon attempted to make small talk, Torval found it little more than irritating.

Now, here on Earth, he felt just as uncomfortable not having anyone to communicate with. Sitting in the restaurant, eating an otherwise thoroughly enjoyable three-piece chicken dinner, he should've been focusing on the mouth-watering tastes tickling his palate. Instead, he worried about where Prelz might be, and fretted over exactly what he was supposed to do next when everyone he knew in the city was missing or unavailable.

There was always the library, but Torval had little need of that place now that he could access the Internet to find answers to all his technical questions. Still, he had nothing else to do and nowhere else to go, so once he finished his meal, he made his way a couple of blocks to the stone structure. Unfortunately, he found the doors locked, and upon close inspection he found a sign indicating the place was closed on Sundays.

So now what? Wander the streets until it was time to report for work? Torval paced back and forth on the library doorstep for a few minutes, trying to sort things out. What he really needed right now was someone to talk to, and that someone had to at least partially understand his current problems.

The first name that jumped to mind was that of Shelly Mendez. In fact, the moment he thought of her, he started to walk toward her apartment. After a few seconds, though, he stopped himself. His human body certainly wanted to visit her again, didn't it?

Well, there was certainly good reason for that, but the rational side of himself resisted. Sure, she would show him a good time, assuming she wasn't busy with some other customer, but did he really want that right now? He should be pursuing Christine, not Shelly. That's one thing the *Book of Dating* had explained quite forcefully—while involved in one relationship, you didn't involve yourself in another. Not that he really considered what he had with Shelly to be a "relationship" per se, but Christine might not agree should she find out. He'd already deceived her once, no matter the reason—he didn't want to do so again.

Torval sighed. So what was he to do next? Who in this vast city could he talk to, who might have the slightest ability to understand?

The idea came to him a moment later, and with a smile he turned on his heels and hurried off, keeping his face turned away from the bitter wind as best he could.

* * *

The last time he had visited this church, the place was all but empty. Torval recalled feeling that the open auditorium, and its collection of neatly placed benches, could house more than just a few people. He saw now that his initial impression was correct. At least a hundred humans, and perhaps more, now filled the pews, all looking forward toward the altar and the robed figure there. The speaker read slowly and forcefully from a book on the pedestal before him.

Torval stepped cautiously into the church. Save for an occasional cough or the muffled whimpering of a small child somewhere in the crowd, everyone was silent. All eyes were on the man in the robes, who Torval recognized as Father Michaels. The priest continued to read, glancing up occasionally and pausing between sentences, as if to let the words sink in:

> *And Jesus said to them, "Did you never read in the Scriptures: The stone that the builders rejected has become the cornerstone; by the Lord has this been done, and it is wonderful in our eyes? Therefore, I say to you, the Kingdom of God will be taken away from you and given to a people that will produce its fruit."*
>
> *When the chief priests and the Pharisees heard his parables, they knew that he was speaking about them. And although they were attempting to arrest him, they feared the crowds, for they regarded him as a prophet.*

Upon finishing this passage, Father Michaels closed the book, saying, "This is the Word of the Lord." The crowd then, in unison, said something in response, although the words eluded Torval. All the assembled people then sat down as one, without prompting, as if having carefully rehearsed the maneuver.

Holding the obviously important book aloft, the priest carried it over to a recess in the nearby wall, placing it there before returning to the altar, and genuflecting before seating himself. Torval realized the book in question must be the Bible that Father Michaels mentioned the last time they met. He had no idea it was such an important tome. Clearly it was something to be revered, from the way he treated it.

The room became silent. Torval, at a loss as to what was going on, decided that standing in the doorway was inappropriate, so he moved to one of the open spaces in a pew near the back. No one gave him a second glance, save the old woman next to him, who shuffled sideways a bit to give him more room. As he glanced her way, she flashed him a toothless smile and then returned her attention toward the front. Torval got the impression something else was supposed to happen, but he wasn't sure what.

After a few moments, Father Michaels stood up again and returned to the pulpit. For a moment he let his eyes meander about the crowd, and it seemed to Torval that more than once that gaze fixed itself directly upon him. Still, the eyes never lingered, so perhaps that was just his imagination.

After a moment, Father Michaels began to speak. He wasn't reading from a book this time, or from any prepared notes. Instead, he just started talking, and everyone else seemed ready to listen. Not sure of what else to do, Torval did the same.

"Friends," said the priest with an affable smile, "I'm sure many of you have heard this particular passage before. It's one of many parables our Lord Jesus Christ told during his short stay on Earth, way back over two thousand years ago. He was very good at this, Jesus was, telling simple stories that illustrated the truth to those around him.

"I'm sure most of you have heard the much longer tale of the man who found the birds in his barn, and, frustrated at his inability to communicate, discovered the only way to speak to them was to become a bird himself. This is another kind of parable, in its own way—it's a way to help you understand why God would visit us as an ordinary human being.

"Picture that, if you will—the most powerful being there is, so incredibly powerful that He can create an entire universe from scratch! But now, He's nothing more than flesh and blood, a weak, frail human capable of feeling hunger and thirst and pain. Can you even begin to understand what that must've been like? And this man, this Jesus, is now faced with the ultimate challenge—how to actually communicate with human beings, in a way they can truly understand. For though he may be human himself, at least on the outside, inside he's still supremely powerful and all-knowing. It would be as if you suddenly became an ant, and then tried to explain to other ants how ... well, let's say how nuclear power worked. They'd all look at you, and shake their little ant heads, and think you were crazy.

"So Jesus had to explain Truth to his fellow humans in ways they could understand. He told stories, or parables, that could reach the simple people of the time. Most of these parables, like the story of the prodigal son, had a message of love and hope. Every now and then, though, Jesus tried to send a warning with his tales. The one we heard today, it was delivered as a message to the scribes and Pharisees—the ancient world's version of corrupt politicians—as a warning. A warning that they had forgotten the Word of God, and that they were doomed to Hell. Then there was, of course, the implied message—if they cared to hear it—that it was not too late to change.

"One thing you have to think about, when you realize the way in which Jesus told his parables, was the situation in the world at that time. The world was a much more primitive place. There was no Internet back then. Yes, I know that's hard for some of you to believe! No computers, no cell phones, no electronic mail—not even any regular mail, in fact. If you wanted to get the word out about something, you had to deliver it by word of mouth. Telling a story was a great way to do that, because stories are quick to be remembered, and then told and retold. That's how we have the Bible today. The stories from that time were told so often they were recorded permanently—and by more than one person, too. That's why we have four Gospels, not just one.

"Maybe it's obvious from the way I've been talking here that I really like parables. I think they're an excellent tool for getting across a message. In fact, I like them so much I'd like to try one myself. Only not one set two thousand years ago, in the time of Jesus. I'll tell you what, I'll set one in the modern era, and I'll even throw in a little science fiction for you, just to make things interesting.

"Okay, here goes." The priest hesitated a moment, flexing and symbolically cracking his knuckles before him, as if gathering his thoughts. This drew a couple of snickers from the crowd.

Father Michaels raised his voice just slightly. "Once there was an alien named, well, let's call him Tor, just because that's the first syllable that popped into my head."

Torval jumped slightly in his seat, for Father Michaels glanced his way just as he spoke that supposedly made-up name. Clearly that choice had been no accident.

"Anyway," the priest went on, "Tor's been watching Earth for a while, from a distance. He watches our media broadcasts and he observes us from above, but he doesn't know what it's really like to walk our streets and meet us for real. Yet he also knows what would happen if he came down in his rocket ship and landed in Central Park. He's seen *The Day the Earth Stood Still*. Heh-heh."

The crowd laughed at this, even though the remark completely went over Torval's head. Father Michaels grinned for a moment before proceeding.

"So Tor decides the best way to meet humans for real is to do what our Lord did, and become one of us. He creates a human body, dresses it in appropriate clothes, and steps into New York City, where he is immediately and completely ignored."

The crowed muttered at this, but Father Michaels, undaunted, went on immediately. "Yes, I said *ignored*, because that's what we do when we pass other people on the street—and not ignored on purpose, mind you. There's just too many other people to interact with them all, unless you have some reason to. So Tor shrugs, figuring that's just the way we are, and starts exploring. He has a few encounters with humans and eventually even makes some friends. He rides the subway, he sees a ball game, he almost gets run down by cab—in other words, he has a typical day in the Big Apple."

Another ripple of laughter went through the crowd. The priest paused a moment to allow this to peter out, then continued.

"But what happens then? Tor spends a few days on Earth, mingling with humans, but what next? What report will he deliver to his fellow aliens back up there in the stars? That humans are strange and unusual people? Certainly, that would be part of it, especially if he spent any time in Central Park." There were a few snickers at this comment, but Father Michaels went on without pausing. "Would he say that we are kind and friendly, or that we're angry and violent? Would he think we are worthy beings, someday destined to join him out in the universe at large? Or that we're little more than children, not yet grown enough to really understand our true purpose?

"I'm sure that each of you hearing me today could come up with a different answer. Each of you, if I asked privately, would tell me something different that you'd think Tor would say if asked about humanity. The thing is, what that alien would think of humans would entirely depend on what he experienced in those few days he spent here.

"So think about that, then, if you will. What if you met someone new today, and he was in reality Tor, the alien from the stars, visiting Earth for just a few precious hours? What message would you want him to take back when he leaves?

"That, then, is the lesson of my little parable, friends. Everyone is special, everyone is unique. Everyone sees the world a little bit differently, and if you show a little kindness, and treat everyone as you would a friend, then you've already demonstrated the true measure of what it means to be human."

At that Father Michaels stepped away from the pulpit and went back to the altar, bowing before it once again before sitting. The room was silent for another few moments, apparently to let this speech sink in.

Torval took the opportunity and contemplated the message as he shifted impatiently in his seat. The priest's words hit uncomfortably close to home. It was as if Father Michaels spoke about him directly—and perhaps he had, considering the name he'd chosen for his "alien" visitor. So was Father Michaels really speaking to the crowd, trying to get across what seemed like a perfectly reasonable message, or was he trying to talk specifically to Torval? Or did he manage to do both those things at once?

The demon remained befuddled when Father Michaels stood, and, apparently automatically, so too did the entire crowd. Taken by surprise, the demon had to scramble to his feet. Furthermore, everyone started reciting some sort of chant, something that Torval had no idea was coming. All he could do was stand there, open-mouthed, pretending to mutter the words lest he look too out of place.

In due course the crowd finished and Father Michaels started saying something else, something obviously pre-prepared, so Torval sighed and let himself relax. Clearly he'd entered some sort of religious ceremony about which he knew nothing. Perhaps it would be best to retreat while he had the chance, before he broke some unknown taboo, if he hadn't already done so. Maybe when the ceremony was over he could get a chance to talk to Father Michaels alone.

He glanced back at the exit, but felt a tug at his sweater sleeve. Surprised, he looked over to see the old woman poking at him with a gnarled, clawlike hand. "It's okay, sonny," she whispered quietly. "First time at Mass? It's fine, nobody's gonna hurtcha."

"Yes, this is my first time," agreed Torval nervously, trying to keep his voice low as well. Fortunately, Father Michaels continued to speak, dominating most of the room's attention. Occasionally the crowd added something, following some kind of invisible script, but no one paid any attention to the conversation in the back row.

"I could tell," said the old woman, smiling up at him through excessively thick glasses that made her brown eyes appear to bulge unnaturally out of her wrinkled skull. "Nothin' to be 'fraid of here, sonny. Just stand'n'sit when we do, ya don't haveta say anythin'. Ya gots any questions, feel free ta ask Auntie June here whatever ya want. I usedta sing in the choir here, y'know, back when they had a decent one, before all this rock'n'roll singin' took hold." She sighed for a moment. "Ah, well, it's a signa the times, I guess. What's yer name, boy?"

"Joe," replied the demon, somewhat grateful to find someone to talk to. At that moment, the priest finished speaking, and the assembly sat back down as one. She looked relieved, clutching at some unseen pain in her back, and shuffled about in the hardwood seat as she tried to get comfortable.

"You ain't Catholic, I get it," she whispered after a moment, raising her voice slightly as somewhere else in the building a choir began to sing. Torval raised an eyebrow at the sudden addition of a pleasant melody to the proceedings, and noted that some of the nearby crowd had joined in, apparently knowing the words to this particular song. Meanwhile, several men started walking up and down the aisles, carrying some sort of baskets.

"Yeah, usually I see a couple new ones here and there, in back like you," went on Auntie June, apparently not seeing the need to join in with the singing. "You ain't Protestant, neither, or you at least woulda known some of this already. Jewish? Nah, don't look Jewish to me. What, then?"

"I follow no specific religion," explained Torval, not sure what else to say, "if that is what you are asking."

"Ah, an atheist, or agnostic, or whatever," she continued. "Curious about the faith, then? Or maybe yer writin' something, is that it? You a writer, researchin' or somethin' like that?"

"No, nothing of the sort," answered Torval. "I wish to speak with Father Michaels, but apparently I have arrived during this ceremony, so now I simply wish to wait until it ends."

"Ah, gotcha," she nodded. At this point one of the ushers arrived with a basket, attached to a long stick. He passed this in front of the startled Torval—the container was filled with money! As he froze, unsure of what to do, Auntie June reached out with her right hand and deposited a small purple envelope, which she'd apparently held at the ready for just this purpose. The usher said nothing, withdrew the basket with a single swift motion, and disappeared through the doors behind them.

Torval realized he'd almost made a huge mistake. Until Auntie June deposited the envelope in the container, he'd contemplated removing some of the money, thinking it might be some sort of gift. Now he knew otherwise—clearly this was some sort of fee levied upon the attendees, and in fact, by not contributing, he may well have broken some unknown rule.

"Oh, don't worry," said the old woman, noticing the look of concern on Torval's face, "that's just a donation. It's optional, and since you ain't in the church, there's nothin' wrong with you skippin' out."

"I see," replied the demon, somewhat relieved by this news. Apparently, the offering baskets held a kind of tip, like the donation jar back at the chess club. Had he more money, he might've attempted to find the usher and his basket, but then, he had in fact missed part of the service, so perhaps he'd just forget about the donation for now.

"Anyways," said the old woman, not missing a beat, "yeah, I like Father Michaels, he's a real what-a-waste, y'know? Hee-hee, that's what I woulda said fifty years ago, anyhow. He's got a good head on his shoulders, though, and a way with words too. Like that homily tonight. Who woulda thought of that? Aliens walkin' around tryin' to learn about people! Why, he's really got me thinkin'." She reached over with one of her scrawny hands, skin so tight on it that it looked like little more than flesh-covered bones. "What if you was an alien, boy? Wouldn't that be a hoot! Why, I better be nice to you, hmm? Wouldn't want you tellin' yer other aliens how mean us humans was! Hee-hee!"

"I assure you," remarked Torval with all honesty, "I am no alien."

"Hee, yeah, I knows that," cackled the old lady. "I'd be nice to you anyways, either way, just 'cause that's how I is. So what do you think, hmm? Of our Mass, that is."

"It is interesting," commented the demon, glancing back at the front of the church, where Father Michaels recited some sort of blessing over several items recently delivered to him at the altar. "I feel somewhat left out, seeing as I do not know the rituals, and you are all able to stand and sit and speak when required."

"That's 'cause we been doin' this every Sunday for all our lives," chuckled Auntie June.

"Every Sunday?" Torval was baffled. "You do this every week? Once a week?"

"Sometimes more often," she pointed out. "It's Lent right now, see? That's a special time of year, and we got a lotta extra holy days. Easter's right around the corner, too. You oughta see this place then, it'll be packed! Come on in then if you want—Auntie June'll make you feel welcome. You can sit right here next to me!" She patted the open space in the pew nearby.

Torval nodded. "Perhaps I will," he agreed without even thinking about it, even though he had no idea what Easter was or when it might be. She just seemed so friendly, it felt wrong to refuse.

"Oh, good!" she responded eagerly. "Okay, now this part of Mass coming up, it's called the Eucharist, y'see? The priest blesses the bread and wine, like he's doin' now, and then ... "

Torval nodded, following along and trying to make sense of it all, and the Mass went on for another twenty minutes.

Chapter 4

"Joe, isn't it? Nice to see you again." Father Michaels shook hands with the last of the parishoners as they made their way out of the church, so for a moment he seemed to forget Torval was there. Only when the demon didn't move away did the priest finally turn his attention back to him.

"I apologize if I am interrupting," said Torval, "but I would like to speak with you if I can."

"Oh, certainly," said Father Michaels with a friendly smile. "You'll have to wait a few minutes, though. Sorry, any other night I'd probably be able to jump right into a private room, but it's Sunday, you see."

"Sunday? Why is that important?"

"Because that's when I say Mass," explained the priest patiently. "Several times on Sunday, and sometimes Saturday night as well, although this week I was off the hook since Father Williston dropped by. Of course, that means I owe him one."

Torval nodded, not really understanding at all. All he really got out of that was that this religious ritual called "Mass" happened on Sundays for some reason or other.

"Anyway," said Father Michaels, "I have to hear a few confessions, and then I'll be free, so have a seat in the back of the church. If you like, pick up and read one of the Bibles to keep you busy. I shouldn't be more than twenty minutes, if you don't mind waiting that long. Sunday is my busy time of the week, you see."

Torval checked his watch. He still had plenty of time before he was supposed to report to the warehouse, so he nodded in agreement and went to find an open space to sit. Fortunately, the entire church had cleared out by this point, so he simply sat back down where he'd been during the service.

For a moment he watched the priest, who said a few words to the remaining people nearby before disappearing into the back of the church. A few minutes later, he reappeared, now wearing only the same black oufit and white collar he'd had on the last time Torval visited him. Thus attired, Father Michaels proceeded across the front of the church, curiously stopping to bow at the altar (as he seemed to do every time he passed by that particular structure) before entering a small sealed chamber near the choir's slightly raised seats. Several other humans waited there, seated on benches, and one of these got up and entered the same little room, only from a different direction.

What was going on in there? Torval had no idea, but apparently it involved confessing something, at least according to what Father Michaels just said. The demon watched for another few minutes, but nothing else happened and the other people continued to wait.

Torval glanced around, already bored. In the racks in front of him, on the back of the next pew, were several books. One of these bore the large words "Holy Bible" in gold-colored text. *Ah, so this is a copy of the Bible*, he thought with a nod. He picked up the black-and-gold-trimmed book, opened it, and started reading.

Naturally, he began with the first few lines of the Book of Genesis, which had numbers in front of them for reasons he didn't understand.

> [1] *In the beginning God created the heaven and the earth.*
> [2] *And the earth was without form, and void; and darkness was upon the face of the deep. And the Spirit of God moved upon the face of the waters.*
> [3] *And God said, Let there be light: and there was light.*
> [4] *And God saw the light, that it was good: and God divided the light from the darkness.*
> [5] *And God called the light Day, and the darkness he called Night. And the evening and the morning were the first day.*
> [6] *And God said, Let there be a firmament in the midst of the waters, and let it divide the waters from the waters.*
> [7] *And God made the firmament, and divided the waters which were under the firmament from the waters which were above the firmament: and it was so.*
> [8] *And God called the firmament Heaven. And the evening and the morning were the second day.*

[9] And God said, Let the waters under the heaven be gathered together unto one place, and let the dry land appear: and it was so.
[10] And God called the dry land Earth; and the gathering together of the waters called he Seas: and God saw that it was good.

Torval continued to read, fascinated by this tale, although he felt the word "and" appeared a bit too often for his tastes. Some of what he read sounded familiar, such as the legend of the Forbidden Fruit, and the story that the world's first sinner was named Cain, who still occupied the original prison block in the First Circle of Hell. The rest was new to him, and some of it sounded highly unlikely, while other details outright contradicted things he knew. Or, at least, he thought he knew.

As he continued to dig deeper into the Book of Genesis, the story of the Creation concluded and moved on into other tales, including some bizarre business about a flood and an ark, which he'd never heard of. Nonetheless, Torval quickly lost himself in the pages. He didn't even notice as each of the waiting humans took their turns in the confessional until the last of them finally departed. Only when Father Michaels approached him in the back pew did he finally look up.

"You're hooked, I see," noted the priest, momentarily startling Torval with his sudden "appearance" nearby. "First time reading the Bible, I suppose? I remember how it sucked me in the first time, too. Amazing stuff."

"Yes, I agree," said Torval, reluctantly returning the Bible to its place on the rack. "Much of it is clearly fanciful, but nonetheless I find the passages quite intriguing."

"Fanciful, huh?" replied Father Michaels with raised eyebrows and a scolding tone. "You know, that book is the foundation of not only Catholicisim, but every Christian religion in the world, and a few others as well. I doubt most worshipers would be all that happy to hear you refer to it as 'fanciful.'"

"Well," said Torval, backpedaling somewhat, "I must admit that not all of it is false. I have heard some of these tales myself. If what I have been told is true, there is indeed a sinner named Cain imprisoned in Hell to this day."

Father Michaels nodded, but still looked surprised, as if he hadn't quite believed that story himself. "There is? Have you seen him?"

"Not personally," elaborated Torval. "It is the tale I was told, of how there was originally just one Circle of Hell, and new layers were added as more sinners arrived, and eventually many more Circles spawned, so that Hell continues to expand without end. Or perhaps they were always there, just unoccupied until needed. Honestly, I'm not really sure on that point, but then, it never mattered much to me, so I did not inquire further."

"Interesting." The priest looked at him eagerly, apparently ready to ask another question, but paused instead, as if unsure if he should press for more information.

Torval hesitated at the same time. He wasn't really supposed to talk about the nature of Hell, was he? No, not really, at least according to Prelz. Perhaps it was better to return to the original subject. "In any event," he went on quickly, "the passages I was reading did have some glaring flaws. For example, according to the first chapter, there were only two original humans, Adam and Eve."

"Ah, yes." Father Michaels nodded immediately. "I know what you're going to say. If there were only two, how did they have families from different parents? Well, don't bother, that's one of the mysteries I figure we just aren't supposed to know the answer to."

"Even so, that seems a difficult obstacle to overcome, unless the story is simply leaving out certain details. I would imagine there were more humans in existence than just this Adam and Eve named in the text. Perhaps when I return I can find out more about this. Surely someone in Hell would know what actually happened at that time."

"I'm sure they would," said the priest, shaking his head as if some part of him couldn't believe he was having this conversation. "Wait, why don't you know? Aren't you immortal, or something? Weren't you created at the same time as the rest of the Universe?"

"No, not any more than you," replied Torval with a shrug. "We demons are not born, at least not like humans, but we do come into being, and work our way up through the ranks. We do not die, but we can be demoted, or consigned to Oblivion when no longer needed."

Father Michaels nodded slowly. "So, you can live a long time," he remarked, "but when you die, it's permanent. There's no Heaven or Hell for you. No final reward or punishment to look forward to."

"No, not that I know of. It is just as well. We have our purpose to serve, and when we are done, and can contribute no more, we no longer have any reason to exist."

"That's a sobering thought," said Father Micahels sadly, "and I apologize for bringing it up. I suppose I couldn't resist inquiring, and look where it got me! Anyway, shall we speak somewhere more privately? I know you must've come here to talk to me about something, and like I said, I'm here to listen, if you need me."

"Yes, please." Torval followed as the priest led him back into the back of the church, past the small room where he and Prelz went previously. There were a couple of other people in there already, having some sort of meeting, and they didn't look up as Torval passed.

Father Michaels stepped into his office, sat down, and motioned at Torval to enter. Once the demon squeezed inside, the priest shut the door and pointed at a wooden stool in the corner. Torval sat down there and took a deep breath, trying to consider what to say. He realized then that he should've already been thinking about this matter, but the Bible proved just too compelling.

"So," said the priest, "what can I help you with, my son?" He then chuckled for a second. "Sorry, it seems odd referring to you like that, when you're probably a lot older than me."

"It does not matter," replied Torval, deciding that perhaps the best way to explain was to just spit it all out. "I have been immersed in what I believe you call a 'moral dilemma,'" he explained. "When I arrived here on Earth, I took a job working in the basement of a nearby warehouse. My employers have been kind to me and done me many favors, but now, I have become aware of something unusual taking place on the premises."

"Tell me more." Father Michaels sat back, crossing his arms. "Keep in mind, I cannot, and will not, discuss this issue with anyone else other than yourself. Even your friend Jake, should he ask me about it."

"Very well." Torval then launched into a full explanation of what was going on at the Roxton warehouse, naming names and bringing up the involvement of the police—especially the strange appearance of Lieutenant McCord at the warehouse that morning.

The priest listened carefully, and when Torval was done, he massaged his temples for a moment and then said, "Okay, that's all well and good, but exactly what is it you're asking me? You gave me a lot of information, but I'm not really sure how I can help."

Torval frowned. He'd really hoped that Father Michaels would just immediately have a solution, but apparently it wasn't that easy. "I do not understand human interaction well enough to know how to proceed," he explained. "The police have asked me to gather evidence from the Roxtons without their knowledge. However, I do not know if the Roxtons are in fact doing anything wrong, and so, if I spy on them, I may do them harm, or weaken my relationship with them. Furthermore, I now know the police are not simply watching the Roxtons from a distance, but are interacting with them directly."

"Not exactly," pointed out Father Michaels. "You know that this Lieutenant McCord is interacting with the Roxtons—no, not even that. You know that he has something going on with Pete Roxton. You don't know if Lincoln Roxton is involved, nor do you know if the rest of the police are working with the lieutenant. He may be doing this on his own, in secret."

Torval remained silent for a moment, mulling that over. Father Michaels was right, of course. Until this point, Torval had just assumed that the lieutenant *was* the police, but that might not be so. He may indeed be doing something privately, without the knowledge of the rest of the police force. Similarly, Pete Roxton might be talking to McCord without his grandfather being in on it, whatever "it" was.

"That complicates things," stated the demon after a moment's reflection on the matter.

"Yes, it does," said the priest. "From what you've told me, I wouldn't be at all surprised if the two of them were involved in something—but only privately, just between themselves."

"So what do I do?" asked Torval. "Do I spy on the Roxtons as the police asked? Do I tell the Roxtons, or perhaps only Lincoln, what I saw in the warehouse today? Do I ask the police for more information about what is going on?"

Father Michaels put a hand on Joe's shoulder. "I can't answer that for you," he said solemnly. "I'm not in your position, and even though I'm reasonably certain you've told me all the facts, I can't really know exactly what's going on. I'll tell you what I tell anyone else in a similar situation—you have to do what you think is right."

"But I am not human," complained Torval. "I do not know what is right. I think I have acquired an understanding of good and evil since coming here, but that is not enough. I have no idea what is the right thing to do."

"I have news for you," pointed out the priest, "neither do any of us human types. All we have is our heart, and our conscience to guide us. And, for some of us, our faith."

"I have no faith," said Torval bleakly. "I have nothing to put faith in."

Father Michaels nodded, a sad look on his face, as if he knew Torval was missing something and didn't even realize it. "Nonetheless," he noted, "you *did* came to me asking for advice. That means you *want* to do the right thing. That's half the battle right there."

"That still does not help me with my problem," groused the demon, growing more frustrated by the moment.

"Well, you don't need to do anything right now, do you? I mean, you don't have to make a decision right this second."

"No, but I do have to report to the warehouse soon," explained Torval. "It would be nice to have an answer by then."

"All right, then, let's at least try to work this out. You say the Roxtons have been your friends and done you favors, right? Well, how do you feel about them? Are they nice enough people? Or is there any chance they're just pretending to be nice because they want something out of you?"

"Well, I ... " Torval let his voice trail off, thinking about that more carefully. The Roxtons had indeed given him food and a place to live, but then, they also did that in exchange for work. They—or more specifically, Pete—gave him a bonus assignment for more money, but then that whole escapade was somewhat mysterious, too. What if the errand he ran for Pete was, as some had suspected, illegal in some way? What if the Roxtons were only using him for some nefarious purpose without his knowledge?

Torval rubbed his temples, which were now starting to hurt again, just as they had after playing chess. There was too much he still didn't know.

"I'm not sure," he finally answered. "I don't know enough about their intentions."

"Well," explained Father Michaels, "interaction is a two-way street. You already told me they paid you to do work for them. That's what I'm talking about. You do work, and they give you money and food. There's nothing inherently evil or inappropriate there. Maybe they really are just trying to be helpful, at least as far as that goes. Somehow I doubt it, though. There's clearly something else going on."

"Yes." Torval nodded vigorously. "I think I know what I should do, at least for now. Pete explained to me that I would be receiving another special assignment tomorrow morning. I will find out what that is, and depending on its nature, I will hopefully be able to better judge the character of the Roxtons. Once I know that, I can decide whether to confront them, or take my knowledge to the police."

"Or do nothing at all," suggested the priest. "That's an option, too. You could simply maintain the status quo. Just let this all play out and see what happens."

"Yes," agreed Torval. "Yes, I suppose I could do that, too."

* * *

Upon arriving at the warehouse, the half-frozen demon hurried inside, shivering. The night had grown much colder with the setting of the sun, and although the snow remained absent, Torval found himself uncomfortably reminded of the first night he'd spent on Earth. As he warmed himself near one of the heater vents just inside the building, he remembered just how much he wanted and needed this job.

He still hadn't decided exactly what he should do. He definitely wanted to do the "good" thing, if possible, because that seemed to be the way things worked on Earth—good deeds begat more good deeds, and so everyone prospered. However, he also didn't want to lose his comfortable place to sleep at night. If he chose to tell the Roxtons about the police, and they were in fact breaking the law and used his confession to escape justice, was that not evil? Yet if he chose to tell the police what they wanted to know, and they used it against the Roxtons when they weren't doing anything wrong, was that not also evil?

In the end, Torval knew only one thing for sure—he didn't have enough information. He couldn't make a decision either way. So, he simply decided to do nothing—which would, as Father Michaels suggested, preserve his comfortable sleeping arrangements for the foreseeable future.

"Ah, there you are," said Pete Roxton, stepping into the entranceway, dressed in a heavy coat that at the moment hung loosely and unzipped over his rugged frame. "Thought you'd never show up. Cold night, eh?"

"Yes, very much so," replied Torval, still rubbing his hands together over the heater vent. His gloves, now tucked away in his pockets, had been all but ineffective against the bitter night wind.

Perhaps, he now thought ruefully, *that's why they were so inexpensive.*

"Well, at least the weather's warming up tomorrow," went on Pete. "Looks like spring's finally here. About damn time. Anyway, head on downstairs when you're ready. Say, what's that you've got there?"

"This?" Torval glanced over at the book he'd set down on the counter upon entering the room. "It is a book called the Bible."

"Yeah, yeah, I can see that. Didn't know you were the religious type." Pete gave him a curious sideways look.

"I am not," replied Torval. "I visited a church today, and the priest there gave me this copy to read."

"Ah." Pete nodded half-heartedly. "Well, you have a good time with that. It's Sunday night, after all, so you can do whatever you want. No work assignment for now, but I'll come back in the morning and send you off on another trip around town, so get some rest."

"No work?" inquired the demon.

"Yeah, well, you should know why, if you read any of the Good Book there," remarked Pete, pointing his finger almost accusingly at the tome. "Remember the Sabbath, and keep it holy—that's one of the Ten Commandments, right?"

Now it was Torval's turn to adopt a quizzical expression. "You have read the Bible?"

"Well, yeah, sure, when I was a kid," said Pete. "Didn't everybody? I mean, even if I don't—well, I mean, you know. Go to church."

"Apparently," commented Torval, "some people go to church every Sunday, throughout their entire lives. Is that not strange?"

"Yeah, yeah, it is," agreed Pete, obviously getting uncomfortable with this particular topic. "Anyway, let's get you downstairs. I got stuff to do, and gotta get to bed early."

Torval picked up the book and headed down the steps. Pete didn't follow, apparently seeing no need to do so. "Your food's in the fridge," he pointed out, "and if you want to practice on the computer, feel free, but you don't have to. I loaded a program on there called 'Sales Master,' and the instructions are there on the table—that book I showed you earlier, just in case you forgot about it. Like I said, though, no big hurry."

"Very well," said Torval, even as the door slammed shut above him on the stairs.

"Goodnight, then," called out Pete from the hall beyond, and then his footsteps retreated into the distance.

Torval headed into the computer room and picked up the manual, which was exactly where Pete said it would be. Initially, he intended to learn what he could about this Sales Master program, but he only got a few pages into the manual before growing bored. Besides which, Pete had been quite clear that any actual work was strictly optional.

So, with that in mind, Torval spent the rest of the night with a different book entirely.

* * *

The morning found Torval asleep on the floor as usual. For once he actually managed to work his way into the hammock, but sometime thereafter he fell out, and simply lacked the energy to stand back up.

The Bible intrigued him, although some parts seemed to drag on and on. For example, there were entire chapters that did nothing more than list a seemingly endless series of names. Also, another section described various types of animals that people weren't supposed to eat. Most of these were defined by rules, such as whether or not the creature had hooves, which made no sense to him at all. What difference could that possibly make?

For a while Torval wondered if perhaps he should be following these rules while in a human body, but after thinking about this for a while, he realized something. The Bible provided instructions for only one specific religion—or, perhaps more appropriately, a group of religions. Humans followed a variety of different faiths, or none at all, depending on their beliefs. Since Torval had no such beliefs, he wasn't bound by the rules of the Bible, which made him feel a little better about his eating habits.

The Bible also set forth other rules for those of its faith, among these the Ten Commandments, to which Pete had referred the night before. That at least explained why Sundays seemed to be special. Many of the other Commandments echoed what he knew of human laws, such as restrictions against killing or stealing, but others, like that business about coveting a neighbor's wife, seemed difficult to enforce. At least Christians seemed to have their hearts in the right place, though, which he supposed was the whole point.

Just before falling asleep for the night, he started reading the

New Testament, the first part of which seemed to be the same story told several different times, by different authors. These told the story of the life of Jesus Christ, which Father Michaels had briefly explained during his first meeting with Torval, and had mentioned again during church service yesterday. The end of the story also explained, finally, the full reason why there was a statue of Jesus nailed to a cross hanging on the church wall. The story proved quite enlightening, and the icon itself quite powerful. No wonder they venerated this man, or aspect of God, if that's what He truly was.

Torval found it strange that he hadn't heard anything about Jesus back while he was in Hell. Other than some mention of Him by the occasional whiny prisoner, there was no mention of the story at all. Of course, all of this took place a long time ago—perhaps before Torval emerged from the Pits as a Fourth Class. Possibly well before, in fact, although the Bible didn't give any actual dates, so he had no way of knowing for sure.

He yawned, stretching, and headed for the shower. As usual, the warm water was total bliss, and served to clear his mind. The Bible explained much about how certain human religions worked, but the time for that was over. Now he had to get ready to do the Roxtons' bidding. After all, what happened today would help him decide what to do next with his current moral dilemma.

While putting on his clothes, he heard the door open up top, but Pete didn't come downstairs. Torval put his hygiene products away, collected his other belongings, and stowed the Bible with his other possessions before heading up to meet the Roxtons. Perhaps tonight he might have enough time to finish off the rest of the New Testament, if he got his work done quickly.

Pete and Lincoln were standing in the break room, chatting among themselves about something involving "rebounds" and "foul shots."

"Mornin', Joe," said Lincoln amiably, taking a sip out of a large ceramic mug that held the steaming brown beverage Torval recognized immediately as coffee. "Grab some breakfast. You've got some traveling to do."

"Traveling?" inquired the demon, immediately gravitating toward the open box of donuts. He took one and munched on it in silence, wondering what task his employers had in store for him.

"Yep," put in Pete, about halfway through his own donut already.

"You get to be our delivery boy again today, if that's all right with you." He stuck out his hand, which held the MetroCard he'd loaned Torval during his last assignment. "Here, I've loaded this up with some extra cash, so you should be able to get anywhere you need to go."

"What am I delivering?" asked Torval between bites. The pastry he'd selected had some kind of amazing yellow creamy center that tasted absolutely fantastic. He shut his eyes, licking his lips, and almost missed the reply.

"Well," said Pete, "this isn't like last time, where we made you lug around a briefcase, or pick up a box of car parts. You'll be delivering ... well, let's just say they're invitations, and leave it at that."

"Invitations?"

"Yes, yes, you could use the mail, I suppose," replied Lincoln with a casual wave of his hand, "but it's vital these all be delivered today, and by hand." He poked at a bag on the table next to him. "The envelopes are all in here, along with the addresses on them. You don't have to knock on the doors or anything, just stick 'em under the door and head out."

"So I am not to knock?" Torval raised an eyebrow. "I just put these in the dwellings indicated?"

"Yes, exactly so," agreed Lincoln. "Now, if anyone does see you, or stop you, just don't talk to 'em and keep walkin'."

"Yeah, and I know we can trust you not to look inside the envelopes," said Pete, with a noticeable tone of warning in his voice. "So that way if somebody does bug you about them, you can honestly say you have no idea what's inside. Got that?"

"Yes, sir," agreed Torval automatically.

"Good, good, we knew we could count on you," commented Pete with a smile. "Oh, and one other thing, they all need to be delivered by noon. Get back here by then, and you get a bonus."

"A bonus?"

"Yep." Pete pointed at him before picking up another donut and starting in on it. "You've been wearing the same old clothes for the last few days, so I'm betting you could use some cash for more, am I right? So yeah, do this little delivery, and you get a hundred bucks ... but do it by noon and I"ll double it. Sound fair?"

Two hundred dollars! Torval half-choked on his donut. That would be more than enough to acquire more clothing, and anything else he might need besides.

Yet, even as he nodded vigorously between coughs, it crossed his mind that what he was doing might still be wrong. Why must these envelopes be delivered so quickly? What was in them that was so important, and who was he taking them to?

The answers could probably be found inside the envelopes themselves, but he'd just been told not to open them. The Roxtons expected him not to—indeed, he'd been given an order, and they would now count on him to follow it.

He picked up the bag of envelopes and looked at them disdainfully. Another accursed moral dilemma! How did humans put up with this, anyway? Their lives were certainly a lot more complicated than he'd ever given them credit for.

* * *

To Torval's immense relief, the day had indeed turned warmer, as Pete suggested the night before. How the younger Roxton knew what the weather would be, Torval had no idea, but then, he still didn't understand most of what these humans were capable of. Predicting the weather seemed simple by comparison.

He stood outside the warehouse for a few minutes, enjoying the warm breeze on his face as he flipped through the various envelopes in the bag. The sky was clear, save for a few wispy clouds, and the coat he wore seemed completely unnecessary. He hadn't even brought his gloves, acting on Pete's recommendation that he wouldn't need them.

Six envelopes rested within the bag, each with a handwritten address on the front. Unfortunately, he had no idea where any of these places were. His instructions involved delivering these to the locations specified, but apparently he should already know where these domiciles were. He couldn't very well ask without revealing his lack of knowledge about the city, either.

He examined the envelopes in detail, glancing over his shoulder worriedly. Each seemed rather thick, and sealed with heavy tape. There was no way he could possibly open them without revealing that he'd done so, which meant he'd have to deal with the consequences should he decide to peek.

Torval shook his head. As much as he wanted to, he just couldn't disobey the Roxtons. All his life, he'd followed orders to the best of his ability. Doing otherwise just felt wrong to him, no matter the reason.

So, with that in mind, he now had to figure out where these addresses were. He remembered the map he'd found inside the subway station, so without any further delay, he headed in that direction, putting the envelopes back in the bag and tucking it safely under his arm.

On the way to the nearest subway entrance, he decided to try one more time to find Prelz. The ex-Tempter might be of some help finding the required addresses, and also, this time the Roxtons hadn't directed him to keep his mission to himself.

He took a side trip to the shelter, looking inside cautiously lest he incur the wrath of Lakisha, but neither she nor Prelz were around. Neither was Christine, but then, he hadn't expected to find her there. At this time of the morning, she would almost certainly be at work.

In fact, come to think of it, if any of these addresses took him near her place of employment, that might give him the opportunity to speak to her without Lakisha's interference. He recalled that during their ill-fated date, she told him where she worked. What was it again? Lawyers, he remembered ... something to do with divorces.

Struggling, he tried to think of the details. She'd given three names, names that at the time meant nothing to him. The first of them started with "H," he was pretty sure, but that was all he could remember. No, not exactly, he realized after a moment. She'd given directions—eighteen blocks uptown from the shelter.

Uptown ... what did that mean, exactly? He didn't know for sure, but perhaps it was a section of the city, and as such, it would be marked on the map. He left the shelter, heading back toward the subway, and that's when he saw Prelz.

The older demon stood at the corner, rattling some coins around in a cup. He looked different, and Torval knew the reason immediately—his normally long, greasy hair was gone. This wasn't any barber's work, though, nor had his beard been trimmed. It looked like someone simply shaved his head, without any attempt whatsoever to arrange his hair in any kind of style. If Prelz weren't wearing a dirty brown woolen cap, Torval would've been able to see the bare skin clinging to his skull.

"Oh, hey there," said Prelz as Torval approached. "Found me, eh? Not that I was hiding or anything."

"Yes, I have been looking for you," said Torval. "Where have you been? What happened to your hair?"

"Well, that's a long story," came the reply. "You got time? I think I've got enough here to get some coffee."

"Not really," answered Torval. "I am on a mission, and if I can accomplish it swiftly, I will gain a bonus payment."

"Ah, another mission!" Prelz chuckled to himself. "I wonder what those Roxtons are up to, anyway? What do they have you doing this time? Robbing a bank, maybe? Or a drive-by shooting?"

"None of those things," replied Torval, completely missing the sarcasm. "I am to deliver invitations to six addresses within the city."

"Invitations?" Prelz laughed and stepped back away from the street, taking a moment to count the coins in his cup. "Yep, almost three bucks. Good enough for now. Anything's better than hospital food."

"Yes, I was told these are invitations," explained Torval, showing the envelopes in his bag, and completely missing the comment about hospital food. "Invitations to what, I do not know. Nor am I permitted to open them."

Prelz took one look at what was in the bag and started laughing heartily. "Yeah," he managed after a moment, "yeah, those are invitations, and I'm an angel from Heaven. Heh-heh."

Torval looked at him curiously for a moment. Prelz was talking nonsense. "What?" the younger demon asked, befuddled.

"Sorry, I'm being unusually sarcastic this morning, aren't I? I keep forgetting who I'm talking to. Anyway, what I mean is, that's as likely to be an invitation as I am to be an angel. In other words, not likely at all."

"Oh. I see. What do you think they are, then?"

Prelz turned one of the envelopes over in his hands, squeezing it momentarily. "I'd say money," he replied after a moment. "Yeah, there's probably more than just a few bills in here. Damn. I could just take this one right here, and I'd be rich! Nobody would ever know."

Torval nodded. "Yes, you could do that, but then I would be unable to complete my deliveries, and the Roxtons would be displeased. I would probably lose my job, and be returned to the street, with more than a week before I can return to Hell."

Prelz looked at him and let out a sigh. "You're pathetic, you know that? Just pathetic." He slapped the envelope back into Torval's hand. "You better be damn glad I'm trying to push my soul to the side of good. Otherwise, I'd have decked you by now and swiped all that cash! I know a dozen different holes I could disappear into in this city, y'know. And don't think I get the irony, either. You, tempting me, a Tempter! Yeah, that's perfect. Just fucking perfect."

Torval put the envelope away. "Let me see if I understand," he said slowly. "By not stealing these envelopes from me, you are actually doing good? You are helping your soul gravitate toward Heaven?"

"No, not exactly. If only it were that easy." Prelz shook his head sadly and leaned back against the nearby brick wall, as if suddenly weary. He put his hand to his head and shook it a few times. "This isn't really a good thing, it's just avoiding evil. Avoiding temptation. Don't tell me you haven't felt it since you got here, 'cause I know you have. You can feel it pulling on you, urging you to do something you know is wrong, something that would benefit yourself at someone else's expense."

Torval nodded. "Yes, this is true. I have thought that I might aid the Roxtons, even if they were breaking the laws of this place, in order to keep my job. That would be a form of temptation."

"Yes, yes it would. You're a quick study, my boy." Prelz sagged to the sidewalk, staring ahead blankly for a moment. "That's what I used to do. I gave people opportunities for temptation. Like I said, though, humans don't need any help. They get enough temptation every day without demons to add to their misery. I'm just glad to know I can still resist, at least a little."

"You know," said Torval, "you will have plenty of additional opportunities to do good, especially if these envelopes do contain money. You could have taken them, and made up for it later."

"Stop with the tempting, already!" snapped Prelz, and then he let loose with a series of coughs. "Besides, I don't exactly have a lot of time left anyway. I'm afraid my time here is running out."

"What do you mean?" asked Torval, suddenly concerned, and finally noticing the rough shape his friend seemed to be in.

"I'm not long for this world," replied Prelz with a sigh. "You see,

I'm dying."

Chapter 5

"Dying?" Torval looked at Prelz doubtfully. "Why would you say something like that? How could you possibly know? I thought humans were not given that information in advance."

"Because that's what the doctor told me," replied the ex-Tempter with a heavy sigh. "After I saw you last, I was out begging on the sidewalk and ... well, I just collapsed. Remember how a couple times I said I felt like I was sick, or dizzy, or whatever?"

"Yes," agreed Torval. In fact, there had indeed been a couple of such occasions, but neither of the demons paid much attention. In fact, Prelz tried to pass them off at the time as symptoms of the same illness that was going around the city, the one that had nearly killed Hal, and had, in fact, killed Joe Sampson, before Torval took over his body.

"Well, it wasn't some passing thing," explained Prelz, whose face had by now gone noticeably pale, and his breathing shallow. "There's something in my head, something ... what was it they said? Putting pressure on my brain. Not a tumor, but ... something else. I can't think of the technical name for it."

"These doctors," said Torval worriedly, "is there nothing they can do? When I was reading on the Internet, it seemed to me that a great many things could be cured by what the humans call 'medicine.'"

"Not this," replied Prelz sadly. "Or at least if there is something they could do, they won't do it, because I've got no money and no insurance."

"What?" Torval was dumbfounded. "They would not help you unless you could pay them? Well, then, perhaps the money in these envelopes will—"

"No!" Prelz interrupted, grabbing Torval's arm before he could take the letters out of the bag. "No, don't do that. We don't know if that's what's really in there. Besides, do you have any idea what brain surgery would cost? Even if that's the only obstacle—and I don't know if it is—it's more cash than you'd find in a few lousy envelopes."

"But surely there must be something that can be done," complained Torval. "You gave up your demonhood to become human, and now your life will end so soon? That does not seem fair!"

"One thing about life," replied Prelz with a weak smile, "is it's not really fair. I knew that going in. Don't worry about me, though. When it's time for it to be over, it'll be over. We all have to die—I'm just going a little sooner than I wanted."

"Prelz," said Torval intently, "you have been a friend to me since my arrival. I have never had a friend before, not in all my time in Hell, so I may not understand the concept properly. However, I am fairly certain that friends are supposed to help each other. That is what I learned from my experience with Hal Sommersby. Therefore, I am going to try to help you, if I can, in any way possible."

"I don't see how you can," replied Prelz, getting back to his feet slowly and with some difficulty. The ashen look on his face faded as his natural color returned. "I appreciate it, but seriously, don't worry about me. They said I've got some time left—a few months, maybe a year, if I'm lucky. These little fainting spells will come and go, though, so I gotta be careful crossing the street and whatnot."

"If you need help," replied Torval, "you have but to ask."

"Much appreciated. It's good to have a friend—I'd sorta forgotten what that felt like. Thank you, Torval."

"You are welcome," he replied, hoping he had the expression correct. That's what he thought he was supposed to say, in any case, and it did indeed feel right.

"Very well then," Prelz went on, wiping his brow with the back of his hand and starting to shuffle on toward the coffee house, "tell me more about this mission you're on, and maybe I can speed you on your way."

* * *

Prelz's instructions were indeed helpful, and thanks to his basic understanding of the subway, Torval had little trouble finding the addresses indicated. Most were in easily accessible locations, and no one gave him any trouble. In fact, few people even glanced at him as he found his way to the various apartment buildings, and in one specific case, an office door in the back of a warehouse. After two hours, he'd delivered all but one of the envelopes, so he still had plenty of time to complete his task, as soon as he finished off the last one.

And now, here he was. Torval looked up at the massive red-and-gray brick building before him, feeling a strange unease. Unlike many similar structures he'd seen back near the shelter, this one seemed rundown and not at all inviting. Not that he expected the construction was unsound, of course. He felt certain it would stay together even in high winds. No, the building just looked ... what? Dangerous? Foreboding?

Yes, that's it—foreboding. The structure looked as if it hadn't been taken care of very well. Some of the broken glass in the windows was held together only with tape, while large, meaningless letters had been scrawled in dull colors on some of the walls. The metal framework surrounding some of the upper floors looked rusted and in some places seemed to be coming apart.

This wasn't all, though. Seated on the steps near the entrance, and leaning against the walls in various places, were men and women dressed in black and gray clothing. Some wore caps that bore a strange symbol embedded in the front, not at all like the "N Y" he so often saw emblazoned on such headgear. Some of the men stood in a cluster, talking and looking over their shoulder, and one of them fingered something that looked very much like a knife. Several women leaned against the railing nearby, smoking.

As Torval approached the front entrance, the men ceased their chatter and looked at him directly. All of them had bronzed skin and belonged to the nationality Torval knew as "Hispanic." One of them, the only one without a sweater, wore a muscle T-shirt and a prominent gold cross on a chain. He had a very thin mustache and no other facial hair, and in his hand he held a small black rod with a slit on one end.

"Whatcha doin' here, bro?" inquired the youth as Torval reached the bottom of the steps. The speaker crossed his arms, fingering the strange implement, while his friends adopted wary stances nearby. The whole scene felt altogether quite menacing.

"I have an invitation to deliver," explained Torval as evenly as he could.

"An invitation?" The man looked around at his friends, who chuckled and took a few steps down the stairway, half-surrounding

Torval. "An invitation for what? A party?"

"I do not know," said the demon. "I was told to bring the invitation to this building, so that is what I must do."

He started to take a step, to move past the crowd, but found there was no way to get through. They'd managed to maneuver to block his passage completely.

"No way, bro," said the mustached youth. "You ain't goin' nowhere till I find out what you's really doin' here. Who you takin' this invite to, anyways?"

"I do not know the name," complained Torval. "Please, let me pass. I must take this envelope to room 215."

At the sound of that number, the men glanced around at each other. A couple took steps backward, but the way up the stairwell remained blocked.

"You got an invite for Julio, eh?" said the man. "Well, give it here, then, and I'll make sure he gets it." He chuckled, but the sound seemed nervous and forced.

"I was told to put this under the door," explained the demon worriedly. So far, he hadn't experienced any trouble delivering the envelopes, until now. He didn't want to fail when he was so close to completing his task. "No one else is to take it," he added, wishing these men would just part and let him pass.

"Dude," said one of the observers, a noticeably overweight human in a heavy sweater. He wore a black bandanna over his bulbous forehead. "He ain't hurtin' nothin'."

"Yeah, Angelo," said another, a thinner man in a leather jacket. "You mess with Julio's deals, you know what's gonna happen."

The one called Angelo eyed Torval carefully. "Somethin' ain't right about this guy," he said after a moment. "I don't know what it is. Show me this invite of yours, bro."

Torval thought about resisting, but there was little point. He was all but surrounded and had nowhere to retreat if this turned bad. Instead, he reached into the nearly empty bag he was carrying and pulled out the envelope, which had the address clearly noted on the front.

Angelo studied the envelope, and then glanced over at his friends. None of them said anything, but the look on their faces said they'd recognized something, or at least suspected what was going on.

"Okay, fine," said Angelo after a moment, "I get yer biz now, bro.

You can go on up, but I'm gonna be watchin'. Go on, get your ass movin'!"

The group of men parted and Torval hurried up the stairs, glancing around worriedly, as if they might suddenly close together and crush him. One of the women nearby glanced in his direction, and he caught sight of her as she drew a puff from her cigarette. She wore solid black lipstick, and gave him an odd wink before looking away.

Torval went up the stairs hastily, passing another man who lay curled up in the corner of the stairwell, skin pale and coated in sweat. Another time Torval might've thought to investigate what ailed the unfortunate human, but not now. He just wanted to finish his mission here and get the heaven out.

As he went down the hall, looking for room 215, he noticed Angelo following him, but keeping his distance. The youth continued to massage that odd black thing in his hand, and then, as Torval watched, he pressed his fingers together, and a thin blade seemed to pop out of nowhere. Torval gulped and quickened his pace.

The room he sought waited at the end of the hallway, near a window missing several panes. He took the envelope, got down on a knee, and shoved it underneath, making sure it was completely out of sight before rising. Angelo stood about halfway down the hall, making that skinny blade flick back and forth into its handle. Torval shuddered. Would the man attack him, now that his mission was complete?

Angelo made no move to approach. Torval hesitated for a moment, wondering if he should attempt to push past, when suddenly the door popped open. Another Hispanic man, this one noticeably older, stood there, dressed only in a pair of jeans and several long gold chains. Several scars marred his muscular chest, along with a very large tattoo of a man holding two pistols in front of his scowling face.

"Who the hell are you?" demanded the man Torval assumed was Julio, waving the envelope accusingly in the demon's face. "What the fuck you doin' comin' round here with this shit? Angelo! Why you lettin' skinny white boys walk right up to my door?"

"Sorry, Julio," replied the youth, whose switchblade had now magically disappeared. "He said he had to bring it to you hisself."

"That is true," explained Torval. "My instructions were—"

"Shut up, boy! When I wanna hear shit comin' outta yer mouth I'll tell ya to open it! Angelo! Next time this happens you come get me, you hear? I don't want nobody in my hall 'less I know who it is! You got it?"

"Yeah, I got it," said a thoroughly chastened Angelo, who didn't wait for any further instructions, but turned and scurried off.

"Now," said Julio, picking up a large gun with his open hand, "let's see what you done brought me." Using his teeth, he ripped one corner off the envelope, then pried the rest open with the barrel of his pistol. Inside, there was a folded note, along with—as Torval had already suspected—a large handful of cash. From what he could see, the notes were hundred dollar bills.

Torval waited while the man read the note, out of the demon's line of sight. He still wasn't sure if he'd get out of here alive, especially the way Julio waved that gun around so haphazardly. Torval didn't want to die, at least not yet. He still had things to accomplish before his vacation ended, not the least of which would come as soon as he escaped this building.

"I apologize for the intrusion," he finally said, hoping against hope that he wasn't about to be shot. "However, I have done what I was told to do. I brought you the envelope, which completes my mission here. Now I shall depart."

He got one step before he found that gun pointed directly at his chest. "Not so fast, white boy," said Julio menacingly. "I don't take too kindly to people I don't know comin' down to my turf. You tell McCord that ain't how things work 'round here. Next time he wants to pay me, he does it the right way, got it?"

"The right way?" Torval asked worriedly. "I do not know what the right way is."

"Well, this ain't it!" snapped Julio. "You tell him that, you got it? And I better not ever see your pasty white face 'round here again or I'm gonna break it good, you hear me?"

"Y-yes, sir," replied Torval anxiously, shuffling toward the exit now that the gun was facing away again.

"Yeah, that's right, you get the hell outta here now," Julio called out as Torval half-walked, half-ran to the stairs. "You better run, boy! Ha-ha! Sir, yep, that's right, you better fuckin' call me sir ... !"

Torval pushed his way past the gang at the entrance, ignoring their fading laughter as he hurried down the street as quickly as he could. At any moment he expected to feel a knife, or perhaps a bullet, in his back, but to his relief he managed to escape unscathed.

* * *

Only when he reached the safety of the subway did Torval finally let himself relax. For perhaps a minute, his breaths came rapidly and he had to wipe the sweat away from his hands and face, but eventually he calmed down.

Fear ... that's what he'd just experienced. Nothing but raw fear. Those men could've killed him at any moment, and yet, for whatever reason, they didn't. There were no police to help him—indeed, apparently the enigmatic Lieutenant McCord was involved in paying them for something, using the Roxtons (and therefore Torval) as intermediaries.

In other words, Torval realized, the Roxtons put him in danger, and did so on purpose! He frowned, rubbing his throbbing temples and trying to catch his elusive breath. Things were becoming clearer, and he didn't like the way this was going. The Roxtons were definitely mixed up in something bad, and so was the police lieutenant. Now Torval was in the middle of it as well.

So what could he do? Well, the safest solution seemed obvious—he could simply quit the job and walk away. In fact, he didn't even have to return to the warehouse if he didn't want to, although he did have some money coming to him for today's efforts. If nothing else, he'd accomplished the Roxtons' task and earned his pay. After collecting the money, he could turn his back on them, and never go back. Perhaps Christine, or someone else, could help him find another job. Or, quite possibly, the two hundred dollars would be enough to secure him lodging until the end of his time on Earth.

Yes, that's a good plan, thought Torval. He didn't like the way it left things incomplete, and left the truth of what was happening a mystery that he would never solve. Nonetheless, it would at least get him out of harm's way. Plus, he'd finally be free of the moral dilemmas that plagued him.

Good, he thought to himself. *That solves everything*. With that decision made, he knew he could now proceed with the one other thing he wanted to accomplish before returning to the Roxtons.

He waited, carefully keeping track of the stops the subway made, until finally he came to the one he wanted. Eighteen blocks uptown, Christine had told him, back when they had dinner. Well, that's where this exit was, at least approximately. Prelz had already explained what "uptown" meant, so Torval felt reasonably sure he was in the right place. Now he only had to locate the legal firm, the name of which he still couldn't recall, except that it started with "H." That's what he remembered, anyway.

He stepped off the subway, climbed the stairs to street level, and disengaged himself from the crowd. The buildings here were a bit more sparsely arranged, not right up against the sidewalks as they were further downtown. Several were set well back from the street, with parks, fountains, and statues emplaced before them, or in some cases, wide swaths of concrete organized into wide staircases or walkways. Some of the shorter skyscrapers bore names or numbers, often just barely visible through leafless tree branches, but none triggered Torval's memory.

The only thing to do was check them all, so he started with the nearest one. As it turned out, most had highly visible directories either on plaques in front of the building, or just inside the wide glass doors. After about ten minutes, his eye caught on one name in particular: "Hochman, Stein & Veehorven, Attorneys at Law."

That's the one, he told himself—he remembered it now, because the third name was notoriously difficult to pronounce. Somewhat anxiously, Torval headed inside the building, where a series of guards insisted he pass between two large metal pylons before he could proceed. He might've inquired further as to why, but his mind was too busy working on what he intended to say when he reached the fifth floor, where the law offices waited. Would Christine be there? Would she even talk to him? Should he even be doing this at all?

He had to at least *try*. His chances of success were low, but they were zero without making the attempt.

For a few minutes he wandered back and forth, trying to find the stairs. Many other people passed by him, most dressed in impeccably tailored suits and coats, but instead of climbing steps, they walked into one of several small rooms along the main entrance path, just past the foyer. These rooms had doors that opened at the sound of a bell, which was very curious, but didn't help Torval out at all.

He was about to give up and ask when he noticed a sign bearing the word "Exit" just over an otherwise innocuous-looking door. As he recalled, similar signs hung over other stairways he'd seen in the past. Sure enough, when he pushed his way through, he found himself in a stairwell, and without any further hesitation he started heading up.

Climbing four flights proved to be quite a challenge. The first two weren't so bad, but the third left him breathless. By the time he reached the fifth floor, his heart pounded and his body dripped with sweat. He took off the coat, used its dry outside to wipe the perspiration away, and waited a minute to collect himself. Only then did he proceed.

Hochman, Stein & Veehorven had a large, well-decorated door midway down the hall. Torval hesitated there, gathering his thoughts, and then stepped inside, where a secretary waited behind a large desk. Beyond her station, he saw numerous cubicles arranged in rows, as well as several corridors leading to other offices. Torval looked around hopefully, but didn't see Christine.

"Can I help you?" said the secretary, an attractive young woman dressed in a navy blue business suit. Her black hair was tied back in a bun and several loose locks dangled down her forehead, draped over a pair of thick tortoise-shell glasses. According to a placard on her desk, she was named Elizabeth.

"Yes," said the demon. "I wish to speak to Christine Anderson."

"Sure, let me ring her for you. One moment please."

Elizabeth picked up a telephone headset and punched a couple of buttons. During the resulting pause, she looked up curiously at Torval. "Whom shall I say is calling?"

"My name is Joe Sampson," replied the demon, wishing he didn't have to give his name. How would Christine react when she heard it? He wished he could see her directly, rather than interact with some intermediary. At least this Elizabeth person didn't seem as hostile as Lakisha, back in the soup kitchen.

"Oh, hey, Christine," said Elizabeth after a moment, speaking into the phone. "Someone here to see you. Says his name is Joe Sampson."

The secretary suddenly jumped, and Torval actually heard the sudden shout come through the headset, even all the way across the desk. He was pretty sure he heard Christine's voice say, with much surprise, "WHAT?"

"I take it you don't want to see him?" asked Elizabeth, once she'd recovered her grip on the phone.

"Please," insisted Torval, "I must speak to her. Can you tell me where I might find—"

"All right, if you say so," interrupted the secretary, setting the phone back on its cradle. "Sorry, sir, I'm afraid she won't see you. She says you should know why, and to please go away."

Torval's shoulders slumped. "I really must speak to her," he insisted. "I wish to ask for another chance."

"Another chance?" Elizabeth looked up at him with sudden understanding in her eyes. "You messed things up with her, didn't you? Yeah, I can tell! And now you just want to say you're sorry?"

"Yes, that is essentially what I wish to do," agreed the demon. "Yet she will not give me the opportunity."

The secretary sighed. "Wow, a guy who's actually willing to admit his mistakes and apologize," she pondered, shaking her head in amazement. "I wish I could help, but I really can't let you see her, not after she told me not to! I'd lose my job, you see."

"I can understand that," replied Torval, crestfallen. "I suppose there is nothing more I can do. I have failed."

"Well, I'll put in a good word for you, if you like," replied Elizabeth. "You seem like a decent enough guy."

"Thank you." Torval started toward the door, but as he did, he remembered one other thing. Perhaps this trip wouldn't be a complete loss after all, if he could trust this human to be true to her word.

"There is one thing you could do for me," he suggested hopefully, reaching into his pocket. "If you could give Christine this, when next you see her. Tell her it is from me."

He opened his hand and let the small object drop into Elizabeth's waiting palm. She looked at it curiously. "A chess piece?" she asked, clearly not understanding.

"It is a pawn," replied the demon, as if that explained everything. "Please give it to her, tell her it is from me, and she will know what it means. Thank you, Elizabeth."

She studied the painted wooden token for a few seconds, clearly confused. "But—I don't get it. What does this—?" she began, but by then Torval had already departed.

* * *

The door to the Roxton warehouse seemed to beckon to him. Torval paused a moment, wondering why he felt such anxiety. After all, he would shortly relieve himself of the problems caused by these people and their mysterious business arrangements. He would no longer be endangered, nor would the police have any reason to harass him. He should feel elated, in fact.

So why did he feel so apprehensive? Perhaps that wasn't the word for it, but something definitely felt amiss. He didn't really like what he was about to do, and that in and of itself bothered him.

The delay seemed foolish, so he pressed on, stepping inside the building. He saw neither of the Roxtons, so he walked around, looking for them. In doing so he passed a few of the other employees, but they all seemed busy with some task or other, so he left them alone.

Finally, not seeing the Roxtons on the main floor, he decided to try the basement, and indeed the lights were on down there. As he descended, he spotted Lincoln, standing at the entrance to the computer room. Pete was there as well, seated at the computer. Both were engaged in conversation, but when they saw Torval, they stopped talking immediately.

"Oh, hey, you're back!" said Pete amiably, glancing at his watch. "Not even eleven-thirty yet. See, Grandpa, told you he'd be early!"

"Yep, you were right. Did you deliver all the envelopes, Joe?" inquired the elder Roxton.

"I did," replied Torval succinctly.

"Excellent. And you didn't look in any of them, right?" asked Pete almost offhandedly, reaching for his wallet.

"I did not look in them myself, no," replied Torval honestly. This much was true, as he hadn't opened any of them on his own.

The two Roxtons exchanged glances. "What does that mean?" asked Pete. "Did someone else open one?"

Torval sighed. Perhaps he should've worded that response differently, but now it was too late. "When I delivered the final envelope," he explained somewhat reluctantly, "it was to someone named Julio. He emerged from the door before I departed, opened the envelope while I watched, and I saw the contents, although I did not read the note within."

Pete rubbed his eyes. "Dammit," he muttered, pacing back and forth. "You weren't supposed to see that, Joe."

"I did not seek to," replied Torval. "I had little choice in the matter. Julio was holding a gun at the time."

"He was *what*?" demanded Lincoln. Then, looking at his grandson, he put his hands on his hips. "Dammit, this has gone too far! What if he'd shot poor Joe here? Pete, this has gotta stop!"

Torval's eyes widened. That wasn't what he expected to hear. In fact, he didn't really know what he'd expected, but that wasn't it.

"It's not my fault, Grandpa!" complained Pete, circling around the room as if being pursued. "I didn't know anything was gonna happen! McCord said it was just payoffs, that's all. They were just supposed to be shoved under doors—no interaction with anybody! I wouldn't have sent Joe out there if I knew somebody would threaten him with a gun!"

"Well, I don't care," insisted the old man. "This is the last time you send Joe on that kind of errand! Delivering records and bank statements, fine, but not payoffs. Not again. You want to do that, you can do it yourself, you hear me?"

"But I—" Pete hesitated a moment, and then hung his head. "Yeah, you're right, Grandpa." Then he did a very strange thing. He reached out and put his hands on Torval's shoulders. "Joe, I'm sorry. I'm sorry I put you in that position. Nothing like that was supposed to happen. From now on, you can carry printouts and stuff, but that's all, okay? And only if you want to. If you don't want to, that's fine, just say so, all right?"

"Yes, I suppose," replied Torval. Sensing an opportunity, he pressed on. "However, I am confused. What is happening here?"

The two Roxtons exchanged glances again. Finally, Lincoln said, in a low voice, "If you want to tell him, go ahead. It's your mess. You might as well do the talking."

Pete let out a long sigh. "All right, fine," he finally agreed. "I guess we can trust Joe—he's the most honest person I think I've ever met. Have a seat, Joe. This might take a few minutes."

Torval moved over to the chair in front of the computer desk and sat down. At long last, he would learn what was really happening! He still didn't know if he should quit this job or not, but at least this would clear up some of the mystery.

"Well," said Pete after a moment, staring at a space on the floor somewhere between himself and Torval, "this is all my fault. You see, in my youth, I had a bit of a gambling problem."

"A bit!" laughed Lincoln bitterly. "That's not the half of it, and you know it!"

"Okay, fine, it was a big problem, okay?" groused Pete. "I'm not really proud of it, but yeah, I placed a lot of bets. This was back before Grandpa came back to work here, back when he was retired, and had passed the business on to me. I made some real bad decisions, you see, and I wound up almost losing the place. If Grandpa hadn't helped me, we would've lost it entirely."

"I should've just let it go," said Lincoln, shaking his head. "That would've solved everything. This was my business, though. I built it myself, and I wasn't going to let it die if I could save it!"

"Yeah, and neither was I," went on Pete. "I told Grandpa here I'd do anything to help him cover the debts. I swore off gambling, and I haven't done it again since. Not one time! Not even basketball—God knows I've been tempted, especially with the tournaments going on, and the Big Dance coming up."

Lincoln put a hand on Pete's shoulder. "It's been hard," he said in a fatherly tone, "but you've really held up, son. I'm proud of you, at least for that."

Torval cocked his head sideways. "I still do not understand," he interjected. "If you have cured yourself of your gambling problem, what is the issue? And what does any of that have to do with me?"

"I was getting to that," Pete went on, resuming his pacing. "You see, I owe a crapload of money on this place. I took out certain loans to cover my debts ... and some of those loans don't involve banks. They were going to come due, and I couldn't pay—but then we got some help from an unexpected source."

"If you want to call it 'help,'" remarked Lincoln, frowning.

"Yeah, well, it sounded like a good idea at the time," went on Pete. "The police came to us one day. Not just any police, mind you, but a real sonafabitch named Lieutenant Jonas McCord."

Torval nodded, and neither of the Roxtons missed the recognition on his face. "You know him?" asked Lincoln immediately.

"I do," replied Torval, but then he stopped. How much should he reveal about what he knew of the lieutenant? Not everything, he decided after a moment. "When Julio read the note, he used that name. He said to tell Lieutenant McCord not to send him payments in this manner again."

The Roxtons both nodded, but also frowned in apparent dismay. "Yeah, that's right, the money came from him," explained Pete. "I don't know what it was for. He wouldn't tell me. He just insisted I see to it that the payoffs got delivered. Maybe he didn't want to risk getting caught with his hands dirty if the exchange went wrong—I don't know."

"I still do not understand," said Torval. "What does Lieutenant McCord have to do with all this?"

"When he came to us, he offered us protection," went on Pete. "He said he'd help us with the loan payments. How he found out about them, I don't know. He has his ways—he's a cop, I guess, so he's got his own little network of informants and snitches. Anyhow, he made us an offer we couldn't refuse. He'd keep the loan sharks off our backs, and all we had to do was the occasional favor for him."

"I see," replied Torval. The arrangement sounded fair enough, as long as the favors involved were legal ... and he was pretty sure, from the way the Roxtons were talking, that they weren't legal at all. "So why involve me?" he inquired.

"We needed somebody," replied Pete with a shrug. "Somebody inconspicuous, with no connections to the business, who could make deliveries. Someone with no idea what was really going on, so if you get picked up by the police—the real ones, I mean, not dirty cops like McCord—you wouldn't know anything. Originally you were only supposed to be delivering transaction records, ones without anything incriminating unless you had access to our main files. That's what you did the first time, and that's what I was going to have you do every week. But then McCord put the pressure on me, and I didn't have anyone else to turn to. I'm sorry, Joe. I should never have done that to you—we shouldn't have done this at all."

"We shouldn't be doing *any* of this," went on Lincoln, "but we're trapped now. If we try to tell the real police about McCord, assuming we could even manage to find an honest cop to talk to, then all that does is stop the payments and bring the loan sharks down on our heads. Assuming he doesn't have us meet with some kind of 'accident' in the meantime, mind you. He probably would, you know. I'm telling you, that man scares the hell out of me!"

"Yeah," agreed Pete, "we can't be sure what he's going to do if we ever try anything like that. So all we can do is press on, quietly making payments when we can, until the loans are all covered and we can put this all behind us. When that finally happens, we can go our separate ways—we wouldn't dare tell the cops about him, and he knows it, and he has no reason to do anything to us as long as we keep our mouths shut."

"But in the meantime," added Lincoln, "that leaves us where we are right now. I'm sorry we didn't tell you all this sooner, Joe, but like I said so very many times, honest people are as rare as hen's teeth in this city."

Torval closed his eyes, thinking. What they just told him sounded reasonable enough, and explained a great many things. Some of the conversations he'd overheard also made much more sense, now that he knew these details. Nonetheless, the Roxtons had put him in harm's way, and despite their apparent desperation, he found that difficult to forgive. Pete Roxton should've been the one delivering those envelopes today, not him. Pete had deliberately sent the otherwise innocent Joe Sampson out there, perhaps not knowing exactly what would happen, but well aware that something might go wrong.

On the other hand, something else still wasn't quite right about all of this. Lieutenant McCord took Torval aside and gave him a mission of his own—to spy on the Roxtons and investigate their records. Why would he do that, if things were the way Pete and Lincoln explained them to be? Did he simply not trust the Roxtons? Perhaps he thought they were treating him unfairly, maybe adjusting the transactions to be more in their favor? Or were they lying to him outright, trying to poison him against the police? Yet even that seemed unlikely, for Julio, clearly a criminal sort, had spoken of McCord as someone who often paid him money. So the policeman was definitely up to something.

Bless it all! This new information should've cleared everything up, and given him all the answers. Instead, all it did was pose more questions.

Torval knew he could still just walk away. In fact, that would still be his best way out, wouldn't it? Even as that thought occurred to him, he found his musings interrupted.

"Look," said Pete suddenly, "I can understand if you want to bail. You've got it lucky, I guess, 'cause you can just walk away if you want. In fact, here's the money you earned today, including your bonus. It's the least I can do."

So saying, he pulled out a handful of bills from his wallet and counted them out. Ten twenty dollar notes, deposited into Torval's waiting hands. Enough to last the rest of the week, if he watched his spending carefully. Enough to get by, at least, if nothing else.

"If you want to stay, though," said Pete as he slipped his wallet back in his trousers, "you're welcome to. I won't ask you to do anything else dangerous, like I said, and you can keep on sleeping here in the basement. I won't even lock you in any more, so you can come and go as you please. If nothing else, you've earned our trust."

"Yes, you certainly have that," agreed Lincoln. "I can understand why you wouldn't trust us, after what we put you through, but we'd like you to stay. A good man like you is hard to find these days."

Torval started to reply. He was about to tell them he was leaving, but the words wouldn't come out.

The truth was, he didn't want to leave. He liked it here. He enjoyed the warmth and comfort of his own private basement, and the link to the Internet, and the food in the refrigerator every night. He was safe from the cold, and what's more, the Roxtons *liked* him. They appreciated him—and that was something he'd never experienced before, not in all his years of bleak existence back in Hell.

There was something else, too. He looked around the basement, at the cracked walls and stacks of files, and the impeccably clean bathroom he'd helped to restore to its full usefulness. This place felt important to him—it felt more than just comfortable. It felt like ...

It felt like *home*.

He'd never had a home before. The cube he rested in, back in Hell, was just a place. There was nothing special about it. He neither liked nor disliked it—it simply provided a place to go when he finished with his route. This basement, though ... for whatever reason, he'd become attached to it, in that strangely human way, and he didn't want to leave.

"Very well," he heard himself saying. "I will stay, at least for now."

"Great!" said Pete, smiling for the first time since Torval had come down the stairs. "Thanks, Joe, I knew we could count on you. I swear, no more payoff deliveries, either. You can enter computer records and that's all you have to do, okay?"

"Yes, that sounds good," agreed the demon, still a bit at a loss. Rationally, he knew, he should leave this place forever, and yet, he knew full well that he wouldn't. He just couldn't, and he didn't know why—and thinking about it just made him feel dizzy and light-headed.

"Well, at least that's some good news today," commented Lincoln. "You might as well head out, Joe, although you're welcome to stay if you want."

Just then, though, a voice yelled down into the basement. "Hey, Joe! You down there?"

"Yes," replied the demon, standing up and moving to the bottom of the stairs. Looking up, he saw someone he didn't know, one of the Roxtons' other employees, judging by the blue-collared shirt he was wearing. "What is it?"

"Someone's here lookin' for you," replied the man with a knowing smile. "I think you want to come see, if you catch my drift. Heh-heh."

The other man disappeared from sight. Torval turned to the Roxtons and said, "I suppose I should go, then. Thank you for explaining all of that to me. I appreciate your honesty."

"Same," replied Lincoln. "Have a good afternoon, Joe."

"Yeah, see you tonight," Pete added, sitting back down at the computer. The two returned to what they were doing, not bothering to follow Torval out as he climbed the stairs.

Somewhat reluctantly, he turned his thoughts away from the Roxtons and toward whoever this might be. Who would come to the warehouse to visit him specifically? Was it Prelz? Or had something happened to him, perhaps, and he was in the hospital again, with word being sent through some intermediary? Or, worse, what if this was Lieutenant McCord, trying to find out what he'd learned about the Roxtons' finances, which of course was nothing at all? What would the policeman do if he thought Torval wasn't cooperating?

He was still mulling over that unpleasant thought when he stepped into the main entrance area and came to an immediate halt. Instantly all his worries were swept away when he saw who was waiting there, dressed in a trim business suit, looking as radiant as the day he'd first seen her, if not more so.

It was Christine.

Chapter 6

"Hello, Joe," she said, a note of uncertainty in her voice. "Do you think we could talk outside? I don't want to run into a certain someone who's probably here in the building right now."

Torval was so stunned by Christine's unexpected presence that he almost didn't realize what she was talking about. Then the rational part of his mind, the part not confused by human emotions, reminded him that she wasn't particularly pleased with Pete Roxton at the moment.

"Um, yes, of course," Torval sputtered after a few seconds of struggling to regain control of his voice. "He is downstairs. Let us go outside, so we are not overheard."

"Fair enough," agreed Christine, turning and walking out to the street corner. She wore a crisply tailored beige two-piece suit and carried a light overcoat draped under one arm, the same arm that held a black leather purse only slightly larger than her hand. Her long brown hair wasn't tied up this time, like it usually was, but instead dangled midway down her back, seemingly tumbling there in little waves. Torval followed her as if hypnotized.

Once she'd gone down the short concrete steps and reached a spot out of the flow of pedestrians, she stopped, taking up a position between a street sign and a newspaper vending machine. She then reached up her free hand and opened it, revealing a certain chess piece Torval had taken to her office a little more than an an hour ago.

"I see Elizabeth gave you the pawn," said Torval, stating the obvious. Mostly he just wanted to say something, if only to break up the uncomfortable silence between them.

"Yes, she brought it in my office and set it on the table," said Christine with a sigh. "She said you told her I'd know what it meant. I have to admit, at first I didn't understand, but then I figured it out. It's right out of 'Queen Takes Pawn.' Very clever of you."

"I wanted to explain it to you directly," replied Torval, "except you would not listen to my words. Therefore, I had to find an alternative way to deliver the message."

She tossed the pawn about a foot in the air, and caught it deftly with a flick of her wrist. "Well, it worked," she went on, briefly smiling before dropping the pawn in her purse. With her now empty hand, she reached out and held her open palm before Torval. "If you want to start over, fine, but let's do it right this time, shall we? No more secrets."

Torval nodded and reached out his arm, accepting the proffered handshake. Instantly her appearance changed. Once again her human guise vanished, replaced by a shining angelic figure, dressed in flowing white robes, hovering ever so slightly above the ground. Her face and skin were smooth and without blemish, and her whole body seemed suffused in golden light.

Her beauty was overwhelming, but even as he gazed at that incredible form, he remembered what he must look like to her. She could see the true Torval now, not the human shell. She looked upon an image that made her recoil the first time she saw it. The worst part of it was, he wasn't even sure what she could see, because, according to Prelz, he'd already changed since arriving on Earth. Whatever his true appearance, though, it would be the very antithesis of her angelic form.

He allowed himself to stare for another long moment before speaking. When he did, he followed her instructions to the letter. "I am Torval, Demon Third Class, Layer Four Hundred Twelve of the Eighth Circle of Hell," he told her succinctly, in as friendly a manner as he could.

"And I am Auralea, Angel Second Class, originally of Layer One Hundred Nineteen of the Fifth Plane of Heaven," she answered, "but presently assigned to New York City. Nice to meet you."

"Yes, the same," answered Torval, reluctantly releasing her hand as she pulled away. Her form reverted to its normal human appearance, and he saw, to his relief, that she didn't appear disgusted or repelled by him this time.

"Now that we've got the introductions out of the way," said Christine inquisitively, "tell me what you're doing here on Earth, and more specifically, in the body of someone I thought I cared about."

Torval sighed, not missing the latent hostility in her voice. "I am here on vacation," he said plainly.

She gave a doubtful laugh. "Nice try, but you'll have to do better than that."

He nodded. "Yes, I agree, it is not exactly correct. To be precise, I was *told* I was being sent here on vacation, but I have since learned that is not my only purpose here. I am Advancing."

She thought about that for a second, and then nodded slowly. "You mean you're evolving to Second Class?"

"Yes, just so."

Christine nodded again, but still looked like she didn't quite believe him. "So let me get this straight," she went on, "when you demons Advance, you're put in a human body and sent to Earth?"

"I do not know if that is how all demons do it," answered Torval. "I have never Advanced before, nor have I ever spoken to another demon about the process. I was not even aware I was Advancing until I came here, and certain things became known to me. I believe that, at least in my case, my superiors found it necessary to place me in this body and set me loose on Earth with no further explanation or instructions to guide me. For whatever reason, that is what they saw fit to do, and since I cannot communicate with them from here, I have no choice but to proceed as I am."

She studied his face for a moment, obviously trying to tell if he was being truthful or not. "That doesn't sound very sensible to me," she commented off-handedly, "but then, you demons have always been a chaotic lot."

Torval shrugged. "It does not seem very sensible to me, either, but I do not understand the entire process, so perhaps there is some hidden purpose that eludes me."

Christine took a deep breath, and leaned back against the newspaper stand to gather her thoughts. Another uncomfortable silence followed. Nearby, the streetlight changed, and several vehicles rolled past, including a very large and noisy city bus, but Christine didn't seem to notice. Even when the wind of its passing threw her long hair into disarray, she reached up and straightened the errant locks automatically, without taking her eyes off Torval.

"When I was a Third Class angel," she finally said, shuffling her feet as if nervous, "I was what we call a Guardian. I visited Earth regularly, in spirit form, to guide children. Not to interfere with what they did, mind you, but to provide comfort when things went badly for them, and to subtly guide their young consciences as they developed."

Torval nodded, but said nothing. She obviously had a reason for telling this particular story, so he didn't want to interrupt.

Christine paused for a breath, and then went on. "Everthing was fine, and I did my job well, without complaint or any alterations in my duties. This went on for many years—I honestly don't know how many, to be truthful about it. Then, one day, I began to wonder why I didn't assist older kids, and help with far more complicated troubles involving teenagers and young adults. My superiors responded by allowing me to observe such humans for a while, and then older people as well, and while I did, I found myself Advancing. The thing was, I didn't realize it until later, when the process was all but complete."

"Why did they not simply explain to you what was happening?" inquired Torval.

"Well, they told me later, it was because I'd develop into a Second Class form on my own," said Christine. "They said what I saw and learned would guide me through the changes, and that if they explained it all ahead of time, it wouldn't go right."

"Then that is what is happening with me," he said, half to himself as he realized his situation was very much the same. "They did not tell me, because they knew that information would alter my development."

"But you figured it out on your own," she pointed out. "So it's already been affected, hasn't it?"

"I suppose," replied the demon with a shrug, "but then, that must've been inevitable. You yourself realized you were changing, as well. You went from a Guardian, into ... what?"

"I am a Redeemer," replied Christine, a definite note of pride in her voice. "I bring hope to the hopeless. What is your task?"

"I am a—or rather, I was ... " Torval hesitated. He didn't really want to tell her what his job was, back in Hell, because he instinctively knew she'd be horrified. Yet he had little choice. She had been honest with him, and now he had to do the same.

"I was a Torturer," he finally admitted.

"A Torturer?" she raised her eyebrows, not horrified at all, but instead merely surprised. "Somehow that doesn't seem possible. You don't seem like the torturing sort."

"Nevertheless, it is true," he explained, glad she hadn't recoiled immediately. "My task was to visit each of the souls on my route, ensuring their punishment was uninterrupted, and reinforcing the environment as necessary."

Christine looked away for a moment, and Torval couldn't see the reaction on her face. He thought, perhaps, that she might then simply walk away from him—after all, what did a creature of such goodness and kindness want to do with someone who spent most of their existence visiting punishment upon sinners?

Instead, after a moment, she looked back at him, nodding as if in understanding. "How, exactly, are sinners tortured in Hell?" she asked, sounding merely curious and not disgusted or repelled.

Torval hesitated again. He wasn't supposed to talk about such things. Nonetheless, he decided to answer, if only because he could then make the same inquiry about Heaven, and that would at least satisfy his curiosity. "Each is placed in a cell," he told her. "A room with no exit. They are then confronted with an illusion, taken from their own mind, and forced to endure various hardships that relate to the sort of person they were in life."

"That's basically how it works in Heaven, as well," she replied immediately, sparing him any need to ask for details. "Except, of course, it's not punishment, but a pleasant reward. Each soul is assigned a personal suite, where they experience Paradise as they would envision it. There are, in fact, angels who do the same sort of thing you do—Caretakers, they're called, who go around and make sure the souls there remain comfortable and happy."

"I see," Torval replied. "It seems to me that Heaven and Hell are not that terribly different, then."

"I suppose not," Christine said with a long sigh. She let that statement hang on the air for a moment before proceeding with her questioning. "Tell me, Torval, what was it that made you change? What made you go from being a happy little Torturer to someone banished to Earth?"

"I saw someone disappear," replied the demon honestly. "He disappeared from his cell."

"You mean he escaped?" Christine looked surprised once again. "It's possible to escape from the Underworld?"

"No, not escaping, at least not precisely. I am told it is called Transcendence. The soul realized what it had done, and felt genuine remorse, and then—well, I suppose, it is like what I am doing now. The soul Advanced—it moved on to whatever comes next."

"I've heard rumors about Transcendence," said Christine quietly, "but, since I'm no Caretaker, I never saw it for myself. Even so, just seeing that wouldn't have changed you, at least not directly."

"I began to think about it," he went on, grateful for the

opportunity to speak about this with someone, even happier that it was Christine—and that she was even listening at all. "I began to have questions about why torture was necessary. When I asked my Foreman about this, he arranged my vacation, which he said would help explain what humans were really like, and why they deserved to be punished. I see now that he only sent me here because he recognized my impending Advancement. I will likely never take up the mantle of Torturer again."

"Then what will you be?" she asked curiously. "What are you turning into, Torval?"

He hung his head, wishing he had an answer, for he'd wondered that himself. Instead, he could only reply, in a forlorn voice, "I don't know."

She did a strange thing, then. She stepped away from the curb and reached out to caress his face. Torval didn't pull away, though the gesture surprised him. Her touch was gentle, and left a strange tingling behind as she ever so softly stroked his cheek. Meanwhile, he found himself mesmerized by her luminous form. She was so beautiful—both as a human, and as an angel, and either shape just took his breath away.

Finally, after what seemed like forever, she broke off the contact and stepped back away from him. "Well, whatever it is, it doesn't seem so frightening anymore," she said with a smile. "When I first saw you, that first time, I have to admit I was a little bit scared. I knew what you were then, and it terrified me—I'm sorry, Torval, but it's true. You have to understand, we angels have always been taught that demons are terrible, evil beasts. It doesn't help that human mythology puts you in a similar light. When I saw a demon's face staring at me, from where my friend Joe Sampson had been, well, I sort of lost it, and for that I apologize."

"Then you do not mind my appearance?" he asked hopefully. "It does not bother you that I am a demon?"

"I won't lie to you," she replied with a sad shake of her head. "It does bother me, and more than just a little. Not just that you lied to me, either—I guess I can understand why you did that. I lied to you, too, after all, because of the Compact. I mean, neither of us could just come out and say what we really were, now could we?"

"No, we could not."

"But now that I know, well, we're not supposed to even interact," the angel went on.

"We cannot come into conflict," corrected Torval. "That is what the Compact says."

"True," she agreed readily, "but you know as well as I do that those specific words also have a deeper meaning. Angels and demons aren't supposed to interact, at least according to the spirit of the rule. That's what has me so worried."

"If that is true," asked Torval, "then why are you even here? Why are you risking having this discussion? Not that I am complaining, mind you, but I must know the answer."

"Because you're not like any demon I've ever heard of," she explained, the corners of her mouth turning up into a pleasant smile. "Demons are supposed to be evil, vindictive, terrible things that go around corrupting souls and wreaking havoc. All you've done is look for a job—something Joe never did, in all his wasted years, God rest his poor, miserable soul—and you've treated me with kindness and respect. A foul and evil creature wouldn't have stood in front of those people in the shelter and told them it was possible to find work and better themselves. A terrible monster wouldn't have helped Hal Sommersby get off the streets and back to his family. Those are the real reasons I came to talk to you, Torval. Those are the reasons I'm giving you another chance."

"I see," he replied with a nod. "Actually, I thought it might have been the pawn."

Christine laughed. "That too," she agreed readily. "That's what really got me thinking, in fact. I must admit, I probably wouldn't have come to this conclusion without it."

"So what do we do now?" he asked curiously, feeling grateful and just a little bit light-headed, considering how well this conversation was going. He hadn't expected anything like this, really. Delivering the chess piece, though premeditated, was nothing less than a simple act of desperation.

"Well," she answered, still smiling in a way that made his knees feel like rubber, "what I'm going to do right now is go back to work. This is my lunch break, and my time's almost run out. After that, we'll see. I have a lot more questions to ask you, and I'm sure you have a lot more to ask me."

"That is true," he agreed at once. "Perhaps we could make another attempt at a date?"

"Sure, but not quite so long this time," she answered readily. "You know, you did pretty well at dating, for someone so new at being human."

"Thank you," he replied, and now he too felt himself smiling. "I read a very good book on the subject."

"I'll just bet you did. So tell you what, I'll get off work about five, and meet you at the shelter just after that, okay? I'm sure Lakisha can do without me for a couple of hours, and we can grab some dinner."

"Very well, but I must be back at work shortly thereafter," said Torval, actually rather disappointed by that particular detail. "Where would you like to eat?"

"It doesn't matter," she answered, looking out across the street and waving for one of the ubiquitous yellow vehicles that seemed to be everywhere. One started to pull over to the curb almost immediately. "Just surprise me, okay? Someplace different—Chinese is fine every now and then, but I like some variety."

"I will see what I can locate," replied Torval. "Thank you, Auralea. It has been a pleasure meeting you."

"The same, Torval," she replied, sliding into the back of the cab. "Oh, and we should probably keep using our human names, if that's all right, Joe."

"Very well," he agreed. "Thank you, Christine."

"You're welcome," she responded with a nod, shutting the cab door and settling in for the ride.

Torval watched the cab drive away, keeping his eyes on the departing vehicle as long as he could. Christine's lovely face stared back at him through the back window, and just before she was out of sight, she gave him a supportive wave. He waved back, smiling, and realized that he was almost giddy with excitement.

She was back! Just like that, she'd given him another chance! His desperate ploy with the chess piece had succeeded, and what was more, he'd managed to arrange another date.

A date with an angel!

He felt like dancing with joy. Perhaps he might have, except that just as he started to turn, intending to head back to the shelter and try to give Prelz this most amazing news, his eyes beheld a sobering sight that immediately shocked him back to reality.

There were two men standing there. Two men he recognized immediately, even though he'd hoped to not have to see them again any time soon. They were Marty and Vince, the policemen who'd shown up once before to drag him off to see Lieutenant McCord.

"So," asked Vince with a hearty laugh, "who's the hot chick?"

* * *

Once again, Torval found himself shoved rudely in the back of an unmarked police car, behind the same fence-like protective screen that separated him from the two irritating officers. Having the shield there actually made him feel somewhat better, though only barely. They couldn't reach through it to physically injure him, at least not without stopping the car.

This time he knew where he was going, although that knowledge wasn't much of a comfort. The last time he was here, he thought he'd broken some law, and would be arrested and incarcerated. This time, he knew he hadn't done anything, and that was exactly the problem. Lieutenant McCord would want some sort of progress report, and all Torval had was questions he didn't dare ask.

"So, if you're not gonna tell us who the babe is," Vince called out from the front seat, "at least tell us where you picked her up. Someone like that's gotta have a friend, or a sister, or sump'in."

"Can it, Vince, you ain't got no shot," laughed Marty. "Did you get a look at her? She's high class, I'm tellin' ya. Oh, you could probably do better, if you had a couple hundred bucks to wave down 'round Bowery way."

Vince smacked his fellow police officer on the arm, chuckling loudly. "Don't let my wife hear you sayin' shit like that," he remarked, before turning back to Torval. "Now as for you, let me tell ya, the boss, he wants to know the scoop. You've had what, two days now? Surely you got some info, right?"

"Actually, I do not," replied Torval honestly. "It has not been enough time, and the Roxtons have not given me any of the data Lieutenant McCord requested. If you could just release me, I will notify you when I have learned something of use."

"Oh, ha-ha, nice try," scoffed Marty, "but you ain't gettin' off that easy! You can tell him yourself, and let me tell you, I don't wanna be in on any part of that there conversation."

"It *was* the weekend, y'know," Vince commented. "I wouldn't be surprised if he's tellin' the truth."

"Who cares? Not our business anyways." The other shrugged and turned to face forward again, seemingly forgetting Torval was even there. "So yeah, after we drop him off, wanna snag some lunch? I'm gettin' hungry."

Torval listened worriedly while they discussed several options for food, which only made his mouth water. With some effort he managed to tune them out, mostly by watching the streets and buildings roll endlessly past out the window. He noted, with some discomfort, that he couldn't even escape this car if he wanted to, for there were no handles to open the door. Somehow he doubted he would have the strength to break the window, either.

Besides, there was no point in running. He would have to speak to McCord again eventually anyway, so it might as well be now. The problem, though, was what to say during the meeting. He could simply admit that he didn't learn anything and ask for more time—that would work, if he thought he could resist the lieutenant's cold, withering glare and powerful, compelling voice. Or, considered Torval, he could admit he knew about the deal the Roxtons had with McCord. In fact, if he did so, he might at least be able to learn more about whatever it was the lieutenant wanted to find out.

Torval's mind drifted further. What if he did, in fact, tell McCord, and he somehow didn't mind that Torval knew such details—what if the lieutenant ordered him to spy on the Roxtons further? What if he asked for even more—to steal from them, perhaps, or sabotage them in some way? Could Torval even do something like that? And what if the policeman didn't want Joe Sampson knowing about his arrangement with the Roxtons, and simply did away with him? Torval had little doubt the man was capable of such a thing—Joe Sampson would just meet with some 'accident,' as the Roxtons had put it, and disappear.

Now is not the time to die, thought Torval ruefully. *Not when I'm finally working things out with Christine. Not when I have so very much to learn from her.*

The car came to a halt in a parking lot and Torval found himself half-led and half-dragged into the station house. He made no attempt to resist as he made his way through the building, past any number of uniformed policemen and a few wrongdoers they had caught, now being processed in some way or other. In due course he found himself shoved rudely into the lieutenant's tiny office, whereupon Marty and Vince made themselves very quickly scarce.

"Close the door, will you," said McCord, not bothering to stand, or even look up from the paper in his hands. He was dressed much as he had been last time, except he didn't wear a coat and his dark blue tie was noticeably loose about his neck.

Torval complied and continued to stand, not sure if he should sit without being invited to do so. There was silence for about a minute while the lieutenant kept on reading, until finally he set the piece of paper down and stood up. A palpable aura of menace surrounded him, as though he clearly intended Torval harm, and would do so at a time of his choosing, without any sort of reason or provocation.

"So," said McCord after another few long seconds, "what have you got for me?"

"Nothing," replied Torval, with as much courage as he could muster. "I am sorry to disappoint you, but the Roxtons did not permit me access to any of their records."

"Really? What a shame," replied the lieutenant in a coldly calm voice. He stepped out from behind the desk, pushed his chair into place, and walked out into the room a bit. With one hand, he took hold of a rod dangling from the nearby wall and twisted it, causing the blinds on that section of glass to fold downward, closing off Torval's view of the rest of the station outside. "Are you absolutely sure you don't have anything for me?" went on McCord, not so much as glancing in his direction.

The lieutenant's voice seemed calm and measured, but the threat was clear. Torval didn't stop to marvel at the way the blinds functioned, or how they seemed to magically seal themselves with a simple turn of a wrist. The only thing he could think about was that in a moment, if the policeman kept walking across the room, he would close off the next set of panes, and then the next ... and then there would be no one to see what was to come.

"I apologize," said Torval worriedly, hoping he could stave off any violence by telling the simple truth as quickly as he could. Even as he spoke, though, McCord was already closing the second set of blinds. "I was given a computer program to study, and was told I would be entering sales data into the computer, starting tonight. I am certain I will be able to find whatever it is you need from those records."

"Do tell," replied the lieutenant, continuing to move across the room. He reached the next set of blinds now, and closed them quickly. The room suddenly seemed darker, and Torval found himself sweating uncomfortably. He wished he'd taken off his coat, but it was too late to do so now.

"I suppose you're going to tell me it was the weekend, so you had no chance to look in any of their files," went on McCord. "You realize, of course, that I'm fully aware you spent the night in that building each of the last two nights? You could've been poking around that whole time. You know, I'm starting to think you don't have the right kind of motivation to do what I'm asking."

"I will be able to look at the records tonight," replied Torval shakily. He still wasn't sure he wanted to do this, but he was ready to say almost anything if it would keep the lieutenant from beating him senseless, or worse. "I assure you, that is what I was told this very morning. You must believe me."

McCord moved closer, peering into Torval's eyes, seemingly enjoying the way his hapless prisoner quite visibly quivered with fear. "Oh, I do, I do," he said with a wicked smile. "I believe you'd say anything right now, Mr. Sampson. Isn't that so?"

Torval didn't reply, but the look on his face gave his answer for him. McCord just nodded and kept right on smiling. "Well, you know what? I think you're lying to me. I don't think you'll really find anything. You'll keep making up stories as long as it keeps me happy, won't you? Well, let me tell you something. Mr. Sampson. I don't like it when people string me along. So let me show you what's going to happen if you try."

With that, he suddenly reached up, grabbed Torval by the collar, and slammed him into the side wall, rattling the wooden slabs and causing the nearby blinds to shake. Torval felt limp, as if his muscles had completely failed him, and he coughed, choking for breath.

Meanwhile, the lieutenant maintained his grip on Torval's coat, tugging it upward, so that he almost dangled in the air. "This could be worse," McCord said forcefully. "So very much worse. I trust I've made my point?"

"Y-yes, sir," replied Torval between gasps.

"Good. Now you'd better not fail me, Sampson, or there'll be hell to pay!"

With that, he reached up with his other hand, and slapped Torval lightly across the face. That's when the truth about Lieutenant McCord finally came out.

In that instant, he *changed*.

Where the policeman stood, Torval saw a twisted, blackened serpentine creature slightly larger than a man. The monster had sharp, curved fangs, a pair of coal-black eyes with prominent red slits, and a forked tongue that flicked in and out like a snake's. Scales covered its head and body, enveloping a humanoid torso and arms that ended in sharply clawed, talonlike fingers. Below the waist, his body was legless, a single, thick tail that rested in a rippling coil.

Torval's eyes went wide, for he knew exactly what this meant. Moreover, he realized with a heavy heart, he should've realized it a lot sooner. He should've recognized the signs—the same kind of intense emotions he felt when Christine was near, only nowhere near as pleasant.

Lieutenant McCord was a demon!

Chapter 7

"Aha!" exclaimed the snakelike monstrosity, holding his hand against Torval's face. "A demon! I should've known! I thought there was something wrong about you! The way you spoke just didn't seem right."

"I—I have been working on that," Torval managed to gasp, for the clawed hand clutching his throat seemed to be gripping him even tighter. "Please—release me," he all but begged.

"Oh, right, sorry," replied McCord, dropping Torval at once and stepping away. Instantly he reverted to his human appearance, which, despite being more ordinary, still seemed just as threatening. "Forgot about that. Anyway, nice to see another demonic face around these parts. About time they sent me an assistant!"

Torval took a few deep breaths, rubbing at his neck to ensure he'd suffered no permanent damage. "That is not my purpose here," he explained after a moment, recovering quickly from the surprise revelation of McCord's true nature. A number of scenarios tumbled through his head in swift succession, but foremost on his mind was the warning Geezon gave him just before sending him to Earth—if Torval encountered another demon at work, he was to depart at once and stay out of his way.

In fact, this solves a lot of problems, realized Torval, suddenly quite relieved that the police lieutenant was actually one of his kind. Before he could say anything to that effect, though, the questioning began.

"Then what *is* your purpose?" demanded McCord, in a tone that suggested he would brook no deception.

"I was sent here on vacation," said Torval matter-of-factly. However, before that point could be argued, he quickly added, "However, I have since divined my true mission. I am Advancing, and I believe I was sent here to Earth to facilitate the change."

"Ah, yes, I was wondering about that," said McCord, taking a couple of steps back toward his desk. "You look like an intermediate form. At least, I didn't recognize the shape. So you're Advancing, hmm? What were you before?"

"I was a Torturer," replied Torval without a trace of pride in his voice.

"Yeah, I was wondering if that was it. The basic body shape is still there, but no tail, and you're standing up straight as an arrow. Wonder what you're becoming?"

"I do not know," admitted Torval.

"Well, obviously, they sent you here to meet me," concluded McCord suddenly, without a shred of evidence to support the claim. "You're here to be my apprentice, hmm? You should make a fine Tempter, then. What's your real name? Identify yourself, soldier!"

The response was instantaneous. "I am Torval, formerly Demon Third Class, Layer Four Hundred—"

McCord threw up his hands. "No, no, I don't care about any of that crap! None of that matters any more. Now you're Torval, Second Class Tempter, and you're my apprentice. How do you like that, hmm?"

Torval shuddered, but quickly hid the involuntary gesture by coughing once and tugging at his now-wrinkled coat. "Sir," he replied carefully, "I appreciate the offer, but I was given strict orders when I was sent here. Those instructions were quite clear—if I encountered another demon, I was to depart at once and have nothing to do with him. I do not—"

"Never mind that," scoffed McCord with a hearty laugh. "That was just to keep you from going around touching every human in sight, hoping to find another demon to talk to! It was inevitable that we should meet. I've been wondering when I was going to get some support from the Lower Realm anyway—surely they must be pleased with what I've accomplished here, in just a few short years."

"Be that as it may," replied Torval, resisting the urge to ask for more details on that subject, "my instructions were quite clear. I must take my leave and avoid you hereafter."

"Who gave you those orders?" demanded McCord. "Was it your superior?"

"It was a demon named Geezon. He was the one who sent me here."

"Ah, and what was his rank?"

"Second Class," replied Torval, a bit sheepishly, for he could see where this conversation was going.

"Well," said McCord with a smile, "surely you recognize my classification, correct? You do know that I outrank him?"

"No, I do not," Torval answered honestly. He truly didn't know McCord's form or task, though he was pretty sure he knew the rank. There was no mistaking the sheer menacing power of that serpentine shape, or the deep-seated authority in the lieutenant's voice.

"Of course you wouldn't," sighed McCord. "Let me introduce myself. My name is Mannoch, and I am a Corruptor. Do you know what that is?"

"No, sir," admitted Torval.

"A Corruptor," the policeman explained, as if speaking to a child, "is a blackener of souls. I seek the righteous, and turn them to evil. I find those on the path of good, and show them a better way. I am what every Tempter secretly dreams of becoming. And, finally, in case you couldn't figure it out, I am a Demon First Class. Do you doubt this? Surely you can feel my power, even from our brief contact."

"Y-yes, sir," agreed Torval reluctantly. There was no denying the sheer magnitude of the aura emanating from the creature called Mannoch. He seemed to radiate demonic strength, even from all the way across the little room.

"Then, since you acknowledge my authority," said the lieutenant, grinning with satisfaction now, "I rescind your earlier orders, with respect to myself only, of course. You will now serve me, and me alone. Is that clear?"

"Y-yes, sir," Torval answered automatically, regretting saying those words but finding himself unable to avoid doing so.

"Excellent." McCord sat down in his seat, still smiling, and leaned back with his hands pressed together. "Now that we have that cleared up, let me let you in on what's going on here. I wish I'd known you were a demon sooner—I could've had you working on tempting the Roxtons instead of just spying on them."

Torval shuddered again. He didn't want this! He shouldn't be here—Mannoch being a First Class demon didn't automatically give him the right to order Torval around. In fact, strictly according to the chain of command, Geezon's orders still held, since he was the Transitioner who sent Torval here on his present mission (such as it was). Mannoch could give his "apprentice" new orders, but only insofar as they didn't interfere with Geezon's instructions. Yet Torval knew if he tried to point that out, it wouldn't matter, even if he could find the inner strength to resist the powerhouse seated at the desk across from him. So instead he did nothing, hoping to figure some other way out of this if the opportunity presented itself.

"Anyway," went on McCord, "here's the deal. I have—well, let's call it an 'arrangement' with the Roxtons. Heh-heh. Yeah, that's it, an 'arrangement.' I love how human words can couch such subtleties, don't you? See, I did them a big favor a while ago, and now they owe me. They owe me so much that I can make them do all sorts of fun things. They aren't the only ones, either. I have a lot of people who owe me favors, Torval. That's what I've been doing here on Earth, you see. Every time I take control of someone like that, that's another notch in my Corruptor's belt. Then that just leads to more and more ways to corrupt others. It's so *easy*, too! Like the humans would say, it's like shooting fish in a barrel!"

"I do not understand," replied Torval, noting in his mind that this basically confirmed what the Roxtons had told him. In fact, this provided an excellent opportunity to gather more information, so he pressed on quickly. "If you have the Roxtons under your control, why did you ask me to spy on them?"

McCord narrowed his eyes. "Good one, very good," he noted after a moment. "That's a very astute question, Torval. You're going to make an excellent apprentice, I can tell."

Torval nodded, but the comment made him squirm a little inside. Being a servant of this snake-demon wasn't what he wanted at all. Still, at least he was on Mannoch's good side, for the moment.

"All right, here's the deal with the Roxtons," McCord went on, apparently having no need to doubt Torval's reasons for asking. "Those little human bastards are cheating me! I don't know how, but they're definitely scraping a little off the top and keeping it buried in the accounting. Every time they make a sale, they keep some of it for themselves. I know it—I just don't have any hard proof yet, and when I do, I'm going to put the smackdown on their little embezzlement operation faster than you can spit!"

"The Roxtons are selling things?" Torval asked curiously. This was the first he'd heard of that particular angle—Lincoln and Pete hadn't seen fit to include him in that detail.

"Yeah, they peddle car parts, right? So me and some other friends, every now and then, when we get a real sweet rod at impound, we take it over there to be chopped. You know what that means?"

"Chopped?" replied Torval, not catching the slang reference at first. Just as his mind made the connection with the phrase "chop shop" that he'd heard several times before, McCord went on with his explanation, instantly accepting Torval's ignorance as fact.

"Yeah, the boys break it down, into its component parts." The lieutenant made a motion like he held some sort of weapon, slicing away at a large invisible object on his desk. "Then we clean off the serial numbers and the Roxtons sell it all. There's real advantages to having a car parts warehouse under your thumb—nobody notices when a few additional items make their way into their inventory. It's the best way to move stolen goods I've ever heard of—and it was all *my* idea!"

"I see," replied Torval, and for once he actually did understand. In fact, everything seemed to click in his mind, like the pieces of a puzzle suddenly fitting together. The rumors of the Roxtons running a chop shop were true, it seemed. They did do that—but only because they were forced to do so by a demon in the guise of a crooked cop.

"You know what the best thing is, my young apprentice?" chuckled McCord. "We make a killing selling those parts! Not that I need money myself, really, except to help corrupt more innocent souls. Money's really good for corrupting, you see. Sometimes it's so easy I don't even have to try."

"Money is the root of all evil," remarked Torval, trying to come up with something that would please his superior, "or so I am told."

"That's it exactly!" McCord laughed, pointing a single finger in the air, as if in triumph. "But you see, sometimes it's so tempting, people even try to steal it from their betters. That's what the Roxtons are doing to me, Torval. They're taking money that should be mine, and I'm afraid I just can't let that slide. It sets a very bad precedent, hmm? I don't know if Pete Roxton's gambling again, or if they're so naïve they think they can pay off their loans themselves, but I don't really care. Whatever the reason, it's gonna stop, one way or another."

"What are you going to do?" asked Torval, trying not to let any trace of concern slip into his voice.

"Me? Oh, we don't need to worry about those little details," came the reply. "It'll involve pain, though. Lots and lots of pain." He chuckled to himself, rubbing his knuckles together in a menacing fashion. "Who knows? I may let them live, seeing as their little operation is so useful to me, but not without a few changes in the way they do things. I may even have you put in charge over there, if you perform well in my service."

Torval gulped and nodded, but said nothing. So that's it, then. He was to betray the Roxtons, knowing that they would be beaten and possibly killed, and if he performed well in this task, he would earn favor with Mannoch! The very idea repulsed him to the core, sickening him so much that it almost felt like pain.

For a moment, while the policeman wrung his hands and grinned, staring off into space as he imagined any number of grisly fates for the Roxtons, Torval realized something. When he first came to Earth, knowing little of good or evil, and caring nothing about humans whatsoever, he might not have minded doing what McCord just suggested. In fact, he probably would've done so readily, if the policeman merely promised him a job and a place to stay.

Clearly, his experiences on Earth were changing him, exactly as Geezon must've intended when he sent Torval here. He still didn't know what he might become, but he did know that whatever it was, it didn't involve the terrible betrayal Mannoch expected from him. Even as he came to that realization, though, McCord chose to explain exactly what he wanted his new apprentice to do next.

"Anyway," said the Corruptor, "enough daydreaming. Time to put you to work. Here's your first assignment, Torval. You're going to go back to Roxton Auto Parts, find out what's really going on with their little embezzling scheme, and report back to me. I don't care how you get the information, really—you've gotten pretty close to them so far, so you'll figure something out. Oh, and while you're there, spread a little temptation, too. You know what I mean. Pete likes to gamble, and he loves the ladies, so maybe you can get to him that way. If you need some advice, I'm always here. Just feel free to ask."

"That will be difficult," replied Torval, hoping to find an excuse to avoid interacting with the other demon as much as possible. "I have little money and no way to contact you. The body I occupy was little more than a street bum, with no resources to draw on."

"Oh, that's no problem. No problem at all." McCord reached into a drawer, shuffled some things around, and drew out a handful of bills. "I keep some extra cash around as a slush fund. Here's five hundred bucks—that ought to tide you over for now. Buy some new clothes, for Satan's sake! That's the same crap you were wearing two days ago, and it's starting to smell."

Torval stared in wide-eyed amazement at the wad of bills on the edge of the desk. Five hundred dollars! That was more than he'd earned in all his time here on Earth so far. He scooped up the money, looked at the collection of hundreds and twenties in disbelief, and finally stuffed it all into his pocket before McCord could change his mind.

"Oh, and here's another thing," said the policeman, "here's my card. This has my number on it—call me anytime. I rarely sleep, and when I do, I don't mind an interruption."

"But I have no—" Torval started, even as he took the business card from his superior's fingers.

"What do you think the money's for?" snapped McCord. "Don't give me excuses, Torval! Go get yourself a cell phone, and make sure it isn't one of those with one of those stupid contracts! In fact, I'll have my boys drop you off at a wireless store on their way back to where they found you. Got it?"

"Yes, sir," responded Torval automatically.

"Good! Now, as much as I'd love having you follow me around the rest of the day, I'm really quite busy. Go get the phone, and call me immediately so I can program your number. Then I want you to get some new clothes so you don't stink up the place when you get back to the warehouse. Tomorrow morning, when you're done with work, I expect a full report. Is that understood?"

"Y-yes, sir," he agreed without protest. There just didn't seem to be any point in arguing—McCord just wasn't going to take no for an answer.

"Excellent. Glad to have you on board, Torval. Now get the Heaven out of my office!"

* * *

As much as he didn't like Vince and Marty, Torval almost hoped they would accompany him into the cell phone store. He had no clue how to even operate a cell phone, although he had a fairly good idea from examples he'd seen in use about the city. Unfortunately, the instant he stepped out of the unmarked police car, the vehicle sped away, as if McCord's human assistants were grateful to be rid of him.

Torval peered through the windows of the little shop, mind still somewhat awhirl. He could certainly handle learning that McCord was actually a demon. Indeed, despite the fact that he knew the creature's name was Mannoch, he found himself continuing to think of him as Lieutenant McCord, which was probably for the best. The last thing he wanted was to accidentally say his demonic name when humans were about.

What bothered him was how he'd been instantly and immediately pressed into Mannoch's service. That went against Geezon's orders, and besides, even if it didn't, Torval had the advantage of free will while on Earth. That's how he continued to associate with Prelz, despite those very same orders. Along those same lines, Torval knew he could simply ignore McCord's instructions and do whatever he wanted, without fear of reprisals from higher in his chain of command.

The problem wasn't that, of course, but the fear of reprisals from McCord himself, and his invisible network of corrupted humans. Were some of them watching him even now? Vince and Marty were gone, but that didn't mean Mannoch didn't have eyes hidden elsewhere in the city. Some of them might be fixed on him at this very moment.

Torval's options were quite limited. He could assist McCord, or at least pretend to, and simply ride out the remaining eight-plus days of his time on Earth. He simply couldn't believe that his true purpose here was to become Mannoch's apprentice, and felt certain that the portal would open as scheduled, eight and a half days hence.

Unless, of course, Geezon lied about that detail too ...

No, that isn't right, Torval insisted to himself. He would've met McCord sooner, perhaps even the first day of his arrival—not halfway through the "vacation," after he'd already begun to change. If Temptation was Torval's destiny, as Mannoch seemed to believe, then why was the first demon Torval met an ex-Tempter who hated the job and refused to continue doing it?

No, it wasn't Temptation, he knew that much. Torval didn't know what he might be turning into, but it certainly wasn't a Tempter. Meeting Mannoch was a mistake—an unfortunate coincidence, and nothing more.

So, what could he do? Pretend to follow McCord's instructions? What other option was there, besides blindly following them, thereby betraying everything and everyone he knew?

Well, he could leave, of course. He had seven hundred dollars in his pocket now, enough to get into one of the hundreds of cabs that seemed everywhere, and purchase a trip to one of the more distant boroughs of the city—or perhaps beyond. He could afford to rent a room somewhere for another week, and wait it out. McCord would never find him.

Unfortunately, that would terminate his budding relationship with Christine, and leave the Roxtons hanging. He didn't want to abandon the Roxtons now, not when he knew McCord intended to visit violence upon them at some point in the near future. And he certainly didn't want to leave Christine, not when things between them seemed better than ever.

There was nothing to do, then, but press on, concluded Torval, stepping into the store. A little bell jangled above him as he pushed through the glass doorway, and a salesman dressed in a white shirt and red tie turned his way instantly. The man had short hair, a freckled complexion, and a pair of glasses so thick his eyes seemed to be popping out of his head.

"Can I help you find something?" he inquired. The name on the tag attached poorly to his front pocket read "Chester."

"I require a cell phone," stated Torval in his usual direct manner. "However, I know nothing about them."

"Hmm, so you don't have any idea what style you want?" asked Chester in a friendly and amiable tone, pushing his glasses up on his crooked nose absently. "Or what sort of plan you need?"

"I mean I do not know what a cell phone is," Torval explained. "I understand that it is a telephone, and that I can use it to call other phones, but that is all."

"You don't know what a—" The salesman stopped himself, shaking his head. He glanced around at some of the displays, selected a small rectangular object from its stand, and turned back to his customer. "Never mind. I don't want to know. Alrighty, then, here's how it works. It's just like a regular phone, but smaller, and you can carry it anywhere. See this flap? You lift up to get to the numbers, and when you punch them in, they show up on the screen. Once you've entered them all correctly, hit this green button, and it dials. When you're done with the call, just hit the red button to finish it, or close the flap like this." He snapped it shut, and offered the device with one hand. "Go on, try it if you like."

Torval experimented with the phone for a few minutes, listening while Chester described various other features, like the ability to store numbers, before launching into an explanation of payment plans. While the salesman prattled on, Torval removed the business card from his pocket and practiced entering the phone number there into the cell phone's memory. The process proved rather easy, and he smiled to himself at his success. This technology wasn't that hard after all.

"So there you have it," said Chester, adjusting his heavy glasses again in what was clearly a standard practice for him. "Now, do you know what plan you needed? I won't bother showing you any of the more complex phones—I'm pretty sure you just want something basic, at least for now. Just remember you can always upgrade whenever you like."

"I will not need the phone long," said Torval honestly. "I was warned not to accept a plan with any sort of contract."

"No problem," agreed Chester with an affable smile. "You can have any of these phones over here on a pay-by-the-month basis. The problem, of course, is you'll have to buy the phone flat out. You only get free ones if you accept a contract. That's just how it works."

"Then one of these will suffice," said Torval, looking over his options. Knowing nothing about the individual features of the four choices before him, he selected the cheapest one—but even that one was almost one hundred and fifty dollars. Fortunately, he was easily able to afford it, thanks to the cash donated by Lieutenant McCord.

"All right, good choice," said Chester, adjusting his glasses once more. "Okay, now I just need you to fill out this form while I get the number activated for you."

The salesman picked up one of the boxes near the display, opened it, took out the phone inside, and turned away. He seemed to be working on the device for some reason beyond Torval's comprehension.

The demon focused his attention on the printed form in front of him. Unfortunately, as he'd feared, it asked for certain details, such as address, home phone, and other things that Joe Sampson lacked. He stared at the paper, at a loss, until Chester noticed his difficulties.

"Is there a problem?" asked the salesman.

"I cannot fill this out," Torval admitted. "I do not have an address or another phone, nor do I know my social security number, or my 'e-mail,' whatever that might be."

Chester glanced around, as if making sure there was nobody else watching. "Okay, I see how it is," he said in a low voice. "You know, we're really not supposed to sell phones without contact information—

it's strictly against the rules. However, for a small additional fee, I could see to it this baby makes its way into your pocket without any other complications."

Torval stared at the man. "What fee?" he inquired curiously, for it didn't make much sense that there should be an additional charge just for that.

"Well," replied Chester with a slight tilt of his head and a knowing smile, "it's a fee for me keeping my mouth shut, if you get what I'm saying. Let's call it an extra fifty bucks—in cash."

Now he understood. There was no true charge—this was a bribe, pure and simple. Torval would pay this man extra money, so that he would look the other way and avoid following the proper procedures.

In other words, Chester was doing evil! He was violating the rules and taking money to do it. Mannoch was right, it seemed—money definitely provided an excellent source of temptation.

"What you are doing is wrong," stated Torval impulsively, wanting to know more about the salesman's motivations. The last time he followed this particular path, with the stolen goods peddler named Zac Turillo, his questioning was eventually rewarded. "Are you motivated simply by greed, or is there something else involved?"

Chester looked stunned. "What the hell is that supposed to mean?" he asked after a moment. "You aren't some kinda cop, are you? This ain't illegal, y'know. I'm just trying to do you a favor!"

"No, I am not a policeman. I am simply curious."

"Too curious for your own good," snapped Chester, pushing up on his glasses again. He seemed quite nervous and agitated now. "Do you want the phone or don't you?"

Torval sighed in defeat. He could tell Chester wasn't going to answer his questions. Besides, he needed the phone, and whether or not the salesman was doing evil didn't change that fact.

"Yes, I will take it," said the demon after a moment, reaching into his pocket for the money. He produced a small cluster of McCord's donated bills, since he hadn't bothered to store them in his wallet, and counted out two hundred in total. "Will this suffice?"

"That's fine," replied Chester, smiling and friendly once more. "Let me ring you up."

* * *

As soon as he got out of the shop, Torval examined the phone and practiced with the buttons. This one seemed just as easy to work with as the sample device he'd tried initially. After a few minutes, he'd managed to store McCord's number, and even enter the name as well. He didn't know how to capitalize the second "C", however, so it read as "Mccord" on the contact list.

Experimentally, he selected that number and pressed the green button. The word "Dialing" appeared on the screen. Torval held the phone up to his ear and shortly after heard the comforting ringing sound that told him he'd done it correctly.

"Hello?" came the Corruptor's forceful voice after a moment, sounding noticeably irritated at the interruption. "Who the hell is this?"

"It is I, Joe Sampson," he answered, deciding it was best to refer to himself by his human name, even into this strange device. "You instructed me to call you immediately."

"Ah, good to hear from you, Joe." McCord's voice immediately softened, but still contained its full measure of authority. "No problems getting the cell phone, I trust?"

"Nothing I could not overcome," Torval replied honestly. "I could not fill out the form the salesman gave me, but he took an additional payment in order to avoid that part of the process."

"Ah, you got him to take a bribe!" McCord gave a hearty laugh. "Already working on your temptation skills! Good work, Torval. I can tell I'm going to like having you around."

"Thank you, sir," he replied, not bothering to correct the obvious misinterpretation. As long as Mannoch thought Torval intended to follow his instructions, the next week would flow that much more smoothly.

"Okay, well, thanks for calling, and I've got your number in my phone now," went on McCord. "Now I've got some juicy corrupting to do. Give me a call tomorrow morning. That is all."

Torval started to answer, but the phone suddenly emitted a rapid series of beeps. He pulled the little box away, looking at the screen, where the words "Call Ended" now appeared. With a shrug, the demon closed the flap, slid the phone into his pocket, and left the store behind.

* * *

Next he had to deal with the gnawing hunger in his gut, so Torval headed back toward the shelter, hoping to find Prelz. He had quite a bit of updating to do, and furthermore, he hoped perhaps the other demon could provide more information on exactly how Tempters operated. After all, if Torval had to continue associating with Mannoch, he'd be expected to know what he should be doing.

He didn't see Prelz initially, but a long line waited for the lunch soup service. Torval knew better than to attempt to cut ahead, so he stepped into the queue, wishing his stomach would stop growling. While he stood there, Prelz came around a corner, saw him, and gave a welcoming wave.

Torval moved to meet his friend, abandoning the line at once. "I'm glad I found you," he said eagerly. "I have news to report."

"Sure thing," agreed Prelz at once. "I was hoping for some lunch, though, and you're not exactly dressed appropriately for this place." He gave a brief chuckle at his weak joke.

"We shall go elsewhere," Torval told him. "I have money again, so I will pay for lunch. What sort of food would you like?"

"Hmm ... haven't had pizza in a while," said the ex-Tempter, licking his lips in anticipation. "Pepperoni and sausage—it's like manna from heaven, except it's Italian."

"Very well, I also like pizza." Torval started walking, heading in the direction of the very same place he'd enjoyed his first slice, back when he'd encountered Hal Sommersby begging on the street. The walk wasn't far at all, and once there, he placed an order and secured a table, which Prelz looked at dubiously. Finally, with a shrug, he walked over and sat down, ignoring the frowns and wrinkled noses of other nearby patrons.

"Okay," said Prelz, eagerly gulping down some of the soft drink Torval saw fit to buy for him, "what's this news you want so badly to tell me that you're willing to buy me lunch?"

"Christine and I are back together," said Torval, smiling proudly.

"Oh really?" Prelz nodded and returned the grin. "Glad to hear it! How'd you pull that off? I thought she didn't want to have anything to do with you."

"I used a pawn."

"A what?" Prelz was clearly confused.

"When I went on my date," explained Torval, "we saw a movie

called *Queen Takes Pawn*. In that movie, a man uses a chess piece called a pawn to indicate that he wanted another chance with a woman. The pawn signified a willingness to start their relationship over, from the beginning, as if they had just met. It seemed to me that Christine and I also needed to start over, since we now knew exactly who the other was. So I gave her a pawn, and she understood."

Prelz finished off the soda, made a sort of hissing noise with his mouth, and wiped his lips off with his sleeve. "You figured that out by yourself, did you? Very insightful, my friend. You'd make a really good human, you know that?"

"If that is a compliment, I thank you," replied Torval, not really sure how to respond to that comment.

"Oh, it's a compliment, trust me. It's not like a demon to make that kind of connection. At least, not a Third Class demon, but then, you aren't exactly Third Class any more, are you?"

"No, I am not," replied Torval with a nod. "The changes in myself can no longer be denied. I am certain now that they sent me here specifically to assist in my Advancement."

"Sounds like something they'd do, especially if you'd spent your entire existence in Hell, without ever seeing Earth." Prelz nodded in appreciation. "You have to admit, it's pretty devious of them. I bet they didn't even know what you were going to turn into, so they let the chips fall where they may."

Torval was about to ask what chips had to do with anything, but at that point a waitress arrived to refill their drinks. She, too, frowned at the odiferous presence of Jake the street bum, but she kept silent, apparently willing to tolerate him as long as there were no direct objections from the other customers.

Once she'd refilled the glasses and moved on, Torval resumed the conversation. "There is one thing I specifically wanted to talk to you about," he continued. "Do you think it is possible that they sent me here specifically to meet another demon—a mentor, if you will? Someone who would train me and help me change into my new form?"

"If so, they failed utterly," laughed Prelz uproariously. "I'm about the crappiest mentor they could've hoped for!"

"No, I am not referring to you." Torval took a sip of his soft drink and let that sink in. "I have met another demon, and he believes I was sent here specifically to become his apprentice. Is there any chance this could be possible?"

"Well, I suppose it—wait, what?" Prelz looked around worriedly. "You met another demon? Who is it? It's not one of those cops, is it?"

"Not one of those specific ones, no," replied Torval, suddenly recalling how Prelz hadn't reacted well to their presence the last time. If he'd thought of that, he might not have mentioned this situation at all. Unfortunately, it was too late to back out now. "I told you, I had physical contact with Vince and Marty, and they are human. The actual demon is their leader, a man known as Lieutenant Jonas McCord."

"A lieutenant?" gasped Prelz. "A police lieutenant is a demon? You gotta be shitting me!"

"No, I am not defecating on you." Torval checked himself. "Oh, wait, that is another human euphemism, isn't it?"

"Yeah," replied a suddenly thoughtful Prelz. "You know, I swore I'd never let another demon come anywhere near me, but now, I just don't feel like running anymore. I'm not going to last much longer anyway. You aren't going to introduce this guy to me, are you?"

"No, I do not intend to," replied Torval. "I will not allow him anywhere near you, and as far as I know, he does not know you exist."

"Good, let's keep it that way." Prelz looked around worriedly, scanning the patrons in the restaurant as well as the cars passing by, especially those that moved very slowly. "They could be watching us now, I guess, but I'm just being paranoid. A few days ago, I'd probably already have bolted, but dammit, I'm sick of looking over my shoulder every damn minute of my life. So tell me about this guy—what kind of demon is he?"

"He is a Corruptor."

Prelz almost choked on his soda. "A—a Corruptor? Are you sure?" he managed to sputter. "Wait, there's no way you'd have any idea what a Corruptor is, so you can't be joking, can you? Tell me, what does he look like? As a demon, I mean."

"He is serpentine in form—" began Torval, but that was all the confirmation Prelz needed.

"Okay, stop, that's all you had to say. A Corruptor ... shit, seriously, you gotta be kidding me! I've never met one, but I know what they are. Remember when I told you that story about the snake in the Garden of Eden, the one that talked the first humans into eating the forbidden fruit? That was a Corruptor—Satan himself, possibly, if the legends are true."

"That would explain the serpentine shape," agreed Torval with a nod.

"Corruptors are bad news," went on Prelz nervously. "They're the ultimate Advancement of the most ruthless Tempters. That's what I could've been, if I hadn't suddenly developed a conscience."

"He suggested something similar, actually," agreed Torval. "I have never spoken to a First Class demon before, although I have seen them, and witnessed them giving orders to a Second Class. This McCord, who is also called Mannoch, has the same force behind his words. He is quite powerful, and all I could do was agree to whatever he said."

"Which was to be his apprentice," Prelz replied with a nod. "Yeah, someone like that would have the ego to automatically think you were his servant, especially since you're so obviously in Transition."

"Yes, just so. He believed I was sent here to become a Tempter, under his direct supervision. That's why I was hoping you would explain to me the precise duties of that posting."

"You aren't thinking of actually doing it, are you?" asked Prelz, suddenly concerned. "Of becoming a Tempter, I mean?"

"No, most definitely not! Perhaps had I met him when I first arrived on Earth, I might have done so, but not now. From what I have seen of humans, your analysis is correct—they need no further temptation. McCord, however, seems convinced that they do. He has, in fact, corrupted a great many humans, by his own admission. He is the one responsible for forcing the Roxtons to operate a chop shop, for example. Through various means, primarily involving money, he controls their actions and forces them to do evil."

"Ah, so I was right about the chop shop." Prelz nodded with some satisfaction. "I wasn't sure, but my buddies who told me that never led me wrong before." Then he hesitated, rubbing his chin as he mulled over his companion's words more carefully. "Wait, so you're saying this Mannoch corrupted the Roxtons? What do you mean, 'he controls their actions'?"

"He found out they owed a great deal of money to someone," explained Torval succinctly, "and preserved their business. Now they have no choice but to do his bidding."

"Ah, right, and since they sell car parts ... yeah, the cops, impounded cars ... okay, I get it. Very nice. Very, very slick, in fact. I never would've thought of that. This Mannoch is a real piece of work!"

"You ... admire him?"

"No, not at all," replied Prelz with a frown. "Well, maybe a little.

What he did is truly evil, and I can appreciate that, if only from a Tempter's perspective. This goes far beyond temptation, though. This is manipulation ... he's taking direct action, intervening personally in the lives of humans, controlling them ... he's not supposed to do that, Torval! Trick them into doing evil, or manipulate events to get them to choose the path of evil, yes ... but force them into it? Use them as puppets, with no free will? No way—not even a Corruptor can do that. It's against the rules."

"I do not recall you mentioning anything in the Compact regarding such things," pointed out Torval.

"I didn't tell you everything about the Compact, dude. You have any idea how big that thing is? Anyway, the rules are clear—you don't personally intervene, and you sure as hell don't mess with free will."

"I do not see how a Corruptor could perform his task without directly involving himself in the lives of humans," argued Torval. "If he could not, he would be powerless."

"Oh, are you taking his side now?" inquired Prelz with a raised eyebrow. "No, no, forget I said that. You're just curious, like always. Sorry, I didn't mean to get so defensive."

"I understand. Nonetheless, my question stands."

"Yeah, right, so it does. Well, it's a pretty fine line you have to walk, when you're assigned to field work," explained Prelz. "I can take a human job, such as when I worked at the post office, and play the part of an incompetent worker, in order to infuriate customers. That sort of thing is perfectly acceptable. If I were really ruthless about it, I could secretly open important pieces of mail, see what they said, and deliver them to the wrong person, in order to cause more trouble. But I couldn't write an incriminating letter myself, nor could I force a human to do so—that would be intervention, or manipulation, respectively."

"I think I understand," said Torval after considering what his friend was saying. "What you are saying is you can assist humans in doing evil, but you cannot force them into it."

"Yes! That's it exactly!" Prelz finished off his second complete glass of soda and slammed the empty cup on the table. "You're getting really good at this, my friend."

"So, then, if that is true," went on Torval, "you are saying Lieutenant McCord is breaking the Compact?"

"It sure sounds like it," replied Prelz. "From what you just told me, it sounds like he has his own little empire going. I bet he's lost it—he's on a power trip, and he thinks he can get away with anything."

Torval nodded, but still looked unconvinced. "Are you absolutely certain of this? Is it possible that you don't understand exactly what a Corruptor is capable of, or is permitted to do?"

"I'm sure," Prelz replied firmly. "Believe me, I know. When I became a Tempter, they told me I might someday Advance into a Corruptor's form. They were very specific about how dangerous that was, because it was so easy to forget the limitations of a demon on Earth. This demon you've met fell into this trap, it sounds like."

"Well, what should I do, then?" asked Torval worriedly. "He wants me to become a Tempter. He wants me to be like him."

"Well, stay away," insisted Prelz. "In fact, get the heck out of here, if you can. No, wait, on second thought—you don't want to blow it with that hot little angel of yours, do you?"

"No, I do not. I most definitely do not."

"Then there's only one thing you can do."

"What?" asked Torval anxiously. "What can I possibly do?"

"This demon wants you to be a Tempter, right?" Prelz replied with a smile. "Well then, you, my friend, are going to become the best Tempter there ever was!"

Chapter 8

"Okay, let me think of another one," said Prelz thoughtfully, rubbing his chin and finishing the very last of the pizza. He washed this down with a quick gulp from his third refill of soda.

Torval waited, sipping idly on his own cup. The pizza didn't last very long at all, once it actually showed up. Prelz turned out to be extremely hungry, downing five of the eight slices, but Torval didn't mind. He knew he'd be having dinner with Christine in just a few more hours, after all, while Prelz's next meal would likely be little more than a simple bowl of soup.

"Aha. Here we go," his mentor finally said, coming up with another situation to test his would-be Tempter student. "You're riding in the subway and you overhear a pusher trying to convince another to try an illegal drug. From where you are, you notice a policeman in the next car, chatting with some other riders on the train. He starts moving toward the door, and the two men don't see him coming. The illegal substance is clearly visible and you know the cop's gonna see it in a few moments. What do you do?"

Torval thought about the scenario for a moment, reflecting on the things Prelz had already told him regarding Tempters, and the rules he should follow. This wasn't about making the *good* choice, aiding the policeman in arresting the drug pusher (and acting as a witness if necessary), or even the *evil* choice, warning the two men about the cop's presence so they could avoid capture. Either of those options would work for an ordinary person, but not a demon. Being a Tempter involved convincing humans to do evil, not to do evil directly. A Tempter should always be a facilitator, and nothing more.

"I suppose," replied Torval after taking another long sip from his glass, "that I would first distract the policeman, and after he passed on by, I would help the seller complete his task, perhaps by extolling the virtues of this particular drug to his potential customer."

"Good, that's exactly right," replied Prelz with a satisfied smile. "I think you've got the hang of this, Torval. You think you can handle it now?"

"I believe so. The task is relatively simple, though somewhat distasteful. I would not wish to be a Tempter, although I feel I could pretend to be one if necessary. I only hope I can perform well enough to deceive Lieutenant McCord."

"Good, good. Glad to know I haven't lost my touch. Now, let me ask you another question, if I may." Prelz gulped down the rest of his glassful of soda, and then tilted his head slightly sideways, so that he looked decidedly curious. "If you were really on that subway, and you saw that situation I described, what would you do? Not as a Tempter, I mean. As you are right now."

"I would do nothing," replied Torval, "except watch the policeman stop the sale and arrest the wrongdoer."

"So you wouldn't get involved, then?"

"I would not wish to risk injury to myself," replied Torval, "and besides, it is the task of the police to uphold the law, is it not?"

"True, true," replied Prelz, "but let's go a step further. What if the cop wasn't there at all? Imagine you're just sitting on the subway, and you hear a drug pusher trying to convince somebody to try cocaine for the first time. Do you intervene?"

"That depends," replied Torval. "What is this cocaine? What does it do?"

"It's an illegal drug. Don't get hung up on the details, please! All you have to know is it's against the law, because it's very addictive, and it can cause injury or death if misused."

"Why, then, would someone want to use this substance?" Torval inquired, figuring he couldn't properly answer the question without additional information.

"Because it makes you high," said Prelz, starting to get frustrated. "It makes you feel incredibly good, for a short period of time. Like ... hmm, what can I use as an example? You like food, don't you? Okay, you really enjoyed this pizza, right?"

Torval nodded enthusiastically. Pizza was one of his favorites, after all. So far he'd enjoyed most things he'd tasted while on Earth, so much so that he wished he could eat far more often.

"Good. Now imagine you could feel that fantastic taste through your whole body, only for an hour or two, or maybe even longer." Prelz paused for a moment, snapping his fingers as he thought of something else. "Or, wait, better example! You know how you feel when you have great sex?"

Torval nodded again, thinking back to his last experience with Shelly Mendez. "Yes, I enjoy that very much. I like both, but sex is more intense, especially at the end."

Prelz grinned wickedly. "Of course it is. You want more of it, right? Well, a coke high is just like that, only the feeling keeps on going, so it's like you're floating, adrift in total euphoria, for hours on end."

Torval sounded intrigued. "You sound as if you know these effects from personal experience," he remarked insightfully.

"Yes, well, the less said about that the better," snapped Prelz, in a tone that suggested Torval drop that particular line of questioning.

"Well, then, If the drug can do that, then why is illegal? Would it not be wonderful for all humans to experience such things? I have only felt that way on a few occasions, and they were very brief indeed. If the taste of food could be extended, or the ecstasy of org—"

"The drug has side effects!" interrupted Prelz swiftly, summoning more patience only by taking a couple of very deep breaths. "It's extremely expensive and horribly addictive! People hooked on the stuff will sell everything they own to buy more. They'll commit any crime they can think of, just for another hit. Plus, while you're under the influence, you can do terrible things without realizing it. Oh, and it causes all kinds of medical problems, and yeah, as the icing on the cake, if you overdose, you're probably dead."

Torval nodded. "I see. So that is why it is illegal."

"Yeah, that's why," sighed Prelz, catching his breath, "and for good reason. Besides which, think about it this way. Which would you rather do—live life like you're supposed to, or be a slave to this drug, existing only to lose yourself in some nonexistent fantasy world where everything is total bliss, but you accomplish nothing at all?"

Torval thought about that for a moment, and realized he could actually imagine such a situation, from his own body's experiences. "That sounds like what Joe Sampson was doing with alcohol," he noted. "Is alcohol similar to cocaine, then?"

"In many ways, it is," replied Prelz. "It's not quite as expensive or addictive, but yeah, when you drink enough of it, you get pretty buzzed. Some people, like Joe and Hal, would use it to forget their old lives, to escape a reality too painful to bear."

"I see," went on Torval. "Then I would not wish to try this cocaine drug any more than I want to use alcohol. However, I do not understand the distinction. Alcohol is not illegal, correct? It seems too readily attainable."

"No, it's not. Like I said, it's a lot milder. In small doses, it's not too bad. Besides, they tried making it illegal once, and that didn't work out so well. So it's sort of tolerated—people are supposed to control their drinking, and there are laws to prevent its misuse, but if you want to get totally trashed and sleep in alleys, that's perfectly fine, as long as you don't mind getting forgotten by society and treated as a nonentity."

"Apparently Joe Sampson didn't mind," pointed out Torval. "I, however, would not like that fate very much. I am accustomed to having a purpose and reason for existing. Lacking that, I believe I would choose Oblivion."

"Strong words, my friend." Prelz clapped him appreciatively on the back. "Strong words indeed. Now, back to my original question, if I may. You see a pusher trying to get someone to try cocaine. What do you do?"

"I believe," replied Torval without any hesitation, "that I would tell his potential customer the various risks and dangers you just described. That way he could make a fully informed choice."

Prelz considered that, running his fingers through his scraggly beard. "That's exactly the opposite of what a Tempter would do," he said after a moment. "How interesting. Why would you do it that way? Why not something else? Pull the customer away, perhaps, or chase the pusher off, or try to find a cop or security guard to do it for you?"

"It simply seemed like an appropriate response," replied Torval with a shrug. "You have been explaining the nature of free will, and I know that as a demon, I am not supposed to force humans down any specific path. I should leave the choice up to him, after he understands all the options."

"But why say anything at all?" pressed Prelz. "Why bother? You're a *demon*, Torval! Why do you care if a human chooses good or evil? What difference does it make to you?"

"Because—well, because ... uhmm ... "

Torval's voice trailed off. He found, to his surprise, that he had no immediate answer. Prelz was correct, of course. Torval shouldn't intervene at all. Yet he knew for a fact that given the information at hand, and the situation as described, he would definitely step up to the potential customer and warn him of the ills of cocaine use. In fact, he would do so without a second thought.

Why? Why would he do that? When he arrived on Earth, cold and alone in the snow, he wouldn't have intervened in such a conversation. What had changed to make him care about the welfare of random humans?

"I don't know," he finally answered. "I cannot explain."

"It's because you're Advancing," pronounced Prelz immediately. Apparently that was the point he'd been aiming toward, and he pounced upon it straightaway. "You're changing, and not just physically. The things you've seen and done here on Earth are altering your perceptions and personality. You're being prepared for whatever kind of demon you're going to become. If," he added with a curious grin, "you're becoming a demon at all."

Torval's eyes widened at that remark. "What do you mean, *if* I'm becoming a demon? How could I become anything else?"

"Well," replied Prelz, almost chuckling at Torval's reaction, "as much as I'd like to take credit for the way you're turning out, I can't say I've been as much influence as a certain other someone. Someone who has long brown hair, stunning blue eyes, and an absolutely ferocious pair of legs."

Torval was taken aback. "Are you referring to Christine?" he all but demanded.

"Of course, my friend. Of course I mean Christine! You've been infatuated with her from day one, haven't you?"

"But what does that have to do with anything?" Torval found himself irritated by this line of questioning, though he didn't know why. Perhaps it was the way Prelz described her physical attributes, although even that shouldn't have invoked such a reaction.

"Well, if you're changing because of the people you've met, and the things you've seen them do, what stronger influence can you think of than the one who helped you find a job, bought you clothes, paid for your shave and haircut, and all that other crap?"

"So what you're suggesting," said Torval, starting to understand what Prelz was getting at, "is that Christine's presence and actions have influenced my Advancement? That they have somehow made me into—into a good person?"

"Yes, exactly!" Prelz nodded vigorously, causing his ragged beard to bounce up and down in an almost comical way. "You're turning good, Torval, and I've never heard of a good demon before."

"That could be a problem," replied Torval worriedly.

"You think?" Prelz's comment was laced with sarcasm.

Torval frowned. In his quest to understand the difference between good and evil, he'd apparently turned to the side of good without even realizing it. At least, that's what Prelz's little thought experiment suggested. The revelation surprised Torval somewhat, though it didn't really bother him all that much, until he started thinking about the ramifications.

"I do not mind being this way," he stated after a moment. "In fact, I find that performing good acts makes me feel satisfied, even content, as if what I've done is natural and proper. Yet if there are no good demons, then what possible task can I perform when I return home? What purpose can there be in Hell for one such as I?"

"I don't know," answered Prelz honestly. "Maybe there's something you can do, as a good demon. They could use you as a barometer to measure against incoming souls, to see if they're headed in the wrong direction. Or maybe you could be a punching bag for demons with a mean streak. Who knows? There's one other possibility, though. One other thing you just might want to consider."

"What is it?"

"Well, there may not be any good demons," replied Prelz, holding up a finger to punctuate his point, "but there are plenty of angels up there."

"What does that have to do with—" Torval started, but halted in mid-sentence as he realized what Prelz was suggesting. A moment later, the ex-Tempter finished the radical thought for him.

"What if you aren't Advancing as a demon any more, Torval?" asked Prelz pointedly. "What if you're turning into an angel?"

* * *

The question left Torval momentarily stunned. The sheer impossibility boggled the mind, and yet, if it could be true ... what would it mean? What would happen to him next? Would he even be accepted into the angelic ranks, seeing as he'd spent his entire existence working for the Other Side?

Did he even *want* to be an angel ... ?

While he pondered, seemingly frozen at the table, Prelz just grinned, greatly amused by the way he'd left his friend so speechless. He was still chuckling to himself when the pizza restaurant's manager arrived to throw them out. Apparently he didn't mind letting them pay good money for food, but the instant they finished, they were unceremoniously shown the door.

Prelz didn't even complain at the attack on his person, for his appearance and atrocious body odors obviously caused the ejection. He was too busy enjoying the way Torval looked amazed, perplexed, and horrified—all at the same time.

The two demons reassembled outside the restaurant, in a nearby alley far from any passing humans, and resumed the conversation. "Well, what do you think?" laughed Prelz. "Torval, Angel Second Class! It has a nice ring to it, I say."

"I do not—I mean, I am not—is this thing even possible?" stammered Torval. "To Advance from demon to angel? Can it be done?"

Prelz shrugged, not bothering to wipe the bemused smirk off his face. "Who knows? I'm not a Transitioner, so I haven't the slightest clue. I was just thinking, you've been acting like such a goody-twoshoes lately, what if you've crossed the line from demon to angel?"

"So you are just guessing, then," replied Torval, sounding more than just a little bit relieved. "You are speculating, nothing more."

"Yeah, but you know, I wouldn't be surprised if it could happen," suggested Prelz thoughtfully. "I mean, if they left you here with no instructions, so that your new form would be based on the people you met and experiences you had, then consider this. Who's the first person you met when you took human form?"

"A bum," answered Torval at once, "lying in the alley with me. He was covered in wet cardboard and had been drinking alcohol."

"No, no, that's not what I mean! Who was the first person you actually interacted with for more than just a minute or two? The first person who became a significant part of your life here on Earth?"

Torval thought back to the first things that happened to him upon arriving. He remembered the freezing cold, the snow-filled alley ... then he made his way to the shelter, where he had some soup, and he saw and spoke to—

"Christine," he finally said. "I met Christine Anderson!"

"There, you see?" Prelz waved a partially gloved finger in Torval's face for emphasis. "That's what I mean! The first person you met turned out to be an angel in disguise. And when you actually did meet another demon, who'd you find but me—a reformed Tempter who's gone human and wants nothing more to do with demonkind! With the two of us as your advisors, you can see how you might be influenced to switch sides, right?"

"I suppose," agreed Torval half-heartedly.

"Of course, it may not even be possible," pointed out Prelz, finally noticing the distraught expression of worry on his friend's face. "In fact, it probably isn't. It's really a wild, off-the-wall theory, but still, if anyone could swap sides, it'd be you."

"I do not think I want to be an angel," complained Torval after a moment. "I admit, I have achieved a basic understanding of the concept of good, but that hardly qualifies me to change sides. In any event, I doubt that Heaven would accept a former demon into their ranks."

"Why not? They're all about redemption up there!" said Prelz conclusively. "Besides, there's not that much different about us anyway."

"What do you mean? We are as opposite as can be." Torval paused for a moment, intending to elaborate, but suddenly found himself unable to really explain in words what he meant. Honestly, he didn't really know all that much about angels, except what Christine had told him, and a few things he'd heard at various times in the distant past.

"We weren't always that way," replied Prelz. "The way I had it explained to me, when the Creator made the world and set the humans loose upon it, he had a suite of advisors—the first demons and angels, in other words. At the time we were all basically the same, except for some variances in rank and responsibilities. Two of these original angels, supposedly named Gabriel and Satan—there are other names for them, of course, but those are the ones recorded in that Bible book that seems pretty much everywhere—well, they had some opposing thoughts about how Man should be allowed to do his thing here on Earth."

"You mentioned this before, after we first met," pointed out Torval. "I was too busy thinking about some other subject to ask you to explain further. Perhaps I should have done so back then."

"Yeah, well, now's a better time," replied Prelz good-naturedly. "You see, the Creator—God, if you like—gave Man dominion over the Earth, but that was before Man gained wisdom from the Tree of Knowledge."

"The serpent tempted them into eating the fruit," remarked Torval. "I read that story myself. It is in the Book of Genesis."

"Ah, good, you're doing your homework," commented Prelz. "So you know what I'm talking about, then. Man was cast out of Paradise and onto Earth, where he multipled and spread rapidly. Well, Gabriel wanted to help Man find his way, to guide him and teach him to be good, so that he wouldn't spoil the world that God had given him. Satan, though, decided that if Man owned the Earth, he should be able to use it however he pleased. In a very real way, the two quite literally represented the opposing forces of good and evil, and each of them drew support from the ranks of the angels, so that pretty soon there were two camps, with two totally different philosophies, arguing and fighting over what Man could or couldn't do."

"There is no mention of this in the Bible," said Torval, "at least, not as far as I know."

"All of this went on behind the scenes, if you will," Prelz explained. "Some of it spilled over here and there. Some of it leaked into old tales and legends, and a lot of ancient cultures picked up on bits and pieces that eventually coalesced into some of Earth's early religions. Check out Greek mythology sometime if you want an idea of what I'm talking about."

"I will do that," agreed Torval readily. *That's something else I can investigate on the Internet*, he told himself.

"Anyway, back to my point." Prelz scratched idly at his beard and shifted his weight slightly. "Initially, the early angels and demons just had opposing philosophies, and put them into practice apart from each other, but confrontations were inevitable. Eventually things began to escalate. You might have read in the Bible that God smote two cities called Sodom and Gomorrah?"

"Yes, I vaguely recall that. Something about someone becoming a pillar of salt. I must admit I did not fully understand."

"Yes, that one. Well, I don't know if the names of the cities are right, but the Creator didn't have anything to do with it. Those cities were the first battlegrounds between angels and demons, and both towns were destroyed in the opening salvoes of the war. Things came to a head after that, and by some accounts God created a flood, or deluge, or a great storm, depending on whom you ask or what religion you follow. It wasn't to scourge the Earth, though—it was to stop the fighting and protect the innocent humans from further interference."

"So that was what the story of Noah's Ark was all about, then?"

"In a way, yes. The Bible got a lot of the details wrong, and the sequencing of events, but whoever wrote that stuff had no way of knowing what was really going on. In any case, God had basically had enough of all this fighting over Man, so he forced angels and demons to draw up a Compact that would ensure we wouldn't directly go to war over humanity again. We split into two camps after that, and things eventually evolved into what you see today. The point being, of course, that if you go back far enough through history, there's no real fundamental difference between angels and demons, aside from the jobs we do and our basic shapes—which, of course, are mostly determined by the tasks we perform."

"If what you say is true," mused Torval, "then it could indeed be possible for me to become an angel, if that is the manner in which my Advancement proceeds."

"Yeah, I suppose that's right," Prelz answered with a nod. "I'm sorry if you don't like it, but that could be where you're headed."

Torval wrung his hands for a few seconds, looking out into the city but not really focusing on anything. His mind kept trying to wrap itself around the possibility that he might become an angel, a luminous creature who dwelled in the Upper Realm—a place he'd never seen, and had no real concept of, other than the stories humans told of a plane crafted of clouds and light. The very idea that his vacation on Earth might end with a portal to Heaven, instead of Hell, made him tremble with apprehension. What would he do when he got there? What would he say? What would his task be, in his new form? How could he possibly perform any angelic job, having spent his entire existence in Hell—an experience that would have no relevance whatsoever in Heaven?

"I do not think I want to be an angel," he finally managed, even though he knew he was only repeating what he'd already said.

"Well, what *do* you want?" asked Prelz curiously. "I mean, have you even thought about that? If you had a choice, I mean, what would you do? What would you want your new job to be?"

"I do not know," Torval replied honestly. "It doesn't really matter what I want, anyway. I will perform the task my new form is suited for, to the best of my ability. That is the reason I exist."

"Well, then, there you go!" exclaimed Prelz, as if that solved everything. "You just want to do your job, right? Well, if your new job is to be an angel, just do it the best you can. If that's what you become, then that must be what your purpose is, wouldn't you agree?"

"I suppose," answered Torval with a sigh. "Your point is valid, Prelz, but I must admit I had hoped I would become something familiar, something I would understand intuitively. Being an angel seems ... well, it seems contradictory to my nature."

Prelz nodded. "I can well imagine why you'd feel that way. I wish I could tell you what being an angel's really like, but I can't. I've never met one—well, not one that I knew was an angel, anyway." He snapped his fingers suddenly. "Hey, that's right, there *is* someone you can ask! Next time you see Christine, you should tell her all about this, and see what she says. If nothing else, she can tell you what being an angel means. Then you can come back and tell me, 'cause I'm too damn curious for my own good." He chuckled to himself, grinning.

"I will ask her," agreed Torval readily. "I am, in fact, having dinner with her this evening after she finishes working, and before I must report to the warehouse."

"Oh, another date? Good for you!" remarked Prelz, slapping his friend on the shoulder by way of congratulations. "Where are you going this time?"

"I don't know yet," answered Torval. "Somewhere different that is not Chinese in nature. I enjoy fried chicken, so I thought perhaps that the KFC would be—"

"No, no, not fast food!" argued Prelz immediately. "You don't take your date out to a fast food joint!"

Torval gave him a quizzical look. "The food is not fast—oh, I see, that must be another human phrase of dubious meaning."

"Yeah, it's referring to the way you can get in and order your food quickly, without spending a lot of time in the restaurant. Anyway, where you take a date should at least have a waiter, and menus you can order from. Forget about places where you go up to a counter."

Torval nodded. "I see. What, then, would you suggest?"

"Don't look at me! I'm a bum, remember? I get spit on just trying to eat pizza! If she likes seafood, though, I hear Lobster Bistro is pretty nice. It's a couple blocks that way if you want to check it out."

Torval glanced down the street, making a mental note of the location, almost exactly opposite that of the warehouse. "I will do that," he agreed. "I must also acquire new clothing, because, as I have been told, wearing the same ones over and over again is not acceptable."

"Yeah, you should probably wash the ones you're wearing, too,"

Prelz suggested, "although you can't very well do that if you don't have anything else to put on. Besides which, one outfit isn't exactly a full load in a washing machine."

"Washing machine?"

"Yeah, they have machines that—oh, never mind, don't worry about it. You won't be here long enough to care. Just get a few more outfits, and rotate them around. You should be good. You going shopping right now?"

"That was my intent. I don't know how long it will take, and I must not be late for my meeting with Christine."

"Okay, I get the hint. I'll take off, then, but I'm gonna meet you later tonight, okay? I want to see how your date went."

"Why do you not accompany me?" inquired Torval. "Your advice on purchases would be most welcome."

Prelz looked down at his dirty, rag-covered body and pointed at himself with both hands. "You think they're gonna let me in a store looking like this? Not likely, my friend."

"You could clean yourself," suggested Torval. "I have enough money to purchase new clothing for you, and if I asked, I believe Christine would allow you to cleanse yourself in her shower."

Prelz shook his head sadly. "Nice try," he said ruefully, "but I can't do that. My place is on the streets, like it or not."

"Why?" asked Torval directly. "Why must you remain a bum, Prelz? You already said you are tired of running. You could take a job, and find a place to live. Perhaps, when I leave, you could even assume my position at the Roxton warehouse."

Prelz just stared at him. "You're really good at that," he said accusingly. "You learn pretty well, but then you had a good teacher."

"Good at what?"

"Okay, maybe not as good as I thought." Prelz chuckled to himself. "Don't you realize you're tempting me right now?"

"But what I suggested is not evil," argued Torval. "I am attempting to help you."

"It may not be evil, but it's still temptation." Prelz let out a long sigh. "Look, buddy, I know what you're trying to do, but I'm just not interested, okay? If I'm gonna die, it'll be on these streets, the same way I lived. That's all I really want."

"But you could be so much more comfortable—"

Prelz held up his hands. "I don't care! I just don't. It's been too long, and I just don't have the energy or desire to change here at the last minute. Plus, if I slip up, and someone notices me, and they find me—I don't want to risk it, not here at the last, when my time on Earth is almost up. That would mean everything I've done would've been a waste. You don't want, that, do you?"

"No," replied Torval sadly. "No, I suppose not. What have you done, though? In what way are you different than Joe Sampson, who wasted his life and accomplished nothing?"

"That's not the point, and you know it!" snapped Prelz, but his head hung low despite his words. "I've done the best I could, with what I had to work with. All I can do is hope it was enough. Now can we please stop talking about this? Thank you for offering, Torval, but my answer is no."

"Very well," said Torval piercingly. "You have the right to make that choice. You do, after all, have free will."

"That I do, my friend," replied Prelz with a knowing nod. "That I do."

* * *

After saying goodbye to Prelz, Torval headed to the clothing store he'd visited previously. He was hoping he'd find Sarah there, as she'd helped him the last time, but someone else stood behind the counter. He looked around for a bit, thinking she might be working elsewhere, but didn't see her. Apparently she either wasn't there today, or toiled elsewhere, someplace out of sight.

Without anyone else around that he knew, Torval was on his own. He perused the various racks of clothing, starting with the pants, for he at least knew his waist size. Jeans were a comfortable choice, and he did like the ones he had on, but he'd observed that humans didn't always wear such clothes, so there had to be some reason for this. Perhaps jeans were inappropriate in certain situations, and he didn't want to break some social taboo that he wasn't aware of.

Looking through the various choices, he did notice that some of the trousers seemed to be of higher quality, which of course resulted in a higher price tag. Well, if he had to pay that much money, he'd only want to wear such things for special occasions. He selected one, a pair of dark brown slacks, thinking he'd don them for dates, such as the one later tonight.

Another date with Christine! He couldn't stop thinking about that, actually. The business with his Advancement, and his concerns about Prelz, and the problems with Lieutenant McCord and the Roxtons all seemed to fade away when he thought of having dinner with Christine tonight. Her angelic status didn't make her any less interesting or intriguing—quite the opposite, in fact. He wanted to spend more time with her, as much time as possible. Their individual work schedules would make that difficult, but he felt that if he could, he'd like to take her to dinner every night. Then there was the coming weekend, too, when they could perhaps spend two entire days together.

He had so many things he wanted to ask her! Just trying to remember all those questions made him dizzy. What she did on the job, what Heaven was like, what other tasks there were for angels ... and most importantly, whether or not she knew if a demon could switch sides.

Although the idea of becoming an angel made him somewhat queasy, there would be one obvious advantage—he'd be able to spend more time with Christine. In fact, if by some chance he became a Redeemer, like her, perhaps they could share the same assignment. That was probably hoping for too much, however. More than likely, he'd be sent somewhere else, perhaps another city, or maybe even to Heaven itself, depending on his ultimate angelic shape. In fact, come to think of it, being an angel wasn't any assurance at all that he'd ever be able to see her again.

The thought of never seeing Christine again made him sad, so he pushed it aside. He still had plenty of time to spend with her. He'd just have to make those hours count, that's all.

He continued to shop, picking out three more pairs of pants of various types and styles, then tried them on. A couple of them felt too tight, and one was too short, so he replaced them with slightly larger ones and tried again. The new ones seemed all right, although one seemed to slip around his waist a bit, but his belt solved that problem easily enough.

With his selection of pants complete, he started to look around for some new shirts to wear. Unfortunately, he had no idea what the sizes meant this time. He tried several possibilities, until he thought he had the right idea. Also, it seemed that shirts came in a much greater variety of styles, something he had no concept of whatsoever. This left him somewhat at a loss.

He was about to start picking shirts at random when he heard a pleasant voice behind him. "Do you need some help, sir?" a woman asked in a friendly tone.

Torval turned, holding a handful of different-colored shirts under his arm. The stack was getting quite unwieldy, actually. He recognized her at once—the friendly checkout girl named Sarah. Apparently she was working today after all, just not behind a register. "I do indeed need help," he admitted readily. "I require several shirts, but do not know which ones are best."

"Don't I know you from somewhere?" inquired Sarah, studying him closely. "Oh yeah, now I remember. You're the tip guy!"

"Tip guy ... ?"

"Yeah, you left me a tip! You're the only one who's ever tried, as long as I've been here. You know, I almost got in trouble for that."

"I apologize," said Torval honestly. "That was not my intent."

"No, no, it's okay, my boss said as long as I don't make a habit of it. Anyway, my friends thought it was pretty cool, and I bought a round of sodas at the bowling alley last night—on you. So thanks!"

"You are welcome," replied Torval. "However, so as to not get you in any further trouble, I will not tip you again."

"That's fine," she agreed with a smile. "I don't need a tip, anyway. I get paid to help people in the store. So you need some advice, huh? Okay, let me see what you've got there."

Torval set down the pile of clothing and she rifled through it for several moments, comparing them with several others on the racks nearby. "Okay, first off these shirts you've got won't go with any of the pants you picked, if that's what you're looking for. These two here, they would go with these over here, and this one ... "

She spent a few minutes trying to explain how the various shirts did or didn't match with his chosen trousers, which frankly left Torval baffled. He did manage to grasp the concept of avoiding different colored solids, and trying to use multicolored shirts that at least partially matched his pants. Most of the rest of Sarah's explanation went completely over his head.

When she finished giving out advice, Torval had three acceptable pairs of pants and a half-dozen shirts, at least two of which matched each of the trousers. Sarah also recommended three sweaters he could wear over certain of the shirts, depending on color, but these were optional, depending on the weather. She also hooked him up with a package of undershirts, as well as a new belt that would look better with the more expensive set of pants.

He considered getting some new shoes as well, but decided first to check how much he owed for his selections. He thought perhaps he'd accumulated two hundred dollars worth of clothes, but when Sarah tallied it all, the price actually exceeded three hundred. *That's enough shopping for now*, he figured, seeing as how he'd already blown a hundred and fifty on the cell phone. That meant he'd now used almost all of the money McCord gave him—and all of it exactly as the police-demon intended.

Smiling at his success, Torval paid for his purchases and said goodbye to Sarah, thanking her profusely for her help. True to his word, this time he didn't attempt to leave a tip.

* * *

Torval left the shop with two bags full of clothes and his wallet considerably lighter. At least he wouldn't have to buy any more outfits for the duration of his stay, which was fortunate since he didn't expect to receive that much more in the way of money—unless Lieutenant McCord saw fit to hand him another heaping wad of cash, of course.

He started the long trek to the warehouse, where he could change clothes for his date and store the others, but then remembered he'd wanted to investigate the restaurant Prelz recommended earlier. According to the directions, it was only one block over. He walked in that direction, noting immediately that the rope-like handles of the clothing bags seemed to cut into his wind-chilled flesh. He had to shift his grip constantly as he walked, wishing he'd remembered to buy better gloves.

He was grateful for the break when he finally located the Lobster Bistro, a restaurant at the corner of a wide, busy avenue and a much smaller road that seemed less traveled. The place looked, from the outside, just like any of the other similar establishments he'd noted during his admittedly limited explorations. Inside, though, it looked much fancier than he expected. The entrance was extremely well decorated, and the waiters and staff dressed in fancy clothing far superior to what he'd just purchased. Instead of tables just scattered haphazardly around, each leaned up alongside rows of flowers, or impressive aquariums filled with brightly colored fish.

Torval nodded to himself. *This place will be acceptable*, he decided, despite the fact that the prices would probably be higher than the China Cottage. He had plenty of money, after all.

With that settled, he left the restaurant and started lugging his purchases in the warehouse's general direction. This took quite a while, as he stopped frequently, switching hands and grips on a regular basis. When he finally arrived, he toted both bags together, held in his arms rather than by the handles. That proved much easier on his fingers, although it did tend to limit his visibility somewhat.

Pete caught sight of him as he made his way down the hall to the stairs. "Oh, hey, let me get that for you," he said, hurrying ahead to open the door.

"Thank you," said Torval, a phrase that felt ordinary to him now. Back home, he never had the occasion to say such a thing, unless directed to in one of the cell illusions. In Hell, no one ever did anything worthy of thanks, as far as he could remember.

"No problem. Wow, what did you do, blow all that cash in one shot?"

"Not quite," replied Torval honestly, making his way down the stairs. "Most of it, however. I cannot continue to wear the same clothes all the time, so I purchased more."

"Hmm, let's see what you got here." Pete glanced inside the bags as Torval finally got to set them down at last. "Hmm, not bad. Good choices, too. I wouldn't have thought an ex-bum would be able to pick out matching outfits, but I guess you had a life beforehand, huh?"

"Yes," Torval agreed, "but I also had help from an employee."

"Well, whatever," remarked Pete with a shrug. "Hmm, dress pants? I guess you got that Bible, you're gonna be going to church now, too, huh?"

"That was not my intent, but I suppose it is a possibility," replied Torval. In fact, perhaps next Sunday, he would go to church with Christine. As an angel, she probably visited such places on a regular basis.

"Well, what then? You got a hot date or something?" Pete gave a sort of chuckle at that, as if he didn't really believe it was possible.

"Actually," admitted Torval, "I do in fact have a date tonight. I intend to wear those pants, as well as this shirt here, because I am told the brown stripes are an effective match."

"Wait, you got a date? Seriously?" Pete's eyes widened. "Well, I guess I can believe it, 'cause you look all right, for an older guy." He laughed at his own joke, for Joe wasn't all that much older than Pete. "Who is it? Anyone I know?"

Torval hesitated at that. Should he even mention her name? Christine and Pete didn't really get along, at least based on what she'd told him. Perhaps it would be best to simply avoid the question.

Before he could reply, though, Pete saw the answer on his face. "Oh, hell, don't tell me, it's that chick that brought you in here, isn't it? That Christine Anderson or whatever. Am I right?"

Torval sighed. No sense denying it now. "Yes," he admitted, hanging his head worriedly.

Pete nodded, grinning. "Good luck with that," he said, clapping Torval on the shoulder. "She's a real cutie. You could do a lot worse."

Torval was surprised. "You are not upset?"

"Why? Should I be?" Pete scratched at his chin, shutting one eye partially as he thought about that comment for a second. "Oh, I get it. She told you we went out, didn't she?"

"Not exactly," replied Torval. "Someone I know observed you picking her up that particular night. She only explained after I asked her directly."

"Oh, right." Pete shrugged and proceeded to explain further. "Well, yeah, we went out, but she ain't my type, y'know? I was just hoping for a little fun, no commitments or anything like that, and I thought I was pretty clear on that point. I took her out, we went to a bar, we had some drinks, you know the drill. She didn't really seem all that interested, so I took her back to her apartment, and that was that."

"That does not sound entirely accurate," remarked Torval, not even realizing the mistake he was about to make. "She said you wanted to sleep with her, and when she refused, you responded with insults. Furthermore, she added that she had no intention of going on another date with you, and that I should tell you so myself."

Pete's mouth dropped open, and he stared at Torval in disbelief. Finally, after a couple of seconds, his face screwed up into a grimace, as if in pain. "She really told you that? Told you all that?" he demanded.

"Yes," replied Torval. "There were few details, and that was essentially the extent of the conversation."

"That *bitch*!" exclaimed Pete suddenly, slamming a fist loudly against the nearest wall. "She said that about me, after I bought her dinner, and drinks too? Okay, fine, maybe I stepped over the line asking if she wanted a roll in the hay, but she was so goddamned hot in that tight dress and boots she had on, and I was so sure—"

He stopped and took a moment to storm around the basement. Torval, meanwhile, remained silent, somewhat surprised and more than a little frightened by Pete's outburst. Torval started to realize that perhaps he'd made a mistake by telling all of that to Pete, even if Christine had, in fact, asked him to do so.

Finally, Pete stopped pacing and looked Torval right in the eye. Holding up a finger, he pointed it almost in the demon's face. "Okay, let's get one thing straight," he commanded. "I did *not* do anything wrong, no matter what that high-and-mighty princess told you! All I did was make an offer, and when she refused, okay, fine, maybe I cursed under my breath a bit, but I was seriously disappointed, you know? I didn't try to push myself on her, or get her drunk, or any of that crap. She drank those cocktails entirely on her own! After she—after she *disagreed* with me, I took her back to her place, and that was the end of it! I thought maybe I might call her later, and apologize, but now, I guess that ain't gonna happen, is it?"

"No, I do not think so," agreed Torval shakily.

"No, it sure as hell isn't!" Pete went on, biting off each word in obvious anger. "I wouldn't call her again if my life depended on it! If you think you got a better shot, you go right ahead, but do me a favor and don't mention her name around here ever again. Got that?"

"Y-yes, sir."

"Good. Oh, and one more thing. I want you here by eight o'clock sharp. That date of yours better not last a minute longer. Not one goddamn minute!"

With that, he stormed up the stairs, slamming the door behind himself angrily, with so much strength that the walls seemed to shake.

Torval sucked in a deep breath, wishing very much that he'd never brought up that particular subject at all. Actually, Pete was the one who had initiated the discussion, simply by asking questions, but Torval volunteered the information about what Christine said regarding their date. He shouldn't have done that, he knew now, but how was he supposed to realize that in advance? He had no way of knowing Pete would react with such hostility.

Actually, the more he turned it over in his head, the more he realized how differently the two of them remembered their date. Christine had been upset enough to grow as angry as he'd ever seen her when she mentioned the subject. Pete, on the other hand, told his grandfather the next morning that things had gone well, when clearly they hadn't. Did he simply lie to Lincoln to salvage his pride, or did he just not realize how much he'd angered Christine?

Unfortunately, Torval couldn't exactly ask. For one thing, Pete had just ordered him never to speak of her in his presence, and for another, that particular conversation—the one between Pete and Lincoln—was overheard through the heater vent, when they thought he couldn't hear. Unless he wanted to admit to his eavesdropping, Torval had to proceed as if he hadn't listened to it at all.

Worst of all, he'd just injured his relationship with Pete, who until now had been friendly toward him. For the next ten minutes or so, while he changed clothes and cleaned himself up in preparation for the upcoming date, Torval tried very hard to think of some way to repair the damage he'd done. Unfortunately, nothing came to mind, and he continued to feel terrible about it, despite the fact that he hadn't intended for any of this to happen.

Another problem to worry about, he realized, even as he finished getting ready and checked his appearance in the mirror. *This whole situation is just another human problem, another example of the kind of issues they must deal with on a daily basis. How can they possibly stand it?*

He sighed again, and not for the first time, or the last. Being human was far more difficult than he'd ever imagined. Ah, well, he'd be seeing Christine again very soon—at least he had that to look forward to.

Not for another couple of hours, though. With nothing else to do, he sat down at the computer and started surfing the Internet.

Chapter 9

Recalling what Prelz suggested regarding Greek mythology, Torval managed to pass the time prior to the date very quickly. In fact, he completely lost track of time, and if he hadn't needed to use the restroom after a couple of hours at the computer, he might've been late. As it was, he still had to walk briskly to reach the shelter on schedule.

Christine wasn't there yet, as it turned out, but he noticed Prelz right away. The ragged-looking demon, still wearing the woolen cap over his shaved head, lounged at a table behind a steaming bowl of soup.

"Hey, Joe," he called out, waving.

"Nah, she's not here yet, if that's what you're looking for. I've been keeping an eye out for you."

Torval moved inside, stepping around the line of bums waiting for their usual handout. Lakisha stood nearby, serving soup with that menacing ladle of hers that doubled as a weapon. Torval avoided her, but despite the fact that she saw him and frowned, she said nothing, for which he was exceptionally grateful.

"I have been reading about the Greek religion," Torval mentioned as he settled in on one of the uncomfortable wooden seats. "It is very interesting. The gods they worship are very much like humans, with many of the same emotions and flaws."

"Yeah, that's part of what I was talking about before," said Prelz, sipping at a spoonful of what looked like chicken soup. Seeing this, Torval realized he felt a bit hungry. "And by the way, nobody worships those gods anymore. That was an ancient religion that's pretty much gone by the wayside."

"That explains why they were constantly referred to in the past tense," remarked Torval.

"Yeah, I guess. Anyway, Christianity and Islam pretty much

muscled that stuff out. Monotheism proved pretty influential back in those days. Anyway, did you get the point I was trying to make about those old myths?"

"That their deities were like humans, but with godlike abilities? I believe I stated that already."

"No, no. Remember, I told you a lot of those old tales were based, in part, on some of the things angels and devils did before the Compact. What does that tell you?"

Torval thought about it for a minute, but didn't make the connection. "I do not know," he eventually replied.

"That they were manipulative little bastards!" exclaimed Prelz with a grin. "Didn't you notice that? In damn near every story, some god or other is fooling around with some poor human's life, or changing the weather or destroying some city entirely at a whim."

"Ah, yes, I see," replied Torval, nodding. "I did read a few myths in which such things happened, but there were others in which the gods simply displayed human frailties and emotions, often to great extremes."

"Did you happen to read any of the *Odyssey*?" inquired Prelz curiously, in between several spoonfuls of soup.

"Not completely. It was too long. I did, however, read a summary that explained most of the characters, and the eventual result. The story was referred to as 'epic,' which I assume refers to its length."

"And its scope," Prelz pointed out. "The *Iliad* and the *Odyssey* spanned most of Ulysses' life, and documented a long and painful war brought on entirely by jealousy and greed. What you may not have realized, if you just read a summary, was how often the Greek gods influenced the story, intervened in the war, and basically mucked things up throughout. Poor Ulysses lost all his men and had to sail the seas for years just because Poseidon didn't really like him. Those ancient gods were the sort you just didn't want to tick off."

"And these were based on the doings of angels and demons?"

"Basically, yes," Prelz confirmed, "although I couldn't give any real examples. That's just what I was told. Apparently, back in those days, angels would try to help humans directly, especially heroic figures, while demons would do the opposite. I'm sure a lot of the tales of monsters actually referred to demons—back then, before the Compact, a demon's true form was plain to see, as was an angel's, although in both cases they tended to look more humanlike than not. Even so, try to imagine a superstitious, ancient human getting a good look at an angel as he invokes some kind of heavenly power, and you can see where these stories of gods could come from."

"That certainly makes sense," said Torval. "I am glad I was not around in those days. Things certainly seem more orderly now."

"Yeah, the Compact was the best thing that ever happened to us, actually. If not for that, we might well have destroyed each other, and most of the world too. Then where would humans be?"

Torval had no answer for that, so he simply considered the possibility in silence. If there were no angels or demons, what then? Humans would be completely on their own. Would they descend into barbarism, or would they rise above it? He had no way of knowing.

While he mulled that over, Christine walked in, still dressed in her work clothes, except that she now carried a tan-colored overcoat over one arm. She saw Torval immediately, smiled and waved, and walked up to the table. In response, he rose to meet her, but this time what he'd read in the dating book never crossed his mind. He simply stood in greeting automatically, without thinking about it.

"Sorry I'm late," Christine said apologetically. "I had to finish up some paperwork for one of our cases."

"I only just arrived," replied Torval with a shrug. "I do not mind, as it gave me a chance to speak with Jake."

"I see that," she replied. "Nice to see you again, Jake."

"Same to you," he answered, staring at her a bit too intently, with his head cocked sideways. Christine couldn't help but take notice of the unusual attention he focused upon her, and said as much at once.

"What's going on?" she asked. "Why are you looking at me like that? Do I have something on my face?"

"It's not that," replied Prelz, continuing to stare. "I just—well, now that I—oh, hold on a second. Joe, a word please. Alone."

Torval frowned. "I have no secrets from Christine," he replied, although he didn't know exactly what his friend was about to do. "You can speak freely."

"Okay, fine, if that's the way you want it." Prelz looked back at her, resuming the intrigued stare. "It's just that I find it funny how I always thought of you as an angel, and now, I find out that's exactly what you are."

Christine looked horrified, flashing an angry glare at Torval. For his part, he was momentarily shocked. He didn't think Prelz wanted his true nature known—certainly not to Christine, and in fact hadn't made any indication that he intended to so casually tell her about himself. Why would he do that? It seemed contrary to his nature, although Torval knew instinctively that there was no way Prelz would do something so radical without a good reason.

"Joe!" Christine spouted angrily, "you didn't tell him who I was, did you? How could you do that? Humans aren't supposed to—"

She suddenly stopped, noticing Jake's tremendous grin, and the crestfallen look on Torval's face. "Oh, dear God in Heaven above," she said with a gasp, "don't tell me he's a demon, too!"

"Not exactly," Prelz replied, still immensely enjoying her reaction. He stood up and extended a hand. "Nice to meet you, Christine, or whatever your real name is."

"I don't think I really want to take that," she replied, nervously regarding the hand in front of her. "Do I?"

"Take his hand," urged Torval, figuring that as long as the secret was out, he might as well embrace it. "You should know the truth. This is Prelz, the one who has helped me adjust to my human form. I met him shortly after I arrived on Earth. Without him, I would have been lost and alone in this vast city."

Christine sighed and shook hands, her eyes going wide. Torval, for his part, saw nothing unusual. Nothing changed, as far as he could tell, but the two of them clearly saw the other's true shape. Christine regarded Prelz as she would a dangerous beast about to strike, while the demon simply continued to stare, wide-eyed, in total amazement. Torval knew exactly how he felt, and imagined he must've worn the same sort of expression when he first saw her eye-catching angelic form.

After a few moments, Christine pulled her hand back, and Prelz just shook his head in wonder. "Wow," he managed to say. "I didn't think it was possibly you could actually look better than you do as a human, but I was wrong."

Christine smiled and blushed slightly. "Always the charmer, Jake," she told him. "It's a shame we never shook hands before this."

"The opportunity never came up," he replied. "Besides, you know how dirty I am. You probably want to wash your hands before you have dinner."

"Oh, I intend to," she laughed. "My name is Auralea, by the way. Since I know your name, it's only fair I tell you mine. I'll keep calling you Jake, though. I doubt anyone else would understand, unless there are more demons around. There aren't, are there?" She looked around curiously. "I'd hate to think I've been surrounded by demons for the last few years, and never knew it!"

"Nah, I'm the only one here, far as I know," said Prelz. "Actually, I'm not even really a demon anymore. I renounced my status and became fully human. That's why I'm living as a bum and not off tempting or torturing people."

"You did what?" she asked, surprised. "I didn't even know that was possible for demons!"

"Neither did I, but you can do it, apparently, because I did," he explained. "I was a Tempter, and truth be told, I just got sick of it. I embraced humanity, so here I am, living and aging like a mortal. When I die, I'll be judged and go to Heaven or Hell, depending on how well I've done at atoning for all those sins of mine when I was a demon."

"Well," said Christine helpfully, "you certainly seem to be doing something right, if Joe here is any indication."

"Thanks!" said Prelz, his mood brightening noticeably. "That means a lot, coming from you. Actually, though, if you have any other advice for me, or know of anything I can do, I'd appreciate it. I know what Hell is like, and I'd just as soon avoid that place if at all possible."

"I'll be happy to help out," replied Christine, a bit of eagerness plainly obvious in her voice. "That's what I do, after all. I don't know if Joe told you, but I'm a Redeemer."

"Well, I could sure use some redeeming," admitted Prelz. "If you don't mind, I'd like to sit down and chat with you for a bit sometime. You think I could do that?"

Now the reason for Prelz's revelation became clear, Torval realized, nodding to himself. Of course he would want the opportunity to talk to an angel about how to get into Heaven!

"Sure," Christine agreed readily. "In fact, why don't you come to dinner with us? You may not be all that hungry, but you could at least keep us company."

"Oh, no, thanks anyway, but I'd be a fifth wheel for sure," responded Prelz, holding his partially gloved hands up in a gesture of refusal. "Besides, they're not going to take too kindly to me where you're going."

"Okay, then, after we're done and Joe here goes to work, I'll come back by here and look for you," said Christine affably. "Speaking of dinner, where are we going, anyway?"

"A place Prelz—I mean, Jake—suggested. It is called the Lobster Bistro, and it is not far from here."

"Yeah, I know that place. It's a bit expensive—you sure you don't mind, Joe?"

"Not at all," he replied at once. This time, he knew he had plenty of money to cover whatever the bill might be.

"Okay, then, sounds good to me. I love seafood, and I bet you will, too. Let's go, already—I'm starving!"

* * *

They left Prelz at the shelter and walked to the restaurant at a leisurely pace, enjoying the gorgeous sight of the orange setting sun shining off skyscraper windows and passing vehicles. As they walked, Christine locked her arm in Torval's, in that curious way she'd done before, and he had to resist the urge to pull her close. Having her there, at his side, smiling at him as they ambled slowly along, made him feel strangely calm and at peace. Her presence seemed totally natural, as if she belonged there. When her eyes met his, all his human problems seemed to melt away.

Not for the first time, Torval wondered if these strange feelings washing through him were a product of his human shell, or something more. Some part of him wanted these particular emotions to run deeper than mere flesh, but he had no way to know for sure if they even could. If, after he went back to Hell, he still felt this way, what then? She would be gone, and he would never see her again. Would that be too painful to bear? Or would the memory of her sustain him, even strengthen him, as he faced whatever his new task would be?

Hopefully, it would be the latter.

"You know what?" she said as they walked. "It's funny, I thought I wouldn't be able to get over finding out you were a demon. Now that I've met another one, though, it doesn't seem so unusual."

"To be fair, Jake is no longer a demon," replied Torval. "He has become human."

"True, but I still saw a demon's shape when I touched his hand," she pointed out. "Anyway, I guess I'd just sort of gotten used to being among humans, with little or no contact with any supernatural beings.

I almost forgot there could be any others."

"You do not talk to other angels, then?" inquired Torval. "I had thought perhaps there were others nearby that you simply did not choose to introduce me to."

"No, I'm the only one in this part of the city, as far as I know," she replied. "Every few years, someone comes and checks on me, and of course I have an emergency phone number I can call if something goes horribly wrong."

"A phone number?" Torval was surprised. "Angels use telephones to communicate?"

"Might as well take advantage of the technology," she replied with a smile. "In the old days, there were monasteries and such scattered around, where one person or another might be an Archangel in human form, but there's no need for that anymore. Now we have the magic of cell phones. Anyway, I came really close to calling that number when I found out about you, but I decided not to."

"That is fortunate," remarked Torval.

"Well, I kept thinking, did I really want to end my assignment like that, just because you turned out to be a demon? That's what would've happened, you know. If I called them, and said I'd met a demon, they would've reassigned me at once."

"Then I am grateful you did not call."

She squeezed his arm. "So am I! Actually, I kept trying to think about how I was going to explain it, and it didn't make much sense. A demon in a bum's body, trying to get a job and get off the streets? I couldn't figure out how to tell them that without sounding like a complete idiot."

"When I arrived on Earth," explained Torval, "I was motivated entirely by the demands of my human body. I was cold and sick and hungry, and all I could think of was finding a warm place to stay and acquiring a supply of food to eat."

"Yeah, I can imagine," she agreed, "but you found out that wasn't all you needed, didn't you? Food and shelter are the basic needs of all humans, but after that, there's a whole lot more to living, isn't there?"

"That is true," he admitted. This was something Prelz also suggested, not so long ago, and the ex-Tempter had been right. "There is a great deal more."

She nodded in agreement. By this point they had reached the restaurant, so Torval stepped ahead of her, opening the door to allow her to pass through. She smiled appreciatively and went inside. There was no wait, so they were quickly shown to a small two-person table set in a recess between a decorative plant display and a large aquarium stocked with colorful tropical fish. Torval waited for her to sit, then followed suit and began to study the menu.

The prices, he saw at once, were indeed high, but he shrugged that aside. He'd still have plenty of funds left after this meal, as long as he kept his purchase on the lower end of the scale. After studying the choices for a minute or so, he settled on something called a "Saltwater Sampler Platter" that offered several intriguing seafood choices. The opportunity to try several different items at once would be most welcome.

After ordering, they made small talk for a while, with Torval describing the simpler events of his day, including the purchase of his new clothing (on which she provided a welcome compliment). She followed suit by explaining several of the cases occupying her time at work, most of which involved discontented couples in the process of divorcing.

"I can understand that humans might become unhappy with each other after a time," said Torval after she finished describing a particularly nasty case involving something called a "pre-nuptial agreement" being hotly contested in court. "However, from what I have understood about love, if two people fall in love, it is supposed to be lasting."

"Well, she replied somewhat sadly, "love can be a fickle emotion. It's hard to describe, really, because I must admit I've never been able to quite grasp it myself. Sometimes what you think is love is just lust—a passionate desire that turns out to be fleeting. Other times, one partner or the other doesn't feel love, but pretends to, or just goes along with the other out of a hope that maybe they'll fall in love eventually. Also, unfortunately, sometimes people fake love in order to get what they want from their partner, and when marriage is involved, that usually involves money."

"Money, again," sighed Torval. "The human euphemism that money is the root of all evil certainly seems well founded."

"Yes, it does." Christine nodded in agreement. "Humans do like their possessions, and you can't acquire possessions—at least, not legally—unless you have money, so there you are."

"But those things are transitory," Torval pointed out. "They do not persist after death. I know that humans don't truly know what awaits them when they die, but clearly it will not involve physical objects they acquire while living. Why do they not understand?"

"You might as well ask why they do anything at all," replied Christine. "Do you remember when you wanted out of the cold? What would you have done then, to acquire warmth and comfort?"

"I do not know. A great many things, for I did not like the cold very much."

"There you go, then. When a human wants something, he's as likely as not to just take it, no matter the consequences. It's all about *now*, not what comes later. And speaking of now, here's our dinner. About time—my stomach's really growling!"

The waiter arrived with their food, and Torval ate slowly, enjoying the intense flavors of each of the different items on his plate. Christine, who had ordered baked salmon, seemed to enjoy hers as well. They said little, primarily because Torval was too busy focusing on his palate to chat, and she just enjoyed watching his comical facial expressions as he sampled each tasty morsel.

After he finally finished, Christine finally spoke up, chuckling softly in amusement. "Ah, that sure brings back memories," she said with a smile. "I remember experiencing taste the first time. So amazing—I didn't know anything could be so intense and pleasurable. There's other things, of course, but food is the easiest one to enjoy."

"I wish we could eat more often," agreed Torval, "but once I am full, the desire disappears."

"It's your body's way of refreshing itself," she explained unnecessarily. "Eating is enjoyable so you're more likely to do it regularly, thereby keeping yourself healthy and well fed. As long as you don't give in to excess, you're fine."

"I do not intend to," he noted. "I must say, this plate contained perhaps the best food I have eaten since I arrived on Earth. I must remember to thank Jake for suggesting this place."

"It ought to be good, it's expensive enough," she replied, rolling her eyes. "How did you get enough money to afford that, anyway? Did the Roxtons make you rob a bank?"

"No, nothing like that," he answered, shaking his head in the negative. "The Roxtons are not criminals, it seems. I know I suggested before that they might be, but it turns out that they are simply victims."

"Oh?" she inquired curiously. "How'd you figure that out?"

Torval started to answer, but paused. How much of this story did he want to tell Christine, anyway? She'd already admitted that she very nearly called her superiors, thereby terminating her assignment here, simply because she'd met a demon. How would she react if she knew there was a Corruptor in a police station just a few blocks away?

On the other hand, she might be able to help him deal with that particular situation. So far, Prelz had given some decent advice, but it would be good to hear the angelic side of things. Perhaps she might even be able to suggest some way to help the Roxtons, or possibly even do so herself—she was, after all, a Redeemer.

"This will take some explaining," Torval said after a moment. "Some of this may be difficult for you to hear."

"Don't worry, Joe," she replied with a smile. "Whatever it is, I can take it, as long as you don't introduce me to any more demons."

Torval frowned. "Very well," he replied, "I will not introduce you."

Christine caught the hidden meaning in his words almost instantly. "Oh, no! There's another demon?" she gasped. "Not one of the Roxtons! Although, if you told me it was that Pete Roxton, I wouldn't be at all surprised. Except he—oh, never mind, you don't need to know about *that*."

"It is not either of the Roxtons," replied Torval. "Let me explain what I know, and then you may ask any questions you see fit."

She nodded, and he proceeded to outline the entire situation with Lieutenant McCord, the Roxtons' debt, and the way Torval had been thrust into the middle of things. This took more than just a few minutes, during which she listened intently, but remained silent.

When he finished his tale, Torval added, "That brings you completely up to date, as of the events of today. However, you must understand, I did not know this McCord was a demon until this very afternoon. I have been attempting to determine what to do, which is part of the reason I have told you all of this. I was hoping you might be able to provide some assistance."

Christine took a few gulps of her drink and leaned back in her chair, wiping her lips with a napkin. "Well," she said after a moment, "that's quite a story, Joe, and it's a tricky situation, isn't it? This Corruptor demon certainly seems to have his hooks in the Roxtons pretty deeply."

"Not literally," replied Torval, "but I believe I understand your meaning."

"If I thought he was violating the Compact, I could take direct action," mused Christine. "Unfortunately, this just sounds like the sort of thing a truly evil demon would come up with. I'm not sure I can do anything directly."

"Prelz said Mannoch *was* violating the Compact," argued Torval. "He said a demon was not able to force humans to do his bidding, nor could he strip them of their free will."

"Well, see, that's the problem right there." Christine took another sip and continued, shaking her head slightly. "See, he hasn't quite taken away their free will—not completely, anyway. The Roxtons still have a choice. If they wanted to, they could pull out of this arrangement. They'd lose everything, and probably go to jail, and if McCord is the slimy weasel I think he is, he'd just wriggle out of any accusations they sent his way. Still, that's just it—they *do* have that choice, even if it's not a very good one. The Compact is thereby upheld."

Torval nodded, disappointed to hear this, for it limited his own options significantly. "I see," he muttered in frustration.

"I know it's unfair," she went on. "In fact, it's absolutely horrible! The Roxtons got themselves into this themselves, though, and now they're stuck with it. This Corruptor you've met seems extremely good at his job, unfortunately for them."

"So there is nothing that can be done?" asked Torval worriedly. "The situation will soon escalate, with or without my help. If the Roxtons are stealing from McCord, he will find this out and injure them."

"Well, maybe they aren't," suggested Christine. "Maybe he's just being paranoid, which I could certainly believe, from the way you've described this particular demon. In fact, a certain amount of paranoia would be very helpful in his line of work."

"If the Roxtons are not stealing, then they have nothing to fear," Torval realized. "That is the solution, then. I must ensure that they are not embezzling funds, and then report this information to McCord. He will then allow things to return to the way they were."

"That won't solve anything, though." Christine leveled those piercing blue eyes of hers at Torval, and they seemed to cut right through him. "That might defuse the current problem, but that still leaves the Roxtons as McCord's virtual slaves."

"This is true," Torval admitted. "I admit it does leave me uncomfortable, but what can I do? I am as nothing before the might of a First Class demon. If I oppose him, I will be destroyed, and when I return to Hell, I will be punished for violating orders and interfering with another demon's work."

There was silence for a moment as she mulled that over, and during the interim the waiter arrived with the check. Torval took it, counted out the cash from his pocket, and paid the man with four twenty dollar bills, advising him to keep the rest as the tip. A hefty sum, but the dinner had been worth it, and he still had almost two hundred dollars left.

Once the waiter moved out of earshot, Christine began to speak again. "Joe," she said in a tone that almost sounded like pleading, "you know you have to help the Roxtons! You can't just let this go on. God knows I have my own personal problems with Pete, but at least he knows he screwed up and is trying to rectify it. If not for him, at least think of Lincoln, who put everything at risk to help his grandson! Can you really sit idly by and watch their lives be destroyed by another demon?"

"I will not lie to you, Christine. It disturbs me greatly that this is happening, but I simply cannot interfere. The best I can do is ascertain the Roxtons' guilt or innocence in embezzling funds, and if they are innocent, I can mediate for them."

"If that's true," she argued in a frustrated voice, "then why did you even tell me any of this, if you've already decided what you're going to do?"

"I did not know that for certain, until you informed me he was not violating the Compact," Torval answered honestly. "In any event, I had hoped you would be able to do something, since it seems I cannot."

"Oh, I see how it is," she replied, tossing her napkin onto her plate angrily. "You can't fix your own problem, so you get me to do it?"

"That is not what I mean," he protested. "Please do not be upset, Christine! I want to do something, but I do not see how I can."

Christine clutched at the napkin for a moment, wringing it back and forth between her hands. "Let me ask you something, Torval," she went on. "Not Joe, this time. I'm asking Torval the demon, punisher of sinners. What if you went back to your old job after this is all over, and one day, you come to a new prisoner, and you find it's Lincoln Roxton? And he's being tortured because he was corrupted by Mannoch into doing evil against his will? Kindly old Lincoln Roxton, who helped you when you were down, is now burning in Hell for all eternity, and when you had a chance to stop it, to help him get free of this meddling demon's influence, you did nothing? How would you feel then? Well? How would you feel?"

Torval stared at her, totally at a loss. He wanted to say that he wouldn't care, because he was a demon, and because he'd have no human feelings when he returned to Hell. Yet he couldn't say that, because he knew it wasn't true. He knew he'd feel terrible. He'd feel as if he let Lincoln down.

In fact, considering the scenario further, he knew he wouldn't be able to do his job at all. How could he torture Lincoln Roxton under those circumstances? There would be no way to bring himself to do it. He just knew he couldn't.

Quite suddenly, he realized that he cared about what happened to the Roxtons. That was the problem—he *cared.*

Damn these human emotions! Yes, *damn* them, not bless them, because that wasn't the correct term after all, was it? Human emotions were a curse, and one he couldn't rid himself of, no matter how much he wanted to. Somehow, in being on Earth, and interacting with people—not just Christine and Prelz, either, but others, like Hal and Shelly and Zac, and everyone else he'd met—somehow, in being a part of this world, he'd developed the inexplicable capacity to *care.*

Torval hung his head. "I would feel miserable," he finally answered. "What is more, Lincoln Roxton would not deserve such a fate. Not when he has no choice but to do evil, unless he accepts a penalty so great that it would destroy his life."

"Then what are you going to do?" inquired Christine quietly, glad she'd made her point. "How are you going to help them?"

"I don't know," replied Torval, shaking his head sadly. "I really have no idea, but if an opportunity presents itself, I will aid them however I can."

She put a hand on his arm, and he shuddered slightly. "I knew you had it in you, Torval. I knew you'd do the right thing."

"I should not feel this way," he told her, his voice laced with melancholy. "I am a demon, not bound by human needs or desires, yet I have them now, and I cannot deny them any longer. Prelz told me this curse I bear is called a 'conscience.'"

"Yes, I suppose it would be," Christine replied, smiling in satisfaction. "I'm glad you've developed one, even if you aren't. It warms my heart to think that even a demon can be redeemed, at least a little bit."

"Yes, you are very good at what you do," admitted Torval appreciatively, understanding now that this is what she did on a daily basis. "I am suitably impressed. Still, you did nothing in particular, other than force me to face a part of myself I had hoped to avoid. Nonetheless, this is a disturbing development, because I can now only wonder how I can possibly function as a demon."

"What do you mean?" she asked, her smile quickly fading, replaced by a look of curious concern. "You aren't going to become human, like your friend, are you?"

"I do not know," he told her. "That is a remote possibility, although it is not my intent to choose it."

"Well," she went on, "I must admit, I've heard something about that before. Among angels, there's a story that if you so choose, you can give up what you are for a human form. We refer to it as 'falling to Earth,' although there's no actual falling involved. Once you make this choice, it's permanent—there's no going back. That's what worries me, Joe. If you were to do that, and then you changed your mind—"

"It is not that," Torval interrupted. "I do not think I could stand to be human permanently. What concerns me is far greater. When Jake and I discussed my continuing Advancement, he proposed that my interest in goodness was influencing my change far more drastically than I ever thought possible."

"What do you mean by that, exactly?"

Torval shrugged. "He thinks I am becoming an angel."

Christine stared at him for a few seconds, and then, she did something he didn't expect. She opened her mouth and started to laugh. The noise immediately drew attention to their table, so she covered her mouth, but couldn't stifle the giggles for several more seconds.

"Why is that so funny?" asked Torval when she seemed to have recovered from the inexplicable bout of mirth.

"A demon? Become an angel?" She chuckled again, several times. "That's crazy, Joe. It can't happen!"

"But I have become obsessed with good," argued Torval. "Furthermore, as has just become obvious, I have developed a conscience."

"Yes, well, that doesn't make you an angel," pointed out Christine. "Besides, your form has a lot more changing to do if you're going to look like one of us before it's done. I think you're giving my influence a bit too much credit."

"But what if it is possible?" Torval asked worriedly. "What if I become an angel? What will become of me then?"

Christine sighed and took his hand. Instantly she shifted, in his eyes, into her angelic form, which smiled beatifically at him. "Listen, Joe, if you do become one of us, I'm sure the transition won't be anything to concern yourself with. I've never heard of anything like that ever happening, but who knows, maybe it's possible. There's nothing in the Compact to prohibit it, as far as I know. Who knows—in this crazy universe, I could almost believe such a thing could come to pass."

"If I do change," Torval went on, holding onto her hand as long as he could, "would you help me, Christine? Otherwise, I would be alone, and I do not think I could stand that."

"Of course I will," she replied readily. "I'll be right here for you, Joe. No matter what happens, just remember, I'll always be here for you."

Chapter 10

Torval glanced at his watch as he and Christine stepped out of the restaurant. He still had plenty of time before the hard deadline insisted upon by Pete, so he was in no hurry to end the date.

She pulled on her overcoat, despite the fact that the early evening wasn't all that chilly, and noticed him looking at the time. "Do you have to leave so soon?" she inquired, sounding disappointed at the possibility.

"Not yet," replied Torval. "I have just under an hour before I must report to work, and I am afraid I must be prompt. Is that enough time to see another movie?"

"A movie? Now?" Christine laughed at the suggestion. "No, those last about two hours, sometimes longer."

"I recall that *Queen Takes Pawn* lasted that long, but was not aware that they are all the same length. Never mind, then. Is there something else you would like to do?"

Christine looked out at the lights of the city, apparently considering the possibilities. "There are some things I'd like to show you," she remarked, "but most places are closed now. Is there anything you might be interested in?"

Torval nodded. "We could have sex," he proposed matter-of-factly. "I believe we have enough time available."

At that, Christine burst out laughing once again. For a moment she managed to catch herself, and looked at him curiously, whereupon she realized he was serious and commenced laughing once more.

"I fail to understand why that is humorous," said Torval once her giggling faded enough that she could hear him. "Do humans not copu—I mean, do they not sleep together after dates?"

"I'm sorry, Joe," she went on between fits of laughter, "it's just—the way you asked me, it was so unexpected, you caught me off guard.

Looking at you, it's easy to forget you're a demon and don't know how we do things here on Earth."

"I understand that there is something of a taboo regarding the subject," he pointed out, "but you and I are not humans. My body is definitely attracted to yours, and judging by the kiss we shared after our last date, yours is similarly afflicted. I merely propose that we allow our bodies to interact more directly."

Christine put a hand on her forehead and winced. For a moment she didn't say anything, until finally she took a deep sigh and looked into his eyes. "How about we go for a walk, and I'll try to explain," she offered. "Central Park isn't too far. Shall we?"

"Certainly," he replied, joining her as she strode off in the direction of the park. "I do apologize if I have offended you, Christine."

"I'm not offended, actually," she told him, quickening the pace slightly to make it through an intersection before the light changed. "Actually, if you weren't a demon, I would've probably slapped you, like I did with—well, with a certain other someone, not so long ago. But as it is, well, I just wasn't expecting you to even bring it up."

"The subject of sex is of some interest to me," Torval explained. "I have observed many souls suffering in Hell for sins related to intercourse, or similar activities. However, since reproduction is such an important facet of the human condition, I could not understand why there would be punishments associated with it. Since arriving here on Earth, I have come to learn many things about the subject, but apparently the finer points still elude me."

"I'll say!" she agreed at once. "You were right about one thing, though. My body is definitely attracted to yours. In fact, when we kissed that night, if I hadn't opened my eyes and seen a demon staring back at me, I may very well have asked you up to my room. God knows I wanted to! You seemed so perfect, a real diamond in the rough, and I was truly wondering where you'd been all my life. Unfortunately, you were just too good to be true."

"I am still here," he pointed out. "I have not gone anywhere."

"You really want to have sex, don't you?" she asked with raised eyebrows. "Well, I suppose you would. That male body of yours probably hasn't had sex in ages, so it's got you pumped up on hormones."

"Actually," he said blithely, "I have had intercourse twice since arriving on Earth. Whatever these hormones are, they are not to blame."

"You had sex twice? Really?" Christine looked surprised, though whether it was because of the act itself, or because of his admission, Torval couldn't tell. "Oh, no, don't tell me it was with that harlot you met at the employment bureau!"

"It was," Torval admitted. "In fact, you were quite correct regarding Shelly's intentions. She did indeed attempt to rob me the first time I visited her apartment."

"I *knew* it!" exclaimed Christine accusingly. "I don't know how I knew, I just did. Sometimes I have feelings about people—call it intuition, I guess. She just seemed a bit too desperate. Why didn't you take my advice? Why did you go see her?"

"Because I was curious about sex, as I told you," Torval explained. "Furthermore, I knew I had nothing of value for her to steal. She was quite upset about this fact, actually, and I felt very bad about her situation."

"What situation might that be?" She clearly didn't have very much pity for Shelly, which didn't seem all that surprising, considering Christine's distinct hostility toward Shelly during their one and only meeting.

"She was in need of funds to pay for her home," said Torval. "In speaking with her, I realized she was only a prostitute because she had no other way to earn money."

"That excuse is as old as civilization itself," sighed Christine, throwing up her arms in exasperation. "It might've worked in ancient times, when women were little more than property, but not today. There are plenty of other things someone like her could do to make money that didn't involve selling her body."

"Yes, she mentioned that she was trying to find ways out of the profession," Torval noted. "I felt badly for her, so when I needed further instruction, I returned to her apartment and purchased a lesson. In that way, I provided her with a less tainted source of funds, and learned something in the process."

"Wait, you did what now?" Christine stopped in midstride and shot him a curious, and somewhat shocked, look. "You went to her for a lesson? A *sex* lesson?"

"Yes, I was concerned about my performance during our first copulation," Torval replied honestly. "She told me I did poorly, and that worried me greatly."

"Why?" asked Christine, starting to walk again. They had, by this point, reached the entrance to the park, and began strolling along a paved path, beneath a row of soft lights. Other humans passed here and there, enjoying the cool evening, but none paid them the slightest bit of attention.

"Because at that point I was scheduled to go on a date with you," explained Torval, "and I was afraid that if we did, in fact, have sex, that I would disappoint you."

Christine blinked, and paused for a moment to contemplate those words. "You mean to tell me," she said slowly, "that you paid for lessons in sex just on the off chance you and I would sleep together?"

"Yes, exactly so."

"Why, I don't know whether to slap you or kiss you!" Christine sighed and shook her head sadly. "That's the craziest thing I've ever heard!"

"You must realize, at the time I did not know you were an angel," Torval reminded her. "I thought you were simply a human woman, and one whom I was very interested in, both physically as well as mentally. I still maintain both of those interests."

Christine nodded, almost to herself. "Well, that's all well and good," she said after a moment, "but all the same, we should probably avoid the physical part."

"Why?" he asked, not angry or upset at all, but simply curious as to why this should be.

"Well, first and foremost, because I'm an angel and you're a demon."

"But these are human bodies we wear," countered Torval. "The bodies desire each other, as we have both already admitted. I could—*we* could both learn more about being human, if we let nature take its course."

"That would be more convincing if I thought it was the real you talking, without the influence of the male sex drive."

"I assure you, I am in complete control."

"That's what they all say." Christine chuckled at that. "Anyway, that just proves my point. As angels and demons, we should know better than to engage in casual sex. Think of all the problems that could cause! What if my superiors find out that I knowingly had intercourse with a demon in human guise? It's bad enough that I'm just talking with you. What if they tried to claim you forced yourself on me?"

"But that would not be the case," said Torval. He did, however, grudgingly admit she was probably right. "Nonetheless, your points are quite valid. I doubt my superiors would be any happier about the situation should they learn we engaged in casual sex."

"Exactly," Christine said, obviously glad she'd made her point. "Anyway, what good would it do, anyway? You've already tried sex, and so have I, even if it has been a while. It wouldn't prove anything, and all we'd do is open ourselves up to problems later."

"I suppose," agreed Torval reluctantly. Curiously, he asked, "You have had sex before, then?"

"Yes, of course," she answered, shrugging it off as though it was unimportant. "Not recently, though. When I first arrived on Earth, I tried it a few times, just to see what it was like. Probably for many of the same reasons you had, actually. What I got most of the time was a sweaty mess and emotional friction from my partner, so after a while I gave up."

"You did not sleep with Pete Roxton, then?" inquired Torval.

"Heavens, no!" Christine exclaimed with a frosty laugh. "Not that he didn't try. He couldn't keep his hands off me. What a pig! Sorry, Joe, I know he's your friend, and the Roxtons have helped you, but when we had our date, Pete wasn't very nice. Well, he was at first, but not after he got a few drinks in him."

"He is under great stress," said Torval. "Perhaps he simply hoped you wanted casual sex, as he clearly did, and when you did not, he just reacted poorly."

"I suppose that's possible," sighed Christine. "Let's just not talk about him anymore, all right?"

"Very well," Torval agreed readily. "I must inquire, if you have given up on such things, why did you even agree to go out with him at all? Why did you bother to go on a date with me, as well?"

They reached a large fountain, where several groups of humans were standing around, chatting amongst themselves. Joe followed closely as Christine meandered through the crowd, until she came to a spot off to one side where the concrete walls surrounding the fountain gave them some privacy. Here she leaned back into a half-sitting position, crossing one foot over the other and running one hand absently through her hair.

"Well," she told him, "I suppose it's because I've always been interested in human romance. Do you know what that is?"

"I am familiar with the concept," Torval replied. "I read a few articles on the subject. In fact, I thought we were experiencing the beginnings of romance during our first date."

"That's true," she agreed, "before we knew who we really were. Ever since I arrived on Earth, and had those sexual incidents I told you about, I've been fascinated by romance. Look around, Joe. Right now, I mean. Look at those people over there, for example."

She gave a subtle point with her left hand, and Torval glanced in that direction, where he saw a man and a woman locked in what looked to be a passionate embrace.

"And those two." She pointed again, and this time, she indicated a pair walking quietly hand in hand. "And over there," Christine went on, and partway down the walkway, he saw a man and woman on a park bench, leaning against each other with arms around each other's shoulders.

"I see them," replied Torval, wondering where she was going with this.

"Those people, they're all in love," explained Christine. "Different stages of love, obviously. The first two, they look like they're falling in love right now—passionately, in fact. The ones walking together, they've been together for a while, and the ones on the bench are probably somewhere in between."

"I understand, but I do not see your point."

"Well, what I'm getting at is, we can see the results, but not what came before. How do they meet? What brings them together? How do they know when they're in love? What do they do once they realize they are, and how do they share their lives? That's what romance is all about, Joe. I've read about it, and watched movies, and all of that, but I've never experienced it for myself. That's why every so often I go out on a date, if I find someone I like, and who seems like a good match for my human self. I was totally wrong with Pete Roxton—but with you, or at least with Joe Sampson, I thought maybe, just maybe, I'd found the right person."

Torval nodded slowly. "I am sorry I disappointed you, Christine."

"You didn't disappoint me," she replied, putting her hand on his arm. "I guess I just should've known it wouldn't work out. I don't think romance is something we're really meant to experience. Not as demons or angels, anyway. If we were human—truly human, like Jake—maybe then. But not now. Not like this."

Torval took a moment to consider those words. He knew, logically, that she might well be right, yet something in her tone told him otherwise. Rationally, what she said made sense, and yet, Torval wasn't ready to give up that easily.

He was pretty sure she didn't want to, either. The way she spoke sounded as though she merely wanted to convince herself of something she didn't really believe.

"Christine," Torval said after a long pause, "since I arrived on Earth, I have experienced a number of human emotions. In fact, I have perhaps sampled them all, except the most intense ones. I have yet to feel hatred, for which I am quite grateful, but on the other hand, I do not yet know love, and in that, I feel diminished."

Where he was going must've been obvious. "Joe," she asked, almost pleading, "please don't do this ... "

"I would like very much to feel this thing called love," he went on, as if she hadn't spoken. "You are the only one on this world who can help me do that."

"I—I can't," she answered, lowering her eyes so that she was staring at the cracked and pitted sidewalk below her feet. "I don't want to fall in love with you. It would be wrong—it would be ... "

What happened next was beyond Torval's conscious control. He didn't even think about it—he just acted. He stepped close to her, leaned down, and kissed her gently on the lips.

She didn't pull away. For a few seconds she simply sat there, not really reacting, until finally she gave in, leaned her head back, and wrapped her arms around his neck. Torval, eyes tightly shut, returned the gesture, hugging her tightly, awash in human feelings, those intense sensations that swept madly through him in spine-tingling waves.

After an eternity, she pulled her lips from his, but kept her hands firmly clasped about his neck. Torval opened his eyes for a moment, enjoying the sight of her radiant angelic face gazing back at him.

"We can't do this," she insisted weakly. "Joe ... Torval ... we can't let this happen! You're going to leave soon, to go back to Hell, and what then? It'll be too painful, for both of us. Maybe you should go. Maybe ... maybe we just shouldn't see each other anymore ... "

"That would be far more painful," Torval countered. "Let us experience this thing called romance, Auralea. Let us learn what love is, even if only for a short time."

"We can't," Christine protested weakly. "What if we ... what happens if ... oh, the hell with it!"

They kissed again, more passionately this time, and after that there were no more protests.

Chapter 11

As much as Torval enjoyed kissing Christine, it had to end eventually, much to his dismay. A part of him actually considered deliberately not going back to work, in order to spend the rest of the evening with her, but he knew he couldn't do that. He had a responsibility there, and simply couldn't turn his back on the Roxtons, despite his feelings to the contrary.

He and Christine walked hand in hand back through the park, making small talk, no longer concerned with seeing each other in their true forms. Torval, for his part, was gratified that his demon shape didn't upset her now. In fact, she seemed quite comfortable looking at him, and of course he didn't mind her appearance at all.

Something about holding hands with her just felt natural and right, which probably explained why so many other human couples did the same thing. He passed a number of them on the way back through the park, and he thought now that perhaps he finally understood some small fraction of what they must feel for each other.

It's dangerous to care this much about someone, he thought absently. The logical part of his mind remained wary, reminding him with little subtlety about such things. Yet he couldn't help himself. He cared about Christine, and maybe even loved her, although he still wasn't entirely sure he understood the full depths of that emotion. What was more, he *liked* caring about her. *That*, his emotional side told him, *is all that matters.*

As they walked, the conversation drifted through some of the details about dying marriages she'd helped to save while working in the legal profession, and from there to some of the more memorable souls Torval had to oversee on his route back home. Christine seemed saddened to hear about those unfortunates, and more than once remarked that at any point during their lives, a few kind and supportive words delivered at the proper moment might've saved them an eternity of torture.

That's what Christine did, in her assignment on Earth—she tried to save souls from just such an unfortunate fate. Torval could understand how that job would be very rewarding, although, in her own way, she interfered in a soul's development just as much as Prelz used to do as a Tempter.

He found himself reminded once again of the concept he'd imagined a few hours earlier—what if demons and angels weren't allowed on Earth at all, and humanity had to make its own way? Did demons and angels simply act as natural counters to each other? Or would the lack of demonic temptation, and angelic redemption, lessen the human experience?

Was it the nature of humanity to experience both these opposing forces, and then, using their power of free will, make the choice of their own accord? That thought intrigued him, but before he could voice it, they arrived at the warehouse.

"Well, this is as far as I go," said Christine with a sigh. "I don't want to get too close to that place."

"It is a shame you and Pete must remain at odds," stated Torval. "I wish you could interact without so much hostility."

"Well, maybe if he apologized," suggested Christine. "Actually, no, scratch that. I can see how part of that was my fault. I may very well have led him on a little, if unintentionally. Maybe I should come in and apologize instead. Do you think I should?"

"I don't know how Pete would react to your presence," Torval told her. "I am afraid I may have made things worse earlier today."

"How?" she asked worriedly.

"I told him what you said during our first date. He did not react well to this news."

"You told him—oh, no, that's right, I forgot about that! I was pretty mad at him then, and I didn't know who you really were—oh, no, if you told him that, then he must be really pissed!"

"Yes, he is," said Torval. "In fact, when he found out about our date tonight, he ordered me not to be late. That is why I have been checking my watch so frequently."

"Oh, so he's mad at me, and takes it out on you," groused Christine. "Way to shoot the messenger, Pete!"

"Nonetheless, perhaps now is not the time to interact with him further," Torval suggested. "I will attempt to repair the damage if at all possible."

"That's fine, just don't make it worse," she said with a clipped laugh. "Oh, one more thing before I go. Have you figured out how you're going to help with their situation?"

"I have not thought of anything," he replied. "The first step is to find out if they are indeed embezzling, and once I know the truth of this, I can decide how to proceed."

"How are you going to find that out?"

"I was told to look through their records," said Torval. "That is what Lieutenant McCord wants me to do."

"If you do that," Christine pointed out, "you'd be going behind their backs."

"Yes, that was my primary concern," admitted Torval, "but there is another problem, as well. Even if I do look at their records, how will I know exactly what I am seeing? Will I be able to recognize something incriminating if I saw it? I have looked at their sales records before, if only briefly, and they are nothing but meaningless names and numbers."

"I see your point." Christine held up a hand. "What are you going to do, then?"

"I suppose," concluded Torval after a moment, "I will simply have to ask them."

* * *

Torval waved as Christine sped away in the cab, quickly losing sight of her smiling face amidst the city lights reflecting off the window. He missed her already, but the sheer joy he felt all but overwhelmed that emotion.

Human romance has its advantages, he thought, almost bouncing up the steps to the warehouse entrance. If nothing else, he felt wonderful! The problems and dilemmas he faced seemed like nothing compared to the euphoric high of blossoming love.

When he stepped into the building, Pete and Lincoln were both inside. He could hear them talking in the break room, though their voices were too low to make out any words. Torval sighed and took a deep breath, forcing himself to focus on the present. He would see Christine again tomorrow, during her lunch break, as they had already arranged. Now it was time to go to work.

He headed toward the voices, still smiling to himself. "Ah, there you are," said Pete, sipping at a plastic bottle of water. "Right on time, too. I guess you win, Grandpa."

"Win?" inquired Torval curiously.

"We had a little bet going as to whether you'd be late or not, seeing as you had a date tonight," replied Pete. "He was right and I was wrong."

"And he did have the date, too," said Lincoln, pointing at Torval's face. "The lipstick tells the tale."

Torval reached up to his face, where the elder Roxton pointed, and wiped at the corner of his mouth. To his surprise, he found a reddish stain on his fingertip. Obviously, some of Christine's cosmetics made their way onto his lips, so he picked up a napkin from the nearby table and wiped them off.

"Don't worry, son," said a grinning Lincoln. "That's been going on since I was a boy. In other words, since the Dark Ages."

Pete chuckled. "Oh, come on, you aren't that old yet! Anyway, it's none of our business what Joe here does on his off time. Or who it's with."

"Now, Pete, we talked about that," said Lincoln sternly.

"Yeah, yeah, I'm getting to it. Look, Joe, I want to apologize for what I said before. I didn't mean to jump all over your case about Christine, and to make matters worse, I think I was wrong about her too. I let myself get a little carried away, y'know? I think I owe her an apology."

"That is good to hear," said Torval. "I spoke with her on this matter this evening, and she also admitted she might have overreacted."

"Yeah, she did, all right," agreed Pete with a grin, "but so did I, so I guess that makes us even."

Torval nodded, glad that the problems between them seemed to have been defused so easily.

"Anyway," went on Lincoln, "enough touchy-feely stuff, it's time to get you to work. You're going to be entering in sales records in our accounting program, Joe, so I hope your fingers are ready for some marathon typing."

He looked down at his hands, and in the process noticed he

still had some lipstick staining his fingertip, so he wiped a little harder until it was completely gone. "I believe I am ready," he stated after a moment.

"Good. What we're trying to do is get all our records from last year onto the computer, so we can do our taxes electronically. You know when Tax Day is, right?"

"Tax Day?"

"Yeah, the day taxes are due. April 15th. That's less than two months away, and there's a ton of stuff to type in, so you should get started right now. I figure if you work for two or three hours a night, you'll be done by the end of March."

"Two or three hours?" Torval raised his eyebrows. "I am here for the entire night. I could work much longer, if you wish."

"No, no, we wouldn't want you getting carpal tunnel syndrome," insisted Pete, using a phrase that meant nothing to Torval. "Besides which, this is going to be mind-numbingly boring. What you can do, if you want, is type stuff in for a couple of hours, then do some filing, or cleaning up around the basement, or whatever you like."

"Plus, like we said before, we're leaving the upstairs door unlocked from now on," Lincoln reminded him. "You can come up, have a look around, and do anything you see that needs doing. Anything that fills the time, really, when you can't stand the data entry anymore."

"The best part is, you're going on the payroll," said Pete in a congratulatory tone. "Like we said before, you'll get a regular paycheck from now on. Four hours a night, fifteen bucks an hour. And yes, before you ask, we're still buying you dinner, too. There's a couple of roast beef sandwiches in the fridge here—since you can come upstairs now, we pulled the small one out of the basement and put it back in the, uh, assembly area."

"How's that sound?" inquired Lincoln, before Torval could ask what they meant by "assembly area." "You ready to get started?"

"Everything you have said is acceptable," said Torval, "but there is something else we need to discuss before I begin work tonight."

"Oh?" asked Pete, exchanging glances with his grandfather. "What is it? You better not tell me you're getting married, or I'm gonna smack you!"

"No," replied Torval, dismissing that idea as a faint attempt at humor. "This is something else entirely. I have, in fact, been extremely worried about this subject, and I am afraid what I tell you may adversely affect our relationship. Nonetheless, I feel I must proceed. You were, after all, honest with me earlier today in describing your situation with Lieutenant McCord."

"Okay," said Pete, "go ahead, lay it on us."

"Yeah, don't hold us in suspense!"

"Very well." Torval took a deep breath. There seemed to be nothing to do but plunge ahead, so he did. "Lieutenant McCord has asked me to spy on you. He wishes to know if you are secretly keeping some of the money you make from the sale of stolen car parts."

Pete and Lincoln's mouths both dropped open simultaneously as Torval spoke those words. For a few long seconds, silence reigned in the little room, save for the humming of the nearby refrigerator. Then Pete quite literally crushed the plastic bottle in his hand, sending water spewing everywhere.

"That bastard!" Pete all but screamed. "That heartless, fucking *bastard*! He's the Devil, I tell you! The fucking Devil!"

Lincoln put his hands on his grandson's shoulders. "Cool it, Pete!" he yelled, raising his voice louder than Torval had ever heard it. "Knock it off! I know how you feel, but breaking things won't help!"

"Goddammit all to Hell!" yelled the younger Roxton, storming around the room, causing Torval to back out into the hall. Pete crushed the bottle in his hand still further, then flung its crumpled remains into the front of the refrigerator, where it flopped to the ground in a broken lump. "Sorry, Gramps, but this is fucking pissing me off! I swear to God I'm gonna kill that piece of shit the next time I see him!"

"Do not do that," Torval interjected. "That would only make the situation worse. Far worse than you know." It would, in fact, doom Pete's soul to eternal damnation, which of course is what Mannoch probably wanted in the first place. In fact, he might even have a contingency plan for such a thing, for all Torval knew.

Pete threw up his hands. "Oh, what's the use? I know I can't kill him, damn his soul to Hell, but I sure wish he was dead! That would solve one of our problems, at least!"

"You know," said Lincoln, "at this point I'd be content to just let the bank foreclose, and get the heck out of here, if I thought McCord would let us off the hook that easily."

"Me, too, but you're right, it's never gonna happen, so now what the hell are we supposed to do? If he finds out—"

"Wait," said Lincoln, putting up a hand. "Joe, why are you

telling us this? If there's one thing I know about Jonas McCord, he wouldn't have tried to get you to spy on us if he didn't have something on you, or threatened you in some way."

"That is true," replied Torval. "He did, in fact, threaten me, but I will handle that on my own. However, I have decided I cannot, in good conscience, spy on you behind your backs. Now that you know the truth, I can ask the more important question—are you, in fact, embezzling funds from Lieutenant McCord?"

The two Roxtons looked at each other for a moment, and by their mutual expressions, Torval felt sure he knew the answer. Had they chosen to lie, he would've known it in a heartbeat. However, to their credit, they made no attempt to do so.

"Yes," admitted Lincoln, bowing his head slightly. "Yes, we are, and we have been for quite a while."

Torval sighed and lowered his head. He'd been hoping otherwise, because this complicated matters greatly. Furthermore, he would now have to somehow keep this fact to himself the next time he spoke to Mannoch. Nonetheless, it was imperative that he have the answer, because he couldn't formulate a plan without knowing the truth.

"Are you going to tell him?" asked Pete after a moment, a very worried look on his suddenly ashen face.

"No." Torval shook his head. "I will lie for you, because if I do not, you will likely suffer great pain, and possibly even death."

Pete looked relieved to hear Torval would keep their secret, but Lincoln clenched his hands into fists. "No," he said firmly. "No, I don't want you having anything to do with that man, Joe! We got you into this, and now, we're going to get you out of it. Get your things—I'll drive you to the bus station, and get you a ticket anywhere you want to go. You can have some spending money, too. You can disappear someplace and forget you ever knew us."

Torval sighed and shook his head. "I admit I have considered that option," he replied, "but I will not run. I will help you with this as best I can, for as long as possible. I can use my position with McCord to help hide your secret transactions, until such time as you can pay your debts and escape his control."

"No, it's too risky," argued Lincoln instantly. "I won't have you doing that for us! You don't owe us anything, Joe, as much as we appreciate it. I don't think I could have it on my conscience if something happened to you."

"The choice is mine to make," explained Torval, invoking the semi-sacred right of free will, "and I have made it. Now, if there is nothing further, I am ready to learn about entering your receipts onto the computer. I will tell McCord tomorrow that I spent all night reading your files and found nothing out of the ordinary, which will, in fact, be true. Is that not so?"

Pete nodded, still looking a little pale, as well as somewhat dumbfounded by Torval's words. "Yeah," he said after a long pause. "Yeah, that's true. Don't worry, everything you're gonna see tonight is completely legit."

"Good," said Torval. "The less I am required to lie, the better. Lieutenant McCord is not easy to deceive."

Pete sighed ruefully. "That," he all but muttered under his breath, "is the understatement of the year."

Chapter 12

Torval needed about fifteen minutes of instruction to learn the basics of the Sales Master program. While he worked under the careful tutelage of Lincoln Roxton, Pete casually rifled through the nearby stacks of files, removing some of them for what he called "safekeeping." Torval felt sure those particular folders contained material that would've been of interest to Lieutenant McCord, but with the offending material removed, Torval could safely claim he never had access to that information, and he would, technically, be telling the truth.

Actually, what he intended to do was, in fact, dishonest (at least as far as Mannoch would be concerned), even if technically "truthful." This was what the humans apparently called a "little white lie"—another of those bizarre euphemisms of theirs—which signified a lie told for the greater good.

So one could lie, something normally considered to be evil, in order to actually do good. Realizing that, Torval wondered if it one might sin in other ways without actually being evil. Could he cheat, steal or even kill if doing so proved necessary or even noble? Would someone who killed a rapist be punished for the deed, or rewarded? What about someone like Shelly Mendez, who took payment for sex in the manner of a prostitute, but did so for good reasons—to teach others the proper ways of pleasing their mate? Was this also good, from a certain point of view?

Perhaps, but he had no way to know for sure. These were questions for someone with experience in such matters. He resolved to ask Christine later, and focused instead on his work.

Once Torval finished learning about the software program, the Roxtons left him alone to enter sales records into the computer. This information had something to do with taxes, a concept he understood somewhat, although the reason for the computer eluded him.

He supposed he didn't actually have to understand—the Roxtons needed the computer for some reason, so that was good enough for him. He sat down and began typing, placing the names and numbers in the appropriate rectangle-shaped spaces on the screen. Upon finishing with one sales receipt, he clicked on a special button in the lower right corner, causing the computer to store the information somewhere—how it did these things, he had no idea—and present him with a fresh, blank data screen, whereupon he began entering the next receipt.

Torval found this task incredibly easy. Typing didn't even cause him any problems—he found his fingers had an almost innate knowledge of the keyboard. Apparently, Joe learned the art of typing at some point in his life, and retained those reflexive skills even after his soul moved on. Without his body's training, Torval would've had to manually hunt for every key, arrayed as they were in seemingly random locations.

For the first hour or so, he had no trouble, but he soon became very bored and distracted. Most of the receipts were virtually identical, with a name and address, one or two items sold, and some numbers indicating the price. Typing all of that in, as the Roxtons warned him, proved quite mind-numbing. He began to take frequent breaks, using the time to walk around, consume his meal, and surf the Internet.

Shortly after midnight, he became very tired, even though he hadn't performed any actual physical activity at all. The numbers on the pages blurred together, and he had to force himself to keep working. The Roxtons told him to complete three hours of data entry, and he doubted he'd done two, considering all the break time.

His body urged him to quit and go to bed, but he refused to do so, for he'd been given clear instructions and the Roxtons would expect him to complete his task. Giving up just wasn't in his nature. Only when he dozed off and his nodding head slammed into the keyboard, giving him a painful welt on his face, did he finally decide he'd satisfied their wishes to the best of his ability.

He was too tired to fight with the hammock again, so instead he simply curled up on the floor, where he dropped off within moments.

* * *

The next morning, Torval woke up to find his eyes dry and surrounded by crusty material that had to be carefully scraped off. He supposed this came from staring too intently at that computer screen, which had a way of irritating his vision. He also had a mild headache, but by the time he finished soaking in the shower, the pain faded and he felt much better.

After drying off, going through his usual hygiene rituals, and putting on one of his new outfits, he headed upstairs for breakfast. Pete awaited him, enjoying a cup of coffee over the usual box of donuts. "Morning," he said amiably. "How'd the data entry go?"

"You were correct," admitted Torval, eagerly sampling a brown-colored donut covered in white glaze. "Data entry is quite tedious. I believe I preferred cleaning the bathroom, where I could easily gauge the quality of my work, and see meaningful progress."

"Yeah, it's not much fun; I figured that," agreed Pete. "You know, when you think about it, though, it's pretty easy work. You get to sit in a comfy chair all night, take breaks when you want, and you don't strain any muscles or get dirty. Lots of people would kill for a job like that."

"I do not believe that killing would be appropriate," Torval remarked.

Pete snickered. "Yeah, not literally, but you know what I mean! Anyway, after you leave, I'll take a look at what you did, though I'm pretty sure you had it figured out. No worries there. Are you meeting with McCord today?"

"I believe so," said Torval. "At his insistence, I acquired a phone yesterday. When I leave here, I will call him, and ask for further instructions."

"What are you going to tell him?" asked Pete, a note of concern in his voice.

"I will tell him I found nothing," replied Torval. "He will insist that I try harder, no doubt, but I have no intention of doing so. I will do my best to convince him otherwise, of course."

"What if he figures out you're lying?"

"Then I suppose there will be violence," replied Torval with a shrug. "I will not resist, as there would be no point. Hopefully, I will not be killed, although it is impossible to rule out that possibility."

Pete gaped at him and shook his head slowly. "I can't tell if you're acting, or if you really don't give a shit what he does to you. Either way, you're freaking me out."

"I do care about what happens to me," replied Torval, somewhat hastily trying to cover up his obvious mistake, "but I do not believe it will come to that. I should be able to avoid physical harm."

"I sure hope so, 'cause if you don't, my grandpa is gonna blame himself for whatever happens to you. Or worse, he'll blame me, since I got us into this mess. So let me give you some advice."

"Please do."

"Okay, then, here's the thing. McCord is a real intense guy, right? He's got this way of intimidating you, like he's gonna crush you under his thumb at any moment. Well, let me tell you, I've played a lot of poker in my time, and I can tell when I see a bluff. And you know what? A lot of times, that's what it is. He's really just trying to scare you into making a mistake, or panicking, or whatever. So unless he has the goods on you, just stick to your guns, and he'll probably back off. Not in such a way that he'd ever look like he lost a staredown, of course, but enough to let you off the hook."

"I think I understand," said Torval, "although I doubt I will be able to determine if he is bluffing, as I have never played this game called 'poker.'"

"Never played ... ?" Pete narrowed his eyes. "That's funny, the way you talk, with that monotone of yours, I'd think you'd be great at it. Nobody would ever get a read on you, I bet."

"I am afraid I have never played," Torval insisted. "I have played chess, but not poker."

"Chess? Really? It's been a while, but I used to play that with my father all the time. He was really good, though. I almost never won."

"Where is your father?" inquired Torval casually. "If your grandfather works here, I would expect your father to do so as well."

Pete sighed and stared at the nearby wall for a moment, a sad look on his face. "I'd rather not talk about it."

"Very well." Torval didn't press the issue, and the room grew silent. He was starting his second donut when Pete finally turned back to face him.

"No, on second thought, I think I will tell you. I should be able to talk about this by now, dammit."

"You do not have to."

"Well, I want to, so there." Pete sighed and took a breath before proceeding. "You see, my father and I had a falling out about ten years ago. It was about the sixth or maybe seventh time I borrowed money from him to pay one of my bookies. He threw me out of his apartment and told me to never come back there again. A few months later, when I tried to hit him up for another fresh helping of cash, he'd moved away. I don't know where he went, and I never really tried to find out, since he obviously wanted nothing more to do with me."

"That is unfortunate," said Torval, not really sure what he should say in response. "You allowed money to destroy your relationship with your father."

Pete looked at him, an agonized expression on his face. "Damn, you just go right for the throat, don't you? Yeah, that's exactly what I did. I fucked everything up. That, this business, my life, everything! Never again, though. I'll never gamble again. Not even to teach you poker, even though I'm pretty sure you'd be great at it."

"If not that, then perhaps chess," offered Torval. "In that game, there is no gambling involved."

Pete nodded. "You know, you're absolutely right," he said after a moment. "I haven't played chess in years. Tell you what, I'll bring in the board, and we can play sometime, okay? Maybe some morning, after you wake up, if nothing else is going on around here."

"That would be very enjoyable," agreed Torval. "I am looking forward to it."

* * *

Shortly after that, he bid Pete goodbye and headed out to the street. Playing chess again would indeed be fun, although his skills would surely be weak in comparison. More practice would be in order if he were to have any chance against the younger Roxton.

With that in mind, he started walking toward the park, hoping to find more chess players there. The day was sunny and warm, with the wind much more noticeable today. A few loose papers fluttered in the morning air, snaking their way down the streets between passing cars and buses. All around him, people jostled along, paying him no mind, intent on their own personal business.

He glanced back and forth at the street as he waited for the light, wondering if Vince and Marty would show up in that unmarked car of theirs. They had a way of coming out of nowhere, when he least expected it. This time, though, he saw no sign of them, and crossed unmolested.

As he walked, he thought perhaps that he should take out his phone and call McCord, but he didn't do so immediately. In fact, he really didn't want to make that call, for fear of the inevitable confrontation. What would happen depended entirely on his ability to deceive the police-demon, but as far as Torval was concerned, either way the result would be bad. Fail, and he would be beaten or killed for attempting to lie to a superior. Succeed, and McCord would be angry that there was no evidence to prove the Roxtons' guilt. What he would ask Torval to do next was anyone's guess.

He got two more blocks before he realized this is what the humans called "procrastinating." Delaying any further served no purpose. The confrontation would come, one way or another, and if he took too long, that would only upset Mannoch all the more.

Torval waited until he found a spot comfortably out of the path of other pedestrians, then took out the phone and dialed the lieutenant's number. The phone rang twice before the noticeably gruff response all but shouted into his ear. "What is it?" demanded McCord. "You got something for me?"

"I am afraid not," said Torval, keeping his voice as even as possible. "I studied a great deal of sales receipts, and found nothing suspicious."

There was a long pause, during which Torval wondered what would come next. Finally, McCord replied, "I guess I shouldn't have expected anything right away. Listen, I've got some things to do just now, but I want to talk to you face to face. Report to my office before lunch—say, about eleven o'clock, all right? There's some things you need to see."

"I will be there," Torval agreed at once, relieved that McCord hadn't been upset at all.

"See you then." A click followed, and the phone beeped twice as the connection ended. Torval smiled to himself as he put the device back in his pocket. Success! He'd deceived Mannoch, and done so quite easily, with no repercussions. Furthermore, he hadn't even lied, at least not technically.

There were different kinds of lies, and sometimes they could be used for good purposes. Glad to have learned about another important facet of the human experience, he pressed on toward Central Park.

* * *

Torval didn't find any chess players this time, but didn't really mind too much because the game did take considerable time to play, and eleven o'clock wasn't that far off. He must've slept later than he thought.

He stayed in the park for a while, watching humans come and go, sometimes alone and sometimes in groups, often just walking and other times on one or another of their strange vehicles. A few even seemed to glide past, riding on tiny wheels strapped to their feet. This looked so easy, and so much faster than walking, that he wondered why more people didn't use that mode of locomotion.

The day continued to warm up, so much so that Torval wished he hadn't worn a sweater at all. Still, the breeze felt pleasant, and he found he simply enjoyed standing in place, letting the air wash over him. Birds flitted about, singing and chirping, and the sound seemed quite soothing. In this place of peace and comfort, he could simply close his eyes and relax.

This is being human, he thought idly to himself. Standing there, in the warm spring breeze, troubles momentarily forgotten, he could only smile. He'd come so far since that first day, almost exactly a week before, when he'd arrived sprawled out on the frozen ground, sick and weak and hungry. Now he had a full stomach, gainful employment, a place to live, and even friends, a strangely fulfilling concept he couldn't have comprehended before coming here.

And he had Christine, a woman and an angel, who at any other time might have been his enemy, but was now quite the opposite. Someone he could share his humanity with. Someone he could love.

Torval realized then that what he felt was sheer, unconditional happiness. *No wonder humans seek this particular emotion*, he thought to himself. *This is what they live for.*

The moment proved fleeting, though. He'd run out of time, for he faced the long walk to the distant police station, where Lieutenant McCord waited. Torval sighed, feeling the pleasant emotion of happiness slipping away, but its memory remained sharp and clear. He could find it again, whenever he needed to, he was confident of that.

Still smiling contentedly, he continued on his way.

* * *

"Ah, good, there you are," said McCord with a frown. Turning to his assistants, who stood uncomfortably in front of his desk, he added, "You two, beat it! Time for me to educate our new friend here."

"Whatever," commented Vince, rolling his eyes. The policemen retreated, shaking their heads, and Torval thought he heard some sort of curse muttered under someone's breath.

The door slammed shut, and McCord motioned toward the chair. "Have a seat, Joe," he offered, smiling. "I hope you slept well."

"I suppose I did," admitted Torval, sitting down in the seat directly next to McCord's imposing desk. "I apologize for not finding anything incriminating against the Roxtons."

"That's okay," said McCord. "It was really a long shot anyway. I'm sure those two wouldn't just leave that sort of thing lying around. You're going to have to dig a little harder, that's all. Here, take this."

He pushed a small, black case across the desk. The rectangular container was about twice the length of Torval's cell phone, with a silver latch on the side. "What is it?" he inquired curiously.

"Well," said McCord, "these belonged to an associate of mine who stupidly decided to cross me. After I shot him, I confiscated these and a few other items I thought might come in handy. Go ahead, open it."

Torval nodded, frowning at the not-so-subtle implication that betraying McCord would have fatal consequences. He popped open the latch and saw a number of long, thin rods with differently shaped metal ends, some of them in odd, jagged shapes. "I do not understand," he admitted, not really knowing what he was looking at. "What purpose do these serve?"

"They're lockpicks, my young apprentice," said McCord with a gleam in his eye. "I have no doubt the Roxtons are hiding things from you, probably locked safely away. These picks should get you through any ordinary lock, which is all they can afford. I want you to spend some time here practicing on these."

With that, he lifted up a large cardboard box, previously hidden behind his desk, and set it down next to Torval's chair. Inside, he found a wide variety of locks, ranging from simple loose padlocks to more complex ones attached to the sides of jewelry boxes and the like.

"I regret to inform you, sir," said Torval after a moment, "that I know nothing whatsoever about lockpicking."

"That's fine, neither do I," chuckled the lieutenant. "It's okay, though, there's no huge rush. You can learn as you go. In the bottom of the box there's some instructions, and if you still have trouble, I know a couple people that can give you hands-on training later this afternoon."

Torval's shoulders slumped. This wasn't what he wanted to be doing all afternoon, but he had little choice. If he wanted to continue pretending to serve McCord, he had to do this task. As long as he could stretch out the deception for another seven days, he could depart Earth without doing any harm to the Roxtons, or interfering in Mannoch's mission here.

He had, of course, agreed to help the Roxtons if he could, thanks to his pesky conscience and Christine's urging, but he still didn't know how to accomplish that. His first goal had to be to appease Mannoch until he could come up with something along those lines.

"Very well," he agreed. "I will do as you ask. However, I cannot guarantee success. Even if I become skilled at lockpicking, the Roxtons may not have the information hidden behind such defenses. Furthermore," he added almost as an afterthought, in the hopes of leading McCord off the track, "they may not even be hiding anything at all."

"Oh, they are, I'm sure of it," McCord insisted. "I'm not an idiot, Torval! I keep my eye on what's going on with anyone who's in my service. I can see they're keeping up with their loan payments, and there's no way they can be getting that kind of money if they aren't skimming off the top."

"They could be—" began Torval, but that was all he had a chance to say.

"They aren't!" snapped McCord. "I'm sure of it! Besides which, even if they aren't, they're paying off their loans one way or another. Do you know what that means?"

"No, sir," Torval answered meekly, even though he was pretty sure he knew exactly what it meant.

"It means their usefulness to me is about over," replied McCord. "The only thing keeping them under my heel is the knowledge that if they fail to do as I ask, they lose their precious business. That's the only leverage I have, Torval, and to a Corruptor, leverage is everything!"

"Well," suggested Torval hopefully, "I suppose you can simply move on to corrupt other souls. After all, surely the Roxtons are doomed to Hell through their association with you."

"No, you fool! Don't you see? It's exactly the opposite! I can't allow them to wriggle free. Not after all this time and all my hard work! Who knows what might happen? With no threat of foreclosure hanging over their heads, or of having their kneecaps broken, they might even use those records of theirs to incriminate me, and in doing so, redeem themselves. I can't permit that, you see. I don't like to lose, Torval, but it's not just that. I'm doing far too well here to let a couple of weak-willed idiots like them bring me down."

"What will you do, then?" Torval asked, a very uncomfortable, sinking feeling in the pit of his stomach.

"Well," replied McCord with a casual shrug, "if I can't get my hands on those records, I suppose the Roxtons will just have to die."

Chapter 13

Torval was stunned. He simply stared at McCord for several seconds, aghast, and trying with all his might to keep his emotions to himself. He knew, instinctively, that allowing any sign of horror to creep onto his face would reveal too much.

"Nothing to say about that?" inquired Mannoch after a moment, grinning widely. "I do believe I've left you speechless!"

"I'm sorry, sir," Torval heard himself say. "It's just that—well, it's not—"

McCord threw up his hands. "I know what you're going to say," he interjected immediately. "You're going to throw that silly Compact in my face, aren't you?"

"Well, yes, I suppose I am," replied Torval, trembling slightly. "I thought that taking direct action against humans was a violation of the rules."

"Oh, normally it would be," explained McCord patiently, "but not with people I've already corrupted. Once they're mine, I can do with them as I will. The Roxtons gave themselves over to me when they accepted my help, so they no longer have any choice in the matter. Once I've milked them for all they're worth, I can discard them at any time. Best to do that before they find a way to escape their Devil's bargain, don't you think?"

Torval nodded slowly, but said nothing. His mind whirled. If McCord was telling the truth, then he really could simply kill the Roxtons at any time, whenever he felt their usefulness was at an end. That meant Pete and Lincoln were, effectively, doomed.

The question at hand now was whether or not they could escape the corruption McCord had already visited upon them. They'd already announced their intentions to try to break free of their servitude to Mannoch, so they were at least trying to find redemption. They had, in fact, exercised their free will to decide their own fate. By choosing to free themselves from him, had they done enough to save their souls? Torval had no way of knowing.

That did bring up another issue, however. From everything Torval had been told, humans had free will, and no one, neither angel nor demon, could deny them the right to exercise it. Despite Mannoch's corruption, the Roxtons could employ free will to leave his service and seek redemption. Could Mannoch truly refuse to permit this and take away their freedom of choice?

Torval didn't know, and that was part of the problem. The conflict must've showed on his face, as McCord frowned immediately. "Look, I can understand your doubts, Torval," he said confidently, his voice assuming a soothing, almost paternal tone. "You were probably told some whiny bullshit about free will and all that, but believe me, I know what I'm allowed to do. I've already punished a few people that tried to cross me, and if I broke the Compact, don't you think someone would've put a stop to it? Nope, no lightning bolts from the sky, or anything like that, so I'm telling you, it's perfectly fine. As long as I'm sure they're thoroughly corrupted, I can do whatever I want. In fact, it'll be nice having you around, because you can keep a close eye on them, and let me know if they're up to anything else."

"Yes, sir," muttered Torval, trying very hard not to reveal any more of the inner turmoil he was feeling.

"In fact," said McCord, "did you get any more chances to try your new tempting skills on anyone? Come on, I'm sure you must've had at least a few opportunities."

Torval nodded slowly, thinking back to what Prelz told him about the job of Tempter. "I was able to successfully bribe the phone salesman," he noted after a moment.

"Yeah, I know about that! What else?"

"Uh, let me think a moment," replied Torval, trying to focus. The memory of the morning's conversation at the warehouse returned to him. "I attempted to talk Pete Roxton into playing a game called poker," he offered hopefully. "He thinks I will be good at it."

"Excellent!" exclaimed McCord. "That's perfect! If he starts playing again, he'll start gambling, and that could lead to some wonderful things. Well, wonderful for me, anyway." He chuckled loudly. "What else?"

"I am sorry, I cannot think of any others," said Torval regretfully. "I did not have many opportunities to interact with humans, as I spent most of the night working in the warehouse, alone."

"Ah, yeah, that's true," agreed McCord with a nod. "Okay, well, still, that's a good start, working the poker angle. Get him to start playing again, and I'll give you a special reward—I'll bankroll you while you're learning the game. Sound good?"

"Yes, sir," agreed Torval automatically, although he didn't quite understand the term. He would have to learn more about this game called poker, obviously.

"Okay, then, here's what I want you to do. I've got to head out for a lunch meeting with some associates of mine, so I'm going to put this box away for now. Get back here in a couple hours, whenever you want as long as it's after one o'clock. I'll put you in a closet someplace and you can practice with these locks. Maybe tonight you can break into a locked file cabinet or something and find what I'm looking for. If not, well, you can keep trying until you get really good at it. Who knows? After we're done with the Roxtons, I can put you to work breaking into all sorts of places. Won't that be fun?"

"I suppose," commented Torval half-heartedly.

"Good!" replied McCord with a laugh, slapping Torval hard on the back, so that he had to cough several times. "This is great! It's so nice to have another demon around to talk to and work with. You know what, Torval? I think this is the beginning of a beautiful friendship!"

* * *

Torval eagerly scurried out of the police station. As he walked away, hurrying so quickly he almost stumbled several times over broken spots in the sidewalk, he realized he'd been sweating profusely. The constant nervousness and gnawing worries made him sick to his stomach. How quickly everything seemed to change, after that peaceful moment in the park!

So much for being happy, he thought ruefully.

He now knew the depths of Mannoch's evil. Corruptor or not, he'd gone too far. Torval hadn't been a student of the human condition all that long, but he knew enough to understand that it wasn't right to use people and then kill them when they weren't needed anymore.

Even a demon couldn't get away with such things, he felt sure. Despite McCord's words to the contrary, he was in violation of the Compact—at least insofar as Torval's limited understanding suggested.

He wished he could actually *read* the Compact, to be sure of its exact wording and intent, but of course that option wasn't available. The only way he could see it involved going back to Hell, and there'd be no return trip, unless he wanted to come back in a different body somewhere else in the world. Unfortunately, as he now knew after surfing the Internet for hours on end, the world was a very big place indeed.

He slowed down after almost running into someone at a street corner. Fretting, he paced about as he waited for the light, afraid to cross against the crowded flow of late morning traffic. What was he to do now? He couldn't continue to serve McCord, not if he knew the demon was in violation of the Compact. He also knew better than to oppose a Corruptor, for that could have only one result. He could simply return to Hell, tell Geezon what he knew, and allow his superiors to deal with Mannoch—but by then the Roxtons could be dead, their souls bound for Hell before they could find the redemption they clearly wanted.

He had to help them. He knew that now. This was no longer some vague possibility he could pursue when it suited him. He had to find a way to help the Roxtons *now*, before McCord decided he didn't need them anymore and got rid of them.

Torval reached the shelter, hoping to find Prelz, but found no sign of the ex-Tempter anywhere. Torval spent the next half hour circling the block, and then the surrounding blocks, but didn't find his friend. After that he had to return to the shelter, in order to meet Christine for lunch.

She wasn't there, either, but a couple of minutes later a cab pulled up and she emerged, wearing a navy blue blazer and knee-length skirt. She looked as radiant as ever, and her smile immediately warmed Torval's heart, driving away some of his worries and fears just as easily as the spring breeze earlier in the park.

"Hi, Joe," she called out as she paid the cabbie, who sped away a couple of seconds later. She all but skipped up to him and gave him a quick kiss, which was more than welcome.

"How was your morning?" she went on after they separated, with more than a little reluctance on his part.

"Not good," he admitted. "I must ask you an important question before I proceed with my explanation."

"Fine, go ahead, but let's get some lunch first, okay? I'm really hungry—I overslept, so I missed breakfast."

Torval agreed and started walking, heading toward the KFC that wasn't that far away. He knew she wouldn't have very long for lunch, so "fast food" would have to do. "Why did you oversleep?" he asked curiously as they walked, arms linked in the comfortable way she seemed to like most.

"Yeah, I was up a bit late talking to a certain demon friend of yours," Christine went on, smiling to let him know she wasn't actually angry or upset about this. "I wish I'd known who Jake really was long before this, Joe—I could've done a lot of things to help him, if only I'd known."

"You have helped him now, then?"

"I think so," she replied. "If nothing else, at least he got the first night he's had off the streets in a long time. I let him use my guest room, and when I got up this morning, I just let him sleep. He might still be there, for all I know."

Torval nodded, feeling at once pleased that Prelz finally agreed to sleep somewhere other than an alley, and a bit jealous that he hadn't been able to stay with Christine himself. "Good," he said, returning her smile. "I am happy for him. When I tried to talk him into leaving the streets, he would hear nothing of it."

"Well, I'm just a bit more persuasive than you," laughed Christine. "Now, as for lunch, it's on me this time, okay? I'm tired of you buying all the time, just because you think you're supposed to because you're the guy. I'm perfectly capable of paying for lunch if I want to!"

"If you insist," agreed Torval. They had by now reached the chicken restaurant, so they took a moment to order. The man behind the counter took her money, collected their food and put it on a tray. Torval carried this to a nearby table, in a corner away from where any other humans could overhear their conversation.

"Okay, then, what's this big important question you have to ask?" Christine wondered as she started in on her chicken sandwich.

"It is about the Compact," said Torval. "I have not read it myself, but you have, is that correct?"

"Yes, I've seen it," she replied. "I read it once, and then an instructor explained what it actually meant. That doesn't really qualify me as an expert, but then, I've been around lawyers for the last few years, so I think I can interpret the meaning of legal documents pretty well. Go ahead with your question."

"Very well." Torval took a deep breath and then continued. "If a human has fallen under the control of a demon, what powers does that demon have over him?"

"What do you mean?" Christine looked confused. "As far as I know, he doesn't gain any power at all. Not that I can remember hearing about, anyway."

"What I am saying," elaborated Torval, "is if a human has been corrupted by a demon, so that he is now that demon's puppet, does he lose his right to free will? If the human decides to break free of the demon's control, is he permitted to make the attempt, or can the demon refuse to allow it by destroying the person in question?"

"What? Oh, heavens no!" exclaimed Christine. "Humans *always* have free will! Nobody can take that away, no matter what!"

"You are certain of this ... ?"

"As certain as I can be," Christine replied. "Without a Compact sitting here to look over, I can't quote you the actual rules, but my teachers were very firm on that point. You can't take away a human's right to free will—*ever*."

"That is good to know," replied Torval, "and yet, it also presents me with a terrible dilemma."

"What do you mean? Why are you asking me that, anyway? I can tell it's not just a rhetorical question—what's going on?"

"Last night, I learned the Roxtons are indeed embezzling money from Lieutenant McCord," explained Torval worriedly. "They are attempting to buy their way free of his influence by repaying their loans."

"Oh, that's wonderful to hear!" said Christine excitedly. "Don't you see, Torval? That's what I was talking about—they have the right to choose to do the right thing, if they want to. It's just like I've always said—there's good in everyone, no matter how bad their situation. Give them a chance, and that good will shine through, like a ray of sunlight through the clouds."

Torval nodded in agreement. "Yes, I too was pleased to hear it," he told her, "and they were honest enough to reveal this information to me, even after I told them I was asked by McCord to spy on them."

"Ah, so you told them that," she noted. "I'm glad you did. That was a secret you didn't need to keep."

"Yes, but I am not finished with my explanation. This situation becomes more complicated as I go."

"In what way?"

"This morning," Torval went on, "McCord confided in me what was actually going on. I now know the real reason he wanted me to find the Roxtons' records. He is afraid they will use that information to implicate him in various crimes once they are free of his control."

"Good, I hope they do," said Christine forcefully, almost spitefully. "It'd serve him right! I'm sorry, Joe, I know he's one of your kind, but what he's doing is ... well, it's just not natural!"

"I am still not finished." Torval sucked in another deep breath before continuing. "McCord told me that he cannot permit them to undermine his activities here on Earth. Therefore, if I cannot find those records soon, he is going to kill the Roxtons."

"Kill them—!" Christine gasped and put a hand over her mouth, eyes wide with horror. "He can't kill them! Why, that would be—oh, my! Dear God in Heaven above, that's *unthinkable*!"

"I agree," replied Torval. He realized then that he hadn't even started on his lunch, so he picked up a drumstick and took a bite. The chicken tasted as savory as ever, but he barely noticed.

"Now I see why you asked me that question when we sat down," Christine went on. "If the Roxtons have chosen to defy him, of their own free will, he can't oppose that choice. It's theirs to make. That's the one thing that truly binds us, angels and demons alike. He can't just kill them because he doesn't like their choice! That's not just a violation of the Compact—it's like throwing the Compact right back in our faces!"

"I was afraid of that," said Torval between bites. "I believe I had already reached the same conclusion, and now you have confirmed it. Unfortunately, this leaves me at an impasse. I must stop Mannoch and help the Roxtons, yet I lack the power or ability to do so. I cannot think of any way to intervene that would not violate my own orders, or result in my human body's premature death."

"Well," said Christine, "you may not be able to do anything yourself, but I might have something we can try."

"What is that?" asked Torval, desperate for anything that could possibly help him with this seemingly unsolvable problem.

"About a year ago," she explained, wiping her mouth with her napkin, for she'd by now finished her own lunch, "I was working on a case where a woman was divorcing her husband becase he was a dirty cop. Among many of the interviews I had to sit in on, there was one that involved Internal Affairs officers."

"Internal Affairs ... ?"

"It's a branch of the force that investigates police misconduct," explained Christine. "They aren't very much appreciated by regular cops, since they help to prosecute fellow officers."

"But if those officers are corrupt," said Torval, "would they not deserve their fate?"

"Yes, of course they do," agreed Christine at once, "but you have to understand something about the police—they're a very close-knit group. Sometimes they depend on each other for their very lives, so they tend to get attached to each other. If one turns bad, the others may not want to believe it, or they may just not understand. So they tend to see Internal Affairs as a bunch of betrayers—a 'rat squad,' as they sometimes call them."

"I see," said Torval. "So this is the group that we would call upon to stop Lieutenant McCord?"

"Maybe," she replied with a nod. "In my line of work—both legally and angelically—it's good to have contacts like these guys. I'll give one of them a call and explain what's going on. This afternoon, in fact, if I can set up a meeting."

"I wish I could attend," said Torval sadly, "but in order to keep up the illusion of cooperating with Lieutenant McCord, I must return to his office in about an hour."

"Don't worry, you don't need to be there with me," Christine went on. "In fact, it's probably best if you aren't. I'll clue him in, and see what he says. There's one thing I know he's going to want, though—he's going to want some kind of evidence."

"I believe the Roxtons have evidence," said Torval, recalling the hastily hidden files from the night before, "but as they are not yet free of McCord's control, they may not wish to turn it over."

"Well, they're going to have to," Christine replied, forcefully enough to get her point across. "If they don't, you know what's going to happen."

"Yes." Torval sighed deeply, shaking his head slowly from side to side. "Yes, I know all too well."

Chapter 14

Lunch seemed to end all too soon, and Christine bade Torval goodbye and hurried to find a cab. Not before a goodbye kiss, though, which made him feel a little bit better. Hopefully she could convince an Internal Affairs policeman to help in some way.

There is the possibility, thought Torval worriedly as he walked back toward the shelter, *that whoever Christine asks will turn out to be just another ally—or pawn—of Lieutenant McCord.* How deep his corruption reached within the police department, Torval had no idea. If the Internal Affairs officer did turn out to be in Mannoch's camp, it would be the end of the Roxtons, and probably Torval and Auralea as well.

Hopefully Christine would choose her contact very, very carefully.

Torval reached the soup kitchen to find Prelz waiting, although he looked almost unrecognizable. The ex-Tempter was clean, for the first time since Torval met him. He wore what looked like new clothes: a long-sleeved flannel shirt, slightly oversized jeans, and white tennis shoes. He didn't have his woolen cap on, so his recently shaved head, now covered in a peach-fuzz layer of very short hair, was plainly visible. Even his beard looked clean and trimmed, a far cry from its usual ragged self.

"Torval!" Prelz called out excitedly, moving up to shake hands, momentarily flashing into demon form as he did so. "I gotta tell you, that was the best night I've had in years! I forgot what real beds feel like. I slept until almost noon!"

"You look well," said Torval appreciatively. "I see Christine provided you with clothing as well."

"Yeah, it's a bit big, but I don't care. I'm so glad I let her talk me into this. You know what? You were right—I did need to get off the streets. I didn't want to admit it, but I think it's 'cause I've been out here so long, and I'm just a stubborn old bastard."

"You are indeed stubborn," agreed Torval, "but I doubt you could be considered a bastard."

Prelz rolled his eyes. "It's just an expression, for goodness sake! Sheesh, are you ever gonna learn? Anyway, who cares, my stomach's full and I'm clean, and the day is gorgeous ... I feel great!"

"I am glad for you," Torval said. "I felt that way this morning, as well. What did you and Christine talk about last night?"

"Oh, you can probably guess," replied Prelz. "First we just sat in the back of the shelter for a while, and I told her all about what I used to do as a demon, and why I quit. I told her what I wanted most of all right now was to help cleanse my soul, and she told me that started with becoming a useful member of society—so I went with her to a Goodwill store, and she bought me this."

"A good will store?" Torval raised his eyebrows curiously. "What is that?"

"Goodwill, all one word," corrected Prelz. "It's a place where people take clothes and other things they don't want, and donate them. They're then either given to the needy, or sold for low prices to make money for charity."

"It sounds like the store is well-named, then," said Torval. "I thought that was just another strange human euphemism, but I see that it is not."

"Nope. Anyway, after that, she said I could crash on her futon, but only if I had a shower, so I did. Damn, I was filthy!"

"I remember," said Torval. "Joe's body was also quite dirty. It took some time to fully cleanse all of it."

"Yeah, I'll bet. Anyway, we talked for a while longer, mostly about things I could do, getting a job, that sort of thing, then she had to hit the sack. I stayed up for a while, watching TV—another thing I really missed from before I became a bum. I gotta tell you, these humans sure put out some good entertainment!"

"I suppose," said Torval, "although I have never used a television. Is it like the movies, or the Internet?"

"It's sort of like a much smaller movie, but you don't pay to watch, so they use advertisements to make money. Ah, I can see you're gonna ask me about that too, aren't you? Never mind, it'll take too long to explain. Just watch TV sometime and you'll see."

"Very well, I shall do that."

"Okay, good. Now that we've got that out of the way, what's going on with you and the Roxtons? Christine updated me, sort of, but that was last night. What's the latest?"

Torval explained what he'd learned since the last time he saw Prelz, including what he and Christine had discussed at lunch. As he told the rather long story, Prelz listened intently, but said nothing, not even to ask for any details. When Torval mentioned what Lieutenant McCord was really up to, and how he'd threatened to kill the Roxtons, Jake's bearded face noticeably darkened, and he spent the rest of the explanation frowning and wringing his hands together, clearly aggravated.

"There," said Torval when he was done, "you are now completely up to date. What do you think?"

Prelz continued to scowl. "Well, I think you just ruined my happy day, that's what I think," he muttered. "Don't worry about it, though, I'll deal with it. This McCord guy is my worst nightmare! You know, I could've turned out that way, if I hadn't developed this overgrown pity gland of mine. Oblivion's too good for the likes of him!"

"He insists he is not violating the Compact," said Torval, "and since I have never seen it, I cannot dispute his claim. I have only what Christine told me to counter his argument."

"Well, don't worry, she's completely right," replied Prelz immediately. "You can't just kill a human if you don't agree with the choices they've made. You can't even hurt them, or even threaten to hurt them. All you can do is try to change their minds. That's what Tempters and Redeemers do."

"Then what does a Corruptor do?" asked Torval. "It would seem their task is highly restricted by the Compact. Why do they even exist?"

"It's a matter of scale," explained Prelz. "A Tempter tries to convince as many humans as he can to commit evil acts, but he's not really organized about it. When I worked at the Post Office, I did all sorts of minor things. I'd lose important documents, deliver them to the wrong places, damage packages, that sort of thing. The worst thing I ever did was convince some guy to tear the top off a box he'd received and send it back like that, so the shipper thought the item was lost in the mail. That was Temptation for you."

Torval nodded. "Well, then, what would a Corruptor do?"

"Probably come into the Post Office and teach ordinary workers how to steal valuables and make it look like they were just randomly lost," suggested Prelz. "Or get people involved in some other kind of mail fraud or billing scam. It's sort of like the old saying about fishing: you can give a man a fish and feed him for a day, or you can teach him to fish and feed him for a lifetime. A Tempter gets a man to sin today, while a Corruptor makes him sin his whole life."

Torval nodded, immediately grasping the difference. "I see. Thank you for the explanation—that makes much more sense."

"You know," went on Prelz thoughtfully, "what McCord is doing as a dirty cop isn't really breaking any rules. In fact, he's actually doing a damn good job of corrupting. The problem is he won't tolerate anyone who refuses corruption, or tries to escape it. You can't have corruption without the possibility of redemption—and he won't accept that. Sooner or later, he's going to go too far, break the Compact in some way that gets noticed—and then who knows what'll happen?"

"Yes, I came to the same conclusion," agreed Torval. "He must be stopped. Unfortunately, I do not know how to accomplish this, unless Christine indeed provides the help she promises, and the Roxtons agree to aid the police."

"Well, I could always just kill McCord's body," offered Prelz, "and he would be returned to Hell, where hopefully he'll be punished for his actions."

"If you kill him, will that not count as a sin against you?" inquired Torval. "Or is this a situation where committing a sin is actually, in fact, an act of goodness?"

"I don't know," Prelz replied with a shrug, "but I'd think the latter. Especially since it's not really a human I'm killing, but a demon who's gone over the edge. I'd be doing the world a service."

"That sounds reasonable," agreed Torval doubtfully, "but why would you be the one to kill him? You should remain uninvolved. This is my problem to solve, not yours."

"Ah," said Prelz, smiling for the first time since Torval updated him on this situation, "that's just it, my friend. This may be just what I need to clear my record! Like your girlfriend said, I need to do something truly good, something important—and maybe sending Mannoch back to Hell is just what the doctor ordered!"

* * *

Allowing Prelz to slay McCord certainly seems like an easy way out, mused

Torval as he made his way back to the police station. For one thing, that would remove the pressure from the Roxtons, and for another, it might well be considered good enough to save Prelz's soul from damnation. However, the more he considered the option, the less Torval liked it.

First of all, Prelz had to actually do the deed. How, exactly, could he kill a police lieutenant? Well, perhaps the better question might be: how could he kill him without immediate retribution from the authorities? Murder, no matter how justified, was still against the law on Earth. Torval doubted Prelz wanted to spend his remaining days rotting in a jail cell somewhere.

Secondly, what if they were wrong about how justifiable homicide worked? What if they assumed Prelz would find redemption, and only succeeded in damning himself to a truly terrible fate? Furthermore, when Mannoch's body died, his demon side would return to Hell. Once there, assuming he wasn't consigned to Oblivion for violating the Compact, he could simply wait for Prelz's soul to arrive, and then exact a swift and terrible retribution. From what Torval knew about Mannoch, he had little doubt the Corruptor would indeed seek just that sort of vengeance, were it within his power to do so.

So perhaps having Prelz murder McCord wasn't a great idea after all. Torval sighed heavily as he neared the station, somewhat annoyed at having to rule out the possibility. Something about it just seemed appropriate, as if a swift death was exactly what McCord deserved.

Torval entered the building and made his way to the lieutenant's office. McCord was there, visible through half-folded blinds, but seemed busy, talking to several people Torval didn't know—a uniformed cop, for one, and several others who looked suspiciously like plainclothes officers. They had a way of carrying themselves that reminded him of Vince and Marty.

After a minute or so, the meeting hadn't ended, so Torval sat down to wait. A few more minutes passed before the humans inside finally concluded their business and departed. At that point McCord stuck his head out the door and called to him. "Get in here," he said gruffly, in that no-nonsense tone he seemed to employ at the start of every conversation. "I've got a couple of things to ask you."

Torval complied, and McCord shut the door behind him before returning to his desk. "You have a good lunch?" he inquired, with what was quite obviously a loaded question.

"Yes, I did," replied Torval, suddenly worried. He suspected from the nature of the query that McCord knew exactly where, and with whom, he'd dined a short while earlier.

"Good," said McCord nonchalantly. "Now, tell me, who's the girl?"

Torval decided not to waste time feigning innocence or pretending he didn't know what was going on. McCord had clearly followed him, or asked one of his minions to do so. "Her name is Christine Anderson," the younger demon admitted openly. "She is the social worker who helped me find a job when I arrived on Earth in the body of a bum."

"I see," replied the lieutenant with a nod. He continued to watch his apprentice carefully, steely eyes fixed on Torval's, as if trying to bore directly into his skull with his gaze alone. "I'm told you two looked pretty friendly."

"We are dating," admitted Torval, only barely avoiding the temptation to emit a telltale sigh.

"Oh, really?" McCord's eyebrows went up. "You have a girlfriend? How interesting. Why?"

Torval was confused by the question. "Why ... ?" he repeated dully.

"Why would you, a demon, go out with a human? What possible purpose would it serve?"

Torval hesitated. What would happen if McCord ordered him to stop seeing Christine, and then had him followed to ensure he didn't violate the command? That would be a disaster! He had to shift the lieutenant's thoughts away from that possibility, and after a moment's thought, an idea occurred to him.

"She is a good person," replied Torval, "and by keeping close to her, I have more opportunities to tempt her into doing evil."

McCord nodded appreciatively. "Smart thinking, but why date her? That seems a little bit extreme to me. You could just drop by and visit occasionally, don't you think?"

Torval paused again. This wasn't going to work unless he could carry the temptation angle even further. He had to think of something even more effective. What would Prelz tell him to do in this situation? What should he do, if he were a Tempter?

Or better yet, what should he do if he were a Corruptor instead ... ?

"The temptations I was thinking of," said Torval after a moment, keeping his voice as level as possible, "require more than just occasional visits. Furthermore," he added almost as an afterthought, "when I learned that she went out with Pete Roxton, that added an even greater opportunity to plant the seeds of jealousy."

"Ah ... I see." McCord scratched his chin for a moment. "Very good, Torval! Yes, that's excellent! You're killing two birds with one stone, aren't you? Tempting two people at once. I'm impressed, and I don't impress easily. Excellent work!"

Torval nodded and forced a smile. The lieutenant's praise didn't exactly warm his heart. In fact, he felt positively disgusted with himself. Yet he had, at least for the moment, thrown the Corruptor off the track.

"Just one more thing, before I set you to learning the fine art of lockpicking," went on McCord. "When I first had you followed, you visited a prostitute named Shelly Mendez."

"Yes, sir." Torval again had to force himself not to give away any emotions on the outside. Why would he bring her up? She'd done nothing worthy of the lieutenant's attention, as far as he knew.

"Why was that, exactly?" the Corruptor went on.

"As I am new to the human experience, I wished to understand the ritual of sexual intercourse," explained Torval honestly.

"Any particular reason? Besides the fact that your human body wanted it, of course."

"If I am to tempt Christine Anderson," replied Torval, almost cringing at what he was about to say, "I need to be capable of engaging in copulation without appearing uninitiated."

"And you told Shelly Mendez this?"

"Yes, sir. I asked her to train me in the proper procedures."

"So it *was* your idea!" McCord slammed his hand down on his desk. "That's absolutely brilliant! You're even better than I gave you credit for, Torval."

"I—I do not understand," admitted Torval, unable to hide his puzzlement.

"Ms. Mendez has gone a step beyond simple prostitution," explained a grinning McCord. "She's opened up her own little sexual instruction school, of all things! When I had a couple of my boys bring her in for questioning, she said it was *your* idea! Imagine my surprise when I heard the name 'Joe Sampson' come out of her mouth. You sure do get around, for someone who's only been on Earth a few days!"

"Yes, sir," replied Torval resignedly. The fact that he'd done something that McCord appreciated made him feel even worse than he already did.

"Well, I heartily approve, my boy," went on McCord with a certain amount of glee. "We're going to look the other way for now, as long as she stays under the radar, but do you have any idea how many more opportunties this opens up for us later?"

"Not really," replied Torval, trying and failing to sound as enthusiastic as possible. "A great many?"

"Damn straight." McCord nodded, obviously pleased. "It's like a gold mine! As soon as we get done with the Roxtons, and a couple other projects I'm working on, I'll be tapping that one, I promise you. I may even put you in charge of it, if you're ready. How would you like that, hmm?"

"It sounds like a good opportunity." Torval wanted very much to end this conversation at once—the longer it went on, the deeper his depression grew.

"The best part is, you can probably get free sex from her anytime you want. She seems like a pretty tasty little morsel, if you can get past all those messy tattoos. Am I right?"

"Yes, sir. That is as accurate a description as any."

"I thought so." McCord flashed him a wink. "Only one more thing, just for the record. From now on, if you do any tempting or corrupting, be sure you tell me about it right away, all right? I want to be kept informed of everything you do."

"Yes, sir."

McCord kept right on talking. "Because," he said in a suddenly harsher tone, "it turns out this Christine Anderson you're hanging around with works for a legal office, and if I hadn't known you were trying to tempt her and Pete Roxton, I might've thought you might be up to something else. You do realize, of course, that if you were to betray me, that once I finished with the Roxtons, and your woman, I would come after you, Torval. Returning to Hell would not save you."

His voice suddenly rose to a level where he all but yelled in Torval's face. "You AREN'T planning anything behind my back," he demanded, "*ARE* YOU ... ?"

McCord stared at his apprentice, slate-grey eyes locked on target like powerful beams of unholy wrath. Torval shuddered and struggled to maintain control. The force of that gaze, and Mannoch's top level authority, seemed impossible to resist. He knew, though, that if he faltered here, and caved in, all would be lost.

Torval felt his will buckling. Somehow, he had to stand up to Mannoch. Flailing about for something to grab onto, his desperate mind dredged up something Pete Roxton said that very morning. Something about the way McCord indimidated others, and how it was quite often little more than a bluff.

A bluff. That's what this was. Mannoch was bluffing, trying to use the power of his intimidating stare to trick Torval into admitting something. That's all he was doing—nothing more.

"I assure you, sir," Torval heard himself say, "I am not up to anything. I cannot disobey your orders, nor do I wish to do so. In your service, I shall become a successful Tempter. That is my purpose now."

McCord nodded slowly and his angry glare swiftly morphed into a satisfied grin. "Excellent," he said in appreciation. "And you have nothing to worry about, Torval. As far as I'm concerned, you're already a successful Tempter. One day, if you keep at it, you may even become a Corruptor like me!"

"Thank you, sir," replied Torval, willing his knees to stop shaking. He felt a strange mixture of relief and despair flood through him.

"You're welcome." McCord's grin faded and he went immediately back to business. "Now, enough of that. Time for you to pick some locks!"

Chapter 15

Torval was glad to be left alone with the boxful of locks, the picks, and a set of instructions. McCord stuck him in a small storage room down the hall from his office, a place where he assured his apprentice he wouldn't be disturbed. The only light came from a single uncovered bulb overhead, shedding a weak glow on the dusty, box-filled chamber.

As soon as McCord departed, Torval started to gasp for breath, hyperventilating in a way he normally did only after climbing several flights of stairs. He knew he'd just narrowly escaped a complete disaster. There were a few seconds there when he almost broke down and blabbed everything to his superior, but somehow, he reached inside and found the strength to resist that powerful gaze.

His human body still shook and trembled, but at the time, he felt as if he'd somehow detached himself from his emotions, so the rational part of him remained completely in control. Exactly how he managed this, he didn't know, but he was glad for it. Furthermore, he now knew he could resist Mannoch, and deceive him if necessary. If nothing else, that knowledge felt empowering.

Torval still didn't understand how he resisted that terrible stare. Mannoch was a First Class demon, of that there could be no doubt, and Torval only Second Class—not even fully Advanced, at that. So how could he possibly defy his superior? Quite honestly, he should've immediately caved in. Doing otherwise shouldn't even be an option.

Did that mean he really *was* changing into an angel? If so, he'd be Transitioning right out of Mannoch's grasp. A demon wouldn't have any power over Torval if he went over to the other side. Yet wouldn't his change be recognizable by now? Mannoch still believed his subordinate was becoming a Tempter. Wouldn't he be able to tell if Torval was now part angel?

Torval shook his head dismissively. He still hadn't quite

completed half of his so-called vacation. He still didn't even know for sure what he might become. Fretting over it served no purpose.

His heartbeat finally returned to a stable level, and his breathing became normal again. Using his shirt sleeve, he wiped off the sweat from his forehead and turned to the box at his feet.

In the back of the storage closet, he found a single lonely stool, so he sat down there and pulled out the instructions. Instantly he recognized that the pages were printed from a website, for they bore a web address and looked very much like a screenshot. Apparently, McCord found these instructions somewhere on the Internet.

With nothing else to do, Torval began reading.

* * *

Picking locks wasn't all that easy. For one thing, the tools proved extremely difficult to work with. Torval's fingers didn't seem to want to cooperate when he tried one of the fine movements needed. Second, his eyesight wasn't nearly good enough for the task. He simply couldn't see if he moved his face close enough to look at the lock mechanisms. Whenever he tried, everything became blurry.

Still, he plugged away, and managed to figure out how to open a few of the simpler locks. In some cases, he simply had to insert one of the tools while twisting another, until he found the correct angle. Others could be opened by using a rod containing several adjustable teeth. One lock in particular could be fooled by using a special implement that shifted its shape to fill in recesses within the mechanism.

The others refused to cooperate, despite Torval's best efforts. Furthermore, to his dismay, the hour was getting late. He needed to depart so he could meet Christine.

Perhaps it's time to face McCord again, he decided, getting up off the stool and opening the door. His buttocks were by now quite sore from sitting on a metal stool, and he had to steady himself for a moment before proceeding. He left the locks behind as he moved down the hall, and when he came to McCord's office, he found to his surprise that the lieutenant wasn't even there.

He glanced around, but didn't see anyone he recognized. There were a few other police about, and they paid him no mind, save for one man who seemed to be studying him closely. Torval decided he should ask before simply leaving without a word, and approached the uniformed officer submissively.

"Can I help you?" said the man, who wore a nametag with the word "Sheffield" on it.

"I am looking for Lieutenant McCord," replied Torval. "He gave me a task and I believe I have completed it to the best of my ability."

"Yeah, you're Joe Sampson, right?" Seeing Torval's nod, Sheffield went on immediately. "He had to take off—something important came up, he said, and he didn't want to bug you."

"I see," replied the demon, mildly irritated that he'd been left to his own devices without explanation, but that seemed the way McCord operated. "Very well, then, I shall depart. The items he left for me are still in the storage room."

"Sure, whatever," said Sheffield with a shrug. "I'll tell him next time I see him, not that I expect him to give a rat's ass."

"What does that mean?" inquired Torval, having never heard that particular, and very odd, expression.

"It means half the people around here don't know what the lieutenant is up to, and the other half only *think* they do. Anyway, you have a nice evening, Joe."

Torval nodded, and didn't miss the note of hostility in the policeman's voice. Apparently, McCord was something of an enigma to the ordinary cops around the station.

"Very well," Torval replied, turning to leave. "If at all possible, I shall do just that."

* * *

Christine was already waiting at the shelter, but she didn't seem to be bothered by the fact that Torval was almost ten minutes late. She occupied a table in the back, chatting amiably with Prelz. The two seemed to be getting along quite well.

"Ah, about time you get here," commented the ex-Tempter as Torval approached. "Busy day, I suppose?"

"I apologize," replied Torval. "I was placed in a small room and forced to pick locks all afternoon."

Prelz blinked. "You know, sometimes I don't know if you're really serious or you're just jerking me around."

Christine giggled. "No, I think he means it," she told him. "McCord really made you learn lockpicking?"

"Yes. However, I am not very good at it. I could only unlock seven of the several dozen locks in the box, even though I worked all day. My eyes could not focus on the small surfaces, nor could these human fingers remain steady enough to do such detailed work."

"Damn, there goes my plan to have you help me crack some safes," chuckled Prelz. "No, don't worry, I'm just kidding! Anyway, your girlfriend here was telling me she had some good news, but wanted to wait till you got here to spill it. So he's here, babe. Spill!"

Christine rolled her eyes and grinned. "Fine, fine, and stop calling me 'babe'!" She exchanged laughs with Prelz and then went on. "Okay, here's the thing. I got hold of the man I know in Internal Affairs. He wants to meet with the Roxtons tomorrow morning. Isn't that wonderful?"

Torval nodded. "I am pleased," he replied, "but there is always the danger the Roxtons will not wish to cooperate."

"I think they will," said Christine hopefully. "I'd like to be there, actually, so I can work my redemption mojo. You can help too, Joe. I'm not so sure Pete will want to listen to me, but I have to try."

"I agree, you should be there," said Torval. "I believe if the two of you exchange apologies, all will be well. In any case, there is another issue. McCord knew you and I had lunch today, because he had me followed. He knows about you—not who you really are, but that you and I are dating. He also has apparently checked up on you, and knows you work for a legal firm."

Christine looked horrified. "What? How dare he spy on me! The nerve of that man—and I use the term loosely! How *dare* he!"

"That could be a real problem," put in Prelz. "If you show up at the Roxton place tomorrow to meet Joe, I doubt he'd care, but if you arrive with some unknown guy, and he's watching ... "

"Yeah, yeah, I see what you're saying." Christine shook her head. "What a mess! I'll have to tell Norm to arrive separately, so he looks like any other customer."

"Norm?" inquired Torval.

"Yes, his name is Norm Campbell. He's a police officer, but he won't be in uniform. He'll be dressed casually. He told me that

Lieutenant McCord is someone on IA's watch list, but so far they don't have any real evidence against him. If the Roxtons cooperate, and are willing to testify, it'll help fill in the gaps. Like I figured, though, he's going to need some real evidence."

"I will tell the Roxtons," replied Torval. "What time will this meeting be?"

"When you get up," replied Christine, reaching into her purse. "Here's his card, so when you and the Roxtons are ready, just call him. He already knows where the warehouse is, or so he tells me. Oh, by the way, that reminds me—didn't you say you had a cell phone?"

"Yes, I do." Torval reached into his pocket and pulled out the little box, which drew a raised eyebrow from Prelz.

"Good. Here, enter my number, so you can call me if you ever need to. Ready?"

Torval nodded and opened the flap. After working the controls a bit, he got to the screen where he could enter a new contact. Christine then read off her numbers, and he dutifully entered them in.

As soon as he finished with that, he recalled he had another phone number as well, on a card he'd placed in his wallet. He removed the business card and entered the information there as well. "What's that?" asked Christine curiously.

"This is the number where I can reach Hal Sommersby," explained Torval as he finished his task and put the phone away.

"Oh? You should call him sometime, see how he's doing," suggested Christine.

"Perhaps I will," said Torval, "but not now."

Christine nodded, and then her face brightened considerably. "Oh, I forgot to tell you the best part about coming to meet with you tomorrow!"

"What is that?" Torval stopped for a second, and then realized what it must be. "You are missing work?"

"Not just that," she replied happily. "I took the day off. We can spend the whole day together!"

* * *

The prospect of spending the day with Christine brightened Torval's mood immensely. In fact, he managed to almost forget about his troubles with McCord and the Roxtons throughout dinner.

Christine told him that since he'd picked the restaurant last night, it was her turn to decide, which seemed only fair. She selected a place called "Adam's Rib" that was known for its excellent meat dishes, particularly steaks and something called "barbecued ribs." Torval thought the name of the establishment sounded rather odd, considering it referred to a story out of the Bible, but he gave it a try.

As it turned out, barbecued ribs were indeed quite tasty. They were, like fried chicken, meat eaten directly from the bones. He could dip them in any of several types of sauces, ranging from a rich tangy flavor to so spicy that he had to follow up each bite with several gulps of soda.

He and Christine spent the evening just chatting and enjoying each other's company. They observed something of an unspoken agreement not to bring up Mannoch or the troubles he caused, and that was just as well. That subject would've just depressed Torval, and he didn't want to feel that way. Not around Christine.

This particular restaurant wasn't all that close, so they had to take a cab back to the warehouse, so Torval wouldn't be late for work. He didn't really want the night to end, even though he knew it had to. He could easily have spent the rest of the evening with her, talking and getting to know her better, sharing the sort of experiences that few other beings would even begin to comprehend. Fortunately, he had all day tomorrow to look forward to.

This time, when they kissed goodnight, they lingered a while, holding each other, enjoying the feeling of closeness that came with physical contact. Torval wished he could hold her far longer, but he knew he had to get to work, so he reluctantly waved goodbye as she climbed into the vehicle and drove away.

The time has come to face the Roxtons, he realized, walking up the steps to the building and hesitating a moment. He'd managed to avoid thinking about this all night, but now there was no more avoiding the issue. Pushing aside the pleasant memory of Christine's lips on his, he stepped inside.

"Right on time again," said Pete as he entered. "And another date with Christine, I see. You two must be getting pretty close."

"Yes," agreed Torval, remembering then that he probably should've wiped off any leftover lipstick. He looked around until he found a napkin and took care of the problem. "Is Lincoln here? I must speak with the two of you about a serious issue."

"Sure, he's in back, sorting some stuff," replied Pete. "Come on, I'll show you."

Torval followed him deeper into the warehouse, where the elder Roxton stood amidst a collection of small boxes, holding a pen and notepad in one hand. He wore a pair of glasses that Torval hadn't seen him use before.

"Oh, hey, Joe," said Lincoln. "What's up? Don't tell me, McCord is harassing you again?"

"I suppose that is accurate," replied Torval. "There is something we must discuss. I believe there may be a way for you to escape the influence of Lieutenant McCord."

The two Roxtons exchanged glances, and Lincoln lowered the notepad and removed the glasses. When he took them off, they dangled over his chest on a silver chain. "What's going on?" he asked.

"Yeah, don't keep us in suspense ... again," Pete agreed.

Torval sucked in a breath. "This may be difficult to hear, but I must tell you. Earlier today, I heard McCord say that if you continued your attempts to free yourself from his control, he would be forced to kill you both."

Neither Roxton said anything, but their faces went pale. Lincoln turned away and started to pace about, chewing on a fingernail, and emitting something that sounded like a moan. Pete remained a bit more stable, but still looked quite distraught.

"I cannot permit this to happen," went on Torval. "Therefore, I spoke with someone I knew could help. As a result, a meeting has been arranged with a policeman from Internal Affairs. If you can provide him evidence that proves McCord's wrongdoing, they will see to it he is arrested, and you will be safe."

Lincoln still didn't say anything. Instead, he just sort of kept walking into the darkened area of the inactive warehouse. As he faded into the gloom, Pete shook his head. "Joe," he replied slowly, "I—we, I mean—appreciate that, but I don't know if we can."

"You must try," said Torval. "This may be your only chance to escape McCord's control."

"We've thought about it before," went on Pete. "Don't think we haven't! What if the Internal Affairs guy just turns out to be one of McCord's flunkies? What if he doesn't help, and McCord finds out? Or worse, what if he does get arrested—what happens to us then? They come after us, that's what, as soon as McCord spills his guts to the cops. We've done things—things we're not very proud of, Joe. Things that would land us both in jail if the truth came out."

"That no longer matters," replied Torval. "McCord will not permit you to leave his service of your own volition. If this goes on much longer, he will simply execute you, and continue doing what he's doing now."

"I don't know," sighed Pete after a long pause. "I just don't know."

At that point, Lincoln emerged from the darkness, still shaking his head. He shuffled forward, hands at his sides, the notepad now noticeably absent. After a moment he put his arm on Pete's shoulder, and looked up at him with a strange, almost pleading expression.

"Joe's right," he said slowly. "We have to do this, Pete. We have no choice. This has gone on far too long. It's time to put an end to it."

"But, Grandpa, what if—"

"I don't care." Lincoln turned away. "I'm an old man, Pete. You shouldn't have to go through this. I'll tell them it was all my idea, and you can have your life back."

"No, you won't!" Pete argued. "I won't let you! I'm the one who got us into this. I should take the rap. Besides, it's better than dying."

"And a lot better than doing that man's bidding anymore." Lincoln hung his head sadly. "How did we let this happen? How did we fall so far? I should've just let the business fold. It's as much my fault as it is yours, Pete. Don't go blaming yourself."

"This is not about blame," Torval interjected. "This is about redeeming yourselves."

Lincoln nodded. "Yeah, I suppose it is."

"Then it is settled," said Torval, grateful they'd made the right choice. "Tomorrow morning, I will call the policeman and he will come here to speak to you. There is one other thing, however. Something I failed to mention."

"What?" asked Lincoln.

"The person I spoke to, in order to arrange this," replied Torval, "is Christine Anderson. I hope this does not cause any additional problems."

Lincoln looked at his grandson, who emitted a heavy sigh. "No," he replied after a moment. "No, I suppose that makes sense. Someone like her, she'd know some cops, wouldn't she? And someone like her wouldn't have anything to do with an asshole like Jonas McCord. Fine, I can handle that."

"Good," replied Torval. "Then in that case, awaken me tomorrow when you are ready, and I will make the call."

"Will do," replied Lincoln. "Oh, and Joe, one other thing."

"What is it?"

"Thank you," he replied, smiling. "Thanks for doing this. You didn't have to go this far for us. It means a lot."

Torval smiled. "You are welcome," he said, and for the first time, he felt like he understood what that phrase really meant.

Chapter 16

Torval worked off and on the rest of the night, alternating data entry and surfing the Internet when typing in receipts became too boring. This turned out to be quite frequently, in fact. He really didn't like data entry very much, but fortunately, he didn't have to do that much of it.

Just after one o'clock, about an hour after having a cold ham and cheese sandwich from the refrigerator, he decided to go to bed. This time, he tried mastering the hammock, which so far had vexed him at every turn. With a little perseverance, he finally managed to get into the webbing without falling out, and once he figured out how to shift his weight around without toppling over, he found it very comfortable. He fell asleep quickly thereafter.

The next morning, at just after nine, the Roxtons woke him up. To his surprise, he hadn't fallen out of the hammock during the night. For the first time since coming to the warehouse, his bones didn't feel stiff and sore when he stood up. Nonetheless, the shower felt just as invigorating as always, although he forced himself to cut the session short, since Pete and Lincoln were waiting on him upstairs.

Before finishing in the basement, he took out his phone and called the number Christine gave him yesterday. "Hello?" a man's voice, deep and throaty, answered on the second ring.

"Hello," replied Torval. "This is Joe Sampson. I was told to call you this morning."

"Yes, I've been waiting for the call," came the reply. "This is Norm Campbell, just in case Christine didn't give you my name. I'm actually just down the street, having a bit of breakfast. I can be there in five minutes."

"Good," replied Torval. "That will give me time to finish preparing for the meeting."

"Cool, see you then."

The man hung up, and after finishing getting dressed, Torval made his way upstairs.

* * *

"Hello? Anyone here?"

Norm Campbell's deep baritone echoed through the foyer. Torval stepped out of the break room toward the warehouse entrance. "We are back here," he called out.

"Ah, right." The man stepped into view a moment later. He was of medium build, with short brown hair, a well-trimmed mustache, and a hawklike nose that looked just slightly too big for his face. He wore a long-sleeved blue-and-green checkered shirt, a pair of navy blue slacks, and black shoes. He didn't look much like a policeman at all, although he certainly spoke like one.

"Hello, you must be Norm," said Lincoln, stepping forward to shake the man's hand. "I'm Lincoln Roxton, and this is my grandson, Pete. I'm sure you know Joe."

"Actually, I don't," answered Norm, exchanging handshakes with everyone in the room, including Torval. This at least proved he wasn't in fact an angel in disguise, which seemed like a definite possiblity. "He and I haven't met before. Christine called me herself. Speaking of which, that's probably her now."

They could all plainly hear the door open up, and Christine's voice called out a moment later. "Joe?"

"Back here," replied Torval. "Join us."

She appeared a moment later, dressed in a dark green pantsuit, wearing a blue scarf and wide leather belt. Her chocolate-brown hair hung loosely about her shoulders and she looked, as usual, fantastic.

"Ah, good, I'm last to arrive," she said with a smile. "I hope you all weren't waiting?"

"No, I just got here," said Norm. "We were just going through the introductions."

"Before we start," said Pete, stepping forward slightly, "I'd just like to say something. Christine, I know things didn't go very well between us, and I admit it's my fault, so I hope you'll accept my apology."

She smiled and nodded. "I had my own part in that too," she

told him. "Let's just forget it, shall we? We've got far more important matters to focus on, don't you think?"

"Definitely." Pete stepped back and resumed leaning against the table, obviously glad that bit of unpleasantness was over. "Honestly, I can't believe you're even thinking about helping us, the way I treated you, but I must say I really appreciate it."

"I'm just happy to help," Christine replied, still smiling, and looking perhaps a bit uncomfortable from all the praise.

"Okay, then," Norm interrupted before things could become any more awkward. "Let's get this started. I think we can keep this brief. First, let me explain that we've been hearing things about Jonas McCord for a while now, but nobody's been willing to come forward with any real evidence. He's rather powerful and has a lot of friends, so we aren't going to make any moves without anything very specific. Unfortunately, the last few times people tried to turn him in, they met with very messy ends. Not trying to scare you here—I'm just letting you know, we're going to take whatever steps we can to keep you safe. That's why I'm having this interview here, in plain clothes, arriving as if I'm a customer of yours. In fact, if you were to let me leave with a car part or two, anyone who might be watching this place wouldn't think anything unusual happened."

"Sure, we can do that," replied Pete. "I'll grab an old alternator or something from the recycle bin."

"All right, good." Norm nodded appreciatively. "Now, the next thing is, I was told you were willing to cooperate, but not whether you had any evidence to help our investigation. If you do have any, I urge you to consider turning it over in—"

"There's nothing to consider." Lincoln took a few steps, over to a briefcase leaning against the refrigerator. Torval hadn't noticed the black case sitting there until now. "Last night, after Joe here told us what was going on, I spent some time collecting what we have. You'll find everything in here—receipts, log files, contact names, everything we could think of. I'd intended to use this stuff as insurance once we'd paid the loans, just to make sure McCord left us alone, but now I think it's better off in your hands."

Norm opened up the briefcase and flipped through the pages therein. "This looks quite comprehensive," he said after a moment, smiling, and perhaps looking a bit excited. "I appreciate your trusting me, seeing as how I could be working with McCord for all you know."

"Well, I thought about that," admitted Pete, "but I don't think you are. If you were, I doubt you'd bother coming—he already would've dealt with us some other way, without wasting any more time. Besides, we're screwed anyway, so there's no point in worrying about it."

Norm nodded. "I won't ask for details, but I assume you've done some things for McCord that would get you in a spot of trouble if the truth came out."

"Yeah, you could say that," admitted Pete. "It's all in there, unfortunately, but Grandpa and I already decided to hand it over and let the chips fall where they may."

"Well," said the policeman in a tone that suggested he completely understood, "I can't promise anything, but if nothing else, you did those things under duress. I'm sure I could convince the judge to take that into account."

"That'd be great," said Pete resignedly, "but you know, I don't even care about that. I just want this over."

"Me, too," agreed Lincoln. "I think it's a given that we've lost the business at this point, at the very least, but that really happened a long time ago. Trying to prolong it was our real mistake."

"I'm really sorry I got you into this," said Pete sadly. "I wish I hadn't—"

"It's water under the bridge," interrupted Lincoln. "What's important is we're doing the right thing now."

"That we are," his grandson agreed. "That we are."

Norm nodded at that, obviously understanding what they were going through. Perhaps he'd seen this sort of thing before. "Well, let me take this back to my department, and we'll see what we can do," he said in a soothing tone, closing the briefcase and holding it at his side. "Honestly, with the amount of information here, we could be able to move on McCord sooner rather than later. As soon as we do, we'll contact you, so you can stop looking over your shoulder. In the meantime, just continue doing what you've been doing. That means *all* of you. I'll be in touch."

"Thanks," replied Lincoln. "We really appreciate it."

"Glad to be of service." Norm nodded in their direction one last time, turned, and headed out of the building. Pete followed him out, making sure he had a spare car part to complete his "satisfied customer" cover story. After that, the younger Roxton returned to the room, taking a deep breath and sighing.

"You know something?" he asked after a moment, breaking the silence that seemed to have settled over the little group. "I feel really, really good. The best I've felt in years, in fact."

"Me too," agreed Lincoln. "It sounds like a cliché, but I really do feel like a great weight has been lifted off my shoulders."

"The only thing that worries me," put in Torval, "is if he does turn out to be on McCord's side. You just gave him all that evidence, and it is everything he wanted me to steal."

"Yeah, well, we thought of that," said Pete with a shrug and a smile. "We're not complete idiots, y'know. There's copies of all that stuff in a safety deposit box at the bank. We put it all in there this morning, before we woke you up."

"Yep," replied Lincoln, mirroring his grandson's grin. "If anything happens to us, at least there's another chance to bring down McCord."

* * *

Torval intended to eat breakfast at the warehouse as he usually did, but Christine saw him reaching for a donut and stopped him. She had other plans for dining that morning, and after they bid goodbye to the Roxtons, she explained why. Apparently she wanted to get to some kind of guided tour, and food would be provided along the way.

Once they left the building, Christine hailed a cab and directed the driver to head for one of the city's piers. "What are we doing that requires a pier?" Torval inquired curiously, once the vehicle started moving and he'd strapped himself in. He still didn't feel completely safe in a car, but at least the seatbelt provided an illusion of security.

"You'll see," replied Christine with a mysterious smile. "You want it to be a surprise, don't you?"

"I am not used to surprises," said Torval, "but I will wait, if you want me to."

She chuckled. "Anticipation adds to the appeal. Anyway, how much of New York City have you seen since you arrived? Any of it at all, or have you been stuck in the middle?"

"I have taken the subway to several locations," replied Torval, "but that is all. Jake suggested on several occasions that I see more of the city, but I have not been able to do so."

"Well, now's the time." Christine slapped him on the knee playfully. "Time to see New York in all its majesty. I think you'll be amazed. I know I was the first time I got a good view."

"I have read about the city," replied Torval, "and I know that it occupies a large island. There are some landmarks I could name, but that is all."

"When I first arrived," Christine explained with a faraway look in her eyes, "I thought the buildings went on and on forever. Central Park seemed like a leftover, a museum piece of what the world was like before humans built skyscrapers everywhere. It's actually quite the opposite, although you wouldn't know it looking out these windows. Someday I should take you out to the country, so you can see what I mean, but not today. We don't have that kind of time."

"We have all day," corrected Torval. "I need not report to work until eight o'clock this evening."

"Well, I've got something scheduled for pretty much everything in between," Christine told him, again smiling mysteriously. "I'm going to be your tour guide today, Joe. You're going to see some of the best New York has to offer. I've got it all planned out."

"And you are not going to tell me of your plans," replied Torval, "because they are a surprise."

"Exactly!"

Torval nodded, returning her smile. "Then I am looking forward to your secret tour. It should be quite interesting."

"Yes, it will," she agreed. "Now sit back and enjoy the ride."

* * *

The first thing they did, as it turned out, was take a harbor cruise. The boats left every hour from the pier, so after purchasing tickets, they had a bit of waiting to do. They used the intervening time to visit a nearby coffee shop for a quick breakfast. Torval enjoyed a buttermilk waffle with maple syrup, which had a taste sweeter than anything he'd ever tried before. Nonetheless, it was quite enjoyable, though not particularly filling. Christine advised him that lunch wasn't that far off, so he chose not to order anything else.

The cruise took place aboard a yellow double-decker boat that superficially resembled the ferry Torval rode on his way across the Styx with Geezon. That rickety craft was steam-powered, while the more modern one used a much quieter means of locomotion unknown to Torval. Presumably a motor of some kind, like cars and buses used, but nonetheless a mystery.

The cruise ship also moved much faster than the Styx ferry, so much so that it whipped the wind through Torval's hair and left him somewhat chilly, despite the brisk spring air. He and Christine spent most of the trip inside the fully enclosed lower deck. Fortunately, the ship wasn't terribly crowded, seeing as the tourist season wasn't yet in full swing, so they had plenty of space to themselves.

Throughout the cruise, which lasted a couple of hours, a voice over the loudspeakers continually described points of interest and historical facts about the sights visible through the windows. Torval listened to these as best he could, but much of what they said made little sense, or discussed events long past that meant nothing to him.

At first, when they set out, Torval thought the harbor wasn't that large, but once out on the choppy water, he suddenly could see the entire city in all its glory. What he saw took his breath away. As far as he could see, from one side of the view to the other, nothing but buildings lined the edge of the water. Apparently the humans decided that this island (which he now could finally see as such) provided a perfect location for stacking massive buildings, and they left not a single space untouched. If they didn't need roads to get around, thought Torval, perhaps the entire island would've been covered with a single gigantic structure stretching for miles in all directions.

In the midst of the harbor sat a small island dominated by a tall green statue of a woman in robes, holding a golden torch above her head. "What is that?" inquired Torval as he spotted it for the first time. "A sculpture of some kind, or a monument to someone important who perished on this spot?"

"Just listen," said Christine, pointing at one of the speakers in the wall above. "They'll tell you. It's very interesting."

He listened while the voice explained Ellis Island's original purpose, and where the Statue of Liberty came from. A gift from another nation, it seemed, now seen as a symbol of freedom all over the world. Immigrants to this country would see this place first when they arrived after a long journey across the sea. Apparently, coming to the United States gave the new arrivals a chance at a fresh start in life.

Torval nodded as the explanation concluded. "This reminds me somewhat of myself," he said after contemplating the statue for a few moments. "I, too, came here to gain a fresh start, though I did not know it at the time. My life as I know it has changed completely. When I return, I will be a different person, and I will undertake a new task on a permanent basis."

"Does that worry you?" Christine asked, putting a hand on his shoulder.

"Yes, somewhat." Torval sighed. "I have not had much time to consider it, but yes, I am concerned. What bothers me most is that I do not yet know what my purpose will be."

"Do you still think you might become an angel?"

"I don't think so, although that fate does not worry me as much as it did before. If I were becoming an angel, I think it would be obvious by now. Take my hand, Christine, and tell me if I look angelic in any way."

She complied, and immediately took on her faintly glowing, heavenly appearance. Torval waited, watching her reaction, and all she did was smile. "You're right, I still see a demon," she told him after a moment, reaching up to run a hand across his head. To him, it felt like she caressed his hair, but she apparently saw something else entirely. "Your horns are close to your skull, curving back and then wrapping forward a bit, over your ears. You have hair, too, in between them, but it's not that long. I don't remember you having hair before."

"I did not," he told her. "I was completely bald, and that includes my entire body as well."

"You actually look more human than demon now," Christine went on. "Your face isn't nearly as bony as I remember. Open your mouth."

He did, and she looked at his teeth. "The incisors are a bit long, but not that sharp. You don't look that dangerous, really. I doubt you'd scare anybody, except for the horns and those red eyes of yours. Even your skin looks more like a human's than it used to. It's not so pale anymore, although I guess that could've been a trick of the light."

Torval considered her descriptive words for a moment. "Do you suppose I could be transforming into a human, then?"

Christine shook her head in the negative. "I don't see how that's possible. You said your friend had to deliberately choose to be human, right? Besides, your horns are pretty prominent for a human head."

"I wonder," Torval went on, still pondering the situation. "Prelz told me he chose to become human, but do you suppose it was more than that? What if he began to Advance, but because of his experiences here, the only path he could take was toward humanity?"

Christine considered that for a moment. "I don't think so, but who knows? He would've been moving up to First Class, right? That seems like a pretty radical shift."

"Unless he directed it that way himself, by his own desire to experience mortality. Would it be possible, then, to force a change on yourself? To Advance to a human form because that is what you yourself most wished to happen?"

"If it is," replied Christine, "then what's the difference? Whether he did it by Advancement or not, Prelz is Jake now, a human, and there's no way to undo that. It doesn't really matter either way."

"No, I suppose not," replied Torval with a shrug.

"Anyway," Christine went on, "let's not bother ourselves with that sort of thing, okay? Let's enjoy the rest of the cruise. See? Look up there, that's the Brooklyn Bridge."

Torval peered out the window again, this time taking in the sight of an impressive structure of metal that crossed the water, connecting two sections of land together in such a way that cars and other vehicles could travel across unimpeded. Another amazing feat of engineering, he realized, shaking his head at the ingenuity these humans had. No wonder the Creator gave them dominion over the Earth—demons could never come up with something like this.

The rest of the cruise was just as spectacular, and after a while he found himself overwhelmed. He sat down on one of the benches along the side of the boat, and Christine joined him. They spent the rest of the ride leaning against each other, just enjoying each other's company.

Once again, he experienced that pleasant emotion of happiness, and at least this time, it lingered quite a bit longer.

Chapter 17

Christine wasn't finished wowing him with the sights and sounds of New York City, either. In fact, she was just getting started.

After the harbor cruise, they stopped at an Italian restaurant and dined on a thick-crust pizza of a type known as "Chicago style." Torval didn't know what that meant, but Christine told him he'd like it, letting it be another surprise for him to look forward to. The wait was worth it, as it turned out. The chewy, cheese-covered crust, packed tightly with meat and thick-cut tomatoes, tasted far better than any other pizza he'd yet tried. This was, as might be expected, reflected in the price, but Torval didn't mind at all. He attempted to pay, but Christine insisted they split the bill, which turned out to be pretty much standard procedure for the day.

After lunch, they went to a special skyscraper called the Empire State Building, at one time the tallest in the world. Torval expected they would simply tour some historical display on the lower floors, but instead, Christine led him into a small room with a wall covered in buttons. He'd encountered chambers like this in her office building, and had seen people entering and exiting with some haste, but didn't know the reason for it. Now he found out.

Christine pressed one of the buttons, and the room began to shake. Torval felt slightly queasy, and for an instant he thought he might be falling. "What is happening?" he asked worriedly.

"It's an elevator," replied Christine. "Don't tell me you've never been in one before!"

"I have not," Torval replied, a bit grateful that no one else shared that little room with them. "Why are my ears starting to hurt?"

"Just flex your jaw," she told him, demonstrating the procedure. "We're going up real fast. The number up there is the floor we're on."

"You mean," replied Torval, "that each number is the equivalent of a flight of stairs?"

She nodded, smiling. "Pretty amazing, huh?"

"Yes," he replied. "I am glad we are not climbing them, or I would be quite exhausted by now."

"You and me both!"

The elevator came to a stop, and they exited, only to get into another of the same type of rooms, whereupon the journey up continued. "Why did the first one not go all the way?" asked Torval, still working his lower jaw to try to pop his ears completely.

"I have no idea," Christine answered with a shrug. "Maybe it was too far for one elevator? This thing was built what, fifty years ago or more? I don't remember exactly, but elevators hadn't been around all that long. In fact, they needed elevators to make buildings like this even feasible. Before that, nobody could build anything taller than maybe ten or twenty stories."

"So the humans invented elevators," Torval supposed. "How do they do such things? Demons are as intelligent as people, yet we have never created anything on our own, as far as I know."

"Well," replied Christine, "there's an awful lot more humans than demons or angels, I can tell you that. Besides which, remember, we don't really need for anything, do we? Humans have to feed themselves, clothe themselves, and improve their lives. Every invention they've ever come up with came out of a desire to do one of those things. Oh, except for weapons, of course, which were used to improve oneself at the expense of others."

"So what you are saying, then, is that demons do not invent anything because we have no need to do so?"

"Exactly." Christine nodded vigorously. "Humans have a saying—'necessity is the mother of invention.' It's very true, when you think about it. I wonder if the Creator had any idea what they would come up with when He put them here?"

"Perhaps He did not," replied Torval. "That, at least, might partially explain why He gave the Earth to them. If everything they invent builds upon itself, who knows what they might yet be capable of?"

"It'll be hard to top what you're about to see," said Christine mysteriously. "Where we're going right now is the observation deck of this building. You'll be able to see the entire city from here, and all I have to say is: try not to faint."

The elevator doors opened, and they had to pay a small fee to reach the observation area, but the price was quickly forgotten. What Torval saw when he stepped outside, into the windswept overlook, was nothing short of breathtaking.

The city stretched out before him in every direction. Buildings, some taller than this one, but most not, seemed to stretch to the horizon. To either side, he could see water, and even the island with the odd green statue that now looked very, very small indeed. At the extreme limits of his vision, he saw bridges connecting the island of Manhattan to the other boroughs.

To get an idea of the scale, all he had to do was look down. There, just barely visible on the streets, were tiny colored rectangles moving about. He realized these were cars, and the far smaller dots nearby were human beings. Everything was so far away, the city looked like nothing more than a complex miniature diorama.

"Remember to breathe," cautioned a grinning Christine from somewhere nearby.

Torval nodded slowly, but didn't even look at her, hypnotized by the view. As he studied the streets and structures, he found himself occasionally spotting familiar places, such as the distinctive design of Rockefeller Center. Using that landmark as a starting point, he managed to locate what he thought must be the Roxton warehouse, though he couldn't be entirely sure. The place was simply too far away, the view obscured by nearby skyscrapers.

He spent nearly twenty minutes wandering around the observation deck, peering through the bars at the amazing sight below. Christine showed him how to use one of the coin-operated telescopes, which he used until its time ran out completely. Looking at the city from above fascinated him in a way he didn't realize could be possible. The place was so massive, so seemingly endless, that to suddenly take it all in at once was overwhelming.

"I remember the first time I came up here," Christine finally said, interrupting his thoughts with a casual hug. "I thought it looked like humans built their own Heaven right here on this island. Everything looks so peaceful and perfect when you look on it from above. Of course, it really isn't, but it's a good enough illusion, don't you think?"

"I agree," replied Torval, nodding. "This is the most spectacular thing I have ever seen. Nothing in all my existence could've prepared me for this."

"This city," Christine pointed out, "has millions of people living in it. *Millions*. Can you even grasp how many humans that really is?"

"I have thought about that before," he admitted, "and no, I cannot."

"And this is just a single city, Joe. There are *hundreds* of cities on Earth. Not all are this big, but you get the picture. There are far more humans than you or I can really understand. We're just tiny little cogs in the Creator's vast universe, you know. Seeing something like this just puts all of that in perspective."

"That may be so," Torval commented, "but we are still important. We have our jobs to do."

"Yes, we do," agreed Christine, "but not right now. This is a day off for both of us, Joe. When they sent you here, they said you were on vacation, didn't they?"

"Yes, but as I have since learned, that isn't exactly true."

"Well," she replied with a smile, hugging him more closely this time, "it is today."

At that, she reached up and kissed him, and for a little while he managed to forget about the view.

* * *

After the Empire State Building, Christine led him a few blocks over to the park, where they spent a while just wandering amidst the budding trees and newly planted flowers. The tours were indeed impressive, and Torval was glad he'd taken them, but quite honestly he felt happier just walking alongside Christine, holding hands and sharing the afternoon.

There seemed to be people everywhere, some just strolling or picknicking on the lawns, while others were exercising, playing with pets, or sunning themselves. Some threw a brightly colored disc around, which baffled Torval until Christine explained it was nothing more than a game.

Further on they found a small band playing steel-drum music, singing with the beat in a kind of half-speaking manner that seemed strange, but nonetheless intriguing. Torval had to wonder how they could possibly say the words that quickly, while remaining in time with the sounds from their odd instruments, but he supposed such coordination came with practice.

After that they took a paddleboat ride out onto a pond, a practice that seemed pointless to Torval until they stopped and began to drift. At that point the trip's true purpose became obvious, as the setting felt quite soothing. In fact, it seemed remarkably intimate, despite the presence of other humans walking around the lake just a short distance away. Nonetheless, he found Christine's nearness irresistible, and soon they were kissing again, alone in the heart of the city.

Eventually they had to catch their breaths, and simply sagged together in each other's arms. She sighed contentedly, clinging to him, and he felt happier than he ever thought possible.

This is what I want, Torval realized now. *This is what it's all about, isn't it?* Of all the emotions he'd felt in all the time he'd spent on Earth, this was the one he'd been searching for all along, without even realizing it.

"Christine," he asked quietly, "is this love?"

She looked back at him with eyes of purest gold. There was a very long wait before she replied.

"I don't know," she admitted slowly, "but I think so. I honestly hope so."

"If it isn't," he told her, "I do not know what else it could be."

"I've been trying so hard to find love," she replied, "but searching for it was all wrong. I should've just let it find me, like you did. Oh, Torval! How can I be in love with a demon?"

"Or I an angel?" He sighed and touched her radiant face, if only for a moment. "It doesn't seem possible, and yet, here we are. Are you not still concerned that you will get into trouble?"

She waved a hand casually, as if to dismiss that thought. "I don't care. I really don't. They can do whatever they like to me, and it won't matter. It's worth it, just to be with you now, just to feel like this."

"I have to agree." Torval leaned up even closer, kissing her again, if only briefly. "I wish this never had to end, and yet I fear it must. In a week, I will have to go. What will happen to us then?"

"We'll move on," she told him, shaking her head. "Something else the humans like to say—'it's better to have loved and lost, than to not have loved at all.'"

"Sometimes what humans say is very strange," remarked Torval, "and other times, it is the voice of wisdom."

"That's true, but please, let's not talk about you leaving, okay? That's too depressing, and I'm too happy to be depressed right now.

Let's look at it this way—I still have seven more days to be with you. I want to make the most of them."

"As do I," he agreed.

"In that case, let's head back to shore." She sat up and started to slowly pedal, causing the paddleboat to slowly make its way across the pond. "Seeing as you like food so much, I've got one more surprise for you."

"Will you at least give me a hint this time?"

"Sure," she replied, grinning. "I'm going to cook you dinner!"

* * *

So far, every meal Torval enjoyed on Earth had been crafted either at a restaurant or at the soup kitchen. In every case, the process was a mystery, taking place behind closed doors, or inside some machine or other. Now, for the first time, he got a look at how food was actually made.

Christine had obviously prepared in advance, for she had most of the ingredients ready. She proceeded to create a meal called "chicken tetrazzini," which required a number of ingredients Torval already knew he liked. Among these were chicken (obviously), as well as cheese, mushrooms, tomatoes, and peppers (which he'd tried on pizza), and a kind of boiled pasta called "spaghetti." All of this was mixed together over heat, and then baked inside a device called an "oven" that apparently became so hot inside that touching the interior would result in painful burns.

Along with the main course, Christine also prepared a side dish of rice pilaf, as well as a mixture of leafy and chopped vegetables referred to en masse as a "salad." Finally, she concluded the impressive array of food with a dessert made of a vanilla-flavored pudding covered in a hard, crunchy crust.

The meal took at least an hour to cook, during which time Torval hovered over Christine, asking so many questions that she finally threw him out of the kitchen. He had to watch from across the room, helping here and there, and amusing her in his pitiful attempts to set the table.

When they finally did eat, the food was by far the best he'd ever tasted, even exceeding the level of the delectable seafood at the Lobster

Bistro. Clearly, preparing dinner by hand made all the difference, and once he was finished with the dessert, Torval said as much.

"Oh, Joe, you say the sweetest things," Christine replied with a smile. "You really mean it, don't you?"

"Of course I do," he replied with a shrug. "Taste is one of my favorite sensations, and this is by far my best experience with it since arriving on Earth."

"Well, I appreciate it. I worked hard on that." She sighed. "I wish I could cook like that all the time, but I'm usually so busy, I don't get the chance."

"I certainly wouldn't mind if you cooked like that as frequently as possible," he agreed readily. "Now that I have seen something of the process, I believe I could be helpful in assisting you."

"You can be more helpful if you wash the dishes later," she said with a laugh. "You've never done that, have you?"

"No, I have not, but there was someone in a cell on my route who washed them in scalding hot water, as punishment for treating others with cruelty during life."

"Well, that's fine, but you don't have to scald yourself. Just turn the heat up a little bit, or the dishes won't get clean."

"I understand." Torval nodded in agreement. "Cleaning up after this meal seems like an acceptable way to repay you for your efforts. Shall I begin at once?"

"No, it can wait," she replied, suddenly concerned about something. She stood, set down her napkin, and stepped over into the main part of her apartment. "Joe, there's something I want to ask you. I've been thinking about it since—well, since the other day. I want you to answer me honestly on this, okay?"

He stood, sensing something important in the air, and approached with caution. "Certainly," he told her. "I see no reason to lie to you, Christine."

"Good." She lowered her head and looked back over her shoulder at him. "The other day, when we were in the park, you suggested something to me, and at the time, I laughed, because it was so off-the-wall, it seemed funny. Now, though ... I've been thinking about it. Thinking about it a lot, in fact."

Torval nodded. He was pretty sure he knew what she referred to. "What do you want to know?" he inquired, beginning to feel the stirrings of anticipation deep inside his chest.

"When you went to see that harlot," she went on, "and took those lessons ... why did you do that?"

"Because she told me the first time that I was very bad," replied Torval, "and I felt it important to improve my skills."

"Because you expected to use them on me."

"Yes, as I explained before, that is so," he admitted, without a trace of reluctance in his voice.

She nodded. "Well, then, my next question is this: Why, exactly, did you want to go to bed with me?"

Now she turned to look him directly in the eye. Torval didn't hesitate, but answered with complete honesty. "Because, at the time, I felt it necessary to repay your kindness to me in the only way I knew how."

"I see." Christine turned away again. "I thought so. That was the only thing that made any sense."

An awkward silence descended on the room, and Torval immediately felt uncomfortable. His admission clearly disturbed her, and he realized it disturbed him somewhat as well. His original reason for the lessons now seemed unimiportant, and even wrong. All at once he understood that being intimate with someone didn't have to be about something as petty as repaying debts.

In fact, the more he thought about it, the more he realized that he finally understood what he'd been trying to comprehend all this time, ever since that day at the library.

"If it means anything," he added, feeling the need to express that fact as best he could, "I no longer feel that way."

She didn't move. "You don't?"

"No," replied Torval. "In fact, quite the opposite. I no longer wish to simply have sex with you, Christine. It was wrong of me to do so. I know that now."

She turned and looked at him with an odd expression, half surprise and half amazement. "Really?"

"Yes," he answered with complete honesty. Suddenly, he found himself nervous again, as he had back when he stood under that flickering light after their first date, trying to work up the nerve to kiss her.

"Instead," he asked shakily, "I think I would ... I mean, if you would consider it, that is—"

"What?" she asked, smiling in that amazing way of hers,

apparently enjoying his difficulties just as much as she had the last time.

"Christine," he managed after a moment, "I would like very much to make love to you."

She walked purposefully toward him, and very carefully and deliberately took his hand in hers. Her golden form was as stunningly breathtaking as ever, and he found himself tingling all over.

"Joe," she answered with a smile, "I would like that very much, too."

Still holding his hand, she led him through the door to her bedroom, and they had no more need for words.

Chapter 18

"You know," Christine sighed happily, "I never really knew why humans were so obsessed by sex, until now."

Torval nodded, enjoying the feeling of her warm body against his. For once, where human nature was concerned, he understood completely.

"Yes," he agreed after a moment. "In my earlier experiences, it seemed like so much work for so little return."

"And so unsatisfying." Christine ran her hand softly up and down his arm, giving him a sudden, pleasurable chill. "But when you care about someone ... "

" ... it is far more." Torval finished her thought for her, and she pulled herself up far enough to give him a quick kiss.

"Thank you," she said with a smile, "for renewing my faith in romance. I thought maybe I just couldn't understand because I wasn't really human, just in a human body. I imagined maybe you had to grow up, and live a whole life as human being, if you wanted to really comprehend what it was like. Now I see I just needed to find someone else like myself to share this with. Someone like you."

"But I am not an angel," he protested.

"Close enough." Christine gave a little laugh and rolled onto her back. "I'm glad it was you, Torval. Maybe it *had* to be you. Who knows? I'm starting to think anything's possible."

"As am I." Torval put his arm around her and turned his head, enjoying the sight and smell of her, her very presence at his side. Lovemaking was so much more than just sex, he now knew. A gift, a game, a contest, a sharing of oneself with another ... it was all these things and more, all tied up in what was, biologically, nothing more than the act of reproduction. Every person had the drive to perform that simple process, but when your partner was someone you loved, it could be so much greater.

Someone he loved ... Torval knew now that he loved Christine, with all his heart. Demon or human or angel—it no longer mattered. He loved her, no matter what he was, or might become. What's more, he felt quite certain that when he returned to Hell, he would still love her. What he felt transcended the flesh—it was now a part of his very soul.

He was about to tell her exactly that when a noise startled both of them out of their mutual afterglow. After a second, Torval realized the repetitive banging indicated someone knocking on the door to Christine's apartment. In fact, listening more closely, he could now hear a voice.

"You in there?" someone was yelling. "I saw your lights were on ... come on, I know you're there! Let me in, already!"

Torval sighed, for the voice belonged to Prelz. Christine sat up, came to the same conclusion, and let out a heavy sigh. "All good things must come to an end, I guess," she complained, climbing out of the bed and reaching for a bathrobe. "You want to let him in while I get dressed?"

"Very well," replied Torval, disengaging himself from the covers and standing up, totally nude. He started toward the door, but decided perhaps it was best if he put on some clothes as well. "I will be there momentarily," he called out.

"Joe? That you?" Prelz's voice went on. "Oh, yeah, right, I should've figured. Take your time."

Torval did just that, pulling on all his clothes except the shoes, which he figured could wait. He let Prelz in a few moments later, as soon as he figured out how to work the deadbolt lock.

"Where the hell have you been?" demanded his friend as he pushed his way inside. "I've been checking the shelter all afternoon, and you never turned up. I was starting to think something happened."

"Christine took the day off of work," explained Torval. "We spent the day touring the city, and then we came here."

"Where she fixed you dinner, I see," Prelz went on, moving into the kitchen and surveying the place. He picked at the leftovers a bit, tearing off a piece of unfinished chicken. "Mmm, this is good stuff. Much better than the soup back at the shelter."

"Yes, it was excellent," replied Torval. "Christine is a skilled cook."

"I can tell. What else did you two do, hmm?" Prelz raised an eyebrow thoughtfully. "You guys get down and dirty?"

"If by that you are referring to sex, then yes," Torval answered without hesitation.

"Joe!" Christine yelled loudly from the back room, stepping into view only partially clothed. Despite her raised voice, her anger was entirely feigned. "You don't have to tell him that! It's none of his damn business!"

Prelz began to laugh, clapping his hands together several times. "Oh, you did, didn't you? That's great! Really great!"

Christine grinned, her face turning somewhat reddish, and retreated back into the bedroom. Meanwhile, Torval just shrugged. "Actually, I should use a different term. We did not merely have sex. We made love, and the difference is quite pronounced."

"I'll just bet it is," laughed Prelz, still chuckling to himself.

"In fact, now that I have experienced it, I cannot understand why a human would bother with what is known as 'casual sex.' It is completely unfulfilling, a pale shadow of the real thing."

Prelz just shook his head. "You're amazing, you know that? One week on Earth and you understand this shit better than most people! Maybe it's all backward—maybe humans should take turns being demons, instead of the other way around. Maybe things would make more sense to them then."

Christine reemerged from the back of the apartment, this time dressed in a loose-fitting shirt and sweatpants. She'd tied her hair back in a ponytail and her face looked moist, suggesting it had just been washed. "That might just work, Jake," she remarked. "You should suggest that sometime."

"I doubt anyone would listen," he chuckled to himself, watching as Christine walked over and took Torval by the arm. "You know, you two really do make a great couple."

"I don't see why you are so surprised by our relationship," said Torval, putting an arm comfortably around her shoulder. "You were the one who encouraged me to continue pursuing her after I discovered she was an angel."

"You did?" inquired Christine curiously.

"Yeah, I did," Prelz admitted, "but honestly, I never thought anything would come of it. Look at you now, though. Damn! What a screwed-up romance this is! Well, I guess what they say is true—opposites really do attract."

"We aren't exactly opposites," Christine remarked, "but you've got the wrong saying."

"Oh, you've got a better one?"

"Sure." She flashed him a knowing smile. "Love conquers all."

Prelz nodded and rubbed his beard thoughtfully. "Yep, I have to admit, I think you've got me there."

Christine smiled and quickly changed the subject. "Okay, then, enough about our love life, what brings you to my apartment? And how'd you get in past the security door?"

"That? Oh, I'm pretty resourceful, y'know."

"Jake, come on ... "

"Okay, okay, I was waiting there, and one of your neighbors let me in. I said I was a friend of yours, and they held the door open while they left. It helped that I'd been in here, so I could describe the place, so they knew I wasn't some random burglar."

"Hmm, well, even so, they're not supposed to do that, but whatever." Christine shrugged. "That still doesn't explain why you're here."

"Well, I wanted to find Joe, but after I gave up looking for him I started coming here. I figured you'd show eventually. I want an update, already! What's going on with the Roxtons?"

"Oh, right! After everything else, I almost forgot." Christine turned to Torval. "You want to tell him? You made it all happen."

"Very well," he replied, and proceeded to report on the proceedings of that morning, telling Prelz all about how the Roxtons agreed to turn over evidence against McCord, and that they made the choice of their own free will. In the process of telling the story, Torval realized he'd all but forgotten about all of that, having lost himself in the events of the afternoon.

"So," said Prelz when Torval was finally done talking, "the police are going to arrest McCord, one of their own, and throw him in prison?"

"That was what I understood," replied Torval.

"Probably not right away," Christine put in. "Norm said he'd be working on the case immediately, though, so I suspect it won't be more than a few days."

"Good," Torval said. "I would like to know the results before my vacation is over."

"Oh, let's not talk about that!" Christine gave him a quick hug. "Besides, it's all going to work out regardless. We've done our part, and that's all we can do."

"Do you still have to go to work?" Prelz asked curiously.

"Yes," Torval replied. "Not for another hour, however. I believe at this point I must engage in a post-dinner ritual referred to as 'washing the dishes.' Where can I find the appropriate materials to perform this task?"

Prelz put his hands up and backed away. "Don't look at me! I have absolutely no idea whatsoever!" His sarcastic tone suggested that he did, in fact, know exactly what the job involved. "You can handle that yourself, my friend. I'm gonna watch some TV."

"Jake," commented Christine somewhat firmly, "you know, I didn't mind you staying here last night, but you aren't moving in permanently! You need to find a job and get your own place, like you promised."

"What do you think I did most of the day?" he complained. "I put in some applications. Nobody hires on the spot, though, unless you're in the company of a pretty young social worker." He flashed a mock glare at Torval. "Anyway, I'm gonna check back to a couple places tomorrow, and the employment bureau too."

"If you like, I can meet you there in the morning," said Christine. "I did the same for Joe, and it worked out well enough."

"Sounds good. What time?"

"They open at eight, but I'd need some extra time to get an appointment for you, so how about eleven? I need to head to work early, to get caught up on anything I missed today, but I should be able to work in a call to Simon by then."

"I'll be there. Actually, I'll head in early, just to get a jump on things, if that's all right. Is it still okay to stay here tonight? If I spend the night on the street, I doubt I'll be all that presentable tomorrow."

Christine sighed. "Fine, but turn everything off this time! You left the TV on and the water running in the sink."

"Oh, right, sorry." Prelz looked chagrined. "I didn't mean to, I was thinking about some other stuff when I left. Like, how much different it felt being clean and all."

"Yeah, well, it took me twenty minutes to unclog my drain," Christine complained. "Ah, well, it was worth it, I guess. Seeing you off the streets, and trying to improve yourself—that's what my job here on Earth is all about. Even if you're really a demon, you're still a soul I can help save."

"Yep, and I appreciate it." Prelz gave a slight bow in her direction. "Now, where's the remote? Ah, here it is."

Christine shook her head. "I didn't think he'd ever stop watching that thing," she remarked.

"I am still not sure what this 'television' is all about," Torval commented. "I was told it was similar to movies, but smaller and with advertisements."

"That's about right. You know, if you want, I can do the dishes myself, and you can go sit with Jake. He'll probably have to explain everything you're seeing anyway."

"No, I will do the dishes," replied Torval. "You have fixed me this meal and shown me such hospitality. It is the least I can do."

Christine pulled him close and planted a kiss on his lips. "That's so nice of you," she told him, running a hand over his forehead. "You know, if not for these horns, I'd never know you were a demon."

Torval kissed her back, and was about to reply, when a sudden buzzing sound made him jump. He looked around for the source of the sound, but didn't see anything. Christine, however, rolled her eyes and reluctantly moved away. "Damn phone," she groused, reaching for what looked like a handle atop a white box near the edge of the kitchen counter.

Torval realized what the noise was now, and nodded to himself. *Just a telephone*, he noted, relaxing.

"Hello?" she asked, putting the device to her ear. "Oh, hey, Norm, how's it going with the case?" She whispered to Torval, "It's Norm Campbell. I think he's got some news."

"I would like to hear it," replied Torval, wishing he could make out the barely audible voice coming out of the headset.

She nodded. "Hang on a second, Norm, would you? I've got Joe here, and another friend of ours, and we all really want to hear this, so let me put it on speaker. One sec."

She pushed a button, and then yelled out into the other room for Prelz, who appeared quickly. "What's up?"

"We've got news on the Roxtons," explained Christine, setting the phone down. "Okay, Norm, we can hear you, so go ahead."

"Okay, here goes," the policeman's voice said clearly, coming out of the speaker on the cordless phone's base. He sounded rather pleased with himself, actually. "You guys ready for this?"

"Sure, lay it on us," answered Christine.

"Right, well, here's what happened," began Norm. "I brought back everything the Roxtons gave me, and we started going through it. It was a gold mine, so I sent some men out to round up a couple of the people they named—one in particular was someone named Brent Maclure."

"I remember him," said Torval. "My first task for the Roxtons was to deliver a briefcase to him, but I did not know the contents."

"I see," replied Norm, pausing for a moment as he digested that admission. "Well, anyway, this Brent fellow panicked the minute we started questioning him, and he agreed to spill the beans on McCord in exchange for protection. After that—well, I had more than enough evidence, and the DA agreed, so we went ahead and got a warrant before any word of this had a chance to get out."

"You mean you've already arrested him?" asked Christine, wide-eyed with amazement.

"Yep," replied Norm with a chuckle. "About an hour ago, actually. He never saw it coming. Didn't say a word while we read him his rights. We also nabbed a couple of his cohorts at the station, too. Hopefully we'll—wait, what?"

Someone else started talking in the background, and rather urgently, but none of them could make out the words. "What do you mean, 'what'?" asked Christine worriedly. "What's going on?"

"Hang on, Christine, someone's yelling at me. Just a moment." The phone seemed to go dead.

"Norm? Norm!" Christine gave the phone a whack, but nothing happened. "Damn, he put us on mute. What's going on?"

"I don't know," said Prelz, "but I was just thinking that sounded too good to be true. This McCord guy doesn't seem like someone who would just let himself get arrested."

"No," replied Torval, "I doubt that he would. He seemed to have ways of knowing everything that was happening, even at great distances from himself. I would not think he could be taken by surprise so easily."

"I'm just shocked they were able to do it today," said Christine, shaking her head. "Usually it takes a while to prepare a case, especially against another cop. If they arrest him, and they're wrong, it could destroy his career. They're usually really careful about that."

"Norm did say they had been suspicious of McCord for some time," Torval reminded her.

"Ah, yes, so he did. Well, I suppose that—"

At that moment the phone crackled and Norm's voice spoke up

again, this time sounding anything but joyful. "Okay, good news over, now bad news time," he said urgently. "I just found out McCord broke out of his holding cell!"

"Broke out?" gasped Christine. "How?"

"We don't know, exactly—it looks like the lock just snapped somehow—and what's more, he took down five officers on his way out of the station. Two are hurt really badly." Norm uttered an incomprehensible word that sounded like a curse. "We're putting out an APB now. He won't get far."

Torval shook his head. "On the contrary," he commented sadly, "I believe he will do just that."

"What if he goes after the Roxtons?" said a horrified Christine. "He might figure out they're the ones who turned in the evidence!"

"I don't see how he could possibly guess that," replied Norm, "but yeah, I can see why you'd be worried. Tell you what, I'll send a cruiser over there just to keep an eye on them till we get McCord back in custody."

"Thanks, Norm, that'd be great," replied Christine, still looking quite concerned. "You don't suppose someone might've told him anything about us, do you?"

"No, definitely not," he reassured her. "I didn't mention you or Joe in my report at all. There wasn't any need to. Oh, and I do want to mention one other thing. I think we've only scratched the surface of what McCord was up to. I've seen bad cops and dirty cops, but never anything like this. Even if he gets away, at least this little criminal empire of his has been broken up. That's already a given."

"Well, at least that's something," replied Christine morosely.

"It's all thanks to you and the Roxtons," went on Norm. "I'll give you a call when we catch him, okay? He won't get away again."

"Thanks, Norm. We appreciate it."

"No problem. 'Bye."

The phone clicked off, and Christine just shook her head. "I should've known he'd get away. It was too easy, wasn't it?"

"Someone must've helped him," suggested Prelz. "That's probably why he wasn't all that worried when they took him in. He knew he'd be set free."

"And yet he injured five other people," noted Torval.

Christine nodded. "Five other police officers attempting to stop him from leaving. Five good men just doing their jobs."

"Yeah." Prelz scratched at his beard absently. "You know, that right there is proof he's gone off the deep end. When he got arrested, he should've known his mission here was over. He should've been looking to get back to Hell so he could deliver his report and get another assignment."

"If that is true," wondered Torval, "then why did he bother to escape? What purpose would it serve?"

"None," replied Prelz, "unless he wanted something else. Maybe he has a fall-back plan."

"Or maybe he just wants vengeance," Torval supposed. "He did, in fact, warn me that if I were to betray him, I would pay a severe penalty."

Christine looked even more worried than ever. "If that's true, and he did find out the Roxtons were involved ... "

"Yeah," agreed Prelz at once. "Yeah, that could be really bad for them. Torval, you got their number on that phone of yours?"

"No, I do not," he replied. "I have never needed to call them."

"I can look it up," replied Christine, hurriedly pulling an extremely thick, yellow-colored tome out of a drawer. She flipped through the pages, which were covered with tiny print, until finally stoping at one entry in particular. "Roxton Auto Parts, here it is," she read, taking the phone in hand and punching the numbers quickly.

The speaker option was still on, so all of them heard what happened next. When the beeping of the numbers came to an end, there was a pause, followed by a strange tone, and then a mechanical voice that said simply, "The number you have reached is not in service at this time. Please try your call again."

"Oh, no," said Christine, looking quite pale. "You don't suppose that—?"

"He cut the phone line?" Prelz shrugged. "Hmm, a power-mad Corruptor out for revenge ... what do you think, Joe?"

"I think," said Torval with a sinking feeling in his chest, "that we should go to the warehouse at once."

The other two exchanged glances, nodding as one. "Then get your shoes on," Christine urged him. "We'd better hurry!"

* * *

The cab ride to the warehouse seemed to take forever. No one spoke, except to try to urge the driver to go faster. When the dark-skinned man replied, it was in a language Torval didn't understand, so whether or not he knew what they wanted, the demon didn't know for sure.

After what seemed like an eternity, they arrived at the appropriate street corner, where they happened to miss the light. Rather than wait, Christine just hurried everyone out of the vehicle, paying the man without a second thought and racing across through a break in traffic. Torval and Prelz followed closely behind.

Night had fallen, and the city was dark, save for streetlamps and passing vehicles. The warehouse, too, had most of its lights out for the evening, save the ones inside the main entrance. As soon as the trio came into view of the door, they realized instantly they were right to be worried.

Thick black smoke filled the inside of the foyer, just barely visible through the glass. A few sooty tendrils crawled their way underneath the door, seeping out into the cool night air.

Chapter 19

"Dear God," gasped Christine, staring in horror at the smoke-filled entryway. "The warehouse—it's on fire!"

Torval hesitated. What, exactly, was burning? He didn't see any flames, and while the smoke was unusual, it didn't seem inherently dangerous. He figured he'd just open the door and let it out, but to his surprise, he found the entrance locked.

"Why would it be locked?" demanded Prelz, trying to help Torval, but failing. "You don't have a key, do you?"

"No, I do not," replied Torval, somewhat at a loss.

"McCord must've locked it," Christine concluded. "Joe! Call nine-one-one, quick!"

"Do what?" Torval had no idea what she was talking about, and only stood there in confusion.

"Oh, never mind, just give me your cell phone! I'll call it in—you two get inside, quick! The Roxtons may still be alive!"

"The door will not open," complained Torval, not really sure what he should do. The others seemed to be frantic, but while the smoke was unusual, he failed to see the urgency. Nonetheless, he handed over his phone to Christine, who anxiously began dialing, and Prelz continued to try tugging hopelessly on the door.

"This isn't gonna work," commented Prelz urgently. "You don't have those lockpicks, do you? No, never mind, it'd take too long. We need something more drastic!"

"I don't understand," replied Torval. "What is happening?"

Prelz started looking around the stairs near the doorway, tugging on bricks and pieces of masonry. "It constantly amazes me how clueless you are," he said in frustration. "Don't you get it? McCord set the building on fire and locked the door! He's probably got the Roxtons tied up in there! This is his revenge!"

Torval nodded, understanding at last. "Then we must get inside at once," he stated. "We must help the Roxtons!"

"Exactly! Now here, help me with this!"

Prelz found a loose chunk of sidewalk, but it was too heavy for him to lift by himself. Torval assisted, and together they were able to heft it up and move to the door. "Okay, on three, we toss it through," said Prelz, swinging the concrete block back on each number, gathering momentum. "One, two, three!"

The glass door shattered with a loud crash. Immediately Prelz kicked the broken fragments out of the way and forced himself inside. Smoke poured out of the entrance, but still choked the foyer, so Prelz stayed low, coughing repeatedly. "Come on!" he yelled. "They could still be alive!"

Torval followed, trying to mimic Prelz by staying under the thick smoke cloud. Even so, he began to cough almost immediately, as the air itself threatened to choke him. He found himself crawling, still hacking repeatedly, unable to answer as Prelz called out, "Anybody here? Anyone? If you can hear me, yell so we can find you!"

From behind him, Torval heard Christine yell, "The fire department's on the way!" Whether she followed, he couldn't see. The building was dark, except for flickering lights ahead, deeper inside the warehouse. Flickering that was ...

A fire! He could see it now—flames dancing in several places amidst the crates and boxes on the stock floor. Intense heat radiated down the hall, oppressive even at this distance. Prelz pushed on just ahead, almost flat on the ground, looking around for any sign of the Roxtons, but found none, nor did they answer his repeated calls.

There's one place they could be, thought Torval—*the basement*. He turned back, crawled a ways, and came to the door, but found it locked as well. "Pete?" he called out. "Lincoln? Are you there?"

Amidst the crackling of the flames, Prelz's constant yells, and his own coughs, Torval thought he heard a moan of pain coming from downstairs. The door wouldn't open, so he did the only thing he could think of—he flipped onto his back and started kicking with as much force as his legs could muster.

"Are they in there?" asked Prelz from nearby. "What is that, a closet?"

"It leads to the basement," said Torval, remembering now that Prelz had never actually seen the inside of the warehouse. "This is where I work."

"Well, okay, I don't know why they'd be down there, but if they're damn near anywhere else, they're screwed anyway." Holding his breath, Prelz stood up, turned to one side, and threw himself shoulder-first into the door. It didn't open, but there was a distinct splintering sound from the area of the handle.

"Damn, that hurts," Prelz complained, dropping back to the floor. He started coughing again. "Come on," he said between gasps, "kicking it ain't gonna work."

"Very well." Torval stood, holding his breath, and repeated what he'd seen Prelz do. This time, the frame around the lock ripped free, and he only barely managed to keep his balance as he nearly toppled down the stairs. On the plus side, though, there were no flames ahead, nor did he see any smoke. The fire hadn't spread to the basement, at least not yet.

Torval hurried down the staircase, coughing a few times to clear his lungs, and looked around in the darkness. Prelz followed closely behind. "Lights don't work," he pointed out. "McCord must've cut the electricity along with the phones. Any luck?"

"I am certain I heard something down here," said Torval, waiting for his eyes to adjust. "Pete? Lincoln?"

"Ohh ... here ... " someone groaned. Prelz and Torval quickly rushed toward the source of the sound—a corner of the room, under a pile of overturned filing boxes. There they found Pete, covered in loose papers that smelled of chemicals.

"Pete!" exclaimed Torval. "Are you all right?"

"Do I ... do I look all right?" he gasped. "Get this shit off me!"

Working together, Torval and Prelz cleaned off the loose papers and open file folders, most of which were quite damp. Underneath, Pete was a mess. His face, barely visible in the darkness, had been beaten, and his breathing came in ragged gasps. From the impossible angles of several limbs, many of his bones were obviously broken.

"What the hell happened to you?" demanded Prelz.

"McCord," Pete managed to say. "Tried to fight him ... threw me down the stairs. He was crazy. Insane. Grandpa ... over there ... get him out ... "

At that, Pete's head lolled backward and his eyes closed. He wasn't dead, though, just unconscious. Prelz tried to get him to wake up, but didn't have much success. Meanwhile Torval moved to the other side of the room, where Pete tried to point before fainting. There he found Lincoln, also covered in chemical-soaked papers. He, too, was unconscious and appeared to have been beaten.

"That bastard," hissed Prelz. "He didn't even kill them outright. He left them here to burn to death in their own building. I swear, if I ever get a shot at him, he's dead!"

"I will not oppose you," replied Torval, for he felt the same way. Demon or not, McCord had no right to do this to human beings, especially ones who'd made a choice of their own free will. Mannoch's absurd thirst for vengeance left Torval sick to his stomach.

The smoke wasn't helping matters, for by now it had started making its way down into the basement. The fire would follow soon enough, and both Roxtons were doused in some sort of liquid that would doubtless burn quite effectively.

"We have to get them out of here," said Prelz, mirroring Torval's thoughts, "and quick! Help me carry him, will you? And be careful, he's not in very good shape."

The two did their best to lift Pete's heavy body. His injuries appeared quite painful, and the jostling he received on the way up the stairs didn't help matters, so he was probably better off unconscious. Nonetheless, the two demons had no choice but to carry him out, as to do otherwise would be to leave him to certain death.

Torval coughed repeatedly as he finally exited into the cool night air. Gasping for breath, he set Pete down on the sidewalk next to the horrified Christine. "What happened to him?" she demanded, eyes wide in horror at the sight.

"McCord threw him down the stairs," replied Prelz. "Come on, let's get the other one!"

Torval hurried back in, instinctively covering his face with his jacket. The smoke seemed even thicker now, and the flames approached the break room. They didn't have much time. Fortunately, over the din of objects burning, Torval heard the welcome sound of distant sirens. Help was on the way.

Lincoln was easier to carry, being much lighter than his grandson, and the two demons made it out with him in relative safety. The elder Roxton didn't look as badly injured, either. Perhaps he hadn't put up as much resistance, but it looked as if he'd simply been pummled a few times, not cast down a stairwell. His face was blackened and swollen, and his jaw protruded somewhat to one side, but he breathed more regularly than Pete and didn't look nearly as pale.

The sirens grew closer and finally an ambulance swung into view, followed almost immediately by a large truck lined with ladders. Torval and Prelz stepped away as uniformed men rushed to the aid of the Roxtons, bearing metal cases and unfamiliar instruments. They didn't pay the onlookers any heed as they started ministering to the wounded. Meanwhile, the firefighters began hooking up their truck to a nearby hydrant, even as flames started to become visible in the smoke-filled windows.

Torval felt his breath coming in ragged gasps. The effort had exhausted him, and his lungs burned from the smoke, but at least the exertion was over. He struggled to control himself, coughing a few more times, willing his heart to stop racing. Even as he did, though, he saw Prelz wavering, holding his hand to his forehead. The other demon began to cough and hack, falling to his knees, and finally sprawling out on the ground.

"Are you all right?" asked Christine worriedly.

"It's nothing," replied Prelz between choking coughs. "Too much smoke ... I'll be okay. Guess you aren't gonna be working tonight, huh, Joe?"

"It appears not," replied Torval, watching as the firemen began aiming hoses at the windows. Several others, dressed in yellow suits and masks, rushed inside, carrying axes and other equipment.

"They'll save the building," said Christine, leaning up against Christine, "but you two did a much better thing. You saved their lives, Joe. You're heroes!"

"I do not feel like a hero," replied Torval. "I did what I had to do. They would otherwise have perished."

"But you could've been killed in the attempt, and that's the point," said Christine. "You risked your life for another. As good deeds go, that's the top of the list."

Torval looked at her. "It does not matter for myself," he said in a low voice, "but do you suppose this act has redeemed Prelz?"

"Maybe." She shrugged. "In fact, I just bet it did."

"That is good, because—" began Torval, but was startled by a ringing sound coming from Christine's hand.

Startled, she held up the cell phone she'd borrowed to call the emergency crews. "Who would be calling you?" she asked curiously, handing over the device.

Torval opened the case. As he'd seen Christine do, he answered with just a single word. "Hello?"

"So, it was you," came an immediately recognizable voice.

"McCord?" Torval was surprised, if not shocked, to hear the ex-lieutenant's voice on the other end of the line.

Christine gasped at the sound of that name. She started looking around fearfully, as if he might appear at any moment. In fact, Torval realized, he must be watching them right now, or he wouldn't have known about the rescue. Where was he? In the shadows someplace, or in a window in a nearby building? He couldn't know for sure.

"It was you," hissed the Corruptor. "I thought it was just the Roxtons, but no, now I see it all. *You* told them! You warned them, didn't you?"

Torval chose not to answer the question directly. Instead, he replied with the simple truth. "The Roxtons exercised free will in defying you. In seeking vengeance against them, you are breaking the Compact."

"I don't care about that," growled Mannoch angrily. "My business isn't done, but never fear, I can finish them at any time."

"They are not to be harmed," insisted Torval. "If you desire vengeance, destroy me if you must, but leave them be."

"Oh, but why stop at just one, when I can kill you all?" chuckled the demon. "Although in your case, I think I'll just make you wish you were dead. Killing you wouldn't be much of a punishment."

"I do not fear you," replied Torval with as much courage as he could muster.

"You should. Oh, you should! I'd come get you now, but not with the police on the way. Another time, Judas. If I were you, I'd be watching my back."

The line went dead. Torval closed the phone and stared at it, frowning, and realizing that he'd lied just then. He did, in fact, fear Mannoch—quite intensely, in fact.

Christine reached out to take the phone from him. "He's just trying to rattle you," she insisted. "You can't keep that, you know. He may be able to track it."

"If you say so," said Torval worriedly, watching as she threw the phone across the ground, so that it slid, bounching and tumbling, into an open sewer grate. In an instant, it was gone into the dark spaces underneath the city.

If only I could be rid of Mannoch that easily, thought Torval with a sigh.

Chapter 20

After the paramedics finished stabilizing both Roxtons, they worked them up onto gurneys and into the back of the waiting ambulance. Seeing Prelz coughing and nearly unconscious, they moved to help him as well, hooking him up to an oxygen tank. After a few minutes, he seemed to recover. Torval suspected the fainting spell was more due to his brain tumor than anything else.

Meanwhile, the first ambulance left and another arrived. The paramedics moved to check Torval as well, after he had a brief coughing fit, and pronounced both of them victims of smoke inhalation. When the medics suggested both demons go to the hospital for a few additional tests, they agreed, and Christine went along for the ride. Torval didn't think he needed any further medical attention, but Prelz might, and besides, at least this got them away from Mannoch.

They also happened to be following the Roxtons, which was a good thing, Torval decided. He could find out how they were doing once the doctors were finished.

By the time he got to the hospital, Prelz seemed to have fully recovered, and Torval felt better as well. A doctor checked them over, but found nothing wrong with them, and wouldn't treat them further unless they filled out certain forms. Lacking the required information, both demons simply refused and walked away.

After some inquiries they found out where the Roxtons were, but weren't allowed in to see them immediately. Apparently their injuries were fairly severe. This left the trio sitting in a waiting room, where Torval finally got his introduction to that human entertainment medium known as "television."

The TV showed some sort of drama involving several people trapped on an island, and a group of others trying to locate that same island. Christine briefly attempted to explain the plot, but it was so convoluted that Torval quickly lost track. Seeing his confusion, she resorted to explaining individual characters as they appeared, which helped slightly, except that there were too many people and all of them seemed to have their own agendas. Torval eventually decided the show's title was well-chosen, for he was indeed completely lost.

Mercifully, about a half hour into the morass of plots, subplots and sub-subplots, a doctor entered the room, dressed in a long white coat and holding a clipboard. "Are you friends of Peter and Lincoln Roxton?" the middle-aged, balding man asked from behind a pair of black-rimmed spectacles.

"Yes," replied Christine, all but jumping out of her chair in her eagerness to hear some sort of news. "How are they?"

"Well," said the man, "Lincoln will be fine. He has some contusions and his jaw was dislocated, but he'll recover. Peter, unfortunately, is in serious condition. Someone did a real number on him, I'm afraid. He has several fractures, one of which is compound, and some internal hemorraging. We have him sedated, and I think he'll make it, but it's going to take some time and a lot of therapy."

"Can we see him?" asked Christine worriedly.

"In a few minutes," the doctor replied. "The police are in there at the moment, interviewing Lincoln. Apparently whoever did this is some sort of cop who went crazy."

"Yeah, we know," replied Prelz. "A real sick bastard."

"I can imagine, and if he really did leave them to die in that building, he's someone I wouldn't want to meet in a dark alley."

"He'd better just hope he doesn't meet me there," commented a very angry-sounding Prelz. "Killing's too good for him."

"I'd rather not hear such things," said the doctor, backing away slowly. "Violence only begets more violence. In any case, if you can just wait here, I'll let you know when the police are gone."

"Wait," said Christine. "Is one of the police a man named Norm Campbell? He would've been in plain clothes, most likely."

"I think someone said their name was Norm, yes."

"I know him. Do you think we could go back there now?"

The doctor sighed. "Well, I'm not supposed to let anyone else interfere, but if you know him, and he doesn't mind, I suppose it's all right. Follow me."

They trailed behind the man as they took a few turns in the hospital's white, sparkling clean hallways. Eventually they arrived in a side room where several police clustered around a bed, upon which sat the battered and bruised form of Lincoln Roxton. His face was wrapped in bandages so that they could only barely see his mouth. As he spotted them entering, his puffy eyes widened and he gave a brief wave with his one free arm.

The Internal Affairs policeman, Norm, turned to follow his gaze. "Christine!" he called out as she entered. "Ah, and Joe, too. I was hoping you'd be around. You were the ones who pulled him out?"

"Not me," Christine replied proudly. "Joe and Jake here did all the work. All I did was call nine-one-one."

"Well, these men owe you their lives, or so I was told," went on Norm. He pointed at Lincoln, and at the bed adjacent to him, where Pete stretched out, sedated and hooked up to some sort of wall-length device with several flashing indicators that apparently meant something important.

"Just what any good citizen would've done," said Prelz sheepishly. "Couldn't very well stand around while the place burned down around them, now could we?"

"I'm sorry I didn't check up on that cruiser I told you I'd send," Norm went on. "I called it in, but apparently, the message never got relayed. Perhaps one of McCord's friends intervened. If I'd followed up, I could've stopped this before it happened. However, we hadn't named the Roxtons as the informants, so how McCord found out, I have no idea."

"It doesn't matter," Christine replied, putting her hand on his shoulder. "Don't blame yourself, Norm. How were you to know he'd be able to escape?"

"That's what blows my mind," replied the policeman sadly. "He shouldn't have been able to. Five men were there, armed, and he was locked in a cage at the time. I got to ask one of them, and he said McCord just ripped the door open with his bare hands. Took them all by surprise. The worst part is, one of them died of his injuries, so now I have to tell Martin Cartwright's family how this happened, and I just don't know what I'm going to say."

"It's okay, Norm, you couldn't have foreseen this," Christine replied soothingly. "Everything will be all right. I'll help you through it, if you need someone there to lean on."

He smiled. "I appreciate that, but I'll survive. It's not the first time I've had to deliver news like this. Thank you, though. Anyway, we shouldn't bother Mr. Roxton any further tonight. I'm going to head back to McCord's office, and see if I can't dig up anything new there. These two men are going to stand guard over this room tonight, just in case that bastard shows up to finish the job."

"Good," said Torval. "I feel better about their safety."

"Yeah, we'll be right outside," one of the uniformed cops replied, "and believe me, I'll be ready. I knew Martin Cartwright, and honestly, I'm really hopin' the lieutenant decides to make an appearance."

"That's fine, Larry, now let's leave these good people alone, shall we? Come on."

The police left, following the doctor as he led them out the way they'd come. Lincoln looked up at them through swollen eyes and tried to force himself to smile, despite his injuries. All he succeeded in doing was wincing in pain. "Ow," he managed painfully. "'ard to talk, shee, I gotsha dishlocated jaw." He pointed with his left hand, which seemed about the only part of him not injured.

"I see that," said Torval. "What happened, exactly? Why did McCord not simply kill you?"

"Joe!" snapped Christine, slapping him on the arm. "You don't have to put it so harshly!"

"Sorry," Torval replied, cringing a bit. "Can you tell us what happened?"

"Sure," mumbled Lincoln through his bandages. "We wash jusht gettin' back from shelabratin', and I wash makin' sure the lasht of the boysh left okay, then I shaw shomeone in the back. Didn't shee who 'twas and he shuckerpunshed me. When I stood up, I shaw he wash shtartin' a fire. He pushed me down and dragged me to the bashement."

"You didn't see who it was?" inquired Torval, not quite sure he understood all of that, but he figured he had the gist of it.

"Oh, I knew who 'twas, L'tenit McCord, that'sh who. I shaw hish face, but he wash so shtrong, I couldn't do anything. Then Pete, blesh hish heart, tried to fight and got thrown down the shtairs for hish trouble. The lasht thing I remember was McCord shayin' it would be fittin' for ush to die in our own warehoush, shince we loved it so much it was worth backstabbin' him over it."

"Did he say how he found out it was you who turned in the information?" asked Prelz.

"Oh, yesh, that," said Lincoln. "He didn't know, not really, he wash jusht there for ush regardlesh. While he wash holdin' Pete in the air, like he weighed nothin', he asked if we'd done it, and Pete shays, he wash glad we did, caush at leasht we shtopped him from doin' anythin' to anybody else. God, I hope he wakesh up shoon sho I can shlap him!" Lincoln started to chuckle, but only ended up grimacing in pain.

"Well, don't worry, you've got police protection now," said Christine helpfully. "I'm sure they'll find McCord soon."

"I'm just shorry we didn't do thish sooner," sighed Lincoln. "All thosh thingsh we did, caush we were so schared of him, and he wash gonna do thish to ush anyway, no matter what. God forgive ush."

"I'm sure He will," replied Christine with a supportive smile. "Did you happen to have the building insured?"

"Oh, yesh, but only barely enough to cover itsh value," replied Lincoln sadly. "At the leasht, we can cover the loansh, I hope. The inventory, though, thatsh gone. Roxton Auto Partsh ish dead, I'm afraid, and thesh doctor billsh ... gonna be bankrupt, I'm shure."

"Well, don't worry, I'll help any way I can," said Christine helpfully.

"Yes, she is very good at helping people," agreed Torval. "She certainly aided me often enough."

Christine gave him a quick hug. "Looks like you're out of a job, though. Guess I'll have to help you some more. I suppose, since you don't have anyplace else to go, you can stay with me."

Torval nodded, and returned her smile. *At least, if nothing else, one good thing came out of all this*, he told himself.

* * *

They spent a few more minutes chatting with Lincoln, who seemed remarkably chipper considering his injuries and the fate of his business. After a while, though, a doctor finally came in and shooed the three visitors out. After promising to return and check on him the next day, Christine and the two demons made their way out of the room and, after briefly becoming lost in the confusing maze of hallways, eventually figured out how to exit the hospital.

"You know," said Prelz, looking back and forth at the parking lot, "I keep expecting McCord to jump out of the shadows at any time and beat the shit out of us."

"I, too, am fearful," said Torval, shaking his head. "However, he could not possibly be capable of such things. He has no way to find us at this point, unless he just happens to run across us by accident."

"There *is* one problem, though," pointed out Prelz. "Something very important about all this, and I'm not sure any of you caught on."

"What?" inquired Christine.

"He killed someone," Prelz explained. "An innocent. That police officer who tried to stop him."

"So?" asked Torval.

Christine nodded, obviously understanding at once. "What happens when a human dies, Joe? Think about it."

"His soul is released to—" Torval stopped in midsentence. Of course! His soul would move on, where it would be evaluated and judged—and if whoever did the evaluating was on the ball, they'd realize at once that a demon, not a human being, caused his death.

"Yeah, you get it now," said Prelz at once. "What do you think will happen once they figure that out?"

"They will realize Mannoch has gone rogue," replied Torval, "and will attempt to stop him."

"And what's the first thing demons do when they try to stop one of their own who's loose on Earth?"

"I suppose," replied Torval, "that they would send hunters to capture him."

"Yep. Exactly. And that's the problem, at least for me. I don't exactly want to be around here if there's cerberi roaming the streets. If they catch my scent, and recognize it as that of a rogue demon, I'm done for."

"What are you going to do?" asked Torval, quite concerned by this. If the hounds caught him, they would send his soul back to Hell before he died naturally, denying his soul a fair judgment—and Prelz had certainly earned that, as far as Torval was concerned.

"Get out of here, that's what," replied Prelz. "I should hop on the nearest bus out of town. I'll give you—well, Christine, anyway—a call when I get somewhere safe."

"You cannot simply leave just like that," Torval told him, a twinge of uncomfortable sadness sweeping through him. "I would ... I would miss you. You have been a friend to me. Is it not possible to stay and simply fight, should the dogs approach? Or perhaps they will not notice you at all, being focused on their true prey?"

"Well, I gotta tell you, it warms my old heart to know you're gonna miss me so much," said a grinning Prelz, "and yeah, maybe they won't spot me, but I'm not gonna chance it. Oh, and fight them? Not a chance. Cerberi aren't that easy to stop."

"Be that as it may," said Prelz, "I do not want you to leave."

Prelz put a hand on his shoulder. "All good things must come to an end, or so the humans say," he commented. "Anyway, I don't have to go right this second. There's no way the demonic bureaucracy, still stuck in the Stone Age as they are, will get a hunt team out here this fast. Besides, you aren't the only one I have to say goodbye to. There's another person here in town who's been a friend of mine far longer, and it wouldn't be right to bail without at least touching base one last time."

"I know who you mean," replied Torval, "but that section of town is uncomfortably close to the warehouse. I am not certain we should risk venturing there, with McCord somewhere loose in the city."

"There's no way he'll know where we're going," Prelz argued. "Besides, I'm not leaving without saying goodbye, and that's that. Now come on, let's find a cab. It can drop us right at the front door."

"Very well," Torval agreed reluctantly. Actually, he was a bit worried himself, but about another matter entirely. He knew that McCord had seen him with Christine at lunch, and managed to learn enough about her to determine she worked for a legal firm. If he knew that much, could he have also figured out where she lived? If so, that meant her apartment wouldn't be safe.

Yet he didn't want to bring that up now, not on the heels of Prelz announcing his imminent departure, so he decided to wait. He could simply mention it later, after his friend was safely on his way. That would be one less thing Prelz would have to concern himself with.

So he said nothing. As he started to follow Prelz toward the front of the hospital, Christine asked, "Aren't you all going to tell me who this mysterious person is we're going to see?"

"Oh, right, you wouldn't know, would you?" replied Prelz. "Someone I met back when I was having my personal crisis, all those years ago. He helped me, much like you did, Christine, except he isn't an angel, just a man."

"That's nice," she replied, smiling. "Who is he?"

"His name is Father Thomas Michaels."

* * *

As the trio stepped out of the cab, Torval looked around worriedly. The church sat about the middle of the block, with the entrance set back away from the street, partially in shadow. McCord could be lurking there—but no, that was just his fear talking. The Corruptor couldn't possibly be anywhere near this place. Even if he'd followed them to the hospital, he would've lost them once they went inside, and the place had several exits. Unless he guessed correctly, happened to see them leave, and somehow followed their cab through the labyrinth of New York City streets, he was far from here.

More than likely, thought Torval with some concern, *Mannoch is even now staking out Christine's apartment.* Torval needed to explain that to her, but hesitated, unsure of what might happen. Would she agree to not return there tonight, or would she insist on going anyway, holding firm in her belief that Mannoch wouldn't dare harm an angel for fear of shattering the Compact?

Quite honestly, Torval wasn't at all concerned for his own safety. Mannoch could certainly cause his human body pain, and even kill him, but what might he do to Christine? He felt certain the Corruptor wouldn't respect the Compact any more than he already had. His lust for vengeance made him capable of anything.

Torval found himself fearing for Christine's safety—an unfamiliar, alien feeling, but at least he knew why he felt that way. Love, it seemed, could be as much a curse as a blessing, damn it all! Yet he knew he wouldn't change things if he could. Human emotions were, he now knew, more than worth the trouble.

As the cab drove away, Prelz said, "Did you happen to tell Christine here about Father Michaels, by any chance?"

"No, I did not," replied Torval. "Should I have?"

"She should probably at least have a warning," said Prelz, moving toward the door. "Make it snappy, I don't want to hang out here too long."

"Warn me about what?" demanded Christine.

"Well," said Torval, "Father Michaels is an ordinary human, but he seems to be capable of seeing demons in their true forms. I suspect that if you were to touch him, such as in shaking hands, he would be able to see your true shape as well."

She nodded. "Okay, that's good to know, I guess. Any idea how he's able to do this?"

"No," replied Prelz, standing at the door and glancing around anxiously. "He's human, though, so it must just be a gift, like second sight or ESP. Now can we get inside? Please?"

They followed him into the church, which, as expected at this late hour, looked quite empty. The lights were dimmed, but a few candles glowed here and there, suggesting visitors were at least welcome.

"You don't actually believe in ESP, do you?" asked Christine curiously.

"Not really." Prelz shrugged. "Who knows, maybe it's possible, but in these days of television and handheld cameras, you'd think it would be better documented. I think it's just like magic—it's either a stage trick, or some kind of scam. What Father Michaels does, though—he really sees us, and that's no joke. I asked him to describe me once, and he was spot on. Ah, here he is now."

The priest finally made his appearance, poking his head around the corner of the vestibule. "Did someone come in ... ? Oh, it's you, Jake! You're looking quite well, I see. And Joe, too. Good to see you again. And who is this?"

"This is Christine Anderson," replied Torval. "She is ... she is a friend of mine. A very good friend."

"Nice to meet you," she replied, smiling and—to the surprise of her two companions—holding out her arm in greeting.

"And you," said the priest, reaching out to take her hand, whereupon he froze, staring in awe and amazement at the angelic vision that materialized before him. He remained in a near-paralyzed state for about ten seconds before suddenly dropping to his knees, covering his face with his hands.

"Get up!" Christine ordered, rolling her eyes. "I'm no deity, priest! I'm just a servant of God, just like you, and these others here. I'm not any more worthy of worship than any of God's other creations."

Thomas slowly nodded and stood, leveling his gaze only with what looked like a considerable amount of effort. When he saw only a smiling woman there, not that angelic image, he seemed to relax. "I-I apologize," he managed, "but I just wasn't expecting that."

"I suppose I should've warned you," said Christine, "but honestly, it was more fun that way." She gave a laugh that quite effectively broke the ice. "So you really can see me as I truly am?"

"Yes, and I suppose I should've known that with demons running around, there had to be angels too," said Father Michaels. "But even so,

I never expected to see one in the company of ... well, you know." He pointed at the others.

"Demons," said Prelz, shaking his head. "We're demons, and proud of it! But yeah, Father, you're right, we normally would keep our distance, but this one's special. She's helped both of us quite a bit."

"I see that," said the priest, indicating Prelz's clean clothes and noticeably improved appearance. Then he turned to Torval. "In fact, when you said she was a very good friend, I must admit I thought you meant something else."

"Oh, you were right the first time," replied Christine, hugging Torval and exchanging a quick kiss with him.

"It is true," agreed Torval, returning the gesture. "For reasons neither of us truly understand, we have fallen in love."

Father Michaels just stared at them for a few long seconds before finally shaking his head in amazement. "Okay, well, I think I can safely say that now I've seen everything," he pronounced. "If the two of you decide to get married, *please* let me perform the ceremony! I've always wanted to do something nobody else ever has, and I'm pretty sure that would do the trick quite nicely."

Prelz laughed and clapped Father Michaels on the shoulder. "I don't think they're planning anything like that, but yeah, I'm sure you'd be the right one to take care of it. Anyway, the reason we're here is about me, Father."

"About you?" He turned away from the Torval and Christine, who were both still smiling over his reaction, and focused on Prelz. "What did you do now, Jake?"

"I helped save a couple lives tonight," said Prelz proudly. "Joe and I literally pulled them out of a burning building."

"You did? That's wonderful!" said the priest, clapping his hands together. "I knew you had it in you, Jake! We may be able to save your soul yet."

"Yes, well, that's just it, I'm afraid I have to leave," Prelz told him. "The two people we saved were the targets of demonic vengeance. The demon in question is after us now."

"Wait, how can a demon try to kill people?" asked Father Michaels, clearly confused. "I thought you told me that's not how it worked."

"It isn't, and that's the thing." Prelz shook his head. "This particular demon has basically gone batshit crazy. Hell's going to be sending hunt teams after him, and I can't be here with hunters roaming the streets. I'm going to take off, Father, and I don't know if I'll ever be back. That's why I came tonight—to say goodbye, and to thank you from the bottom of my heart for everything you've done for me."

"You're leaving, just like that?" The priest was clearly dismayed. "Without any warning?"

"Yes, I had the same reaction," put in Torval.

"I'm afraid so," Prelz replied, looking quite sad now. "I'm sorry, but all of this just happened tonight, and it kinda took us all by surprise. I'm going to head to the bus station right now, but I'll call as soon as I get somewhere safe."

"I understand," replied Father Michaels. "Well, then, good luck to you. I wish you well, and keep working on that redemption. It's not enough to get to Heaven through a single good deed, you know."

"Yeah, I didn't think so, dammit," chuckled Prelz. "It's been real, Father. I'll call you soon."

They shook hands, and then hugged each other, one last time. With a final wave, Prelz separated, clearly with some reluctance, and started making his way to the door.

"That reminds me," said Torval as they stepped outside. "Do you remember Hal Sommersby?"

"Of course I do," replied Prelz. "You said he went back home with his daughter. Why?"

"He said if I needed anything, I should call." Torval reached into his pocket and pulled the wrinkled business card out of his wallet. "I believe this could be one such time. If I asked him, I believe he would help you, at least until you can find a job and a place to live. Furthermore, you would be safe from the hunters."

"Well, I wouldn't want to impose, but ... yeah, I suppose I could bug him. He was always a good one, that Hal."

"I would call him now," said Torval, "but it seems my phone has wandered off."

Christine gave him a playful shove. "Oh, come on, you know that was necessary! We wouldn't want McCord to be able to—"

She was at the curb at that point, a few steps ahead of them, already looking into the streets for a cab, when suddenly a pair of loud, terrifying howls split the night. The noise, which clearly came from some unearthly throat, was close—far, far too close.

"Lucifer be damned!" moaned Prelz, all but paralyzed with fear. "The hunters—they've found me!"

Chapter 21

Before any of them could move, or even think of moving, two large shapes stepped out of the shadows between the church and the building adjacent to it. The beasts looked vaguely like mastiffs, only larger, and with red eyes that glowed like flaming embers. As they stepped ever so slowly closer, they each emitted another ear-piercing wail.

"Get inside," hissed Christine. "Now!"

Prelz didn't hesitate—he turned and dashed for the door. Torval started to follow, but stopped, torn between his desire for safety and his instictive need to protect Christine. As it turned out, she didn't need his aid at all.

The dogs started to lunge forward, but she jumped in their path, holding up a hand. "Halt!" she yelled loudly. "You cannot pass! These two are under my protection!"

The dogs screeched to a stop, eyeing her warily. They seemed to be trying to work up the nerve to attack, but were unsure of whether or not to proceed. Christine, meanwhile, began to back up slowly, until she all but ran over Torval.

"Go," she urged through pressed lips. "I can't hold them for long."

The dogs, meanwhile, separated and began to circle, obviously intending to rush past her, toward their true prey. Perhaps they wouldn't attack her directly, but she had no real power over them, so all they had to do was elude her entirely.

Torval realized this at once and hurried through the door, which Prelz held partially open. Christine followed a moment later, sucking in a deep breath as the door slammed shut behind her. "That was close," she breathed. "I can't really hurt those things, but they don't dare attack me. I doubt they'll enter while I'm here, but we can't be sure."

"Well, what now?" complained Prelz. "They won't leave, as long as they sense I'm inside. I'm screwed now!"

"What is it?" asked Father Michaels. Having heard the commotion, he returned to the main part of the church to investigate. "What's going on? I thought you were leaving!"

"Hunters," hissed Prelz. "Cerberi—the hounds of Hell, in the bodies of mortal dogs. They're right ouside."

"Will they hurt me?" asked the priest worriedly. "Perhaps I could drive them away."

"They're real dogs," explained Prelz. "They can act just like any wild dog could, so yeah, if you step out there, you better have some kind of weapon."

"Better than that," said the priest after a moment's thought, "I'll just call Animal Control. Once they take care of the problem, you can go." He retreated back into the back of the church, obviously heading for a telephone.

"I guess," said Prelz, pacing about worriedly, "but that doesn't change the fact that there's a hunter demon out there, too, and he's gonna be wondering what his dogs are doing at this church."

"If a Hunter arrives," offered Torval, "I will delay him while you escape. Perhaps if I simply explain the situation—"

"You can't explain, or deal with them!" argued Prelz. "When he realizes he's got a fugitive in here, you won't be able to stop him. Damn, I'm really screwed!"

"Just stay behind me," Christine told him. "He won't be able to attack me, so I'll run interference for you."

"Thanks, Christine," he replied, taking a deep breath. "Okay, fine, I won't panic, then, but only because you asked so nicely. Besides, I have a hole card I can play."

"A what?" asked Torval.

"A little insurance," explained Prelz. "Something I was going to use on McCord, if I ever saw—"

"SOMEONE CALL ME?"

The voice was so loud, so unexpected, that they all just froze for an instant. In that moment, the church doors burst open, revealing a tall, angry-looking man in what had, at one time, been a nicely pressed police lieutenant's uniform. The outfit, now torn and dirty, dangled in tatters, and the tie hung partly askew, as if in mockery of what this man had once been.

Christine uttered a short, terrified scream, backing up to a position just behind Torval. Prelz managed to mumble two somewhat predictable words: "Oh, shit!"

Torval, for his part, simply stared in horror. Lieutenant McCord had found them!

* * *

McCord's evil grin looked like it would split his face. He stepped boldly into the church, chuckling to himself at their reaction to his presence. Behind him, two char-black dogs waited, eyes glowing, seated on their haunches. One thing was clear—they weren't after the ex-lieutenant at all. They were, in fact, guarding the exit for him.

"Surprised?" he asked loudly, as the others backed away from him, eyes wide with terror. "You were expecting someone else, perhaps? The policeman who had me arrested, maybe? Oh, yes, I know about him, too. I know about everything. I must admit, though, I didn't know about you, Torval—or should I just call you Judas?"

"If you wish," Torval heard himself say. He was afraid, yes, but he had to fight back that emotion. Pete told him most of McCord's intimidation was just a bluff—Torval forced himself to focus on that.

"I never expected another demon to betray me," said the Corruptor, advancing far enough that the church doors slammed shut behind him with a loud bang. "I thought we were all on the same team, Torval. Now I see what happened, though. There's another Corruptor at work here, only she works for the other side. Don't you?"

He leveled his accusing gaze at Christine, who met his eyes with as much courage as she could muster. Squeezing Torval's arm for strength, she stepped out from behind him and tried to stand as tall as possible. "If you know what I am," she said firmly, "you know I am beyond your reach."

He threw back his head and laughed. "You think I care about that ridiculous Compact?" He continued to cackle madly. "It's not worth the stone tablets the Creator inscribed it on! It's worthless—meaningless words that hold no power. I could destroy you now, and nothing would come of it. Nothing!"

"Then do it," she replied, swallowing heavily as she mustered the strength to defy him. "Come on, if you think you can. Destroy me!"

"I will," he replied at once, "but at a time of my own choosing. First you will see your friends beg for death!"

She stepped in front of the others. "You'll have to go through me."

"Christine," said Torval, putting up a hand, "this is not your fight. Neither of you should be involved in this. It's between me and Mannoch."

The Corruptor laughed again. "Oh, my, such nobility, from a Second Class demon!" he cackled. "Is this what you do, wench? Turn demons into pathetic, honorable shadows of what they should have been? Ruin all that we are? Yes, you shall meet a painful end, indeed!"

"She did nothing," insisted Torval. "I chose this path of my own free will."

"Oh, free will again!" Mannoch continued to laugh. "It's always about free will! Don't you see, Torval? She corrupted you, with her goodness and kindness—it makes me sick! I can see you aren't to blame for your own actions, though. No, it was all her doing. I will send you back to Hell, where perhaps someone there can deprogram you."

"This has nothing to do with goodness or kindness," argued Torval. "It has to do with what is *right!* You, Mannoch, despite your rank, are not above the Compact. You have broken it, by your own admission, and for that you must pay the penalty."

He stopped laughing and narrowed his eyes. "Torval," he responded slowly, "I'm offering you a way out of what will otherwise be a very, very painful fate. Do you honestly refuse it? Of your own, since you like the phrase so much, free will?"

"I do," replied Torval sincerely. "You must face your punishment, Mannoch. Your time on Earth is finished."

"Very well," he glowered. "So be it. Since you prefer to make your own choices, it seems fitting that you select your own fate."

He settled into a crouch, and began to circle Torval warily. Torval gulped and tried to take up a similar stance. Just about then he remembered, much to his dismay, that he didn't know a blessed thing about fighting.

* * *

As the two demons squared off, Father Michaels chose that moment to return to the room. "Okay, I've called the Anim—wait, what in God's name is going on here?"

Christine rushed to his side. "You should leave, Father," she urged him. "That's the demon we were telling you about—and this is going to get ugly real fast!"

"Violence? In my church?" The priest didn't hesitate, marching out in front of the altar and holding up his arms. "Both of you! Cease this at once! This is a place of God, not a boxing ring!"

McCord regarded him with the same sort of look a man would give an annoying fly or mosquito. "Stay out of this, priest, or you can join them," he commanded.

"I know what you are, beast," said Father Michaels forcefully. Glancing around, his eyes fell on a decorative pole topped with a crucifix. He hefted this into the air and waved it in Mannoch's direction. "You have no place here. Begone!"

"You've been watching too many movies, Father," chuckled McCord. "You think I fear you? That this hallowed ground holds any power over me? I think not!"

Suddenly, with a speed that surprised them all, he rushed toward Father Michaels, who made a weak attempt to fend off the advancing demon with his improvised staff. He might've struck a brick wall for all the damage he did. Instead, Mannoch stepped right up to him and dealt the priest a wicked backhand, sending the unfortunate man flying. He landed with a loud thump against the back of the altar, groaning in pain.

"Leave him alone!" yelled Torval, leaping recklessly into the fight. He honestly had no idea what he was doing, for he'd never tried anything like this before. All he could do was hope his human body had some sort of reflexes he could draw on.

He tried to jump onto McCord's back, but the demon shrugged him off as if he wasn't there. Torval managed to get off two swings with flailing fists, both of which missed horribly, before Mannoch laid him out with a powerful haymaker Torval never even saw coming.

He lay sprawled out on the ground, momentarily stunned and face throbbing with pain, when Prelz made his move. The other demon, until now utterly silent, had obviously been waiting for this opportunity. A knife flashed in his grip—surprising Torval, for he hadn't known about this weapon—and Prelz pounced, striking McCord square in the back. The dagger all but disappeared from sight, buried to the hilt between the former policeman's shoulder blades.

McCord stood straight up, eyes wide with surprise and pain. He reached back, struggling to reach the weapon, but failed. After a moment, he sagged to his knees, and then toppled forward, eyes still wide open in shock.

"Ha!" laughed Prelz, almost dancing with glee. "See there? Told you I had a surprise for him! Surprise, McCord! Didn't see that coming, did you?"

"You—you had a knife?" asked Christine in amazement.

"Yeah," replied Prelz, grinning with satisfaction. "I picked one up yesterday, on the off chance I might have a shot at this asshole. Good thing, huh?"

Nearby, Father Michaels stood up groggily. He saw the body on the floor and shook his head. "Normally," he said, wincing in pain, "I'd say you needed to go to confession now, but that was no man you killed. I saw his true shape for an instant when he struck me. The stuff of nightmares, indeed!"

"He was a Corruptor," said Torval. "The very worst of us. Hopefully, now that he has returned to Hell, he'll be disciplined for his crimes."

"Not very likely," a mocking voice rang out, shocking them all into silence. "No, not likely at all!"

McCord laughed boldly as he stood, sending a chill through the room. The knife slid out of his back, clattering harmlessly on the floor, and all they could do was stare at him in horror.

Chapter 22

McCord's body stood, but did so stiffly, as if forced against its will. His face was an emotionless mask, the eyes dead and lifeless. Torval felt sure Prelz's blow had been successful in slaying the policeman, and yet his body still functioned, even in death.

"You didn't really think you'd won that easily, did you?" Mannoch hissed at them. "I am a First Class demon, the most powerful being to walk the Earth! I cannot be destroyed by some puny human weapon!" He picked the bloody knife up, regarded it with contempt, and flung it across the room.

Torval backed away, completely taken aback by this development. Prelz, similarly, shifted behind the altar, while Christine moved down off the dais entirely. Only Father Michaels remained in place, clutching his useless staff and refusing to move.

Mannoch ignored the priest entirely and advanced on Torval. "Now," he hissed, "it's time to show you some true power."

The remains of McCord's human form came apart, literally ripping at the seams until it fell away, dissolving on the ground in a bubbling pool of slime. For the first time since arriving on Earth, Torval saw a demon in its true shape without coming into direct physical contact. Mannoch seemed to grow, skin blackening, body twisting into a serpentine form, moving with a swift slithering motion instead of on two legs. His arms extended themselves, the hands twisting into claws, and before Torval could dodge, they slashed at him. He looked down to see three long gashes across his chest, torn straight through his clothing, leaving deep furrows in his skin.

The pain was as sharp as it was surprising. He'd never felt a sensation quite like this. His flesh all but screamed, causing him to clutch as his chest involuntarily. However, much to his amazement, his mind snapped into clear, crisp focus.

Mannoch took demonic form, on Earth! How was that even possible? Not that the means mattered—he'd done it, and the Corruptor meant to slay him, and everyone else in this room. There had to be some way to stop him—but how?

"Joe!" yelled Christine. "Keep away from him! He'll cut you to pieces!"

That sounded like excellent advice, so Torval ducked in amongst the church pews. Mannoch, in his much larger form, couldn't follow. Instead, he circled, looking for an opening. After a moment, he seized upon the idea of simply ripping the benches out of the floor, which he did with surprising ease. As he tore each one free, he lobbed the broken pieces across the room at either Prelz or Christine, both of whom swifly took cover as best they could.

"Stop this madness at once!" yelled Father Michaels suddenly. "Foul demon! This is a house of God!"

"Do you have a death wish?" cackled Mannoch, flinging the next piece of broken furniture at the priest, who barely dove out of the way in time. "I already told you, you have no power over me!"

Christine pulled him back behind the altar, which seemed safe for the moment. "Father, please! You should get out of here, or he'll kill you just for sport!"

"What about you?" he asked worriedly. "If I leave, you'll all be killed!"

"We'll just be sent back where we came from," she told him. "Don't worry about us. It's the way things work."

"He shouldn't be doing this!" complained Father Michaels. "Demons aren't allowed to do battle here, on Earth, and certainly not in my church! Besides, if he wins, who knows what he'll do next? No, I won't run, not if there's any way I can help."

"You can't," Christine insisted, pointing at the rampaging demon, who by now had torn up half the room. Torval continued dodging about, avoiding the larger demon's blows, but it was obvious he'd run out of time soon enough. Prelz, for his part, threw books and other items at Mannoch, but he didn't even seem to notice.

Father Michaels pointed at the ornate Bible on its stand nearby. "The Good Book tells us that at one time demons roamed the world," he said, "but holy men had the power to exorcise them. Catholic priests, too, have a ritual for that, but I lack the authority to compel a demon ... unless I have help."

"Father, no!" replied Christine. "He'll kill you!"

He nodded slowly. "Perhaps," said the man, "but it is my choice to make, is it not?"

Christine started to argue, but stopped in mid-word. "Yes," she was forced to admit. "Yes, it is. You have that power. The power of free will."

Father Michaels stood, summoning his courage. "Well, then," he said with as much confidence as he could find, "I must try."

* * *

Torval hopped over the last of the pews, keeping it between himself and Mannoch. There were only a few hiding places left. Soon he'd have little choice but to engage the creature in hand-to-hand combat, and that would be the end of him.

"Christine," he yelled out, "this is almost over. Go with Jake and flee as best you can. If you can find a cab, or reach the subway, perhaps you can escape."

"Not likely," laughed Mannoch. "My hounds have their scent. Imagine, someone sending cerberi after *me!* As if someone of my strength couldn't simply take control of them. Fools!"

"What will you do?" inquired Torval, trying to buy as much time as possible for the others to get away. "You cannot return to Hell. You must know this."

"Maybe not now," hissed the Corruptor, "but who cares? I can take over another body any time I like, you see. McCord's is gone, obviously, and too bad—that was one of my favorites! Those doubters back in Hell will realize soon enough that I'm better like this, anyway. I can find a new place, start all over again, corrupt more souls—why, I could keep this up for all eternity!"

He laughed in triumph and savagely tore away the last of the pews, flinging it against the wall with a loud crash. Torval backed up to the same wall, certain he was about to be sent involuntarily back to Hell. He was about to call out to the others to run when he noticed, to his chagrin, that Father Michaels had stepped up behind McCord. The priest held the crucifix staff again, but didn't intend to swing it as a weapon. Instead, he thrust it out in front of himself, as if in warding. In his other hand, he held a small, black-bound book, something

Torval had never seen before, and as the demon watched in complete befuddlement, the priest began to read.

"We cast you out," began Father Michaels, speaking evenly and with a great intensity, "every unclean spirit, every satanic power, every onslaught of the infernal adversary, every legion, every diabolical group and sect, in the name and by the power of our Lord Jesus Christ!"

Mannoch, upon hearing this, slowly turned in place to regard the priest as he might look upon a meal he intended at any moment to devour. "What is this?" he roared. "What are you doing?"

"We command you," Father Michaels went on, "begone and fly far from the Church of God, from the souls made by God in His image and redeemed by the precious blood of the divine Lamb. No longer dare, cunning serpent, to deceive the human race, to persecute God's Church, to strike God's elect and to sift them as wheat. For the Most High God commands you, He to whom you once proudly presumed yourself equal; He who wills all men to be saved and come to the knowledge of truth. God the Father commands you!"

Mannoch threw back his scaly head and began to laugh. In fact, he laughed through most of the verses Father Michaels was reciting. "Why, my good priest," he managed between uproarious guffaws, "are you actually trying to *exorcise* me?"

Father Michaels kept right on going. "God the Son commands you," he continued, raising his voice over Mannoch's unholy cackling. "God the Holy Spirit commands you. Christ, the eternal Word of God made flesh, commands you, who humbled Himself, becoming obedient even unto death, to save our race from the perdition wrought by your envy; who founded His Church upon a firm rock, declaring that the gates of Hell should never prevail against her, and that He would remain with her all days, even to the end of the world."

"You have no power," laughed Mannoch, raising his claws and moving toward Father Michaels, who didn't move even as the demon struck. The mighty blow sent the priest tumbling head over heels, so that he dropped the book and the staff. "The word of God means nothing to me, priest! You are just a single, insignificant human, with no authority over such as I!"

"That's true," said Christine suddenly, stepping out from behind the altar, "but you see, I'm *not* just a human. In fact, I happen to be a representative of some of the very powers Father Michaels is naming, and I, Auralea, Angel of Heaven, grant him that authority."

With that pronouncement, she tossed the book back to Father Michaels, who clambered to his feet, ignoring the deep cuts on his shoulder and chest. Retrieving his staff as well, he re-opened the book and stepped boldly forward once more.

"The sacred mystery of the cross commands you," he resumed, holding forth the crucifix, "along with the power of all mysteries of Christian faith. The exalted Virgin Mary, Mother of God, commands you, who in her lowliness crushed your proud head from the first moment of her Immaculate Conception."

"Fool!" laughed Mannoch. "Do you think I fear your ridiculous church? Your meaningless, ancient rituals do not frighten me! You have earned only a swift death!"

He started forward again, but suddenly, from almost out of nowhere, Torval intervened. He stepped right in Mannoch's way, startling him, and for an instant the Corruptor stopped. That instant was all the time Torval needed, but he wasn't looking at the snake-demon at all. Instead, his entire attention was focused upon Father Michaels.

For in that brief moment, Torval knew exactly what he had to do. He felt a sudden rush as a sense of meaning, and renewed purpose, flowed into him.

"Auralea has granted you the authority of Heaven, Father," he called out firmly, "and I, the demon Torval, grant you the authority of Hell itself. Drive this creature out, Father, for he has broken the Compact, and for that he must be destroyed!"

"No!" screamed Mannoch, grabbing Torval and flinging him across the room as easily as if he were a feather. Torval felt intense pain as his body slammed into the wall, and there was a definite crack as something important in his chest snapped. He fell, searing agony dancing through his brain, but even so, he didn't take his eyes off Father Michaels.

"The faith of the holy apostles Peter and Paul and the other apostles commands you," the priest uttered, no longer looking at the book in his hand, stepping forward with staff held out, crucifix jutting forward like the tip of a spear. "The blood of martyrs and the devout prayers of all holy men and women command you!"

"This cannot be!" cried a suddenly fearful Mannoch, backing away until pressed into a corner. "You cannot—this is impossible!"

Father Michaels lowered the book, and a smile of satisfaction crossed his face. He seemed, for an instant, to glow with a faint white light, although that could've just been the pain screaming through Torval's mind for all he knew.

"What is more," the priest said with infinite confidence, *"I* command you. I, Father Thomas Michaels, a human being, command you. By the authority of Heaven and Hell alike, I command thee, BEGONE!"

"NO!" screamed Mannoch, suddenly lunging forward. Both his clawed hands came together, slamming directly into Father Michaels' chest and abdomen. The priest stiffened, and a trickle of blood appeared in his mouth, but the smile of triumph never left his face.

He reached out with the crucifix and lightly touched Mannoch's head. Instantly the demon began to scream. He tore his claws free, sending blood spurting amidst the wrecked pews, but even as he clutched at his face, he was already stiffening. His body swiftly blackened, hissing and charring as if on fire, though there were no flames at all. Mannoch writhed and wailed, threw his head back, and let out a final moan.

Then his serpentine form petrified, for a moment freezing into a statue before finally collapsing into ash, which itself swirled, hissing, dissipating until there was nothing left, not even a single grain of dust.

Chapter 23

"Someone want to tell me what the hell just happened?" demanded Prelz, cautiously emerging from where he'd been hiding by the door.

"It is over," proclaimed Torval, rising from where he'd fallen, breathing only with great difficulty. "Mannoch is destroyed. Not just sent back to Hell—he was consigned to Oblivion."

Prelz nodded. "Couldn't think of a better fate for—oh, geez, Father Michaels!"

He rushed forward, along with Christine, to the side of the fallen priest. Father Michaels bled profusely from a number of deep, vicious-looking wounds. Thick red fluid also poured from his mouth, staining his face and the white collar about his neck.

"Is it ... is it done?" he asked through the bubbling froth on his lips.

"Yeah," said Prelz worriedly. "It's over, Father. You did good."

"So ... so we won?" he sputtered.

"Yes, we were victorious," said Torval. "You defeated him, Father. You destroyed a great evil this day."

He nodded slowly, looking up at the three of them. "Then ... then my job is done here, isn't it?"

"You'll be okay, Father," Prelz insisted. "We'll call an ambulance, and get you some help. Just stay with us, okay?"

"No, it's all right," he told them. "I'm ... I have to go, Jake ... looks like I'm the one leaving you, not the other way around, huh?"

"No, you'll be fine," insisted Prelz, but already tears flowed down his face. He wiped them away absently. "I—I thought I knew how to risk my life for somebody, but you got me beat by far."

Father Michaels smiled at that. "I always wondered," he told them, beginning to gasp for breath now, "w-why I had this ability ... why I could see you, Jake. Now I know. I was put here ... f-for a reason ... "

"You showed me," whispered Prelz. "You showed me the way. I

see now. I understand."

The priest smiled and looked over at Torval, who was trying to think of something to say, but couldn't come up with any words. "It's good," said Father Michaels with his dying breath, "t-to know you have a purpose ... isn't it ... ?"

"Yes," agreed Torval, even as Father Michaels' body went limp. "Yes, it most certainly is."

* * *

Prelz tried for a few minutes to revive the priest, but it was clearly too late. The force that once animated that body had departed. The wounds, though not that serious-looking, pierced something important deep within his chest.

"He's gone," said Christine sadly, hanging her head. "We shouldn't be sad. There can only be one place someone like him could go. Rarely have I seen any soul more deserving of a heavenly reward."

"Yeah, well, whatever, that doesn't change the fact that he's dead! I just can't believe it!" muttered Prelz, pacing around the body. "He sacrificed himself, for us! Why didn't he just leave when he had the chance? He could've just walked out of here, and that would've been fine!"

"He did it of his own free will," Christine reminded him. "He chose to intervene, so Mannoch wouldn't be able to spread his evil any further. I didn't even talk him into it—he came up with the idea himself."

"He was your friend," added Torval. "He knew what he had to do. He knew his purpose, as I now do."

"What do you mean by that?" demanded Prelz.

Torval sighed, clutching at his injured chest, which almost certainly had at least one, and perhaps more, broken ribs. Just breathing was painful, but he knew that wouldn't matter much longer. He could see the evidence already forming in a spinning whorl against the back wall of the church, where the unfortunate Mannoch met his end just a few moments before.

"When I gave the authority of Hell to Father Michaels," said Torval plainly, "I finally understood, Prelz. I know what it is I am to do. I know what I've changed into."

"Changed into ... ?" Christine eyed him warily. "Why are you using the past tense? Aren't you still changing?"

"Not anymore." Torval shook his head. "I have completed my Advancement."

"How can you possibly know that?" she wondered, reaching out to take his hand, immediately assuming her angelic shape. "You look the same now as you did yesterday. Maybe a little bit better—did I tell you how handsome you look like that? Those horns of yours are really sexy, you know."

He drew her close, taking a moment to enjoy what he now knew would be among their last moments together. "I appreciate the compliment," he told her, planting an appreciative kiss on her faintly glowing forehead, "but you mustn't change the subject."

"Yeah, seriously, get a room, you two," insisted Prelz. "How can you think you've finished your Advancement? You said it would take two weeks, not one!"

"I felt it happen," explained Torval. "I felt the shift complete. I understand now why I have been so obsessed with good and evil, Prelz. Ever since arriving here, I have wanted to understand those two opposing facets of human existence. Furthermore, I have experienced the full range of human emotions, including perhaps the most intense of all—the love of a woman, and an angel besides."

He and Christine embraced again, causing Prelz to roll his eyes. "Do you guys want me to wait outside? Oh, wait, never mind, those dogs are still out there."

"They will not be for long," said Torval. "They are here for me, not you, and when I go, they will lose their purpose and return to Hell."

"What do you mean, when you go? What are you blathering about?"

"I was attempting to explain," insisted Torval, "but Christine keeps interrupting me. Not that I'm complaining."

"It's not my fault!" she argued, giving him a mock shove. "Get on with it, you!"

"As I was saying," Torval went on, "there can be only one explanation for my acute interest in the opposing forces in human existence. I required an understanding of those forces in order to perform my new task."

Prelz looked at him thoughtfully. "Which is?"

"Is it not obvious?" Torval replied. "I have become a Judge."

* * *

"A Judge, yeah," replied Prelz at once. "I can see that. Sure. Never met a Judge before, 'cause they're pretty rare, but sure, it makes sense. That's why you look mostly human. You have to be almost human, in order to judge souls effectively."

"Yes," agreed Torval, "and Mannoch was my first judgment. When I told Father Michaels to destroy him, that was justice being done. In that single moment, I completed my Advancement. I am now Torval, Demon Second Class, judge of all that is good and evil in the souls of men."

"Wow, congratulations," said Christine with a gleam in her eye. "That's quite a title, Torval. Did you come up with that yourself?"

"Basically, yes," he told her with a smile. "It seems to fit me well, don't you think?"

"Sounds good to me," replied Prelz. "Now, back to the matter of the hounds of Hell sitting outside ... "

"That," said Torval, "is the one downside of all of this. You see, now that I've completed my Advancement, there's no further reason for me to remain on Earth."

"Yes, there is!" insisted Christine. "You still have a week to spend with me! That's reason enough to stick around, isn't it?"

"I would like nothing better." Torval sighed, again wincing in pain. "However, it seems I will not be permitted that luxury. See, the portal is already opening."

He pointed at the back of the church, where a dark swirl occupied the space along the wall. Its purpose was unmistakable, as it was exactly the same as the vortex that brought him to Earth in the first place. Geezon told him to watch for this when his time in the Middle World was over.

"I don't see any portal," snapped Prelz.

"Me either," agreed Christine. "You sure you aren't imagining it?"

"It is there," said Torval. "I can already feel its pull. I must enter it, unless I wish to go rogue, and meet the same fate as Mannoch."

"No, that's not fair!" complained Christine. "Torval, you can't! You still have a week left! That's what they told you, isn't it? They can't deny the rest of your vacation now, just because you got done early!"

Torval shook his head. "This was never about a vacation, Christine. The entire reason for my coming here was so that I could Advance. Prelz and I figured this out early on, but I didn't really grasp the full meaning of it until now. This was no vacation, but a mission with a single purpose, and that mission has been achieved. Thus, I must go."

"You—you can't!" Christine was almost in tears. "You can't go! We—we just found each other, and now we're free of—of everything else, and—oh, please, you just can't!"

"Christine," he replied sadly. "Auralea. I love you with every part of me that is capable of doing so, but I cannot stay."

"You—you could, if you wanted to," she replied, tears flowing down her cheeks. "You could stay. You could ... choose to stay. Stay with me."

Nearby, Prelz shook his head and gave a half-hearted smile. "Now, now," he told her with a wag of his finger, "no tempting, please! That's *my* job!"

Christine looked momentarily horrified, and put a hand to her mouth. "Oh, no! Oh, Torval, I'm so sorry! I shouldn't have—I didn't mean to ... "

"It's all right," he replied with a smile. "I would've been disappointed if you hadn't tried. I can't stay, though. You know I can't. You helped me find myself, my true self, and we must be content with that. I cannot deny what I am, any more than you could deny you are an angel."

She hugged him, still crying softly. "I know," she whispered. "I know ... God help me, I understand, but I don't want to—I don't want to lose you, Torval. Not now!"

"Auralea," he said quietly, "I do love you, but I must go. My time on Earth has come to an end."

They embraced again, one last time, and shared a lasting kiss that served as their final goodbye. Torval lingered as long as he could, resisting the tug of the portal, enjoying the touch of her, the tingling sensation that swept through him whenever they were close, and the knowledge that, at least for a while, he had found someone he cared about even more than himself.

Then he stepped away. She was still softly weeping as he backed into the portal. His last sight on Earth was of her, raising her hand in a finishing wave, and then he no longer needed his human body.

The corpse of Joe Sampson slumped to the ground, a single tear glistening on his dead cheek, and Torval made his way home at last.

Chapter 24

Torval blinked.

He recognized the room immediately. Almost exactly one week ago, this was the last place he saw before leaving Hell. Now he had returned, standing in front of a rapidly closing portal, looking at the same black-skinned demon who had sent him to Earth in the first place.

"Welcome home, Torval," said Geezon with a toothy grin. "Sorry to end your vacation early, but that's the way these things work out sometimes."

"You are not sorry," noted Torval, looking down at himself, seeing his new form for the first time. He did indeed superficially resemble a human, but with thicker skin and no body hair whatsoever. His hands had no talons, or even fingernails for that matter. He couldn't see his face, but a touch of his head confirmed he had a thick mane atop his head, as Christine had mentioned, as well as curving horns that swept back to sharp points just behind his ears.

"No, I suppose I'm not," agreed Geezon with a shrug.

"You misled me," Torval stated emotionlessly, "regarding your true purpose in sending me to Earth."

Geezon nodded slowly. "I am a Transitioner," he replied, as if that explained everything. Perhaps it did, at that. "I suppose you realize now why you were really sent there, hmm?"

"Yes," agreed Torval. "The truth of my mission became obvious only days into the trip. Why did you not tell me in advance, if it was that easy to figure out?"

Geezon grinned again. "It screws up everything if you know beforehand," he explained. "When you left here, just beginning your Advancement, you were like a malleable chunk of clay, ready to be sculpted. The experiences you had on Earth pulled and pushed at you, twisting you, changing you slowly into the demon you were to become."

"Then you did not know when I left what I was changing into?"

"No, of course not," sighed Geezon wearily, obviously having had to explain this to many other demons in the past. "When your superior heard you ask that fateful question, all we knew is your Advancement had begun. That's why I hurried you along so quickly—we didn't want anything you did here to influence you any further."

"Question? What question?"

"What? Oh, that." Geezon tilted his head slightly. "It's very simple. You asked your Foreman *why*."

"Why what?"

Geezon shrugged. "I wasn't there, but he said you asked him a question that started with 'why.' That's what they look for, you see. Third Class demons never ask why, they just do what they're told."

Torval nodded, considering that explanation carefully. He hadn't thought about the actual event before, but of course, that's exactly what happened. He had asked Landri why humans had to be tortured—and that's when this whole vacation nonsense began.

"When I was on Earth," said Torval a bit worriedly, "I changed events. I influenced humans. I experienced emotions. I made friends, and enemies." The fate of Mannoch flashed before him, and he wondered if perhaps he'd get in trouble for that particular bit of unpleasantness. "I did some ... questionable things."

"I'm sure you did, but that's fine," replied the Transitioner with a shrug. "Honestly, I don't really care what you did. It doesn't matter, at least not to me."

"Then you are not aware of the exact events that transpired? You were not watching my progress somehow, from your post here in Hell?"

"Are you kidding? Like I have time to keep my eyes on every demon in Transition? I've got better things to do! Besides, it's not like you broke the Compact or anything." Geezon narrowed his eyes. "You didn't ... did you?"

"No," replied Torval honestly. "In fact, if anything, I believe I ensured the Compact was upheld."

"Not surprising, seeing you as you are now." Geezon smiled that toothy smile of his. "Look at it this way, Torval. For a week, you were human, with all the freedom mortality brings, and see what it's made you." He pointed at Torval's new body. "You've Advanced, as you can see. You're a Second Class demon now. You have a new purpose."

"Yes, I believe I do."

Geezon nodded, apparently glad he didn't have to explain any further. "Then are you ready to begin?"

Torval nodded, taking one last look around the room. The portal had disappeared completely by now, but he imagined, for a brief moment, he could still see Christine's lovely face smiling at him through the nonexistent vortex.

"Yes, I am ready," he finally said, wondering if the pain of loss would ever go away.

"Good." Geezon smiled. "Follow me, then, so you can begin the next phase of your existence."

* * *

Of course, Torval didn't leap immediately into being a Judge. Just as when he'd first advanced to Third Class, he needed training in his new task.

Geezon took him to a large structure at the junction between the First and Second Circles, a place called the Chambers of Judgment. Here, souls that descended to Hell were studied, evaluated, and finally sentenced to their final punishment. Torval expected that, as a Judge, he'd be required to determine their fate, as he had done with Mannoch, but apparently one did not leap directly into such a role.

Instead, he found himself assigned—temporarily, Geezon told him—to a Second Class demon named Arbiter Kylee. She frowned at the initial sight of Torval, rubbed absently at the corkscrew-shaped horns jutting out of her bony head, and shooed Geezon away. "Fine, fine, whatever, I'll take care of it," she muttered, as if having to deal with Torval was some sort of burden.

"I have just Advanced," he explained unnecessarily. "Where should I go now?"

"Nowhere," Kylee snapped. "Your job now is to follow me and watch the procedure, got it? When you're ready to actually do something, I'll tell you, and not before."

"Very well," replied Torval. She held the same rank as himself, so she had no direct authority, but still, she was the one who knew how things worked here, so he deferred to her experience.

At first, she showed him the scanning and evaluation process, where souls had their lives examined and their many sins tallied. There were demons called Recorders who created a file on each soul and its misdeeds, just in case some problem arose later. Such things were rare, explained Kylee, but they did happen. Also, sometimes the fate of one soul was closely intertwined with that of one or more others, and on occasion, they would share similar or even combined fates. In that case, careful records were needed to identify the other souls and determine an effective mass punishment.

The job of a Judge, it seemed, was to consider all a soul's sins, rule on its final fate, and recommend a certain level of torment. Then, another demon called a Sentencer would prepare the proper cell illusion from an appropriate fragment of the soul's life experiences. A Judge could give suggestions, and in rare cases could even decide there were mitigating circumstances that brought a soul to Hell by mistake. That, it seemed, explained why Torval needed a thorough knowledge of good and evil, and what it meant to be human.

After studying the process, Torval felt ready to start working—if not by himself, at least under the tutelage of an actual Judge. However, Kylee vehemently disagreed. After asking Torval a few questions, which he felt sure he'd answered properly, she threw up her hands in exasperation. "Hopeless!" she complained. "You're supposed to be a Judge, and that's the best you can do? Maybe in a decade, if you're lucky."

"But I am certain I—" Torval protested.

"Do you think I care what you think you did?" she barked. "Do I *look* like I care? Oh, all right, I guess maybe I can find something for you to do—go over to Recording and get yourself a temporary position. I'm sure you can make yourself useful, if you really want to. Go on—go!"

Torval hung his head. He didn't know what he'd done wrong, but he followed her orders. If he still had a tail, it would've been tucked between his legs.

* * *

Recording was incredibly boring. In fact, it reminded him very much of doing data entry for the Roxtons. All he did was sift through a soul's experiences, flowing past him at high speed, looking for the darker, more evil acts. Since these almost always stood out as black marks (in his perception, as least), they were easy to spot and not the least bit challenging.

Worse, he knew his talents were being wasted. With each soul that came through, he found himself attempting to judge it, just for practice, and to see if he really understood the procedure. He kept an eye on the results of each imagined recommendation, and found that in nearly every case, the actual judgment almost always agreed with his advice. After a few days of this, Torval had his success rate down to nearly one hundred percent.

He tried to get Arbiter Kylee to let him move to a Judge's position, but she wouldn't even talk to him. Frustrated, Torval found himself performing less and less effectively. His thoughts kept drifting back to his experiences on Earth, and the people he met there. Some of them, like the Roxtons, had their lives changed dramatically thanks to his presence, while others were affected only slightly. What was Shelly Mendez doing now, for example? Was she still trying to teach her unique skills to others? What about Zac Turillo, or others he'd met just as briefly, like Sarah, Brent, Vince, Marty, and more?

He had no way of knowing for sure. The only way he'd ever know is if their souls passed through here and he had a chance to review their lives. And what about Prelz? Torval kept an eye out for that particular soul, but he didn't see it at all, or any record that it had passed this way. Clearly Prelz was still alive, at least for now.

Torval's mind continued to wander. He thought often of Christine, and found that despite his concerns to the contrary, his human emotions didn't fade once he returned to Hell. He still loved her, and missed her terribly. He wanted very much to see her again, but of course that was impossible. There was no way he knew of for a Judge, or even a Judge trainee, to go back to Earth.

Perhaps, he mused, *I should've stayed on Earth after all. If I'd accepted humanity, at least I'd be with Christine now, even though I'd be permanently locked in a human shell.*

Surely that'd be better than my current fate, he thought morosely.

* * *

Many days later, he found his mind wandering, as it often did when he slogged his way through the drudgery of his new post. For the first time since returning to Hell, he thought about Joe Sampson, the unfortunate man whose death in the frozen streets of New York City made his own transformation possible. Whatever became of that particular soul, anyway?

Fortunately, Torval worked in a Recorder's office, so during a break, it was a simple matter to search those records for a man named Joe Sampson who died on a specific day, not so very long ago. Finding only one such candidate, he pulled the file. Reading through it, Torval frowned. Joe had been judged guilty of wasting his life, and was sentenced to relive his uselessness in an eternal winter.

Torval's eyes widened as he saw where the soul had been sent—Cell 10,498 of Layer Four Hundred Twelve in the Eighth Circle. Torval didn't even need to look up where that was, for he recognized the location automatically. Joe's soul now languished in the cell formerly occupied by none other than Michael Rubin!

This couldn't be a coincidence—Joe's soul went to that specific spot for a reason, or at least by someone with a very fine sense of irony. Torval studied the record further, trying to figure out why Joe might be placed in that particular cell. Reading the recorded instructions, he noted that the location in question, having recently been vacated, was simply filled according to "normal" procedures.

Torval gave a derisive snort. There was nothing normal about that—unless it was the biggest coincidence in the history of Hell itself!

Furthermore, the sentencing record looked deliberately vague. What, exactly, were Joe Sampson's sins? Other than the brief mention of a "wasted life," he hadn't done anything specifically evil. Even when he killed those two people in the trucking accident, it was just that—an *accident*. He certainly didn't deserve to be trapped forever in Hell just to work off that particular debt. If anything, he should be somewhere else entirely, for his life had been mostly a good one.

Torval fretted about this for the remainder of his shift. It bothered him greatly that Joe, the man who unwittingly loaned Torval his body, should be treated so unjustly. After a while he realized that it didn't even matter that Joe had done Torval a favor (so to speak). What mattered was that a soul had been trapped in Hell by mistake. Torval intended to correct this error, and he didn't bother asking for permission to do so.

He waited until it was time for his rest cycle, but rather than return to his room, he instead boarded the next transport to the Eighth Circle.

* * *

Foreman Landri regarded Torval with a sense of obvious amusement. His ever-present rolls of fat jiggled often with each of his loud chuckles. "You honestly think this soul is imprisoned here unjustly?" laughed the enormous demon. "Really, Torval, I though I trained you better than that."

"This doesn't involve my former status in any way," replied the would-be Judge, somewhat amazed by the difference wrought by his new rank. Before, he always deferred to Landri, almost cringing in his presence. Now, for the first time, Torval could treat him as an equal. "What I tell you is entirely accurate."

"Well," replied the Foreman, "if you say so. It's no skin off my stomach." He rumbled with laughter again, scratching at his immense belly. "I will, of course, be reporting your interference to your superiors."

"Do what you must," replied Torval with a shrug. "You don't need to accompany me. I know the way to that particular cell."

"I'm sure you do. In fact, when they put that one in there, I rather suspected you might check in on it someday. In any event, try not to stumble over your successor on the way out there. I just finished training him last week, and he's pretty dull, even compared to you."

"I will avoid him," agreed Torval, hoping that this was the last time he'd ever have to deal with Landri. Once, the corpulent demon had the power to awe and terrify him, but now, he seemed merely annoying.

Torval made his way through the corridors lining the cells, keeping an eye out for any Third Class demons, but saw none. The chances he'd bump into one were low, of course. There were hundreds of cells on each demon's route, after all.

No such encounter occurred, and soon he found himself standing before the cell in question. This was the place where his life began to change, all those weeks ago. Sighing at the memory, he pushed through the wall and stepped inside, to find himself once again on Earth.

The familiar sight almost chilled him with its eerie similarity to his arrival in the Middle World. Snow fell on the alley where Torval first awakened in Joe's body. At Torval's feet, Joe Sampson huddled under a stack of flimsy, half-soaked cardboard, guzzling futilely at a wine bottle. He didn't look up when the demon appeared, now cloaked in the illusion of a ragged street bum.

"Joe?" Torval called out. "Joe Sampson, is that you?"

"What?" demanded the wino, sitting up and shivering. "Leave me be, damn you! Let me rot in peace!"

Torval studied the man. He looked exactly as he'd remembered from his own image in Christine's mirror, with the same heavy beard, thick hair and wind-scarred face. There was something very pitiful and pathetic about him.

"I've come to help you," said Torval after a moment. "Surely you must agree that you need help."

"What I need is some alcohol that actually works!" argued Joe. "This stuff is like water! Why can't I get drunk? Give me some of that and you'll be doin' me the best favor I could hope for!"

"No," Torval replied firmly. "No, I won't give you that, Joe. I have come to give you something far greater."

"Drugs?" begged Joe. "A kick to the head? Something to make me—something to help me forget? Dammit! Why can't I forget? Why, oh why, oh God, please, let me forget ... "

"Joe." Torval leaned down, reaching out his arm, holding his palm in front of the pitiful wretch before him. "Joe Sampson. Take my hand, and let me show you something. Let me give you what you need—what you've always needed."

Joe looked at his visitor, and his eyes widened. At first he hesitated, but then, trembling, he reached out and grabbed hold of Torval's hand.

The snow stopped falling, and the city melted away. In its place, the morning sun shone down on a grassy field filled with small monuments of stone. A cluster of people, dressed in black, surrounded a pair of intricately carved wooden boxes suspended over holes in the earth. The mood was somber, and someone began to speak, reading with quiet reverence from the Bible.

"For God so loved the world, that He sent his only Son ... "

Joe emitted a choking cry. "No!" he screamed, for he now wore a crisply tailored black suit, his hair cut short and face clean-shaven. He seemed ready to flee in a panic, but Torval, now similarly dressed, held his companion's arm firmly. All Joe's strength seemed to leave him, and he sank to the ground, sobbing.

"No, please, don't make me see this again," he wailed. "Please, no, whoever you are, take me back!"

"I will not," insisted Torval firmly. "Do you remember when

you were here before, Joe? At this very funeral?"

"Of course I remember, damn you!" he snarled. "I—I watched—from right here ... and I couldn't—I couldn't face those people! That family—I killed that man's wife and little girl! I killed them, oh God, I'm so sorry ... so, so very sorry ... "

"Then go to them," Torval replied, pointing in the direction of the mourners. "Go, and tell them that. That is what you've always wanted, Joe. What you've always wished you could've done, when you had the chance. Do it now, Joe. I'm giving you that chance, at long last. Do what you must."

He let go of Joe's hand. The man stood, looking around like a caged beast who'd been set suddenly free. He started to run, but then, in an instant, he saw before him a snowy street corner, the frozen nightmare of an endless winter in New York, an eternity trapped in what he now knew for certain was Hell.

He swallowed and looked back at the mourners. The verse from the Bible came to an end, as the coffins were lowered somberly into the ground. Everyone remained silent, save for a few muffled sobs. This was, indeed, his last chance—a chance he thought he'd never have again.

In that moment, the tortured soul of Joe Sampson made a choice. He clutched his hands into fists and, steeling himself, forced his wobbly feet forward, one step at a time, gathering momentum until finally he reached the knot of people, where at last he collapsed to his knees, tears flowing freely down his cheeks.

"I'm so sorry," he wailed pitifully. "This is all my fault ... all my fault ... I'm so sorry ... "

As one, the crowd surrounded him. Hands came down to rest softly on his shoulders, and the mourners were weeping too.

"I forgive you, Joe," said one, kneeling down next to him, and he saw, even through tear-filled eyes, that it was the husband of the woman he'd killed. "We all forgive you."

Joe collapsed into the man's arms, sobbing, and in that moment his soul was freed. He flared into pure white light, rising rapidly upward, escaping the confines of the cell, bound for where he truly belonged at last.

Chapter 25

Torval watched Joe depart, and realized he was crying, too. His ability to feel emotions clearly hadn't left him. He felt a great, soul-lifting joy at the sight of a wronged soul finding redemption, and yet, a part of him pitied all of Joe's wasted years of self-torture that so easily could've been avoided.

The cell's environment faded back to its normal, neutral state. He took a deep breath, flexing his fingers. He hadn't been sure, when he came to this place, if he'd be able to actually change the illusion like that, but then, he hadn't actually done it himself. All he did was invoke another of Joe's memories, allowing the soul to create the funeral scene around him exactly as he remembered it. That's why it looked so perfectly realistic—it all stemmed from a point in time burned indelibly into the memories of Joe Sampson.

Torval so no reason to remain here any further. He turned to leave, and came up short. To his surprise, someone else stood in the back of the cell, where the mourners were before they faded out. If the observer had been Landri, or even Torval's Third Class successor, he might've understood that, but instead he saw someone totally unexpected—Arbiter Kylee!

She enhanced his surprise still further by holding up her hands and clapping. "Very well done," she told him, smiling. "Better than I would've thought for a first-timer."

"What do you mean?" asked a confused Torval. "What are you doing here, Arbiter?"

She shrugged. "Oh, I've been waiting for you to come here for some time now, actually," she told him. "I knew you'd get curious about Joe Sampson eventually, and when you saw the cell number I knew you'd come running."

"That doesn't answer my question," Torval replied impatiently.

"I know, but you have to allow me these little pleasures. They don't come that often, you know. Anyway, what do I mean? I should think that would be obvious. This was a test, Torval."

"A test ... ?"

"Of course," she explained. "We can't just let any randomly Advanced demon jump right into Judging, at least not until we're sure they're going to be fair about it. We had to be sure you'd learned enough about good to do the right thing. Most demons wouldn't, you see. Most demons just wouldn't care."

"A test," repeated Torval, somewhat annoyed by this. "You deliberately forced Joe Sampson to endure Hell in order to test me?"

"Not all sentences to Hell are permanent, Torval," she explained patiently. "Sometimes, a soul has something it needs to finish, some truth it needs to realize, before it can receive its final Judgment. That was the case here—we weren't torturing Joe, you see. You can check the records for yourself, if you wish—no Punisher ever visited him, not once since he got here. Eventually, without the alcohol to make him forget, his mind would've forced him to make peace with himself. All you did was come along and speed it up a little. I'm sure if he could, he'd thank you for that."

"I see," replied Torval, nodding in understanding. "Will he receive the comfort he so longed for in life, then?"

"I'm sure he will," said Kylee. "That's what Heaven is all about, or so they tell me. I've never been there myself, of course, but if I ever meet an angel, I'll ask, and let you know."

She chuckled at that, and Torval just nodded. She was joking, of course, but Torval had actually met an angel, and asked her something similar, and if what she told him was true, then Joe really was in a better place now.

"If I have passed your test," he asked after a moment, "what happens now?"

"Now?" She smiled and took him proudly by the arm. "Now we see about fitting you with some Judge's robes."

* * *

Torval settled into the responsibilities of Judging with little fanfare. There were no trumpets or congratulations, just a new office where

Third Class demons brought him souls to receive Judgment. In each case he would review the notes provided by Evaluators, study the soul in detail as necessary, and finally produce a recommendation. Then it was on to the next one.

He could take as long as needed with each case, for it was vitally important that each soul receive a proper Judgment. Sometimes, he found ones similar to Joe Sampson, who needed only to realize something about themselves in order to move elsewhere. These were sent to open cells, with no further punishment required. Most of the time, though, souls were quite noticeably evil, so producing a Judgment wasn't that hard. Occasionally, though rarely, he found a soul that didn't fit the usual patterns, and these he spent the most time with. Every now and then, he'd find that a supposed sin really had a noble purpose, or there might be some other mitigating factor. He felt a sense of distinct pride at catching these mistakes and sending such souls where they truly belonged.

One day, a soul came in that the Evaluators said was a particularly tricky case. Torval examined the initial notes, and saw no reason why this soul should even be in Hell at all. There was some evil early on, but then, it redeemed itself, primarily through good deeds and even some actual heroism.

Torval left his office and cornered the Evaluator who'd worked the case. "Why is this soul here?" he demanded. "Why did you bring it to me?"

"I apologize, sir," said the thin, wiry demon, looking more than a little frightened at being addressed so harshly. "The soul is not human, sir. It is a demon soul, and it was brought to you because we felt you would best understand this specific case."

Torval nodded, starting to get an inkling of what this was all about. "Very well, then, continue your work." He turned and hurried back to his office, whereupon he examined the records in detail. After a few minutes of study he found what he was looking for and smiled.

He stepped over to the soul. He had the power to examine the life's memories directly, or even cause them to manifest in physical form. He willed this particular soul to take its most familiar shape.

A human appeared out of the glowing light. The man wore jeans and a simple T-shirt, and his head was shaved bare. He glanced around, saw Torval, and grinned.

"Torval!" he called out. "Good to see you, buddy. Guess I'm in Hell after all, huh? Ah, well, at least I passed your way."

"Hello, Prelz," replied Torval with a grin. "It's good to see you again, old friend, even if you did have to die to get here."

"Yeah, well, we all knew that was coming," replied Prelz, looking down at his partially transparent self. "Ah, I remember when I looked this good! Those were the days, I guess. Unfortunately, I kinda faded fast when they started the chemo. Hal's kid set all that up, you know. She's really amazing. Hal's got a good thing going, too. He's really back on his feet. You shouldn't be seeing either of them here, I bet."

"That's good news," replied Torval, pleased to hear it. "And now I must know—how is Christine?"

"She's fine," Prelz told him. "She came to see me at the hospital a couple of times, before the end. She still loves you, y'know."

"And I still love her," replied Torval, feeling the pain of loneliness stab through him once again. "I hope she has moved on."

"No, she hasn't," Prelz told him. "I think she's waiting for you. If there's any way, any way at all, you have to get back there. Find her again, if at all possible."

"I cannot go," Torval told him. "I'm a Judge now. This is my purpose, my reason for being. In fact, I'm quite good at it."

"How good?" asked Prelz curiously, if not a bit hopefully.

"Good enough to spot when someone doesn't belong in Hell," replied Torval with a smile. "Apparently they sent you here because you had a demon soul, but that doesn't matter as far as I'm concerned. A soul is a soul, and should be judged on its own merits, not how its existence began. You don't belong here, Prelz."

He smiled and breathed an obvious sigh of relief. "I was hoping you'd say that," he said gratefully. "I tried really hard, you know. I really did. It's not about how hard you try, though. It's about the kind of person you are, deep down inside. You know, I think I really understand now what being good is all about."

"From what I can tell, you succeeded quite well." Torval closed the Recorder's notes and pushed them aside. "Your soul will be released to Heaven, Prelz. I hope it's as good a place as they say."

"Me too," he agreed. "At least there I won't have to worry about tempted humans, red-eyed dogs or ticked-off Corruptors."

"Let's hope not," replied Torval with a grin. "Oh, and while you're there, if you happen to run into Joe Sampson, tell him thanks for letting me borrow his body."

"Will do," agreed Prelz with a grin. "Thanks, buddy. I knew I could count on you for a fair trial."

Torval inclined his head. "You're welcome," he said, nodding. "After all, it's the only type I know."

* * *

The wide door awaited, and Torval stood there, for a moment, considering what to say. He'd been anticipating, and dreading, this meeting all week. He would finally learn, once and for all, whether or not he'd ever have another chance to see Christine.

There was no sense waiting further. He pushed the portal open and stepped inside. Geezon stood there, doing something to the intricate controls that operated the black gateways to the Middle World. "There you are," said the Transitioner impatiently. "I got your message. What did you want to discuss?"

Torval sighed. "This will be difficult for me," he explained unsteadily.

"You do look a bit stressed," replied Geezon, nodding and picking at his needle-like teeth with a thick claw. "What's the problem?"

"While I was on Earth," admitted Torval, "I met a woman, and we fell in love."

Geezon emitted a sigh and shook his head sadly. "Oh, by Lucifer's twisted beard, not this again!"

"Again ... ?"

"Yes, it happens a lot," sighed Geezon. "Your first trip to Earth, you've never met a real human woman, so she looks exotic and beautiful, and one thing leads to another ... I've heard it all before, trust me."

"This is no ordinary woman—" started Torval.

"Oh, of course not, she's perfect, indescribable, gorgeous, et cetera, and so on! Heard. It. All. Before."

"But, this is different," Torval tried to explain, but the Transitioner would hear nothing of it.

"Look, Torval," said Geezon in an almost fatherly tone, "whoever she is, she's just a human. A *mortal.* You're a demon, see? The two of you can't have a future. You won't age, and she will. She'll move on to other men, and then you're just a memory."

"I assure you," said Torval, wondering if he should take the time to explain Christine's true nature, "that is not the case here."

Geezon nodded, emitting a long sigh of surrender. "Okay, fine, if you say so, but it's always the same, trust me. Even if I send you back, you're only in for disappointment. Just remember her the way you last saw her—it's for the best."

"You mean," asked Torval hopefully, "that you *can* send me back? It's possible to go back to the same place I visited before?"

Geezon shrugged. "Anything's possible, my friend," he replied, smiling cryptically. "Well, almost anything, I suppose, but you get the idea. I certainly can't do it now, of course. Not without a good reason."

At least, thought Torval, *there's a possibility, however faint it might be.* That, if nothing else, gave him hope.

"I will see her again, then," he promised, speaking almost entirely to himself. "I don't care what it takes."

"We'll see," replied Geezon with a shrug. "Come back when you have it figured out."

Torval nodded as he turned to leave. There *was* a way back to Earth, and no matter what, he would find it!

Epilogue

The late spring evening remained rather warm, so Christine didn't bother with her jacket as she stepped out of the shelter. She waved a quick goodbye to the other volunteers and stepped over toward the curb, looking for a passing cab to signal. There didn't seem to be any vehicles heading in her direction at the moment, probably because of the red light at the corner, so she simply stood and waited.

A man stepped out of the darkness nearby, startling her with his presence. She glanced his way for a second, then looked again. He seemed somehow familiar, though she didn't know his name. She'd seen him before ... earlier that night, in fact. He'd been sitting in the back of the shelter, but he wasn't in line and didn't take any soup. In fact, he was dressed much too nicely to be a bum, with a decent coat and nicely tailored slacks as well as what looked like expensive dress shoes. His sharply angular face, barely visible in the shadows, could clearly stand a shave.

"Something I can help you with?" she inquired, wondering if perhaps he was some sort of stalker, although she doubted that. More likely a reporter, looking for someone to interview for a human-interest story.

"I've been waiting for you to finish work," said the stranger. "Honestly, I was just enjoying watching you. It has been a while—too long, in fact."

She narrowed her eyes. Something about the way he spoke reminded her of ... no! It couldn't be ... could it?

She stepped forward, eyes wide and hopeful. "Torval?" she asked, almost pleading with him. "Is it really you?"

He took her hand, and his appearance shifted, transforming swiftly into that demonic shape she thought she'd never see again. "It is I," he told her, eagerly pulling her close. "Hello, Auralea. I've missed you so much."

She hugged him for a while, hopping up and down in utter joy. "Oh, Torval, I didn't think I'd ever—but how? How did you do it? I thought you couldn't come back!"

"I couldn't stay away," he replied, smiling. "I'm really not supposed to be seeing you—they warned me not to, but I had to try. I still have too much to learn from you, Auralea—about humanity, about angels, and about love."

"Me, too," she agreed readily. "Well, where should we start? Actually, I think I know ... "

"That's easy," replied Torval. "I've been away from a human body for a long time. There's only one thing I want right now. One thing and one thing only."

"Oh, I think I can guess," Christine said, smiling suggestively.

"That's right," he told her, "I require food! Take me to a restaurant—any will do."

She poked at him and laughed, for that hadn't been the answer she expected. "Same old Torval! Always thinking with your stomach! Okay, mister, I know just the spot. Soon as I can flag down a cab, we'll head over there. You still haven't told me, though ... how did you get here in the first place?"

"Oh, that?" He laughed, holding her close, just happy to be in her arms once again. "It wasn't that hard, really."

She punched him lightly in the arm. "Tell me, then!"

"Well, as it turns out," he replied, planting a tender kiss on her waiting lips, "every so often, I'm entitled to a vacation."

Made in the USA
Charleston, SC
02 February 2014